Dinah Lampitt was born in Essex but spent her childhood in a seventeenth-century cottage in Chiswick. She was educated at Putney High School and the Polytechnic and was fired with her love of history by an inspired teacher. She subsequently worked in Fleet Street for *Woman* magazine, *The Times* and the *Evening News*. She also undertook financial research for City Research while writing short stories for the *Evening News* and features for *She* and *Woman's World*. She has a daughter and a son and lives in Tunbridge Wells, Kent.

By the same author

The Silver Swan
Fortune's Soldier

DINAH LAMPITT

Sutton Place

This edition published 1994 by
Diamond Books
77–85 Fulham Palace Road
Hammersmith, London W6 8JB

First published by Grafton Books 1987

First published in Great Britain by
Frederick Muller Ltd 1983

ISBN 0 261 66548 0

Set in Times

This book is dedicated to Bill Lampitt – my Love and my Inspiration – whose faith and encouragement I will always remember

and to

Jacqueline Getty, who gave me the key to Sutton Place, and Geoffrey Glassborow, who unlocked the door.

My thanks are also due to Margaret, Duchess of Argyll; Father Gordon Albion; Dr Clive Mackenzie and Mrs Barbara Wallace for their help on the last days of Paul Getty

and to

Shirley Russell and Eddie Campbell, Ronin Kent, Erika Lock and Charles Purle for their advice and many kindnesses.

Author's Note

Although the story of the strange events of the Manor of Sutton is presented here as fiction most of the incidents are, in fact, true and a matter of recorded history. Furthermore, nearly all the principal characters actually lived and died in the way I have described. The legend of the curse, therefore, must be judged on the facts.

Prologue

The richest man in the world was dying and as he wandered in that wild never-never land that lies between the end of life and infinity he dreamed.

The dream came in pictures, clear and sharp. This, the last dream he would ever have, was a mirror without distortion.

He saw a boy, crisp-cheeked in the autumn air, thrusting newspapers into mail boxes. Heard him shout with pleasure at the silver dollar in his small square hand. The flash of that coin so much more brilliant than any of the millions that were to follow.

Now the boy was grown, running swift in the hills and loving the earth that would one day reveal its secrets to him. And now followed the man, sleek-haired, sharp-faced, the trappings of wealth about him. But alert, waiting for the moment that must be enacted – the moment when he would be made richer than any other man alive. The moment when he would stoop casually – taking his time with destiny – and pick up a handful of common soil and see in its depths the dull black glow of oil.

Now came the panoply of immense wealth. The old man saw himself as the guest of Kings, the friend of the beautiful and the famous, the lover of women. He saw extravagant house parties, fast cars, luxurious swimming pools and red smiling lips; heard the tinsel tumult of the twenties, the shouts and whispers of the thirties. Saw the meaningless ceremonial of marriage and himself emerge on to sunlit steps five times and each time with a different woman on his arm. Five brides, all nestling close, each vow to last for ever; each to end in the dreary familiarity of divorce.

He saw five sons – one to die as a boy. Oh, that draped coffin, so small to go into the greedy-mouthed grave. But four young men were alive, and one, his first-born, was developing as he had done, watchful, knife-sharp in business, playing hard – the true heir to his boundless empire; another self.

And now the dream changed. Far away he glimpsed a house – not clearly but swathed in mist. And then as he hurried towards it the grey vapour lifted dramatically and before him was a masterpiece of Tudor architecture, towering against a sapphire sky. Amber and rose was the brickwork – diamond the mullioned windows. He knew that his quest had ended; that he and the great house were to own one another utterly and inseparably. Here was the consort that he had sought all his life. No woman could give him this feeling of completion. Symbolically, in the way of fantasy, as he crossed the courtyard a huge door swung open.

The dream altered course once more. He saw his eldest son, mature now, groomed and ready to take over. It would all be his – the house and the fortune. The heir apparent stood smiling, waiting to stretch out his hand.

And then it seemed to the old man that he fell a little further into darkness. For without warning his son was no longer there and in his place waited a pale girl from some time so far in the past that the old man could not even guess who she was. Slowly and sadly she shook her head and he saw that she was weeping, tears running into the hair that hung round her shoulders; hair the colour of wild strawberries.

Now he heard a tinny voice repeating over and over again, 'George is dead, George is dead'. And his heart shrank inside him for, with these words, he knew that all his striving had been worthless. Everything finished. The oil emperor with nobody to succeed to the glittering throne. Sad cypress, come away death. All his riches couldn't buy him George's life. Nor his own.

And then he could see nothing – only a chorus of voices saying 'June 6'. He puzzled about it and then realized that that was the date of George's strange, tragic end. And he felt too that there was another reason why it was important which he could not as yet fully understand. The dream was slipping away from him and he knew that he must wake before he died, force his leaping soul to be patient a little longer.

Why were the voices saying 'May 17', he wondered. What had he in common with that date? And then he remembered that in the history of his great house it had some significance. On June 6 his son had gone and on May 17 some past heir to the house had also died. Very dimly he began to see a pattern emerge but he was too near the threshold of the world to fear or even to care.

'I must see you once more,' he whispered to Sutton Place and it seemed to him that he was helped by hands centuries old as he spiralled down into his body. The dying man's eyes flickered lizard-like, and slowly opened . . .

1

To the prisoner in the Tower the first rose thread of dawn was a blasphemy. His last day on earth should have been beneath ominous skies, less difficult to leave than the clear sweetness of a budding May morning. But from his small window he could see a gentle mist rising from the Thames which confirmed that the day would be fine and alive with bird-song.

He had been awake all night, called from his rough pallet bed almost as soon as he had lain on it. In the gloom he had heard the heavy drawing back of the bolts of his cell door and an anonymous voice saying, 'Your confessor, Sir Francis'.

He had thought, 'Christ have mercy, so this is the time. I shall die on the morrow.' His body had drenched with sweat as his mouth had dried. He had mused on that momentarily; the dampness and the parching simultaneously.

The priest had been old, bumbling, but kind. He had sat on the crude chair, groaning a little as some rheumaticky joint somewhere had responded to the dampness running down the walls.

'Why, Sir Francis,' he had said, 'I know your dear mother. A true follower of the old faith.'

His voice had lowered a little for now with King Henry VIII as the head of the Church, instead of the Pope in Rome, one had to be careful. Francis Weston had fallen on his knees before him and then, shamefully, he had buried his face in the old man's lap and wept. The knotted hand – after a moment's hesitation – had gently stroked the young man's hair.

'My son, my son,' he had said. 'Death is not so dreadful. Go to God with thy soul purified and He will receive you at His right hand.'

'I do not weep from fear, Father. 'Tis the waste.'

'Waste, my son?'

'Mine has been a wasted life.'

The priest thought that from what he had heard Sir Francis Weston had indeed squandered his time on earth but it was not his role to criticize. He was here, in this dreadful room, to comfort the dying, to absolve the soul of guilt and to give absolution.

He handed the young man a rosary.

'Let me hear your confession, my son.'

So it was in the darkness, Francis kneeling on the stone floor, that they mumbled through the familiar prayers together and Francis, the rosary clutched tightly in his hands, thought back over what had been so that he might go to the axe with his spirit as shining as the blade that would be raised over his defenceless neck.

'I believe my first sin to be cheating at cards against my sisters, Father. That and stubbornness with my parents.'

In the blackness the old man smiled and Francis saw again his childhood; his home in Chelsea, the glittering Court of his King, Henry, the eighth to bear that title – but above all, Sutton Place. To even think of it now brought the too easy tears stinging again at his eyes. His father's beautiful mansion would have been his by inheritance. The stately pleasure of owning that jewel of Renaissance design had been his to grasp but the executioner would end that on the morrow.

He had ridden away from the great house, up the winding drive to Court, as an unworldly boy of fifteen. Could it really be only ten years ago? But when he had

12

come back the following Michaelmas his manhood had begun – Lucy Talbot, one of Queen Katharine's maids-of-honour had seen to that. How she had tumbled him in her bed! He spoke of it haltingly before the celibate priest but there was no tone of reproof in the reply.

'My worst sin, Father, was gambling. That coupled with my debts. Oh Father, I go from this world owing money.'

The items flashed through his mind – arrears for his clothes, for gaming, for personal loans, what an extravagant charade. And yet he had not felt himself at any time to be immoral. He had not cheated since he was a child; he truly loved his wife, Rose – his mind quickly flitted over his one infidelity to her – he adored his child, admired his parents. The indignation of his death made him suddenly rise and pace the tiny room.

The priest, misunderstanding, said, 'My son, list your debts and ask your father to discharge you of them. He will do so for the salvation of your soul. Cease to carry this anguish with you.'

All was pitch black now and out of it Francis spoke.

'Father, I go to die falsely accused.'

In the darkness he could hear the priest twitch. It must be the fate of every confessor, Francis thought, to learn the truth on the eve of execution. An incredible situation for them – knowing all and yet unable to speak, bound by the vows of the confessional.

'My son?'

The voice was shaking with the sheer import of the moment. The Queen of England – the mighty Anne Boleyn – she who had severed the English Church of Rome from the Pope, was to die accused of adultery with five young men, one her own brother, and here was a member of them giving his deathbed confession that it

13

was not true. Father Dominic trembled with the responsibility of it all. Then he spared a thought for his four brothers of the cloth, admitted at the Watergate of the Tower, mist-shrouded and doleful, that same night. All five of them with one purpose – to prepare a chosen prisoner for death by execution, commuted from hanging and disembowelling only by the clemency of King Henry VIII himself. To ensure that heaven would await the victim, purified of guilt. But here was a great turnabout. Sir Francis Weston was denying the charge. Were the other priests hearing the same?

Trembling Father Dominic persisted.

'My son – Sir Francis – I must ask you. Have you committed adultery?'

There was a pause and then from the direction of the window Francis spoke.

'Yes, Father, I have.'

'And Sir, was it with the Queen?'

'I have just told you that it was not.'

There was a fraught silence and the priest thought it politic to remain quiet.

'There was a woman, Father; Madge – Mistress Shelton. It was while my wife was with child and would not permit me her bed. I did not love the whore – forgive me Father – but my desire was sharp. You would not understand as a man of God.'

'Oh, would I not,' thought the priest. 'So he thinks it is easy for a normal man to subdue his passions. Just because God has called us, makes it no simpler to abstain.'

'Sir Francis,' he said aloud, 'you come as a penitent, therefore God will forgive you. Do you truly regret your sin?'

'Aye I do. I loved Ann . . . Rose . . . Ann. I love her and will beyond death.'

Staring out of the window at the black Thames, Francis's eyes fastened on the solitary light of a late home-going boat. He thought of his initial meeting with Rose Pickering, his father's ward, and how surprised he had been to feel his body react with pleasure at the first glance from those wondrous cornflower blue eyes. He had never been in love with anyone else since. Ann, of the nickname Rose – his love – his bride – mother of his son.

But the priest was clutching at straws.

'Anne, my son?' he said.

'Aye, Ann, Father. Ann Weston – not Anne Boleyn.'

He regretted his bitter tone. The old man was trying his hardest. It was his duty to extract information in order to forgive. There would be no further betrayal. The mockery of a trial at which – as one of the judges – had sat the Queen's own father, Thomas Boleyn, the Earl of Wiltshire, was over. Francis crossed to the priest and knelt down beside him.

'You are wondering, Father, if I loved Her Grace.'

'Yes, my son.'

'I did, Father' – there was an intake of breath from the old man – 'but not with my body, not ever. Nor did I love her as I loved my wife. You see, Father, it was impossible to be her friend and *not* love her.'

How did one explain to a pious man the effect of a glance from those slanting black eyes; the lips that curved into laughter; the excitement of that thrilling voice which caressed each cadence as it sang or spoke. Just as he remembered his first sight of Ann Pickering so now Francis thought of the first time he met Anne Boleyn. It had been March and the wild tresses of black hair were whipped by the wind as she ran like a forest creature among the daffodils. He had fallen under her spell then.

'You are contradictory, my son. You say you loved both your wife and the Queen?'

'But differently, Father. I loved Ann my wife as a lover, a husband. The Queen fascinated me. She was not like any other woman alive.'

Father Dominic thought, 'So she was probably a witch. The King swears 'tis so.'

He decided there and then to see if he could glimpse her before the night was out.

'Then there is nothing on your conscience with regard to Her Grace?'

'Nothing, Father.'

The priest called for a candle as it was too dark now to see the scriptures and the formal ritual of Confession and Absolution was begun. By three in the morning Francis had laid his carefree life bare. Father Dominic forgave him all in the name of the Trinity. It was over – he was ready for death.

'Will you be there tomorrow?'

'Today, my son. Midnight has gone.'

'Will you be there?' Francis repeated.

Father Dominic hesitated. How could he tell the young man that he detested executions, that they actually made him fall to the ground vomiting. After his one and only embarrassing experience, he had never been asked to attend again.

'Er . . . I may be. But I believe the Archbishop will be present.'

'I will hope to see you, Father.'

He knelt and kissed the priest's hand.

'God bless you, my poor boy.'

The words were out before the old man had had time to guard his tongue. Francis shook his head.

'It has been a wasted life,' he repeated.

'You have fathered a son, Sir Francis. Think of him.'

16

The priest was in the doorway.

'What date is it? One loses count of time in this dread place.'

'May 17, my son.'

'Goodbye, Father.'

'Goodbye, Sir Francis.'

Now there was nothing left to do but make his will. He sat at the rough table, picked up his quill pen and by the guttering light of the candle wrote, 'Father and mother and wife, I shall humbly desire you for the salvation of my soul to discharge me of this bill and to forgive me of all the offences that I have done to you. And in especial to my wife . . .'

Rose . . . Ann – always so jealous of her namesake, the Queen. How could he explain that to him one was a goddess, untouchable; the other a girl whom he desired in his arms, in his bed – all too late now anyway. Too late for anything except this wretched list of extravagant tomfoolery.

'Item to my shoemaker £46. Item to Bridges, my tailor, £26. Item to a poor woman at the Tennis play for balls, I cannot tell how much.'

Dear Jesus, what a wretched idiot he had been. A little tinsel courtier playing in a darkening whirlpool that he had not even noticed.

'Item to Mark Smeaton, £73.6s.7d.'

Oh well, that was one debt his father wouldn't have to pay. For poor simple Mark was to die today as well. The Queen's musician – a carpenter's son made good because of his ability to sing and play and compose. And because of his humble station they had put him on the rack and he had sung a different song. He had confessed to adultery with the Queen's Grace and doomed them all. Francis wondered grimly how long it would have been

17

before he had screamed 'Yes, yes, yes' if they had racked him.

A ray of light fell on the floor. It was dawn and it was then that he crossed to the window and saw that it was going to be a glorious day. Now he must hurry. With the sweet birds in full throat he completed his will.

'Item to the King's Highness £46, won of the King at Dice. Item, £6.3s. won of the King at Imperial.' A great many entries of that nature. Francis recalled a conversation with his father, Richard.

'Francis, you win too often. It is not wise with a man of the King's temperament.'

How right Sir Richard had been proved. If he had deliberately lost a little more would he be facing the death sentence now?

'So all is finally reduced to ifs and possiblys,' thought Francis.

But it was growing lighter by the minute. He put his quill to paper and wrote the final sentence.

'I desire for the love of God to forgive me, and to pray for me, for I believe prayer will do me good. God's blessing have my child and mine.' He thought for a minute and then altered the word child to children. They had had such loving before he left her for ever that possibly another babe dwelled, secret and hidden, in her belly. 'By me a great offender to God, Francis Weston.'

He addressed the will to Sir Richard Weston, Sutton Place, Guildford, then he rose and went once more to the window. The Thames was sparkling now. He stayed there until he heard the bolts draw back on his cell. Sir William Kingston – the Lieutenant of the Tower – stood in the doorway.

'Come, Sir Francis,' was all he said.

'How easy,' thought Francis. 'Come! How glib. Come

18

to thy death is what he is saying and it rolls from his tongue as simply as a call to dine.'

Behind the Lieutenant he saw the faces of his old friends Sir Henry Norris and William Brereton and, supported by soldiers on either side, Mark Smeaton. The musician was a human wreck – head hanging, chin sagging – disfigured to an idiot by the rack. Francis joined his fellow accused and they marched, Smeaton with splayed dragging feet, to collect the last of the party. In his cell, disdainful to the last, George, Viscount Rochford – Anne Boleyn's brother – lolled in a chair.

The four men exchanged glances – Mark Smeaton was beyond all human feeling – and each knew the others' thoughts. Throughout the trial and finally now they acknowledged silently that they were to be sacrificed to the monstrous ego of Henry VIII. Anne Boleyn had fallen out of favour because she could not bear sons – primrose-pale Jane Seymour stood waiting to make her entrance – those that were in the way must be disposed of.

'God save the King,' said George and though Sir William Kingston might shoot him a black glance there was nothing in the Viscount's expression to which any exception might be taken.

As they were escorted out into the open of Tower Hill, Francis saw that a vast crowd had turned out. He did not look up, afraid that he might shake. He really must try to make a good end. He fixed his eyes on George Rochford's sauntering gait. He knew all was affection but who cared aught? Each man must approach his own dying in the way which gave him most courage.

Overhead a blackbird burst into sweet song amongst the May blossom, the beauty of the sound in counterpoint to the brutality of the scene below. Rochford mounted the scaffold steps. He turned to his friends.

'Die courageously,' he whispered; then he launched into a speech about hypocrisy amongst those who studied the Gospels, his eyes fixed firmly on the clerics who stood in attendance. Francis vainly searched among them for Father Dominic.

'Humble old man,' he thought. 'It would have surprised me if he had been here and yet he had a kindly face.'

George was busy now forgiving his enemies and praying that the King might have a long and happy life. He was still smiling when he died. Norris mounted the steps. Francis looked at the sky as the axe blade rose and fell.

The push at his elbow told him it was his turn to climb up.

'Goodbye Sutton Place – now I shall never inherit thee; goodbye old friends – all dying with me; goodbye my son – never to remember his father.'

To the people he made a short speech protesting neither guilt nor innocence. He knew that, even now, a word badly placed, a nuance in the voice, could bring reprisals against the family he was leaving behind.

As he was about to kneel he saw Father Dominic looking quite dreadful – green-faced and sweating profusely – hurrying to the scaffold steps. The priest gazed up at Francis and smiled.

'The old man is more in dread than I,' he thought.

The priest prayed, 'God, my Father, do not let me puke like a babe. I have come especially to help young Weston – give me courage I beg.'

Aloud he shouted, 'Go to God, Sir Francis,' and made the sign of the cross.

Francis nodded, knelt down and died without flinching. Overhead the blackbird carolled his requiem and Father Dominic gave a prayer of thanks that, though he had been forced to look away, public disgrace had been avoided.

Up on the scaffold, Francis's head and body were put into a plain coffin; he was buried in a communal grave with Henry Norris. Father Dominic intoned prayers for the dead in a dreary voice – dangerous to show too much emotion in these turbulent times.

At Sutton Place the silence was intolerable. Neither Sir Richard, Lady Weston nor Rose had spoken above a whisper all day. The only cheerful sound came from the baby, Henry, gurgling to himself in his cradle.

Since they had been curtly refused permission to visit Francis in the Tower there had been no word from London at all and this, in its way, was worse to bear than knowing the actual date when he was to die. Early morning waking brought its own nightmare and each setting of the sun with no messenger the horror of another agonized tomorrow.

At dusk on May 17 it was almost a relief to hear the awaited horse's hooves cross the quadrangle. Sir Richard, seated alone in the Great Hall, his head in his hands, straightened himself. He thought, 'So he's dead, my poor, stupid, harmless son. If only he'd listened to me. I warned him; if the King could turn against Wolsey he could turn against anyone. But, sweet Jesus, I loved the boy, for all his foolishness.'

And he, who had not cried throughout the whole ordeal, felt the unfamiliarity of wetness at his eyes. He brushed the tears aside. He would need every ounce of control now to support his wife and daughter-in-law.

'God's head, I dread it,' he thought. Since Francis's arrest he had not only endured his own misery but witnessed that of the two women. If he had been one ounce less resilient and tough a fighter he would have cracked but over the years he had steered his unerring course deftly through treachery and intrigue and an in-built hardness had resulted. Sir Richard Weston was

21

thought of as one of the coldest men alive by those who did not really know him.

Lady Weston was at that moment standing in one of the large rooms at the back of the house overlooking the gardens. She was too far away from the courtyard to hear the messenger arrive but suddenly she was certain that Francis had died that morning. Looking round her in the lengthening shadows she thought, 'This is a room of death. People will die here in time to come. I know it.' She crossed herself and went down the short corridor to the Great Hall.

Rose Weston had remained all day by the window at the end of the Long Gallery. From there she could see the parkland and anyone approaching the Gate House. For two days she had stayed thus only leaving to answer nature's demands or when it was too dark to see any more. Then she had gone to the bed in which she and Francis had consummated their marriage and lain open-eyed in the darkness or drifted into wild, desolate dreams.

She had eaten scarcely nothing, despite all urging.

'Won't my Lady have something of this lark pie I have made especially for her?'

She had longed to scream, 'Throw your lark pie to the beggars for aught I care. My only love lies rotting in the Tower,' but she had simply smiled and shaken her head.

Lady Weston had insisted on her drinking wine and this she had done so that now, on the second evening of her vigil, she felt light headed and faraway. The speck in the distance, just visible through the trees, meant nothing to her at first and then, in an instant, she was utterly sober, clinging to the window sill with hands like claws. It was the rider from London – Sir Richard's man – but he could have been the Reaper himself sitting astride that horse. Rose threw back her head and opened her mouth

22

to scream but no sound came out. She was frozen, a gargoyle, an obscene caricature of her own beauty.

Downstairs, Sir Richard and his wife held each other silently. The messenger stood before them, tears and sweat making childish rivulets in the dust on his face.

'He died bravely,' was all he managed to say before he wept.

'Did he speak?'

'He said . . . he said, "I little thought I would have come to this."'

Lady Weston, her voice seeming over-loud in the vaulted roof of the Great Hall cried, 'But I thought it would come. Sutton Place is cursed, Richard. You never believed, but I did. This house is built on accursed land.'

The word 'nonsense' was on Richard's lips automatically.

Lady Weston rounded on him.

'So 'tis nonsense is it? Do you realize the date? It is May 17; does that mean nothing to you? Today Francis stood on the very spot where the Duke of Buckingham was beheaded exactly fifteen years ago to this day. And what is the date on the grant of the Manor of Sutton, Richard? Also May 17, is it not?'

'Christ!' Sir Richard had gone white.

The mention of Buckingham brought back the dark secret he had stored in the remotest part of his mind. He had been involved in the Duke's downfall, actively plotted with Wolsey to see the man go to the block and the Manor of Sutton had been his reward. And now his own son had died on precisely the same date in the same place and in the same manner. At last Sir Richard was unnerved.

'I tell you,' said Lady Weston, her voice hoarse, 'Sutton Place and all who dwell here are plagued by the curse of Queen Edith.'

For once Richard Weston was silent.

Through the thick forest of Sutton a cavalcade of riders, their rain-soaked clothes streaming, their faces set and determined, cantered forward. In their midst a young woman clad in sombre grey stared solemnly at the neck of her horse, her gaze never moving to look at her escort. The rain, lashing into her face, ran down her cheeks like tears, hiding the fact that she was indeed weeping.

With each miserably uncomfortable jolt she thought, 'I hate him. I hate him.' But sometimes she grew confused and found she was saying 'I love him' instead. And here lay the truth. In her bizarre relationship with her husband – Edward, crowned King of England in 1042, known by the people as the Confessor – she was no longer sure what she felt. Never would be sure – every emotion confused.

When he patted her on the head and gave her sweet-meats and admired her tapestry work, or brought her a clear-voiced song bird for her room, all was sunshine and she would run to hug him. And then when he drew back from the embrace, tensing his body and moving away quickly, the sadness came, and she would berate herself for never learning, for always being anxious to please, for still hoping – in the face of constant rejection – that one day he would hold her tightly to him and love her like a man. It had always been the same. She, for ever eager and affectionate; he, kind in his fashion, but quite incapable of giving the love she wanted. She had grown from a young girl to a woman in this atmosphere and to him she was still a child. He even addressed her as 'daughter' when he wasn't thinking.

Edith remembered her wedding night. Her father, the mighty Earl Godwin – friend and adviser of the great Knut, Viking warrior who had crossed the seas to conquer

England – had personally taken her hand and placed it in Edward's.

'I give you my flower, sire,' he had said.

And then in the royal chamber, with the clean sweet rushes on the floor, in her new white nightshift stitched by her mother, Edith had climbed into the King's bed. She had undone her plaits and her hair, the colour of strawberries that grew wild in the forest, hung loosely over her shoulders. Edward had picked up a strand of it and held it delicately in his thin fingers. He had looked at her, his gaunt, hollow face softened for once.

'Beauteous child,' he had said and then – after kneeling a long while in prayer – he had blown out the candle. Edith had lain in the dark waiting for something to happen. The fact that he was over forty and she still nineteen did not worry her. She was excited. She had learned from her parents that love was enjoyable; there had hardly seemed a time when Gytha, her mother, was not with child. And her father had made no secret of his lustiness. He would kiss his wife, smack her buttocks, cuddle and caress her, and all in front of the ever-increasing family. Then he would sweep her off to their chamber and the laughs and sounds of pleasure would ring out without inhibition. The Godwin children had taken it all in their stride; to have lived with their boisterous father and had any shyness left would have been an impossibility.

And now this. Edward lay still beside her, his breathing deepening into sleep. Edith had cautiously put out a hand and touched his arm. The instant response had been to sigh and turn away. And so it had continued for a week; every night she had suffered the same humiliation.

Finally she had plucked up enough courage to speak to him.

'Remember, you are the Queen of England,' she kept telling herself.

She had been dancing in the garden while one of her ladies had plucked the strings of a lyre. Edward, giving one of his rare smiles, had come up to her, clapping his hands.

'Do I please thee, sire?' she had said, curtseying respectfully.

'Of course, my sweet daughter.'

'But husband,' Edith had said, 'I am your wife and I desire to be so in every way.'

As the colour had heightened in her cheeks, so it had drained from his. He had started to walk away and Edith had been forced to run along beside him. He had stopped dead in his tracks and given her a look that made her tremble with fright.

'Do not speak of it,' he had said in a violent whisper. 'Chastity is a virtue and the soul is purified by abstension. You must never talk of it again.'

He had hurried off and her words 'But we married . . .' had died lamely on the air. That night he had not come to her room and she had learned from the servants on the next day that he had removed to another chamber.

After two months of bitter distress, Edith had gone to her parents.

'What!' her father had roared. 'The craven wretch! Has he left thee untouched, girl?'

'Aye, father.'

'By the Gods, I'll swear he's not capable of it.'

'He says that it is a virtue to remain pure.'

Godwin's eyes had bulged in his head and his face had turned an angry mottled shade. It was he who had arranged the marriage and even at the time a doubt about the thin ascetic who was to be his son-in-law had crossed his mind. He had thought he might prefer men to women

26

but that the King was impotent – or chose to be – had not occurred to him. In fact Godwin had fondly imagined, as Edward had slipped the wedding ring on Edith's finger, that he would be the grandfather of England's future King and founder of a great dynasty.

'The praying fool,' he bellowed. 'If he spent less time on his knees and more in his wife's bed 'twould be a better thing for England.' And he had hit a nearby table so hard with his clenched fist that it had broken in two.

It could have been a portent, for the strange partnership of the pious King and red-blooded Earl who, between them, kept England in a state of peace, was never the same from that moment. Godwin took to sniping at Edward – deliberately going out of his way to make caustic remarks. If these could contain a reference to potency and virility all the better. In return Edward developed a petulance, an obstinacy, and as his word was finally law he was able to thwart the Earl at every turn. In between the two was Edith, detesting the situation, still hoping that one day Edward would consummate the three-year-old marriage; wishing her father would hold his tongue or that God would do something to help her.

She had always found it difficult to reconcile Christianity with the old pagan beliefs. Her father was indifferent to religion. His contention was that life on earth was the one to enjoy and that the after-life could take care of itself, could not but rub off on his family and reduce his praying son-in-law – the King – to a state of nervous alarm. But from their mother Gytha, sister of the Viking warrior Earl Ulf, the Godwin children had heard many times the stories of the old Gods – Odin the all-powerful; Thor with his red beard and mighty hammer; Freya, paramour of the Gods, going to her trysts in a carriage drawn by cats. Of them all Odin had stirred Edith's imagination most; tall, one-eyed, hunting by night and yet governor of mysticism and the soul's yearnings, a great and formidable sorcerer. She had sometimes thought, most secretly, that if anyone could take on Edward's God and send her husband to her, it would be Odin. But such ideas were forbidden and she had always ended up on her knees praying to the Christian God for forgiveness.

But neither the Christian God nor Odin listened, and finally Godwin lost the last vestige of patience with his son-in-law and the scene was set for a monumental quarrel which was to have the most devastating result.

Edith had been present when the King – all control and majesty gone – had screamed at her father, 'Murderer, murderer! I accuse you of causing the death of my brother.'

'Lies!' Godwin had thundered. 'I stood acquitted of that charge twelve years ago. You enfeebled fool! That my poor daughter should be condemned to a life with an incapable husband sickens me. A state of war exists between us.'

And in a highly dramatic gesture the Earl had thrown down his hunting gloves at the King's feet. Looking as if he was about to have a seizure, Edward had hissed menacingly, 'So be it, Earl Godwin.'

Whilst the two factions had mustered on opposite banks of the Thames, Edith had been confined to her apartments, uninformed as to events. And then one day her door had been thrown open unceremoniously and Edward had stood in the opening. She had not seen him for several weeks and it occurred to her at once that during this time he had become slightly demented. He was thinner than ever and his eyes looked crazed – a great deal of the whites showing.

'Out!' was all he said.

Edith curtsied; still dutiful, still obedient, still wanting love in the face of disaster.

'What has happened, sire?'

He gave a mirthless smile and she thought, 'They are all dead; my father, my brother, everybody. Now I have nothing!'

She managed to whisper, 'My family?' but he either didn't hear or did not wish to. Still with that dreadful grin on his face he said, 'Let us speak of you, Edith. You are to enter a nunnery.'

She looked at him mutely.

' . . . a nunnery. To spend the rest of your life praying and purifying your soul of lustful thoughts.'

'May Odin forgive you, Edward.'

It was a slip of the tongue but he pounced on it.

'Odin! May the one true God forgive *you*. You are going to a Christian community and you shall remain there until your death. Every day, for the rest of your existence will be spent on your knees in prayer.'

'You may as well condemn me to death now, it would be more merciful.'

'You prefer death to prayer? There speaks a true Godwin.'

He turned to go but she called after him, 'Aye and proud to bear the name. At least they are men.'

She had said the most cruel words of her blameless life and she watched him shudder. He spun round and she had never seen him so strained. The rage that had possessed him had, like a fever, gone beyond burning point leaving him cold and dangerous.

'For that I will bring you even lower,' he said. 'You shall be stripped of your possessions, lands and title. You will own nothing but the clothes in which you stand.'

He went to the door.

'I hope that I never set eyes on you again,' he said.

Within minutes, servants had come and her jewels and clothes had been carried out in chests. She had only just been in time to hide two rings in her headdress – one a valuable gem and the other her 'magic' ring. It had been given to her at birth by a well-beloved aunt, Estrith, King Knut's sister. It was a strange-looking object – bronze shafted with an oddly shaped green stone – and it still bore the marks of the teething bites Edith had given it as a baby. It was family legend that it had been given to their forebear, Svein Forkbeard, by the Elf King and that it contained powerful charms. Edith had worn it since childhood on a chain round her neck, for it had been too big for her finger. As she slipped it into concealment she thought, 'Even now I am doing what Edward would hate. How he would abhor the thought of me keeping a talisman.'

And now she was on her way to Sutton Forest in driving rain, to beg and plead. For herself she might not have bothered but she had learned from her serving women that there had been no battle between the King and her father; the Earls uninvolved in the argument had simply refused to fight other Englishmen. Nobody had wanted civil war and Edward and Godwin had been forced to climb down.

'But what of my father and brothers?'

'Banishment, Lady. They are to leave England in two days' time – for ever!'

So Edith's gemstone had gone as a bribe. The first part of her journey had taken her up the Thames but now they had changed to horseback and the leader of the escort – richer for the Queen's ruby ring – was taking his party out of its way; to the King's hunting lodge in the Forest of Sutton in Surrey.

The beautiful red deer abounded there and nothing pleased Edward better than to be in the thick of a pack of barking hounds, riding hard till his hapless quarry were all slain. Edith considered wryly that hunting had been the only thing to awaken any form of excitement in her husband; one glimpse of horse and hounds and he was transformed, almost animated; one glimpse of his wife in any state of undress and he was hastening to pray.

'Pathetic, peculiar creature,' she thought and then felt amazement that she could still have feelings of pity after all he had done. But that was the way it was – love and hate for ever intertwined – wheel gone full circle.

The rain-heavy trees were thinning out now and in the distance Edith caught sight of the clearing where the lodge was built. She wondered if her husband was there or if he was sheltering in the forest somewhere, caught in the storm with his huntsmen and dogs. In either event she intended to wait until she had seen him face to face. She no longer had anything to lose. It was not in Edward's nature to condemn to death – exiling was the ultimate form of punishment as far as he was concerned – so nothing could be made worse for herself, for Godwin or her brothers. Let darkness come and go, she cared nothing; she could wait for years.

As they drew alongside the vaulted stone building the leader of the escort held up his hand and the party drew to a straggling halt. He dismounted and bowed to Edith, the rain running from his hat and down his nose as he did so. A ridiculous, hysterical urge to laugh rose in her throat but she fought it away.

'Lady, let me see if the King is there,' he said. 'Take what shelter you can beneath those trees.'

As he entered the lodge there was a further cloudburst and the party were glad to huddle together beneath three sturdy oaks. Looking down, Edith saw that they were beside a well which presumably gave the hunting lodge its water supply. The constant rainfall had filled it to overflowing and the ground around it was soggy and churned up by the horses' hooves. She was just thinking how muddy and unpleasant the water looked when one of the soldiers dismounted and rubbed some of it into a wart on his hand.

'What are you doing, fellow?'

'Why, this is holy water, Lady. All water belonging to the King can cure ills. It's because he's so pure.'

Edith thought, 'I know enough about his accursed purity to choke me. If it were not for that none of us might be here now.' But it was true that cures were claimed in Edward's holy name and she had been both disgusted and furious to see the servants bottling his discarded bath water in order to sell it to the gullible. She had taken the matter up with him declaring it to be a filthy practice but he had said, 'It would seem that the halt and the maim are sometimes healed, daughter. Is it right that we should put a stop to it? I will pray for guidance.'

After searching his conscience he had decided that it would be wrong to deprive the benefit of his curative powers from those who sought them as God had been gracious enough to grant him this gift.

The escort leader came out of the lodge and ran through the downpour towards them.

'The King is at mass, Lady, and cannot be disturbed.'

It was typical of Edward, Edith thought, to pray before he went off to kill; what a saintly slaughterer the man was. A mood of depression and dislike was settling on her. She supposed that all had been well – if that word could be used at all about a woman condemned for life to the nunnery – while she rode. Now that she was still, she seemed to be giving in to despair. She huddled close to the other riders, the flanks of the horses rubbing damply against one another. The air smelt of wet leather.

Through her thick cloak and gown Edith could feel the rain running next to her skin. She was very near to tears again.

After what seemed hours there was a sign of life. The King's groom appeared leading a horse round to the door and a minute or two later the hounds, on leashes and baying for the chase, came clamouring into view. Then the lodge door swung open and there he was – bearded, hollow cheeked – an air of sadness about his whole bearing.

'Edward,' Edith called out, 'Edward!' But the beating of the rain made her cry inaudible. Disregarding her escort she broke free and her horse crossed the few yards that separated her from her husband. The King had mounted and his eyes were level with hers as she approached.

'Edward,' she said – and her voice was hard with the feelings that were beginning to rage inside her.

The gaunt face turned to her.

'You must forgive us. It is still in your power to revoke sentence on the Godwins. Edward, in the name of Christ, for once show your Christian charity. Remember I have committed no sin against you – all I asked was your love.'

The cold eyes never flickered and the King's face remained expressionless. Without a word he tugged his horse's reins and spurred, with his huntsmen, into the forest, leaving her staring after him.

Intolerable and final rejection. The hate and the love that constantly warred within Edith were both stilled. From the darkest part of her soul something transcending both was rising in a maelstrom of evil.

The escort leader watching her tumble from her horse thought that she was having a fit. He felt vaguely responsible, more than usually so for a man of his mentality. He had fulfilled his obligation after all. The bargain had been her ring in return for taking her to see the King – and that had been done. It was hardly his fault if the cold-hearted bastard had rejected her. But seeing her writhing on the ground like that was unnerving. Anyway, according to his wife, who worked in the palace kitchens, the poor thing had had no life to speak of. Year after year with that impotent old man and doing her best to keep cheerful. It was outside his line of duty to question events but it was hardly surprising to him that Earl Godwin had declared war. What man would tolerate that sort of treatment for his daughter?

He knelt down beside the Queen and was horrified by her ghastly expression and the saliva flecking her lips.

'She's possessed,' he thought and crossed himself.

Deep in her throat she was growling and that frightened him even more. He felt unable to cope with the situation alone.

'Will! Tom!' he called. 'The Queen is ill. Look to the Lady.'

They came and crouched beside her, one trying to bathe her forehead with water from the well. What happened after that later became confused in their minds so that the three of them, in years to come, told different versions of the story and the legend of the curse grew distorted. What they did agree on was that from somewhere Queen Edith produced a Viking ring – so mighty that it must have been worn by a great warrior. Will said that the ring glowed as if it were on fire and Tom that the waters of the well boiled and hissing steam rose up, as she threw it in. The escort leader saw neither of these things but he had to admit that he was looking at Edith's distorted face.

They all heard her call to Odin to avenge her and Tom – a descendant of the raid that had brought Knut the crown of England – said she called out to the Norse Elf

King as well. Everyone differed as to exactly what was said next, with one exception. All three heard her curse the Manor of Sutton for time immemorial, with the words 'May it know death, madness and despair.' Will thought that she cursed the Lord of the Manor too and this would have made sense for King Edward was lord at that time. But the frightened men all witnessed that when the malediction was done Queen Edith's body went into violent convulsions and she lost consciousness.

'The Devil has left her,' said the leader. 'Jesus protect us all.'

'Amen.'

'We must take her to the nuns with all speed. God grant that her soul be safe there.'

They lifted her gently on to a horse and the leader got up behind her, holding her limp body in his arms. Looking down at the drawn face, the wisps of strawberry coloured hair escaping in wet strands from beneath her headdress, he shivered violently.

'This is a dread place. Let us away.'

After they had gone there was no sound except for the rain beating into the well. But in the depths of its swollen waters the Viking ring moved restlessly; by ancient ritual the powerful forces of pre-Christian magic had been invoked, the spell which would affect men and women for centuries to come had begun its relentless progress.

2

It was May 17, 1521, and all England lay beneath a lucent sky. The earth had grown hard and in the streets of London – stinking beyond the endurance of even the most hardened nostril – an astrologer had been stoned for saying it would never rain again.

In Sutton Forest a family of red deer stood drinking at the ancient water hole which had once served the hunting lodge of King Edward, their velvet tongues glistening with drops of water, their ears moving constantly for the slightest sound of an approaching hunter. For that was all that would disturb them now. The lodge had long since fallen into ruin and the manor house, built by the great Bassett family in the Middle Ages had also crumbled into decay. To look at the scene it seemed that little had changed in the five hundred years since Queen Edith had been taken to a nunnery. Only the fact that the manor house had been abandoned bore silent testimony to the falseness of the picture. The beauty and peace were merely an illusion, the truth was that no human being had found it safe to dwell there. The place had been returned to the forest creatures to whom it had originally belonged.

On Tower Hill the smell of the crowd who had turned out to see the execution of Edward Stafford, Duke of Buckingham, wafted towards the scaffold and Richard Weston – present in an official capacity – raised a sachet of lavender to his nose. He kept it there as the head – still pumping blood – fell on the straw; the heat and the stench of the mob far more offensive to him than the death he had just witnessed. All that Stafford's flowing arteries meant as far as he was concerned, was that a fool had been disposed of; a fool who had not only menaced the throne but who had goaded Richard's patron, the great Cardinal who sat in Hampton Court Palace.

The axeman raised the head aloft and turned it round slowly so that everyone should have a good view. Looking at the rather surprised expression on the face, Richard thought, 'Only *you* could be surprised, jester! Your head was lost the day you spilled water in Wolsey's shoes. Nobody who wants to live touches – let alone slaps – the King's right hand.'

And this is how it was in England. Next to the King, Cardinal Wolsey was the most powerful man alive and those who wanted to advance stayed firmly in his faction. Naturally Weston, with his unerring gift for choosing the right pack, had become the Cardinal's man, controlling his face admirably during the ceremony at which, with the entire Court present, Buckingham had managed to spill the contents of a basin he held for the King's ablutions straight into Wolsey's shoes. The smirks and guffaws that followed had marked the start of the campaign to see the Duke dead and though Richard had longed to shout with laughter also, he was too seasoned a campaigner to so much as twitch a lip.

Richard thought back to a conversation he had held with Wolsey two months previously. 'When I was only twenty, my Lord,' he had said, 'I took arms against Richard III at Bosworth. And my father, Edmund, provided ships and money for the father of the King's Grace – Henry Tudor – at the same campaign. It is the tradition of the Westons to support the Tudors.'

He picked his words carefully.

'Is there any way, my Lord, in which I may continue to further the Tudor cause?'

37

Wolsey's bleak little eye had caught his and Richard had known he had spoken well. The Cardinal had risen and gone to look out of the window. With his back turned he said, 'The man's a traitor and plotter. He must be brought down, Richard. I say he must be brought down.'

'Death to the King's enemies, my Lord.'

The Cardinal had turned from the window with a ghost of a smile on his lips. He said nothing but Richard was already bowing and leaving the room. The game was afoot and the plan which would bring Edward Stafford to the block was, even now, taking shape in his mind.

And here the culmination on Tower Hill. Buckingham, the loud-mouthed descendant of Edward III was dead; Richard Weston was alive and already turning away to his horse. In that movement alone, outwardly so callous, was summed up the pattern of existence at the Court of Henry VIII.

He swung into the saddle with ease. For all his fifty-six years he was as tough and strong as the leather on which he sat. He believed in preserving his health, eating sparingly and riding and exercising regularly. To be active in body and mind was his constant goal. Secretly he despised his royal master for his excesses. Too much food, too much everything – and quite unable to sire a boy in wedlock. A little less pleasure and a little more attention to diet would have given England the prince it desired.

As he set off for Hampton Court, Weston thought of his own son, Francis. Richard had brought his wife to bed with the child when he had been forty-seven, and he was still an active man, a virile man in every sense; provided he kept a cool head on his shoulders he saw no reason why this state of affairs should not continue for many years to come.

It was a long ride in the heat to the Cardinal's palace but Weston pushed himself and the horse hard. His excitement was concealed beneath his secretive face with the widely spaced, flint-blue eyes, hard jaw and thatch of thick, curly hair, grey streaked, but still mainly black. The Cardinal's rewards for favours were generous, and this one in particular had been of the highest political importance. Richard knew that some prize lay in store for him but no hint at all had been given as to what it might be. He wanted above all else to be elevated to the peerage, but perhaps such a reward, at this stage, would be a little obvious. Yet he was sure that one day Henry Tudor and his Cardinal would recognize his value to them and satisfy the mighty ambition that was in him.

Sir Richard smiled to himself as he clattered into the great yard at Hampton Court. He knew that he was one of the coming men. He also knew that he would be used and rewarded only as long as he wanted to do no more than accumulate personal wealth. One step out of line, one hint that he could be looking too high, and a monarch's patronage could be withdrawn as fast as a hand from a glove. But he was nobody's fool. He knew exactly how far he dare push.

Aware that unseen eyes had already reported his arrival to Wolsey, he took his time before appearing, first visiting the jakes and washing the dust from his face and hands. He still smelt of the journey but there was little he could do about that without stripping, and that would have ruined the fine timing of his entrance – long enough to make Wolsey feel the prickle of anticipation, short enough not to arouse anger.

Wolsey sat behind his desk, cluttered with papers. He was the *alter* Rex, omnipotent, unbeatable.

'Well?' he asked.

'He's in a bad humour,' thought Richard. 'Tread warily.'

'The King's enemy died this morning, my Lord,' he said.

Without looking up, Wolsey's red-gloved hand, heavy with rings, searched among the papers on the desk and found what it was looking for. Still continuing with his work, he thrust a document unceremoniously forward. Richard took it and saw at once the King's seal. Carefully he opened the scroll. It bore that day's date, and at the bottom was the King's own signature.

So Richard's prize had been immediate. He wondered if the King had signed and the messenger had been despatched with the document even before the head had rolled, or if he had waited for confirmation, picked up his quill and sent a man with a swifter horse than Weston's to Hampton Court?

No matter, it was here. His eyes ran over the contents. No peerage but for all that a rich reward. The grant of the Manor of Sutton in Surrey with all the forests and land appertaining thereto. Somewhere to build, a place for his family to pass down from father to son. In his mind's eye he saw a great, mellow manor house.

He caught the Cardinal looking at him, amused; the atmosphere had thawed.

'You're pleased?'

Weston bowed low.

'My Lord Cardinal. It has always been my dearest wish . . .'

'I know, I know. You've been patient; waited for your own land. That's your strong suit, Richard, you proceed slowly. Teach your son – what's his name . . . ?'

'Francis.'

'Francis – the same tricks.'

'I will endeavour, my Lord.'

'Then we'll have another loyal courtier to call upon.'

Wolsey's frosty gaze was the nearest it could get to anything approaching merriment.

'You know Sutton, of course? It's royal land. This gift is a very personal one from the King's Highness.'

Richard adopted a suitably gratified expression.

'It once belonged to St Edward the Confessor,' Wolsey continued. 'He hunted there. It has passed through many famous hands. Now it is yours for ever.'

Sir Richard went down on one knee and kissed the extended red glove. His face allowed only the merest smile but his heart beat with the power of attainment. Royal land was now his.

After eating and drinking alone – the Cardinal excusing himself – Weston set off for his home in Chelsea. Wolsey had offered him a night's lodging but he was anxious to return; to see his wife's face when she realized she was a Lady of the Manor. With the document safe in a leather pouch, he rode as the sun set and finally reached home in the darkness of midnight.

Anne Weston had gone to bed and came down the stairs in her nightgown. At forty-five she was still a fine-looking woman; hair more golden than grey and very beautiful long-lashed blue eyes. Richard thought wryly how typical it was that Francis should have inherited his mother's soft looks while the girls favoured his own tougher appearance.

Pouring himself some wine, Richard read solemnly to his wife in the flickering candlelight.

'King Henry VIII, by Letters Patent, dated at Westminster May 17, 1521 – today, Anne! – in the thirteenth year of his reign, grants the manor of Sutton with its appurtenances and all the knights fees thereto belonging, villeins, goods and services, waifs and strays, wardships and rights, woods, meadows, pastures, fisheries, water, vineyards, ponds . . .'

Anne threw her arms round his neck and kissed him joyfully.

'Wouldst smother me, woman? Hear how the King finishes. To his noble and well-beloved Privy Councillor, Sir Richard Weston, Knight, his heirs and assigns.'

They kissed on the lips.

Three days later the entire family, accompanied by two servants, set out to see their new property. They conducted the journey in four stages, spending two nights at Guildford. Lady Weston travelled in her litter while the children and the manservant rode with Sir Richard. There was great excitement. The sun gleamed on Francis's fair hair as he chased his sisters' horses, not content till they had raced and he had been allowed to win, indulged as usual.

Sir Richard's slate eyes were untypically expressive as he looked at his son and heir. 'Now he will have something worth calling an inheritance,' he thought, and he thanked God that he had been potent enough to sire a healthy boy late in the marriage and that Anne – despite being thirty-five – had been safely delivered. Now, with a younger wife, there would have been more than just one boy trotting along beside his father . . .

But he dismissed such disloyal thoughts. Anne had been good to him; if her change had come upon her early it was only nature's way. A vague idea of taking a mistress crept into Richard's mind and shafted through it like the rays of sun that were falling on them through the gaps between the mighty trees of Sutton Forest. But by the time the little cavalcade left the cathedral-like atmosphere and saw before it the rolling parkland and the river out of which a single silver fish jumped again and again, Richard

42

Weston knew that his life was destined to be that of a great land-owner and builder without other diversions.

The beauty of the scene brought them all to a halt. The scent of May blossoms delighted the nose. The burbling of the river, in which the exultant fish swam, mingled with the honey-warm sound of bees and nearby doves and seduced the ear, whilst the sight of the lush green grass and wild flowers combined to make it seem like paradise – a far cry from the blood-soaked straw at Tower Hill that had been the necessary ugliness to obtain perfection.

'Where is the house?' asked Francis.

'About two miles further. But it's only a ruin now, built in King John's day.'

'I'll race you there,' the boy said, and kicking his heels into his horse's flanks he was off at full canter. Although only ten years old he was already a good rider, spirited and strong, and his father had no fears for his son's safety as he went after him. But to his surprise, when he caught up with him, it was to see that the boy *had* fallen and was washing his bloodied hands in an ancient well.

Sir Richard dismounted.

'Are you all right?'

'Yes, Father. My hands and knees are scratched. I came off over his head.'

'How did it happen?'

'I don't know. He shied at the well. He was frightened by something.'

'But there's nothing there.'

Francis threw back his head suddenly to gaze at a diving swallow and Sir Richard thought how fragile his neck looked.

'You're lucky, you foolish child, that your neck wasn't broken.'

His words made him think horribly and violently of

Tower Hill and the death of Stafford, and for no reason at all he felt a sense of foreboding.

In the distance he could see the others were approaching.

'Don't tell your mother,' said Weston abruptly.

This was a strange spot, he thought, quiet and still, in contrast to the park which had been teeming with life. Even he – hard and shock-proofed – found it a little eerie.

It was then that he saw before him the ruin of what he assumed had been King Edward's hunting lodge. There was little left except the bare outline of the place which the Saint had used on his hunting expeditions. And then on his right, a hundred yards away, he saw the ancient remains of what had once been the manor house – the home of the Bassett family – now crumbled to nothing but a shell. Sir Richard had an overwhelming sense of the past; he had acquired part of England's heritage on which to build. Thinking to himself that he was behaving very oddly, he stepped among the stones of the hunting lodge and thought, 'Edward, King and Confessor, once prayed here.'

At the nearby well Francis was still washing his scratched knees. Concentrating in the manner of all small boys, his tongue poking from his mouth, it took him a second or two to realize that despite the fact that the sun shone brilliantly he had become cold – so cold that his teeth began to chatter. He looked up and became rigid at what he saw. The blurred outline of a woman stood between him and the sun. It was difficult to discern her features or even her shape properly but he was more afraid than he had ever been in his life.

And then, with her body undulating and formless, he saw her throw herself on the ground and writhe and twist like an obscene serpent, as she hurled something into the

44

well. Even worse was to come for slowly, slowly that terrible head was turning in his direction and from the amorphous face two great hollow eyes fixed their dreadful gaze upon him.

The gurgling sound in Francis's throat released itself. He screamed as he had never screamed before in his life. From the ruined lodge Sir Richard ran like a man of twenty.

'In the name of Christ, Francis, what is it?'

He snatched the boy up in his arms but the screaming continued. He administered a sharp slap to his son's face. The noise turned to a whimper.

'What is it?' Richard repeated, his eyes rapidly scanning every tree for possible assailants.

Against his father's shoulder, which always seemed to smell of leather, Francis whispered faintly, 'The woman.'

'What woman?'

'She was standing by me at the well and then she fell on the ground and . . . Father, it was a ghost. She looked at me and her eyes weren't there – only the sockets. It was the walking dead.'

Despite the warmth, Richard felt every hackle on his body rise and he broke into a cold sweat – it was the words the child had chosen, they were ghastly. Nevertheless he did not believe in ghosts and he was sure that logic lay behind all this.

'Come now,' he said, 'you know as well as I do that ghosts are for old women and small girls.'

'But it was not like that!'

Francis's voice was peevish and Richard felt himself becoming irritable. Obviously the boy had imagined the whole episode for, in fact, nobody could have hidden so quickly and there was certainly no one at the well now. Sensing his father's annoyance Francis began to cry loudly.

Overcoming an urge to hit him, Sir Richard looked round. In the near distance Margaret and Catherine – Francis's sisters – had seen that something was wrong and were trotting their horses forward. Lady Weston and the servants were still mercifully some way behind.

'Curse the child,' he thought, though he had to admit that the boy had obviously been frightened by something or other. Too much imagination – just like his mother. An expedient lie seemed the only possible course.

'Francis, I tell you – and I will *not* be denied – that it was a beggar drawing water.'

A look at Sir Richard's expression told Francis that further protestation was pointless, and now the rest of his family was arriving. First his sisters, bright-cheeked from the ride, and then his mother – enraptured with her new estate – smiling and beautiful, as she was helped down from her litter.

Margaret, the eldest, was opening her mouth to ask if all was well with her brother but Sir Richard cut across. 'I am hungry,' he announced decisively. 'Wife, I wish to eat.'

So Lady Weston's attention was distracted as she supervised the unpacking of cold food from especially prepared baskets. Fowl – for Sir Richard's delight – pies, fruit, cakes, wine and ale; the last for the servants.

They all began the outdoor meal but Lady Weston could not help but notice that Francis had completely lost his appetite and was staring over his shoulder, apparently at a disused well. She was about to ask him what was amiss when her attention was arrested by the arrival of a stranger, trudging in their direction from Sutton Forest.

He was short, with hair cut in the shape of a fringed basin, big widely-spaced teeth and bright blue eyes. The stained appearance of his skin, beneath its natural coating of dirt, suggested Romany extraction. Sir Richard and the manservant Toby rose to their feet protectively but any idea of menace was shattered by the man doing a somersault, then a cartwheel, and finally a split jump, ending up on one knee before Sir Richard.

'Good morrow, my Lord.' His accent was Romany all right. 'Giles of Guildford, if I can be said to come from anywhere. A humble tumbler by trade, a strolling player, a fool. In exchange for a meal, your Ladyship . . .' – he looked longingly at the remainders of the food – 'I will dance for your children, tell tales of great doings, sing songs of love.'

Normally, Richard would have sent him on his way but today, looking at Francis's drained face, he considered the idea. He glanced at Anne and she gave him a smile and a nod.

'Very well, fellow.'

The man kissed Sir Richard's hand.

'God's blessings on you for ever, my Lord. No food has reached my sad stomach these last three days.'

And with that he fell to, munching and drinking voraciously, sitting all the while a little apart with the servants and occasionally bowing his head in the direction of his patrons. He looked so strange as he chewed and bowed, and bowed and chewed, that Catherine and Margaret began to laugh. And shortly a smile came to Francis's face. Sir Richard, thanking God for the lightening of the atmosphere, called out, 'Some shillings for thee, man, if you entertain us well. Are you ready?'

'Ready, aye, my Lord, I am,' and thrusting a huge piece of cheese into his mouth, he approached them.

Swallowing convulsively, he addressed himself to Lady Weston.

'If my Lady will forgive me, I will tumble for you later. On such a full stomach, so recently empty, I fear I may be prone to the evils of wind.'

47

Francis was just the age when any mention of nature's functions sent him into uncontrollable laughter. In this he was joined by his sister Catherine. Lady Weston and the elder girl, Margaret, looked shocked. Sir Richard said hurriedly, 'Then tell us a tale, man, and no coarseness, do you hear!'

'Begging your Lordship's pardon – not meaning to give offence. I thought there would be more offence in the wind, sir.'

Francis shrieked joyfully.

'Oh, get on with it,' said Sir Richard, impatiently.

'My gypsy blood tells me, sir, that I address our new Lord and Lady of the Manor.'

'How did you know that?' interrupted Anne.

'I am in touch with things beyond your ken, my Lady.'

'More like in touch with the landlord of the inn at Guildford,' thought Richard but he said nothing, for his wife's eyes were glistening. She was excited by strange phenomena and had consulted astrologers before the births of all three children. Richard also suspected her of visiting soothsayers from time to time.

'I should very much enjoy hearing the history of the Manor of Sutton,' she said. 'All I know of it is that King Edward the Confessor once had a hunting lodge here and that it has been royal hunting land for many centuries.'

A quite extraordinary expression passed over Giles's face. 'There is very little to tell, my Lady,' he said hurriedly. 'As you say, it belonged to King Edward so long ago it's all forgotten now.'

'How disappointing.' Anne Weston was speaking. 'It would have given me so much pleasure to have heard the chronicles of our Manor. Giles, if you should come across a fellow in Guildford who knows the tale tell him that Lady Weston will give him a good purse for the telling.'

Giles's expression changed again. Richard Weston

48

thought, 'God curse the rogue. He is hiding something, though what I cannot fathom, and yet his greed plays at him like cat with mouse.'

Giles thought, 'How can I tell them that this Manor of theirs is accursed? Sir Richard would not believe me; my Lady would; the children would be afeared. And yet there is but one farthing between me and starvation.'

He decided on his course. They would have a story and it would be the facts, told without hints of underlying evil. Aloud he said, 'Well, my Lady, I *do* know a little of the history. Wilt give me a purse if I speak well?'

'I will judge that,' said Richard.

'What an interfering ear-piercer,' thought Giles. 'If the curse of the Manor falls upon him 'tis divine justice.'

He smiled obsequiously. 'Now where shall I begin?' he said. It was all going to need careful phrasing wherever he started.

'Begin before King Edward,' said Catherine Weston as she moved nearer Giles, her round blue eyes in her twelve-year-old face large with anticipation.

'Well, before King Edward these lands were as they are now. Vast forests loved by the Saxon Kings. King Edward, he was a great hunter. He thought highly of this place and he built himself a hunting lodge which is now that ruin yonder.'

'Did his son inherit it?' asked Francis.

'He didn't have a son,' said Giles. 'Come to think of it, I don't believe he had any children at all.'

His eyes wandered innocently over Sir Richard's face but there was no reaction.

'So he left this land to a friend of his – a fellow who'd been a good servant while the King was alive. He had a strange name. Wenness – Wennitt – I can't remember. No wait, it was Wenesi.'

'What happened to him?'

'Well, it was 1066, my Lady and he was called to Hastings.'

'And . . . ?'

'And he gave up his life to protect England from the Norman Bastard.'

Anne Weston could visualize the scene. The two armies encamped on the night before the battle; Harold, son of Earl Godwin, determined to stop the Norman invader; Duke William, tough and committed to ravaging England. And somewhere in the English camp, a simple man called Wenesi, Lord of the Manor of Sutton, with only another twenty-four hours to live. She noticed Giles looking narrowly and she wondered why. ''Tis a good tale,' she said.

' I believe Duke William then gave Sutton to the Malet family. William Malet had been a friend of King Harold and he had a horrible job to do.'

'What?' asked Francis.

'From that terrible battlefield – laden with naked corpses – Duke William had the dismembered parts of Harold's body removed and wrapped in a purple cloth, and there on the Hastings clifftop, William Malet buried them under a heap of stones. He put a slab by the mound bearing this inscription: "By command of the Duke, you rest here a King, O Harold; that you may be guardian still of the shore and sea."'

'I don't think I like this story,' said Francis. Richard Weston hesitated. He was actually interested to hear the chronicles of his land, learn of the men and women who had lived out their lives on the Manor that was now his property and that of his heirs. On the other hand he could see that the imagined happening at the well had unnerved his son and that any account of battle or blood – and what place did not bear some reference to that in its annals? – would probably set the child weeping.

Looking rather crossly at Giles he said, 'I think Toby should take Francis riding, Anne.'

Giles appeared decidedly miserable and thought, 'This will be the hardest purse I've ever earned.'

Sir Richard, watching his son and the manservant departing said, 'But King Harold lies buried in Waltham Abbey, fellow.'

'They say not, my Lord. They say he was buried by Viking rite.'

And even as her husband made a snorting, scoffing sound Anne's imagination was at work. She saw William Malet laying the last stone in place as the sun set over the stark cliffs; could smell the salt air; hear the scream of the wheeling gulls as they yelled Harold's obituary into the darkening sky.

'Of course, Sir Richard, you may be right. Who is to say? Indeed, there is another legend that King Harold lived on. Now that is a good tale . . .'

His buffoon's face was an anxious walnut as he willed them to ask to hear it. But once again Sir Richard – whom Giles considered a total and meddlesome nuisance – interposed.

'So the Malet family built the manor house? I had been told it was the Bassetts.'

'Yes, it *was* the Bassett family, my Lord.'

'How did it come into their hands?'

'Er . . . I do believe, that Robert Malet and Henry I had some disagreement. Who knows what?' He smiled thinly.

He looked at them but they still had not suspected. Had no inkling that Robert Malet had had to run for his life. 'It was King John who granted the Manors of both Sutton and Woking to Gilbert Bassett.'

'And was that his house?'

It was Catherine who spoke, her china blue eyes gazing at the ruin that lay to their right.

'Aye, young Gilbert built that – not that he had long to enjoy it, God rest his soul.'

Giles hadn't been able to help saying that. He knew the history of the Manor inside out and sideways. His father had been a player and tumbler before him and found it the best tale to tell, not only in the county of Surrey, but wherever he went. And Giles had learned it from him, word for word, and then added his own embellishments. Small wonder he had accidentally gone into the version reserved for open-mouthed bucolics who were always responsive, particularly of a winter's night when the story was invariably accompanied by ale and the smell of roasting crabs.

Four pairs of eyes were regarding him.

'He died young?' asked Lady Weston.

'A hunting accident, my Lady. Most unfortunate.'

'But it passed to his son?'

Giles's heart sank like a millstone.

'Well, it was an ugly business all round. The baby boy died within a few days of his father. A tragedy.'

The assembled company had grown a little quiet, Anne Weston being most affected. She knew, as surely as if she had been there, what that dreadful funeral had been like; that the setting had been bleakest midwinter, the gravediggers' shovels sparking against the frost, a solitary bell tolling and a black figure, ravaged with grief, following two coffins – one man-sized, one minute – through the biting cruel cold.

'But it remained in the Bassett family?'

'Yes, my Lady. Gilbert's brothers inherited.'

'Brothers?'

He had done it again.

'It is not possible for more than one brother to inherit,'

52

said Sir Richard putting his know-all's nose in again. The player suddenly lost his patience, if his purse was withheld, so be it.

'I *did* know that, sir. What I meant was that the estate descended unusually fast through the Bassett family. Gilbert's second brother was killed in battle, the third brother – Fulc, Bishop of London – died soon after inheriting and Philip, the last brother, was imprisoned for life.'

'They seem to have been very unfortunate,' said Lady Weston. 'Were they accursed?'

'I don't know, my Lady.'

'Then why was the Manor deserted?'

'Begging your Ladyship's pardon but I do not think this last part of the story suitable for the ears of the young ladies.'

Both Richard and Anne Weston were agog. Some mighty scandal had obviously taken place. They reacted just as Giles had envisaged and hopes of a good payment rose once more as the girls were despatched to walk with the serving woman.

'Well?'

'My Lady, Philip Bassett only had one surviving child – a daughter called Aliva.'

'You say surviving. Did his other children die?'

'Aye, they did. In your words, my Lady, they were very unfortunate. But be that as it may . . . Anyway, Aliva Bassett married Hugh Despenser and she had a son also named Hugh. It was he who became the lover of Edward II. Hugh Despenser, the son, inherited the manor house and the King came to stay with him here.'

Giles had his audience now and nothing further to fear. The truth could not come out from this story of men in love. Skilfully, he painted a word picture. The high-pitched male laughter; the girlish rompings in the King's bedchamber, the whiff of sweet scents as the two men chased each other through Sutton Forest, probably dropping down at the old well to drink – exhausted with play and passion. Then the merciless Isabella – Edward's French wife – loathing her perverted husband and taking the lustiest man in England, Roger Mortimer – Earl of March – for her lover. The plot to rid themselves of the homosexual who stood in their way, for once and for all. The terrible end. Hugh Despenser, Lord of the Manor of Sutton, strung up on the gallows; his father beside him. Their bodies jerking together in the dance of death. And then the King, hunted down like an animal, and a red hot poker inserted into his rectum, searing his bowels to a cinder as he screamed his way to death.

Anne Weston shivered. 'How unspeakable. For all he had done, no human being deserves to die like that.'

'And that was the end of the manor house, my Lady. After this it fell into disrepair.'

'And the ownership?'

Giles rose. He had said enough. He could tell them no more without betraying the secret.

'I know no more, my Lord. With the fall of the house so falls too my knowledge. The story is at an end.'

He made a bow. 'Have I pleased you, sir? And your good wife?'

Sir Richard nodded. 'Aye, 'twas well told.' He threw him a bag of money.

'Why did the Bassetts have such ill fortune?' said Lady Weston.

Giles shook his head.

'I must be on my journey, Lady. I've to tumble in Woking this night. Only for the village people but it could earn me a farthing or two.'

He kissed Sir Richard's hand. 'I thank you for the purse, sir.' And he was off, disappearing into the forest as abruptly as he had first arrived. Once out of sight he began to chant in a strange tongue. It was the Romany call to the 'unseen people' to ward off the evil eye. He had rather liked Lady Weston and the boy and as for Catherine, that delicious little woman child . . . . As far as Sir Richard was concerned, Giles did not care for him at all. The man would have to take his chance.

That night Anne Weston said to her husband, 'Richard, I do not wish our manor house to be built on the site of the old one. I feel – laugh at me for a foolish hen-head if you will – that the Bassetts knew too much unhappiness there; too much of death and strangeness. I believe that these things can leave feelings behind. May we build in the parkland?'

Richard sat thoughtfully. He was remembering Francis's face at the well, drawn and strained. He wondered if Anne could be right. He had found the place unsettling himself.

'I think we should start afresh,' he said. 'Let us build in the meadow sweetness. Let us build a house to delight posterity.'

Anne sighed, relieved. 'And what shall we call it, husband?'

'I think we should call it Sutton Place.'

3

King Henry was dancing. Dazzlingly dressed in bejewel-
led white, his strong legs elegantly gartered, he knew that
he was the centre of attention and this night he felt
eighteen again; the cares of monarchy lifted. He wasn't
quite sure why he felt so. Was it the extra fine wines he
had drunk? Or was it that he was enjoying his role as
Ardent Desire in the masque arranged by Cardinal
Wolsey? Or was it that earlier in the evening he had
raised his eyes to find his look returned by that of a thin
delicate girl with hair as black as midnight, who moved
amongst the dancers with such presence and a style all
her own?

And what eyes she had; dark but filled with golden
lights that spoke of mysteries and excitements that would
entrance any man. Henry felt a rush of blood. He hurried
forward to take her hand, for the moment had come for
Ardent Desire to rescue the Fair Maidens. The long
sleeves she always wore slipped back as he held her arm
and he saw with amazement something that he had never
noticed before on the few occasions he had seen her
around the Court. Her left hand was malformed. From
the little finger grew another tiny finger complete with
nail. The witch's mark! With deftness the girl slipped the
hand back into the hanging sleeve. She looked up at the
King and slowly she smiled. He thought that if this was
her witchery, he would be a willing victim.

Standing as he was, near the dancers, Richard Weston
noticed the exchange of glances between Henry and
Thomas Boleyn's daughter, Anne. And he also noticed

something that he had seen before, and more and more frequently of late. There was, in the King, a restlessness; a seething discontent, a gnawing, so it would seem, at the man's whole approach to life.

He had not been the only one to realize it, of course. In the Court's innermost circle it was discussed – voices always discreetly low, hiding places examined first for any unwanted observer. They were sure, too, that they knew the cause. The King not only desired an heir for England but he was out of love with his Queen.

Richard, with his totally accurate instinct in matters of diplomacy, thought the situation highly charged, believing that a discontented monarch led to a discontented country. But his set of friends – with one or two exceptions – disagreed. The King was making the best of things; enjoying life as fully as he could; there was no danger lying ahead.

Richard looked at the dancers again and thought, 'There's certainly no danger in that little thing. Why, she's all eyes – nothing to her. All the beauty in the family had gone to her sister.'

His watchful face did not change as, the dance done, the girl – who could not have been more than fifteen or sixteen – joined a group of her contemporaries without a backward glance at the King. Richard was aware – as he made it his business to be aware of everything – that the group consisted mainly of young men and that, as she joined them, there was what could only be described as a ripple amongst them. They eddied on a little tide of pleasure though, for the life of him, Richard couldn't think why.

She certainly moved gracefully and her voice, with its distinctive French accent was melodious but as for looks – no. Strange, though, that she had returned from the Court of Queen Claude in France only a few weeks earlier and had already attracted a small coterie. Surely not because she was the sister of the King's mistress; that would make no sense for Mary Carey, born Boleyn, was not the most popular girl at court.

Richard looked round and saw that another pair of eyes were following his – Sir Richard Jerningham, his friend and fellow member of the King's Chamber, was also studying Mistress Boleyn.

'Intriguing,' said Jerningham.

'Anne Boleyn?' Richard was startled.

'Her father, Tom, made sure I met her the other day.'

Richard knew exactly what Jerningham meant. What a pusher Boleyn was! Nosing in everywhere, ensuring that his daughters met the right people. He must be cock-a-hoop, thought Richard, that Mary Boleyn stepped straight from her marriage bed with William Carey into the King's.

'And what do you think of her?'

'She is beautifully mannered – in the French way of course – and, more than that, she is good company. She made me laugh.'

Richard was astounded. That anyone could amuse the solemn Jerningham was unusual but that it should be that plain little bag of bones . . . .

Richard Weston's duties at Court were heavy that spring of 1522. Within a few days of Wolsey's imperial reception he was at Greenwich Palace, this time for a small investiture involving himself. In company with Jerningham and three others he was to be appointed the King's cup bearer.

His wife, richly gowned in green and silver, was looking her best that evening and Richard was thinking to himself how pleasurable it would be to lie with her in their big bed, when his delightful train of ideas was interrupted by the Queen's principal page bowing before them.

'The Queen's Grace requests your presence in her apartments, Lady Weston.'

As she followed him Anne Weston thought, 'How like Katharine. She never forgets a friend!' And she recalled the times they had shared together; in fact, at most of the great events of Katharine's life, Anne had been present. She remembered their first meeting. She had been plain Mrs Anne Weston then, a twenty-five-year-old lady-in-waiting to Queen Elizabeth of York; Katharine had been fifteen, the pretty Princess sent from Spain to marry Prince Arthur. How formidable it must have been for her. The Yorkist Queen, blonde and austere, seated on her dais – her ladies grouped round her – watching the plump little Spanish girl walk the length of the room and make her curtsey. Frozen faced, Elizabeth of the White Rose had received the kiss of welcome. Katharine had searched round frantically for a friendly look and had caught Anne Weston's eye. The liking had been mutual and instantaneous and the lady-in-waiting had been rewarded by a sweet smile from the daughter of the Queen of Castile.

Within a few days Katharine had been married and Richard and Anne had been present as she had walked to St Paul's, holding the hand of Prince Henry, but taking in marriage that of Henry VII's elder son, Arthur. It seemed but a blink of an eye before the bridal white had been exchanged for widow's black; the loving Princess into a small, desolate figure.

Then Anne had not seen her. The girl had been away from Court during her mourning. The next occasion, she remembered, had been at the death of Queen Elizabeth in childbed. As she thought of it now, Anne could recall the hushed voices, the subdued light, the grave expressions of the physicians, but above all the Queen's face – whiter than the whitest rose of York – and the frail hand patting the head of her sobbing young daughter-in-law, who was whispering in her broken English, 'Do not die – you must not die – it is your birthday.'

It had been a pathetic, almost ridiculous remark but the Queen *had* died and it *had* been her birthday. She would have been thirty-seven years old. The baby girl – named Catherine after the Spanish Princess the Queen had grown to love – was already dead.

After that the Princess – uncertain of her future in England – had lived humbly on a meagre stipend, eking out a boring existence in Durham House and wondering if she would ever marry Prince Henry, to whom she had been betrothed on his twelfth birthday. And Anne had been away from Court. Three depressing miscarriages had followed one another until, in 1507, Margaret Weston had been born safely.

Then in April, 1509, Henry VII had died. Within six weeks Henry VIII had married Katharine and Anne Weston had named her new-born daughter Catherine – the English version of her name – in the young Queen's honour.

Vividly she recalled the Coronation. Anne, up only a few days from her lying-in, had been grateful to sit during the double crowning. But Richard, liege man of the old monarch, had stood with pride. His fears that the new King might turn against him, think him past good service because Henry was barely eighteen and Richard forty-three, had been totally allayed. Within two days he had received three honours – Keeper of Hanworth Park; Steward of Marlow, Cokeham and Bray; Governor of Guernsey, Alderney and Sark.

Anne thought how happy the reign would have been for them all if it had only been blessed with a Prince. As a Queen's Gentlewoman she would normally have been in attendance when Katharine's second child – the first had been stillborn – had struggled into the world on the first day of January, 1511, but Anne herself was expecting a child in February and was awaiting the event at home.

Richard had not told her of the tragedy that followed until Francis was born, healthy and well, at the end of the month. His imperturbable face was unusually grave as he said to her, 'The Prince of Wales is dead. He only lived a few weeks.'

Weeping, Anne had held Francis to her heart, almost guilty that her son was alive whilst Katharine's lay like a wax doll in a tiny coffin.

And now it was over. At the age of thirty-one, as Anne Weston wiped her brow and rubbed her hands, Katharine of Aragon had finally given birth to a child that lived – Mary. Then in 1518 one final confinement – a stillbirth to add to all the other dead royal babies. She had whispered to Anne, 'I have failed England.'

Anne had replied, 'Nobody who could produce a daughter as clever as the Princess could be said to fail, your Grace. But there may still be a Prince. Give nature time.'

But now, as she stood outside the doors of the Queen's apartments, Anne reflected that six years had passed since Mary's arrival and it was obvious to all that there would be no more children for the Queen.

The page, bowing in the entrance, called out clearly, 'Lady Weston, your Grace' and Katharine rose from her chair, crossed over to Anne and took both her hands in her own.

'My dear Anne,' she said. 'It is such a long time since we last met. How well you are looking.'

Anne thought, 'I wish I could say the same about you, dear friend.' Poor Katharine's many pregnancies had swollen her body and made her face puffy. She looked a great deal older than her thirty-seven years.

Anne curtsied to the floor and answered, 'Thank you, your Grace. I trust that you too are in good health.'

'Come, sit down.' Katharine was patting a chair next to hers and the other ladies withdrew to a discreet distance.

'Now, Anne, I hear that Sir Richard has been given the Manor of Sutton. I visited it once, many years ago. There were some ancient ruins there that I found interesting. Are you intending to build on that site? Or perhaps you have already started?'

'We have had some plans drawn, your Grace, but no actual work has begun. We thought we would build a new manor house in the parkland rather than on the old situation. Richard thought of the name Sutton Place.'

'I like that,' said the Queen and for a second her familiar girlish smile flashed across her face.

'We have seen some times,' said Katharine. 'Some happy, some sad. Come, Anne, you shall walk with me.'

And together they proceeded to the chamber where the investiture was to take place. The King, looking boyish and rather more cheerful than he had of late, stepped forward to greet them.

'Lady Weston, how very fine you look.' Yes, he was extremely jovial Anne decided as she curtsied. She thought she knew the cause. In a far corner of the chamber, standing with her ineffectual husband and another girl was 'the Hackney'; Mary Carey had earned the nickname at the Court of France – and from the French King himself in return for distributing her favours amongst the Court gallants.

Anne watched her surreptitiously; the great trollop was following Henry's every move with her round blue eyes, her tongue moistening her lips from time to time. She reminded Lady Weston of a well-fed cat. The King, however, was keeping his back turned and studiously ignoring her.

And then Anne's attention was caught by the girl with the King's paramour. A thin, young creature with flowing black hair and huge dark eyes that seemed to slant at the outer corners. She was not pretty, in fact she was plain, but yet so . . . Anne struggled for the description and alighted on 'enchanting'. And with the word came the quite absurd notion that the girl was, in fact, a woodland fairy and was weaving a spell now, here, in the ante-chamber at Greenwich. For as she moved away from Mary and walked amongst the courtiers, almost as if she was unaware of them, every head turned to look!

Anne was so startled by this impression that she forgot herself and said to the Queen, 'Who is *that*?' Then hastily added, 'Pardon me, your Grace.'

But Katharine was oblivious of any impropriety for she was also watching the two young women.

'That is Sir Thomas Boleyn's other daughter, Anne. She has only recently returned from the French Court. She is not like her sister, is she?'

Anne Weston dropped her gaze. She was seeing too much in the Queen's expression. As one, the two women looked again at Mary Carey, whose devouring eyes were still fastened on the King. Neither had the remotest idea that the cause of the downfall of them both was in the room and was not Mary at all but the dark-haired ondine who stood so quietly, her hands hidden in her sleeves, saying nothing, observing everything.

The simple ceremony over, Henry, with Katharine on his arm, led the company through to the banquet. Behind him, Sir Richard and the other newly-appointed Bearers bore his cups. Anne Weston walked with the wives and through the incessant burbling of Lady Herbert – who was deaf and untypically muttered as a result – she heard

63

a beautifully pitched voice with a noticeable French accent. Glancing behind her she saw the dark girl again. Aware of someone's gaze Anne Boleyn looked up and Anne Weston saw closely the velvet quality of her eyes and her thick jet lashes.

The young woman dropped a polite curtsey and looked demurely away but not before Lady Weston had an overwhelming impression that concealed in that slight form was a strength, a power and an iron determination far greater than any man's.

That night in bed Anne broached the subject.

'Richard, what are your thoughts on that young woman new to the Court?'

He knew at once who she meant, which struck her as significant.

'Anne Boleyn?'

'Yes.'

'I do not find her pretty at all – all skin and bone – her eyes are very arresting, though.'

'And her hair. But have you noticed something else?'

'She has a deformed hand.'

This surprised Anne who had not seen it.

'How is it deformed?'

'She has six fingers on one.'

Lady Weston drew a breath.

'The devil's mark.'

Richard laughed in the darkness.

'Aye, maybe she's a sorceress come amongst us.'

For no particular reason Anne trembled and at that minute Francis screamed in his sleep. It was a moment that Lady Weston would remember for the rest of her life.

She did not see Mistress Boleyn again until the Christmas celebrations. Joining Richard at Greenwich Palace for the Twelve Days she experienced amusement tinged with the faint unease that the girl seemed to arouse in her. It was obvious that Anne's star was now in the ascendant, her clothes and manners copied by all the other young women – long sleeves being quite the height of fashion – and in watching the turn of Mistress Boleyn's head, the extension of a hand in a formal dance, she saw great beauty.

Her thoughts were interrupted by the call for all to step forth. No refusals were allowed for this was the Eve of the New Year. Lady Weston stifled a laugh. Richard's jaw was like an outcrop of rock as he gritted his teeth for the ordeal. He detested dancing above all else but Queen Katharine herself was before him, as the viols and sackbuts burst forth in a great cheerful chord.

Anne Weston found herself partnered by young Harry Percy, the Earl of Northumberland's son, presently attached to Cardinal Wolsey's household.

'What a vast shambling boy he is,' she thought.

He was extremely tall with huge hands – and feet too – for one crunched down on to Lady Weston's toe making her wince with pain.

'Harry!' she said sharply.

He jerked round mumbling apologies and going red, the epitome of love-lorn youth. It was little surprise to Lady Weston to see that his worshipping eyes had been fixed on none other than Anne Boleyn. It was then that the observant Anne Weston noticed something else. The subject of Harry's passion was dancing with the King, her dark eyes laughing, her hair reflecting blue beneath a pearl headdress. And on the King's face was a look vaguely reminiscent of Harry Percy's. Not blatant adoration, but interest and . . . .

'Desire,' thought Lady Weston. And it occurred to her that the Boleyns played a great part in the King's life.

She looked to see if Richard had noticed and sure enough she was just in time to see her husband's widely spaced eyes – as expressionless as ever – flick over the couple and then look away.

She had no opportunity to ask him about it then and was on the brink of doing so the following morning when a knock came on the door of their apartments. Toby answered and Anne saw standing there two of the King's pages and one of the Queen's. On being bidden to enter, the boys placed twelve boxes before Richard and one before Lady Weston. They were New Year gifts from Henry and Katharine.

Anne's box contained a beautifully worked headdress – blue velvet with small sapphire encrustations. With it was a note in the Queen's own hand.

'It would please us greatly if you were more at Court.'

Though discreetly worded it was a royal command.

Richard's boxes contained twelve pairs of shoes. The King could not have chosen better. Though not a vain man and caring little for fashion, Sir Richard had a weakness for good shoes. As merry as a child he pulled on a pair of fine red leather and stood up to admire them.

'Hey ho,' said Anne. 'I see I must call thee gander feet.'

'Thou wilt not,' he retorted and chased her round the room calling, 'Come, old goose, let me pluck thy feathers!'

Anne saw Toby, crimson with mirth, vanishing through the door eager to spread the news of Sir Richard's lusty intent.

'Richard, no,' she called but he had caught her up and had her held firmly on the bed, tickling her ribs. Then he kissed her.

'Will you love me, wife?'

She shook her head laughing.

''Tis the morning.'

'I care not,' he said and kicked off his new red shoes.

Lying in his arms later, Anne said, 'You still desire the old goose, then?'

'Aye.'

The reply was brief but there was a kiss on the nose to accompany it.

'More than Mistress Boleyn?'

'The Hackney?'

'Nay, she is Mistress Carey. I mean Mistress Anne Boleyn.'

Richard gave her a curious look. With everyone else his eyes were always expressionless for it was only in this way that he had perfected the art of close scrutiny – a trick that Lady Weston had learned from him. But with his wife he was not so careful.

'Why do you mention her?' he said.

'I saw you watching her last night.'

'What do you mean?'

'His secrecy is becoming a habit,' she thought. Impatiently she said, 'Richard do not play cat's feet with me. You noticed how the King looked at her. I saw you.'

''Tis not the first time,' he said and he recounted Henry's behaviour at Wolsey's masque the year before.

'How old is she?' said Anne.

'Nearly sixteen, I'm told.'

'Too young for the King?'

It was said as a question not a statement.

'Let us hope so,' said Richard grimly.

In accordance with the Queen's wishes, during that year of 1523 Anne Weston adopted the custom of spending two weeks with her children in Chelsea and two at Court. Everywhere there was talk of the impending war with

France and Richard was preparing to raise a contingent to cross the Channel.

The building of Sutton Place was proceeding at a snail's pace. Of the many Italian architects at work in England Richard had chosen one of the King's own – Girolamo da Trevizi. But though the man had visited the site frequently and embellished and revised his designs, the actual clearing and brick laying had been delayed by Sir Richard's preoccupation with the war. So much so that Anne found herself increasingly in charge of the project.

One day she walked in the parkland alone except for Toby and her serving woman. Holding da Trevizi's plans in her hand, they actually trod step by step through each place where the great chambers and halls would be situated. It was the sheer énormity of the future mansion house that daunted Anne. It would be larger than Thomas Boleyn's home in Kent – and he called that a castle! And it would be greater too than Penshurst Place. She was to be mistress of a dwelling suitable for a peer of the realm.

'I don't really understand these drawings, mam,' said Joan, peering over Anne's shoulder and screwing up her eyes for she was not the most intelligent creature in the world. Anne had found her begging in the streets when she had been newly wed to Richard, the girl little more than eleven, and had taken her in out of pity. The resulting relationship had been gratifying for the child had grown more comely and presentable under Anne's care. And in return Anne had won herself a love and loyalty that had been a great comfort to her through the years.

'It's the writing,' Joan continued. 'I think he writes very odd.'

Anne looked at da Trevizi's exquisite Italianate script and inwardly sighed. She had worked very hard with

Joan's reading and writing but she had to admit with only limited success.

'Let me explain. Where we are standing now there will be chambers for the family and on the floor above them Signor da Trevizi plans to build a Long Gallery where we may exercise on wet and dreary days.'

'That's a new notion.'

'Aye. There will be a lot of original things in Sutton Place.'

'But won't we shiver in that Gallery in winter, mam?'

'We are going to have four fireplaces.'

Joan clapped her hands in delight.

''Twill be a merry sight when they're all ablazing. Why, we could run from one to the other. There'll be some high jinks with the children, I reckon.'

Anne smiled to herself. Joan's simplicity was refreshing after the whispered cruelties of Court chit-chat. Yet that night, as she helped Lady Weston undress in the principal bedroom of the Angel Inn at Guildford, the servant said, 'I still can't think of that great big house somehow, my Lady.'

'What do you mean?'

'It's all so bare now, trees and grass and emptiness. Did you notice the emptiness, mam? It's hard to think of a house in its place.'

As she got into bed Anne thought of Joan's words. What strange things servants came out with. Emptiness!

She fell asleep almost at once but the night was not destined to be restful. She dreamed that she was standing outside Sutton Place completely built and magnificent, but in some way menacing. Etched sharp black against a setting blood-red sun, the huge tower of the Gate House loomed above her like the entrance to a grim castle. The feeling of fear was sharpened by the knowledge in her dream that she had lost Francis.

69

The Gate House keeper was not a man but Joan and to Lady Weston's frantic enquiries as to Francis's whereabouts, she answered, 'You won't find him in there, mam, it's all emptiness.'

'But it isn't,' Anne had protested. 'Look it's lit up.'

'That's only the sun shining through the windows,' and Joan had vanished back into the Gate House refusing to believe her.

In the terrible way that nightmares have, it seemed to take Anne hours to run across the quadrangle. It was as if her legs refused to obey her will and she remained constantly in one spot. Eventually though, she reached the door that led to the Great Hall. She pounded on it shrieking, 'Where is Francis? Richard, help me!'

In the dream, the last rays of the sun were lighting the courtyard, turning it into a fantastic pit of crimson and indigo. Anne was still beating on the door when, to her surprise, it opened so suddenly that she almost fell inside. Mistress Boleyn stood there.

'Where is Francis?' Lady Weston repeated but the girl only smiled and shook her head, raising one hand to show the sinister deformity. As if it had a life apart, the extra little finger began to squirm back and forth and turned into a minute serpent.

Screaming, Anne Weston fled across the length of the Hall and up a staircase at the far end. She found herself in the Long Gallery. It was almost pitch black, the only light coming from two candles at the far end. In the gloom she stumbled forward, straining her eyes to see what object it was that stood there. As she drew nearer she was amazed to find that it was an altar and before it knelt a figure in prayer.

'Francis!' she called.

The black figure did not move. Anne was suddenly so afraid that she stopped dead – but too late. She had been

70

heard. Very slowly it turned its head and she saw the wild, sad face of a woman peering out from a great bush of unbrushed silver hair.

'Who's there?' said the creature. 'Oh my darling, have you come back to me?'

And she rose from her knees and began to creep towards Anne who noticed that her dress was most eccentric – not of any fashion that she knew.

'You are not he,' the old woman was shouting. 'Get out of my house! Help! Intruders!'

Once again Lady Weston was running, the old woman panting after her. But Anne was too fast for her and the noise of pursuit ceased halfway down the Gallery. This time she turned left at the bottom of the stairs and searched the rooms of the east wing but they were all empty, some of them not even furnished. There was no alternative but to cross the Great Hall once more. Mistress Boleyn, however, had vanished.

Standing still to catch her breath, Anne heard the hum of voices. Men and women were talking and laughing. She followed the sound into the west wing where it grew louder and louder. Throwing open a door Anne found herself in a panelled and tapestry-hung dining room. She stopped still in amazement for seated at an extremely long table were the strangest collection of people she had ever seen. The men all wore black jackets and white shirts, with little black bows at their throats – the women were shamelessly bare-armed – some even bare-shouldered.

Despite being startled she spoke. 'I am looking for my son,' she said and then added with dignity, 'What are you doing in my house? Are you guests of my husband?'

To her surprise they all ignored her. Then from a vast chair at the head of the table came a strange drawling voice.

71

'That door has opened again. I gotta get it fixed.'

'I'll shut it, Mr Getty,' said a man dressed in black who seemed to be a servant, and he advanced towards her. Horror-stricken, Anne realized that he couldn't see her.

'I'm dead!' she thought and she began to scream . . .

'What is it, mistress?'

Anne awoke to see Joan leaning over her anxiously.

'You've had a nightmare, mam. You've been shouting and bellowing this last few minutes.'

Lady Weston clutched at her.

'Oh, Joan! It was so terrible. I dreamed of the house. It was full of strangers. And Francis was lost – in danger somehow.'

'There, there, my Lady. Master Francis is safe in London. It was just a nightmare.'

But it depressed Anne all that day. The dream had been so vivid that she felt it must have some significance. And when a few weeks later she started to dream again, she deliberately woke herself up. After that she became more wakeful, afraid that it should come once more to torment her.

Thoughts as to the meaning of the nightmare were going through Anne's mind, as they often did in the darkness while Richard slept beside her. It was May and they were guests of Cardinal Wolsey at Hampton Court Palace. From their apartments she could hear the soft sounds of the Thames flowing close by and, wide awake, she rose and went to the windows. Opening them she leant out and breathed in the gentle air of early summer.

Everywhere there was moonshine playing amongst the May blossoms. It was irresistible. Feeling like a girl and smiling at herself, Lady Weston dressed and crept from the bedroom. All around her the Palace slept. Except for the softly murmured conversations of the guards, the clamour and bustle of the day was completely stilled. She walked through the long silent corridors, made magical by the moon reflecting the colours of the stained glass windows on to the walls and tapestries, and out into the formal knot garden that lay behind Hampton Court.

The night was enchanted; the sky so black, the moon so bright, that everything in the garden and beyond seemed transformed by a master confectioner's hand. Each flower and tree was made of spun sugar, each blade of grass a delicate strand of icing. And to add to the spell came the heady scent of blossom – the bewitching aroma from a fairies' summer banquet.

'Foolish woman,' said Anne to herself, but nonetheless she filled her lungs and stood still, enraptured, before finally making off in the direction of the river. Picking her way through the elaborate knot – tended so lovingly by the Cardinal's gardeners – she came to a less formal part of the grounds. Here were green lawns and an abundance of trees, both blossom-heavy and leafed. So sure was she that she was alone on this glorious night that the sound of lowered voices, somewhere close by, frightened her beyond all reason. So much, in fact, that she actually stifled a scream and drew back into the shadow thrown by an apple tree, pressing herself against its rough bark.

After a moment she relaxed again, for clearly visible in the silver light were two lovers, their arms wound round each other, walking back to the palace. She recognized the tall body of Harry Percy and the slim shape of Anne Boleyn pressed close to his side. To her horror, for she had no wish to be an observer, they stopped right by her hiding place and Harry turned the girl towards him.

'Anne, my love witch,' he said and Lady Weston thought it a poetic turn of phrase for that great Northumberland creature whose ancestor and namesake had fought at Agincourt. He pulled the girl almost off her feet as he bent his head to kiss her. The rapturous way in which their bodies melded together told Anne Weston everything. This was no Court flirtation with games of lust as the play and bed as the prize – the couple genuinely loved.

A sense of relief filled her. Anne Boleyn had seemed to her a *strange* girl and it was reassuring to think of her safely married and bedded and out of the way in Northumberland. Embarrassed she saw Harry slip his hands intimately over the girl's breasts. The expression of joy on both their faces was too intense to watch. Lady Weston turned her head away but she heard Anne Boleyn say, 'No, Harry, no!'

'But I love you so much,' he answered.

Lady Weston looked up, startled. So the younger Boleyn girl was no Court whore like her sister. And Harry was no advantage taker, for he did not persist but simply kissed the dark hair that rippled like warm silk in his big hands. In that unearthly light Anne Boleyn, her eyes slanting and her face aglow with love, was beautified. Lady Weston was not surprised to see Harry Percy's cheeks wet with tears. For all his strength, there obviously dwelt a sensitive creature within him, and this sprite of a girl had moved him deeply.

In August, Sir Richard sailed for France with a troop of several thousand soldiery under the command of the King's brother-in-law, Charles Brandon, Duke of Suffolk and it was Anne who was left to supervise the laying of the foundations of Sutton Place. In September, as the leaves blazed, she went there accompanied by her elder daughter, Margaret, and two servants. The workmen were labouring under the personal supervision of da Trevizi who stood in his shirt sleeves, poring over his plans and swearing occasionally in Italian.

As he saw them ride up he attempted to struggle into his doublet but Lady Weston shook her head and so he greeted them dressed informally, kissing the women's fingers and murmuring 'Lady' and 'Bella Signorina'. He was small and black-bearded, with clever and beautiful hands. In one ear he wore a diamond. It occurred to Anne, without unduly flattering herself, that his Italian blood was stirred by both mother and daughter and, if they had been women of low birth, he would happily have tumbled them both. But as it was he had to content himself with shooting them as many meaningful glances from his brilliant dark eyes as propriety would allow. Though he had a reputation as a womanizer he was accepted by everyone at Court because of his great genius as a master builder.

As he spoke of Sutton Place and how it would rise from his designs, majestic and noble, Anne listened enthralled.

'It will be an innovation, m'Lady. One of the first manor houses to be built without fortifications. No moat – nothing. I am going to build for you a house that will last for ever; that will delight the eyes of all who gaze on it.'

He kissed his thumb and forefinger and gave Margaret a sideways glance.

'A house should be like a woman' – now he was bowing to Anne – 'beautiful in all seasons. Exciting in its prime – ' he turned back to Margaret, 'and in its first bloom.'

Lady Weston saw her daughter blush. She made a mental note to speak to Richard about young Walter Dennys. He would be a good match and she had almost forgotten the passing of time. Margaret was now sixteen and Walter two years older.

'High time they met again,' thought Anne. 'As soon as

Richard is returned from the French campaign there must be a meeting.'

But her train of thought was interrupted. Margaret, pink as a rose, was saying, 'Oh Signor da Trevizi, I cannot wait to see it built. How long will it take?'

'For full completion – two years.'

'Could it not be sooner? Mother, are you not anxious to see it?'

Margaret, aware of those burning Italian eyes, was trying to draw her mother back into the conversation but Lady Weston hesitated and both the girl and da Trevizi noticed.

'Is something wrong with my plans, m'Lady? You are silent. What displeases you, bella Signora? For you I would change a palace.'

Margaret said, 'I know what it is. Mother had a fearful dream of the place and something in her is afrighted.'

Da Trevizi wiped his brow with his shirt sleeve.

'I, too, have dreams of every house I build. I dream that they might fall down!'

Anne did not smile and the Italian immediately composed his features into a serious expression.

'M'Lady, I take no notice of these things. Of the houses I build, half have a story of a bad dream, or a curse, or a bewitchment. I built a castle on an island in Lake Como once. The Princess who owned it told me that she first of all dreamed of centaurs, then saw them, and finally that they owned the island. She made me build a special garden house for them – and went to live in it herself.'

'What happened to her?' asked Margaret.

'She went mad.'

Da Trevizi laughed and Anne could have sworn that his hand shot out and squeezed Margaret's, but on second glance it seemed merely that he was searching for his lace kerchief.

In October – on her fortnightly visit to Court – Lady Weston was shocked to hear that Mistress Anne Boleyn had been dismissed and sent home to Hever in Kent. Furthermore, the Earl of Northumberland himself had physically removed his son, Harry Percy, back to the wilds of Northumbria. The love affair was over and, according to gossip, Wolsey himself had intervened, haranguing Harry so cruelly that once again the youth had wept – though this time with despair.

A strange suspicion was growing in Lady Weston's mind but she had no one to whom she could voice it until Richard returned from France – his force badly routed – in December. As soon as he recovered from his sullen mood at the Duke of Suffolk's infamous defeat, they fell to discussing the Boleyn affair with vigour.

'But why, Richard, why? She and Harry seemed so suited.'

'It seems that he was betrothed as a child to Lady Mary Talbot – Shrewsbury's daughter.'

'But that kind of arrangement can be changed. It couldn't *just* be that and, even if it were, why should the Cardinal intervene personally?'

Richard's expression was as impassive as ever, but in his mind's eye he saw again the King's big, handsome face as he partnered the girl in the role of Ardent Desire. How apt a name it seemed now.

'Is it your belief, wife, that the King's Highness asked the Cardinal to intervene?'

Anne nodded, looking very satisfied with herself.

'It is, husband, it is.'

'Then it would seem, even though he beds her sister, the King does not wish to see Anne Boleyn belong to anyone else.'

The Westons looked at one another. The full realization of the first step that England had taken towards its destiny

– a step that would disrupt the world – had not yet dawned on them but they shared a sense of misgiving.

'I feel in my heart that the King will not stop until he has her for himself,' said Anne.

'That should be easy enough,' Richard answered.

How many times in the years to come was he to remember those words with bitterness.

4

The emptiness had gone and the house had taken its place. In the 'meadow sweetness' – as Richard Weston had described it – now stood one of the most beautiful dwellings in England. Da Trevizi had used moulded alabaster and rose-coloured bricks for its exterior, so that in the early morning sun Sutton Place still maintained the glow of dawn. There was no doubt that the Italian had been as good as his word – he had created a mansion to delight posterity.

On horseback, a quarter of a mile away, in a perfect position to see the whole structure and assess its overall design, were Richard Weston, Henry Norris and da Trevizi himself. The architect, especially clothed in plum-coloured velvet in honour of his patron's visit, was listening to their praise with unabashed delight. In the two years since he had first put pen to paper and drawn the initial sketchy outline of a square manor house without a moat, Sutton Place had fired him with a strange joy. The combination of his Italian romanticism and the sturdy approach of his English workmen was producing something rare. He felt sure that this was the work by which he would be remembered. A nagging notion that the house would one day be far more famous than he, he dismissed. However he made a mental note to ensure that Sir Richard wrote down the name of his designer on some important document. The thought that people in the future might not be certain about the identity of the creator of Sutton Place was disturbing to say the least.

'It is a masterwork,' this from Norris. 'Da Trevizi, you have excelled yourself.'

The Italian spread his small hands and bowed his head.

'I would say you do me too much honour, Signor, but on this occasion I must agree. I believe Sutton Place to be my finest achievement – so far!'

Richard Weston smiled one of his rare smiles. He was pleased. The house was everything he had hoped it would be, combining a stately strength with a certain delicacy and beauty of thought; an intangible quality that set it apart. His wife called it ethereal, his daughter – Catherine – a fairy palace. Francis had said, 'It suits you. It is noble.'

Now all that was needed was the status to go with it and that was rather a worry these days. Since his return from the unsuccessful campaign in France in December, 1523 – nearly eighteen months ago – there had been no advancement. He had worked hard at his various appointments, remained on most friendly and cordial terms with the King and Cardinal – but nothing. He had heard, as early as March, that there was to be an investiture in June at which Henry Fitzroy, the King's illegitimate son by Elizabeth Tailebois, was to be made Duke of Richmond. And he knew that others were to be ennobled at the same time but no mention of his name going forward had reached his ever attentive ears. Surely he had not built a home fit for a man of great rank, for nothing?

Da Trevizi was saying, 'Sir Richard, Sir Henry, may I show you more?' and the three walked their horses forward to the Gate House.

Everywhere craftsmen were creating fascinating exterior carvings and mouldings. The Italian's imagination had run riot – fruits and flowers abounded – whilst above the arch in the seventy-foot gate tower was a band of naked and grinning winged cupids holding rosaries. At first glance Norris was shocked. It seemed to him the height of vulgarity but on closer inspection he changed his mind – there was a certain charming innocence about the little figures – Sir Richard had wanted something original and he had most certainly got it.

By the time he had crossed the quadrangle and reached the huge door that lead into the Great Hall, Norris was openly smiling. Not only were there more of those wicked little amorini but in moulded quoins round the door the initials R.W. above the design of a tun. He looked at Sir Richard sideways. The cunning old fox certainly wanted everyone to know who owned this dazzling display of Renaissance virtuosity – even down to the pun on his name. Wes-tun! He shook his head and laughed.

'Well?' Sir Richard was looking at him.

'Most original, Richard. R.W. and a tun. I must confess I've never seen its like.'

'And the house?'

'Magnificent is the only word.'

And Harry Norris was sincere. It was true that he had been brought up to admire a simpler form of design, yet this in no way detracted from his enjoyment of the ornate concept of Renaissance thought. He was, he admitted, rather too unadventurous a person anyway; partly by nature and partly encouraged to a deliberately blinkered outlook by the very essence of his situation at Court. And, though he longed in many ways to be a freer spirit, he knew that it was this very simplicity that had earned him one of the most coveted posts in the land. For it was he – and only he – who was allowed to attend the King in his bedchamber. Not only that, he slept in the same room; his bed between that of the monarch and the door. Literally the King's bodyguard; he who, by ancient tradition, would die rather than let attackers molest

Henry VIII at rest. But that was only the old custom. In reality he must be the totally trustworthy listener; the observer who saw nothing and everything; the perceiver who knew to the finest reckoning the time when he should absent himself so that the King might be free to roam at will.

At fourteen, Norris had gone into the King's service as a page of the Chamber. Always a quiet young man, he had gone about his work steadily and conscientiously, not really looking for advancement. When it came he had been amazed.

'Why me?' he had said to William Carey, a fellow member of the King's personal suite.

'I think, Harry, because you can keep your mouth shut more firmly than anyone else,' William had said.

Neither he nor Norris could have guessed that one day Harry would have to exercise that very discretion over Carey's own wife, Mary.

Harry supposed that to a more volatile man his job would have presented enormous difficulties but he simply got on with it, without thinking too much. Henry frequently changed his loves though, admittedly, in all those years of marriage, only Elizabeth Tailebois – mother of Henry Fitzroy – and Mary Carey had been serious affairs. But recent events had been a little unsettling. All the visits to Hever 'to hunt'. Yes, the King was hunting all right, Harry thought, but deer were not the quarry. If he was reading the signs aright it was that little dark thing that graced Tom Boleyn's household with her presence – the youngest child, Anne. Anne of the exciting laugh; Anne of the million enchanting glances; Anne who went swirling through a man's dreams like a midnight fairy.

'Jesu,' thought Harry, 'insanity lies along this path. One day the King will offer her something she will not be able to resist and I'll have to make myself scarce. God help me.'

He realized that Sir Richard was inviting him inside, pushing open the vast door. As he stepped into the sheer majesty of the Great Hall, Norris felt that he was entering a church. The vaulted roof soared above him; the stained glass windows – two with glaziers still securing the glass panels – glowed like a prism in a waterfall, whilst above the fireplace blazed the colour of the pomegranate. Richard Weston had had Queen Katharine's device moulded and painted round the mantelpiece.

As the tour of Sutton Place continued – da Trevizi now having joined them again, to point out the finer details of the interior carving and the use of terra cotta moulding – Norris grew more and more amazed. He had no doubt at all that he was seeing a man's vision made reality; it seemed to him that da Trevizi must have had divine inspiration.

He was so bemused with the sheer size of the Long Gallery – something he had never seen before but which would be copied by every architect in England within a few years – that he was forced to sit down in gasping admiration on reaching the far end. As there were no chairs he sat on the floor and gazed round, totally lost for words.

Richard Weston laughed, his expressionless eyes for once animated.

'I see you're in favour.'

'It is the most original thing I have ever come across. I believe you'll start a fashion. Why, you can use it for dancing and music and mummery.'

'And to walk in in the winter. Come, Harry, let me offer you some refreshment. I have had one little chamber in the north wing made ready. The rest is awaiting completion of work.'

'When will it be finished?'

'In the autumn.'

Leaving da Trevizi, the two men proceeded down a turreted spiral staircase and out into the quadrangle where, through a smaller doorway, they entered the Gate House wing. Here Sir Richard had had a room furnished and on the dresser Harry saw that two hogsheads of claret had been placed on supports.

'The man intends to show his mansion to anyone who'll come to see,' he thought. But, God's life, he had something to show!

Sir Richard was pouring wine and saying, 'Tell me about the investiture in June.'

Norris sat down and took the proffered glass. 'The main object seems to be to ennoble Henry Fitzroy. He is to become Duke of Richmond.'

'Surely His Grace cannot be preparing him to succeed to the throne?'

As always with any mention of the King an automatic shutter came down in Norris's mind. His position as principal Esquire of the Body was sacred – gossip, on however high a level, was something in which he could never indulge.

'I have no idea,' he answered. And the reply was fair. Henry VIII's predicament of a legitimate daughter and a bastard son was something that occupied the minds of most at Court. But whether England would accept a King born out of wedlock was the question nobody could answer.

'I believe others will be receiving honours,' said Richard, a fraction too casually.

'Yes, the King's nephew is to become Earl of Lincoln and two courtiers are to be made peers . . .'

The fury Richard felt expressed itself only by a tightening in his stomach, outwardly he showed nothing.

'. . . Sir Robert Radcliffe is to become Viscount Fitzwalter and Sir Thomas Boleyn, Viscount Rochford.'

It was like a game of chess. Richard's expression still did not alter and yet Norris could have sworn that very slightly – so slightly that only someone trained to sense the King's changes of mood almost before they happened would notice – Weston tensed.

'Of course the King hunts a great deal round Hever Castle these days,' Richard remarked, sipping his wine and looking vague. 'I must invite him here when the house is ready. These are great hunting forests – always have been.'

Norris thought, 'He'll get to the point in a minute. I wonder what he wants to know?'

Aloud he said, 'I've heard the red deer are more bountiful here than in any other place in England.'

''Tis perfectly true.' Richard paused then said, 'I'm glad for Tom. The Boleyn family service His Grace well.'

There could be no doubt now as to his meaning and Norris thought that this was not Richard Weston at his most subtle. He had a sudden feeling that the man was hiding a seething discontent.

'And while we speak of them, how are Tom's family, Harry? I hear that the Mary Carey business is at an end.'

'Yes,' said Norris. It was common knowledge and he was revealing nothing.

'And the other girl, Anne? How is she faring since she left Court?'

'Well,' said Norris.

'Well!' What a fatuous description for a slip of a thing who had the King of England besotted, had driven Harry Percy to the brink of despair and was never out of his – Henry Norris's – mind.

Feeling Sir Richard looking at him strangely he added, 'In good health.'

'God damn the man,' Richard thought. 'He'd rather go to the rack than reveal his mother's name!'

He gave up. Norris was immovable, he should have known better than to try and extract information. But the fact that he had been overlooked for advancement had made him behave uncharacteristically, lower his guard. With an inward sigh he turned the conversation to generalities.

Da Trevizi had left the Long Gallery and followed Sir Richard and Sir Henry down the spiral staircase and out into the courtyard. The exterior decoration of Sutton Place was being executed entirely by English craftsmen under his personal supervision. With the house only a few months away from completion he was present on the site several times a week and did not hesitate to get into any one of the work cradles and haul himself up to run his expert Florentine eye over the finer details of the moulded alabaster and carved stone.

He stood now in the quadrangle and gazed about him at where, on all sides, the men were chipping and fashioning the shapes he had designed for them. One in particular caught his eye, for, though he was sitting at one of the highest points on the east wing, he was rumbling away in a melodious baritone, quite regardless of the drop beneath him.

The accident, when it happened, was so quick that for a second the Italian – the only man on the ground able to help – was frozen to the spot. It seemed that the song and the scream became one continuous sound as the rope snapped and the wretched fellow crunched on to the cobbles of the courtyard, as broken and as finished as a trodden ant.

The incidents of the next few minutes were to be relived by da Trevizi until his dying day; he quite literally never forgot them and as he did die – old and celebrated and in the arms of the young woman he finally took for a wife – he saw them again and the last thing he ever said was 'Talitha!'

He began to run forward to the stonemason – though he could see from where he was that the man's neck was broken and he was beyond help – and even as he ran there was a pounding in da Trevizi's ears and a blackness round him as if he were about to faint. He reached the dead man's side and then it appeared to him that he entered a tunnel. Sutton Place was reduced to a faint outline and there was nothing but him and the corpse by which he knelt and this strange bright cavern in which he found himself. Looking up from the dead man's face – the lips still formed into the shape of the song he had been singing – he saw, only a few feet away from him, a girl. It seemed that she had wandered into the tunnel too for she looked as startled to see him as da Trevizi was to see her. Her hair was long and straight and dark and she was dressed in what the Italian could only think was a Greek boy's tunic, for her legs showed to the thigh. They looked at each other in horror without saying a word. Round her neck was a gold band forming letters. With difficulty the Italian spelt out the unfamiliar script.

'T-A-L-I-T-H-A. Talitha.'

He must have said it aloud because she said, 'Oh God, who are you? Paul!'

From what sounded like an echoing vault, a voice said, 'What?'

'Look. Can't you see it?'

'See what? There's nothing there.'

'Talitha!' called da Trevizi and as she opened her mouth to scream, he lost consciousness and fell forward.

That was how Richard Weston found him; lying over the dead stonemason in a faint so deep it resembled a coma. He and Norris carried him into Sutton Place to the little bedchamber that the architect had furnished for himself. He was still in the same state when they rode off for London some hours later, leaving him in the charge of a physician who had hastily been sent for from Guildford.

It was two days before the Italian regained consciousness and this only after Dr Burton in sheer desperation, had administered several pints of water from St Edward's Well; he being a local man and knowing the ancient story of its curative powers. The normally ebullient da Trevizi, after resting for another day, put the work of Sutton Place in the hands of his senior apprentice – Carlo of Padua – and set off without telling anyone where he was going or commenting on his mysterious illness.

He rode throughout that day and night, stopping once to change horses, and on arriving in London went straight to a house in Cordwainer Street, standing next to a hostelry called the Holy Lamb. The servant who answered the door said, 'You'll have to wait. Dr Zachary has a great lady with him.'

Da Trevizi did not reply, merely collapsing into a chair, paler and more exhausted than he had ever been in his life. He may have waited one hour – two; he wasn't sure for the girl kept filling his tankard and he allowed himself to doze off, feeling that at last he was safe.

He was awoken by the door being flung wide. A man stood in the opening, half hidden by shadow, and though he could not see his face, da Trevizi knew that he was being observed. No, more than that – scrutinized, read like a book, stripped bare. The Italian got to his feet.

'Dr Zachary?' he said.

With a swirl of his cloak the man bowed and it was as if a rushing wind was in the room; such power generated from the figure that stood before the architect. As the man straightened his face came into the light and da Trevizi gaped, quite stunned by what he saw. Of course he had never actually met the famous soothsayer and astrologer, nor had he heard him described – but this was quite amazing.

'He's not much over twenty,' thought the Italian. 'Men of learning are mature. This boy can know nothing.'

He looked at the great mass of curly hair, the squarish face, the straight nose; felt the raw energy emanating from the youthful figure before him.

'You *are* Dr Zachary?'

Da Trevizi simply could not credit it.

The man bowed again, his cloak a black velvet torrent.

'Signor da Trevizi, do not be surprised. I am he whom you seek. Old age is not the only qualification for those who have probed the dark secrets of nature.'

'How did you know me?'

Dr Zachary grinned, suddenly imp-like and said, 'I have seen you at Court, sir. I did not read it in the stars.'

The Italian stood wondering. He had not consulted an astrologer before, though it was a popular pastime in Court circles. And the name spoken by those who dabbled in the occult to any extent was always that of Dr Zachary. Da Trevizi had heard it rumoured that he was in truth a Howard – a bastard son of the Duke of Norfolk's family – though nobody seemed to know whether he was the child of a man or woman of the house or who his other parent had been. Yet this wild boy with his tangled curls and amber eyes was so foreign to all the architect's preconceived ideas of a man of great wisdom, that he still hesitated.

Dr Zachary still read his thoughts.

'Signor da Trevizi, why remain? I regret my lack of years and your lack of faith. Farewell!'

He turned to leave but the Italian was forced by desperation to speak. 'Doctor, stay – I beg you. I have had an experience so strange that I need help.'

'Are you accursed?'

'I don't know. She did not seem evil. She looked as terrified as I.'

'Come.'

For no rational reason da Trevizi was afraid as he followed Dr Zachary up the shadowy and spindly staircase that led to the top floor of the gaunt house. Yet what had rationality to do with fear of the dark, of the unknown, of the threat of the inexplicable? For here was uneasiness taking him by the hand and leading him into the sloping attic which served as the astrologer's cloister. How many famous feet, the Italian wondered, had trod this way before in search of the knowledge that was denied mankind; the hidden – or would a better word be forbidden – secret of his identity.

In the dim light he saw charts upon the walls, ancient symbols inscribed beneath, showing the signs of the zodiac and dominating the room a dark-clothed table on which lay a pack of strangely drawn cards, some stones with unusual markings, some more maps of the heavens with measuring devices and in the midst of all a crystal glittering in the light of the candles.

The astrologer motioned him to a chair and then sat down himself.

'Tell me what happened,' he said.

The Italian began with the accident to the stonemason but Zachary interrupted him, 'No, before that. Tell me of the house you have designed.'

Da Trevizi began to speak of Sutton Place and was surprised at how often the astrologer stopped him with questions: Where was it situated? Had the land been lived on before? What of its history?

The architect answered as best he could. He knew very little of Sutton's ancient past, only that he had visited the old ruined manor house a couple of times and seen the well known as St Edward's.

'I am told that it was water from there that brought me back to consciousness. It is supposed to have healing powers.'

Dr Zachary raised his brows and nodded his head so hard that the tousled hair shook, but made no comment.

'But let me speak to you about what happened,' said da Trevizi. 'Let me tell you about the tunnel of light and the woman.'

Zachary thought, 'Strange that Lady Weston should have consulted me about a dream of the place and now here is the designer.'

But he said nothing and da Trevizi plunged into a vividly Italianate description of the fatality and the incidents following. Dr Zachary sat for a long time without saying a word, finally he began to gaze into the crystal, his shoulders hunching, his square face changing, softening with a faraway quality quite at odds with his earlier alertness.

'Talitha was the name round her neck, wasn't it?' he said at last.

Da Trevizi's heart began to race. He had deliberately refrained from mentioning that. Foolish perhaps, but he had wanted to set some kind of test for the man; hadn't really believed in him despite all that others had said. Something in his Italian blood had disliked the thought of a charlatan taking his money; been made angry by a youth posing as a sorcerer. But now he was shaken.

'Yes,' he said, and his voice was trembling.

'Talitha – written in a strange script.'

'Is she a witch?'

An extremely odd expression crossed Zachary's face – his features contorted with apparent rage.

'No,' he hissed. 'Talitha will be no witch.'

'What do you mean, Sir?'

'She is not yet born.'

Da Trevizi went very white and crossed himself.

'Christos,' he said. 'What are you saying?'

Dr Zachary looked beyond the crystal and into the corner of the room. He seemed to have shrunken into himself; his face shadowy beneath the wild hair.

'I am saying, Signor da Trevizi, that you saw a ghost from the time that is still to come. Talitha will be born with great beauty, she will achieve great wealth and she will die most tragically. But there is nothing about her that is evil – you are not bewitched.'

He almost spat out the last words and the architect thought, 'Something troubles him. Witchcraft makes him afraid. Surely he cannot be patronized by the greatest in the land and still dread persecution.'

Dr Zachary hunched his shoulders even more and thought, 'They see a witch in everything. And so my poor mother died in agony as they burned her alive. For all my father's power, he could not save her.'

He recalled his ordeal as a ten-year-old boy, as vividly as if it had taken place yesterday. He had kicked and fought his way through the crowd till he had reached the front, only to see the woman who had given birth to him, with her head dropped forward, fumes choking her, blonde hair blackened by smoke. He had opened his mouth to scream 'Mother' but unexpectedly a hand had clapped over it.

'Are you her child?' a voice had murmured in his ear.

'Yes.'

'Then keep silent or they'll kill you too.'

So, without making a sound, he had watched his mother burning to death till he was able to bear it no more and had turned his head and buried it in the coat of the strange man beside him and blocked his ears so that he could not hear her terrible screams.

Afterwards, when the crowd had dispersed, he had gone with the stranger and collected the forlorn ashes – all that was left of the loving girl who had been his sole companion for ten years – and put them in a box.

'Come, I'm taking you to your father,' the stranger had said.

'But I have no father. He was dead before I was born.'

'He is alive and no more than a mile from here. Come!'

The strange sixth sense that had always been part of him – his mother's gift – told him at once that it was true. He had been swung up to sit in the saddle in front of the man and they had gone at speed to Kenninghall Castle and even before he saw him Zachary had known that his father was the Duke of Norfolk himself.

When he entered the room and saw the powerful square face, the large straight nose, the determined jaw, he knew where his own looks had come from. All but the mass of black curls. His father was looking at those too, for he said, 'So there's Romany in you, all right. Your mother was so fair I was not sure.'

'Did you love her?' said Zachary.

The Duke looked startled. Thomas Howard had not expected the bastard he had not seen since it was a baby to answer him like that. But nonetheless he thought of the rose sweetness of his honey-skinned love who had walked barefoot in the meadows at night, picking the herbs and flowers she needed for her potions, and singing her strange, plaintive songs; thought of the pleasure in her arms, greater than there had ever been with any woman before or since.

'Yes, I loved her,' he said.

The boy held out a small box to him.

'That's all that's left of her. I want that put in your family vault, Lord Duke my father.'

A strange feeling had come over Norfolk. He had wanted to say no, thinking of the tedious explanations if a box containing ashes were discovered in the place reserved for the long dead of the Howard clan, but the boy's amber eyes were staring fixedly into his and he was holding out the casket as if he would stand like that for ever if need be.

'There will be a priest, too,' continued Zachary. 'My mother was no Mistress of Satan. She was a herbalist who could cure people's ills.'

'But what of her fortune telling?'

'She was born with the gift of clear sight, as I have been. We need no pact with the devil for that.'

Thomas felt uneasy. He was quite sure that his son possessed great power, could feel the child's influence over him even now, as he agreed to put the dead woman's ashes in the Howard vault with due Christian ritual.

'She called you Zachary, didn't she?'

'Yes, Lord Duke my father.'

It gave the Duke the strangest feeling to hear himself addressed thus by this wild boy.

'Well, what am I to do with you, Zachary Howard?'

'I could make my own way, sir.'

'No, that you'll not do. I have given her money these ten years past to feed and clothe you and now that she's gone you'll need help.'

'But I have the gift of sorcery.'

The Duke nearly said, 'If you continue you too may yet be burned', but changed it to 'It would be dangerous for you to stay here. I shall take you to London with me. You shall live with a good tutor and study diligently. I shall see you whenever I can, for I am often at Court.'

'Then send me to someone who can teach me of the

stars and the natural laws, and I will make you not ashamed to be my father even though we must never speak of it before others.'

And it had come about just as Zachary had said. In almost exactly ten years from that night he had achieved the position of a Court favourite and it would bring a smile to Norfolk's lips when he heard his bastard described as the greatest astrologer living.

Da Trevizi, watching Dr Zachary's face, thought that perhaps he had gone into a trance but out of the gloom the sorcerer spoke. 'No, you are not bewitched, my friend. Tell me the date, place and time of your birth and I will chart your life for you by the stars. It will take me many days, but it shall be done.'

Da Trevizi was seized with a strange idea.

'Is it Sutton Place that is accursed?'

Dr Zachary hesitated.

'Perhaps,' he said.

5

In the silence of a summer evening, the rhythmic sound of oars pulling at a pace neither leisurely nor yet anxiously hurried, mingled with the cry of a heron, and in the garden of the Westons' Chelsea home – which sloped gently down to the river – both Sir Richard and his wife moved very slightly, while Francis and Catherine shot a surreptitious glance at their sister Margaret.

It was a night made for lovers. The softness of the sunset throwing a beautifying light on the earth; the scent of flowers seducing the warm breeze; the rippling river turning to scarlet and gold as the boat bearing Sir William Dennys of Gloucester, his wife and son, came round the bend in the river and eased into the mooring alongside Sir Richard's barge.

In the dew covered grass the Westons' feet were silent as they walked forward to the jetty.

Margaret thought, 'I cannot show my face for I am not as pretty as Catherine and Francis and he is bound to be handsome. I wish I could fall into the river and drown or become a nun or simply remain at home.'

And so it was standing thus, slightly breathless and quite definitely flushed with anxiety, she found herself face to face with Walter Dennys, the young man it was most earnestly hoped by her parents she would marry.

'Oh dear!' she said.

His only response was a strangled sound from somewhere deep within his throat. This so startled Margaret, who had sunk into a curtsey, that she looked up and saw to her amazement that the lanky young man in front of her was crimson with embarrassment and was bowing again and again, as if he could not stop.

Somewhere behind her she heard Francis give a muffled laugh and this made the situation worse. For Walter Dennys heard it too and blushed even more deeply so that Margaret, standing up, felt obliged to give her brother a kick on the ankle.

Naturally the noise caught the attention of both sets of parents and Margaret found herself the subject of a withering look from Lady Dennys.

'Walter,' she called sharply and Margaret saw him stiffen.

'Y-y-yes, Mother?'

'What are you doing?'

'N-n-nothing, Mother.'

And much to her own surprise it was Margaret who spared him further agony by walking up to Lady Dennys, giving a most respectful curtsey, and saying, 'Forgive me, I accidentally kicked my brother, Madam.'

Lady Dennys sniffed and Walter bowed again and this time he smiled and she noticed that his eyes, which were a most pleasant shade of green, crinkled at the corners when he did so.

And that night, as Margaret's maid was brushing her hair before retiring, Lady Weston came to her. Dismissing the servant, she tucked her daughter into bed herself and then sat down.

'Well, my child,' she said, 'what do you think of him?'

'I think,' answered Margaret quietly, 'that he will be perfectly all right when he comes from beneath his mother's thumb.'

'You are quite correct of course,' Anne said. 'Because she is Lord Berkeley's daughter the woman considers herself high ranking and it is my opinion that she has worried that boy into a state of over-stretched nerves.'

They kissed each other goodnight.

In the bedrooms set aside for guests a similar scene was being enacted. Sir William Dennys was sitting on his son's bed and saying, 'She's a sweet-natured girl, Walter. If you weren't so wretchedly nervous.'

'I know, but I can't help it.'

It was typical of the whole situation that Walter never stuttered when talking alone with his father.

'Well, must she be wooed. Now go to it, boy. Go to it.'

'But Father, how?'

Sir William twitched his shoulders irritably and went out muttering.

The answer, when it came, was so delightfully simple, that neither Margaret nor Walter could have guessed at it nor imagined the hours of infinite happiness that it would give them in the future. Up early, unable to sleep, and dejectedly wondering how a dullard like himself could set about pleasing such a kind and pretty girl as Margaret Weston, Walter almost fell over her, kneeling tending the herbs in the garden specially made for that purpose.

'E-e-excuse me,' he said, blushing miserably. 'I didn't s-s-see you.'

'I shouldn't really be here, this is gardener's work. But I love it so much.'

Forgetting that he was betrothed to her she went on, 'If ever I have a house of my own I want to design and plan a great garden all round it. Shady walks with willows and open walks planted with wild thyme and watermint. And of course, a maze. And a rose garden and a lake big enough to row upon between the shrubs.'

He squatted down beside her, his elbows resting on his knees and his big hands hanging relaxed.

'But this is my very hobby,' he said excitedly. 'When I . . . I mean i-i-if you are so good as to marry me, I am to have a h-home of my own and it is my w-w-wish to have the most beautiful garden in England.'

'With fountains?'

'Aye. And more than one labyrinth. And topiary. And I shall wish to oversee all.'

'If we marry may I work alongside you?'

'Oh, Margaret, w-would you really d-do so?'

Her eyes were bright.

'I would like nothing better in the world.'

By the end of the week all was arranged. The wedding would take place in the autumn after the Westons had moved into Sutton Place; Sir Richard's dowry for his daughter would be generous and in return Sir William guaranteed Margaret a liberal jointure, including property, in the event of Walter's death. These important matters were negotiated by the fathers while Lady Weston was left with the more difficult task of trying to entertain the unbending Lady Dennys.

But in the knot garden, quite uncaring, their heads bent together, Walter and Margaret sat on the stone seat in the sunshine and his great hands – so delicate as they drew – sketched while she talked. And drawing after drawing of the garden they would make at Haseley Court in Oxfordshire emerged.

Her laughs of happiness and the shower of rose petals she threw at him set the seal on their future relationship and guaranteed for posterity one of the most exquisite gardens ever to be created.

Anne Weston knew that Richard was angry by the way he set his feet down loudly as soon as he was through the front door. The clumping as he came up the stairs and towards the room where she and Joan were putting valuables into chests, in preparation for the move to Sutton Place, confirmed her suspicions. Joan mouthed

'Oh' and Anne responded by rolling her eyes to heaven and sighing. She had no time for moods, with the move only a week away. But nonetheless Richard, after his terrible disappointment over the June investiture, could not have had an easy time at his interview with Cardinal Wolsey. She composed her features into an interested smile but her mind was wondering where she had packed a set of silver spoons that had been given to her by Elizabeth of York.

As he came in he slumped into a chair and shouted at Joan to pull off his boots.

'The Cardinal was difficult I take it?'

'No,' answered Richard surprisingly. 'No, he was not difficult. In fact I think he thought he was doing me a great service.'

'Then why so gloomy?'

'Anne, he has given me the Treasurership of Calais.'

'Oh, dear God, no.'

She sat down as abruptly as he had done.

The French town and its surrounding land still belonged to England, just as did the Channel Isles, and to become its Treasurer was honour indeed – but now, at this time, with Sutton Place just completed! Sir Richard had built his mansion only to be denied the privilege of living in it. Anne could have wept.

'When do you go?'

'In two months – when we have settled into Sutton Place.'

'Settled in,' said Anne bitterly. 'You'll no sooner be settled in than settled out again.'

'But I shall return every month.'

'Small consolation.'

'Sweetheart, you could come with me.'

'And leave the running of Sutton Place to servants? Richard, you know that could never be.'

But on their first night in their new home their minds were taken off the problem of Calais by the re-appearance, after four years, of Giles of Guildford, the strolling player. He came through the Gate House arch with the same plodding gait, his back laden with his entire worldly goods. Sir Richard, in highly benevolent mood, sent him to eat with the kitchen lads and invited him to entertain them that evening after supper.

So, after the family had dined in the Great Hall – Richard sitting in the master's chair at the high table, happier than he had ever been before as he enjoyed the satisfaction of possessing and living in Sutton Place – they retired to the Long Gallery. Here Anne had had every candle lit and all four fires lit to welcome the Lord of the Manor on his first evening in his new home with his household.

Giles had an audience ready to be pleased as he leaped in with a great jump and traversed the Gallery's considerable length with a series of cartwheels and somer-saults that surprised even himself. Then, his belled cap ringing, the little head on the end of his jester's stick grinning in a humorous copy of Giles's own face, he burst into song. In a loud but tuneful voice the sound of 'Pastime in Good Company' – the words and music written by the King himself – echoed down the huge space. Then followed jokes and finally another song and display of acrobatic skills.

Exhausted, he knelt before his patron, the sweat streaming off him.

'Well done, Giles.'

Sir Richard had forgotten all about his initial dislike of the player in the good atmosphere. He sat, leaning back in his chair, looking about him. Everything he could see was his; had been earned by his endeavours, kept by his side by his attention, or – in the case of his children – was actually part of him. And after all, to be Treasurer of Calais was almost on a level with a peerage.

'Have I pleased you, my Lord?' It was Giles speaking.

'So well that I have an idea for you.'

Giles stood up but Sir Richard motioned him to a chair and a servant poured the player a glass of wine. He gulped it down as if it were ale.

'And what is this idea, master?'

His face was a little anxious. He was in his usual impecunious state and he was hoping that he was not about to be offered a gift in place of money. That would mean the general time-wasting business of having to sell it and get the right price, whilst his stomach groaned for food.

'Don't frown, fellow . . . .'

Giles obediently turned his face into a grin, an action so idiotic that Francis and Catherine started to giggle without restraint.

' . . . what I have to offer will please you I think.'

Through his fixed leer, Giles said, 'Oh yes?'

Even Sir Richard was beginning to see the funny side of it. Poor Giles sitting on the edge of his chair, his face a mask of unfelt jollity, his jaw rigid as he spoke for fear of cracking his set grimace.

'I am inviting you to become my Fool. Permanently. A wage, a bed in the kitchen lads' chamber, free food. Now what do you say?'

Much to Richard's surprise the grin, instead of becoming genuine, fell away entirely. Rather annoyed, Richard – unused to having offers of a place in his household met with such obvious lack of enthusiasm – said, 'You are not interested?'

'Oh, it's not that, my Lord. Not that at all,' Giles babbled. ''Tis just that I'm overwhelmed. Yes, that's it – overwhelmed. Speechless, in fact. Yes, I'm speechless.'

To himself he thought, 'Dear Christ – of all the ill fortune. The idea's been going through my mind these six months past to find some permanent lodging. I'm getting too old for the outdoor life, though I can still tumble and jest with the best of them. But this! To live on cursed land.'

He knew they were waiting for his answer. His thoughts began to fall over themselves. Would his Romany blood protect him? If he wore the carbuncle blessed by the wise woman, who lived near the mystic monoliths of Stonehenge, would he be all right? Had his invocation to the 'unseen people' for Lady Weston been heard? A certain ritual he knew might do the trick. Oh God, should he risk all in return for the coveted position of Sir Richard Weston's Fool?

Then something Lady Weston said decided him.

'Why Giles, if you become our Fool you'll have a chance to show your paces before the King's Grace for he comes to Sutton Place to attend Margaret's wedding in November. And you'll be able to compete against Will Somers.'

Will Somers! There was a name to conjure with. The King's new jester – new this very year but already with a formidable reputation. His repartee was even now spoken of as the wittiest in the land. To pit himself against such a giant; to have the opportunity – he, humble Giles – to perform for the King. Better learn some new songs. His Grace had an ear for a good tune.

'My speech is returned, my Lord,' said Giles. 'I thank you. It will be an honour to serve you and your Lady.'

It was Margaret and Walter's wedding feast and the most sumptuous of banquets was being served. At the upper end of the Great Hall was set the high table beneath which lay a magnificent red carpet for the King's feet. It had been woven in Turkey and brought to England by

Sir Richard's own trading ship and was, Anne Weston thought, quite the most exquisite floor covering she had ever seen in her life. Lower down, another huge table, with not quite such a good carpet beneath, was set for the Court.

The Hall was garlanded and decorated with as much greenery as the November garden would yield and, in the trailing branches, winter roses had been skilfully woven alongside early holly berries. Anne had wanted as glistening an effect as she could muster to honour Henry and Katharine and the bride and groom. The musicians – resplendent in doublets of crimson with gold slashed sleeves – were jammed together in the two musicians' galleries above the Hall, bursting forth with the most cheerful sound.

In the Queen's fireplace – as the family now called it because of Katharine's device – a vast log fire was sending out a terrific heat and the light from this, and the hundred blazing candles, reflecting in the gleaming facets of the goblets and wine flagons, seemed almost as vivid and brilliant as the jewelled and glittering assembly itself.

Before the King – who sat with Katharine on one side of him and Anne Weston on the other – stood a concoction of iced sugar in the shape of a galleon, the strands as delicate as a cobweb, the sails sparkling frost. On the other side of the Queen sat Walter Dennys with his bride beside him. He had made the garland for her hair with his own hands and the flowers that lay before all the principal female guests he had fashioned the day before.

Lower down the table Francis sat between his sister Catherine and Ann Pickering, a girl he had not met since he was a child but to whom, his father had informed him, he was one day to be married.

On hearing the news a few days earlier, before she had arrived, he had said, 'I'll warrant she's ugly.'

'I'll brook no insolence from you, Francis,' Sir Richard had answered. 'She is an orphan and my ward and she is also the richest heiress in Cumberland. Be civil, do you hear?'

So the day after the King's arrival Francis had stood in the Great Hall listening to the heiress of Cumberland's escort jangling over the quadrangle and watching, with thudding heart, as the door of the middle entrance was thrown open and a small figure had been ushered in. He had dropped his gaze, wiped his damp palms surreptitiously on his doublet and made a bow. The figure curtsied before him and then did something that only somebody raised away from Court would have dared. She looked up and stared him straight in the eye.

Francis had looked and fallen madly in love. A mass of red curls, which simply refused to be constrained by a headdress, tumbled round a creamy skin that was only enhanced by the delightfully freckled nose. But it was her eyes that captured Francis and held him for the rest of his life; blue as meadow flowers, wide and with a twinkling in their depths that simply nobody could resist.

So for the last week he had been longing to touch her – just the merest meeting of hands would have been enough – but had been far too nervous, her very presence making him shake. And he was doing it now – here, at the high table, only a few feet away from the King – trembling so much that the wine glasses tinkled as they rattled together.

Hearing the noise, Lady Weston looked over and Queen Katharine, following her gaze said, 'What beautiful children you have, Anne.'

A very small sigh escaped from her lips. Why had God turned his face against her and only allowed Mary to live? She would have given ten years of her life – twenty

105

– to have Anne Weston's three healthy offspring for her own.

'Your Grace is very kind.'

'It is true. Margaret makes a wonderful bride and as for Francis and Ann Pickering – why they are the prettiest couple in England. I have never seen a boy so handsome in all my life. If my son had lived he would be the same age, for were they not born within weeks of each other?'

Unable to take her eyes off him the Queen went on, 'And his eyes, just like a lake. Anne, now that you and Richard are no longer at Court I think you should send Francis to us. Henry, wouldn't he make a handsome page?'

Henry VIII looked down the table towards the boy.

'Probably the best looking courtier of all,' he said, and he called out, 'Hey, young Weston.'

Francis rose and bowed.

'Yes, your Grace.'

'Would you like to come to Court next year?'

'Indeed I would,' Francis answered and in that simple sentence took his first fateful step towards death.

But now the banquet was drawing to its end and a host of servants were removing the topcloths from the two big tables, baring the undercloths embroidered with lace and gleaming crisply beneath the bowls of fruit and nuts and flagons of burgundy. It was time for the entertainers and tonight was to be Giles's great chance. On the previous night – the wedding eve – Will Somers had held his audience entranced by his brilliant chatter and Giles, listening in the background, had wisely decided that in this field the man was unbeatable. No, he would concentrate on something that Will could not do as well – singing and tumbling – for, though there were better singers, there were few acrobats in England as accomplished as Giles of Guildford.

But this night his voice sounded more clear and true than it ever had before. As he sang a Romany love song – for he knew the King's weakness for sentimentality – he felt inspired; uplifted almost. It was a sweet melody of a knight and his beauteous dark lady of the forest, and watching the King's face Giles saw that it had some special meaning for him, though he had no idea what. How could he know that the words transported Henry to Hever Castle and to *his* dark lady, Anne Boleyn.

Swept away by the words and the sound of the lute, Francis at last found the courage to do what he had wanted to all week. Beneath the table he took Ann Pickering's small child-like hand in his and squeezed. He felt himself grow dizzy as she moved imperceptibly nearer to him.

The notes of the song soared up to the rafters of the Great Hall as Giles came to the last verse and for a moment all the beauty of the occasion seemed frozen into one jewelled droplet of time. All was still and at one, listening to the wild, haunting sound. Then the lute struck its final plaintive note and there was silence. The spell which had held them all was broken. It was never again to be repeated.

6

'And this, young Weston, is where you will report each morning to learn what errands His Grace has for you.'

Francis and Sir Harry Norris were standing in the King's private apartments in Greenwich Palace. These were the rooms known as the Privy Chamber and only the staff directly serving the King were allowed access to them; no other courtiers were even permitted to cross the threshold. Francis was trying hard not to show his excitement. At fifteen he had become one of the King's personal retinue; the new Page of the Chamber and one of the favoured few allowed to enter the sacred precincts of His Grace's rooms.

'There are six gentlemen-in-waiting,' Norris continued, 'Sir William Taylor, Sir Thomas Cheyney, Sir Anthony Browne, Sir John Russell, William Carey and myself and we are the only ones allowed to sleep within the Chamber. However, I have a further post – Principal Esquire of the Body – and, as you know, this means I am the sole person permitted to attend His Grace in his bedchamber. I sleep in there to act as his guard. You are not allowed in, do you understand?'

'Yes, Sir Henry.'

'Now, you will share a room in another part of the palace with the Chamber grooms – they are the two Brereton brothers and Walter Welsh and John Carey. You will rise at six sharply each day and help the grooms clean the Privy Chamber and light the fire. At seven o'clock the Chamber ushers – Roger Ratcliffe and Anthony Knevett – will arrive to guard the door. Shortly after that the yeoman of the wardrobe will bring the King's doublet, hose and shoes. He will hand these to one of the grooms and it will be your job to help warm them by the fire and take them to the gentlemen-in-waiting. You are at no time allowed to touch His Grace. Is that clear?'

Francis nodded. He was frankly overawed.

'Your other duties will be to clear away after Penny the barber has trimmed His Grace's beard and hair. Then you must make yourself useful to anyone who needs you, His Grace's wishes always coming first of course.'

'Of course,' echoed Francis.

'The Head of the Privy Chamber is the Marquess of Exeter and you will be directly responsible to him. Briefly, Francis, the rules are that we do not gossip about His Grace. If he goes to bed early, if he goes late or if he doesn't go at all, it is not our affair. We don't talk about his friends or what he does. In short, nothing that we see or hear must go beyond these walls. Can you keep a still tongue?'

'I think so, sir.'

'Well, it's going to be essential if you want to keep your post.'

Francis gulped. It was only three days since he had left home and he had arrived at Greenwich on the previous afternoon. His father – on brief leave from Calais – had ridden with him but had, after a few hours' sleep, taken his leave. Francis had watched that familiar back riding away with mixed feelings. It was the first time that he had ever been away from his parents and he was starting his career with one of the most difficult – and yet one of the most potentially rewarding – posts at Court. To be a member of the Privy Chamber meant that, for good or ill, one was always under the King's eye. Tact, discretion, all those things were essential. As Sir Richard had disappeared from view Francis had felt the oddly mixed emotions of fear and gratification. Glad that he was now a man in a man's world; apprehensive that he no longer had his family to turn to if anything should go wrong.

He had dined alone that night, feeling rather depressed, and had been asleep by the time the four Chamber grooms had come to bed after late-night gaming with the King. He shared with them a large, pleasantly furnished room on the first floor of the palace, overlooking the Thames. At six the general commotion as they rose had woken him but he had scarcely had time to exchange a word as they hurried off to clean the King's apartments.

'You are excused duties this morning,' William Brereton had shouted over his shoulder. 'Go to the Yeoman of the Wardrobe. He'll fit you with a livery. At the end of the long corridor. Then Sir Henry Norris wants to see you in the Privy Chamber.'

Even at that early hour the palace had been bustling with activity which was just as well for Francis promptly got lost and found himself wandering in the general direction of Queen Katharine's apartments.

'What are you doing here, young man?'

Francis bowed.

'Excuse me, madam, I arrived at Court yesterday and must confess that the Palace is still a labyrinth to me. I am trying to find the Yeoman of the Wardrobe.'

'Well, well – you must be young Weston.'

He looked up to see a rather beautiful fair-haired girl of about twenty regarding him with a very bold look.

'We had heard that you were coming and that you were the prettiest man in the Kingdom. It's said you only got the post in the King's Chamber because His Grace thought you would decorate it so nicely.'

Francis turned pink. Other than the one secret kiss he

had managed to snatch from Ann Pickering before she left for Cumberland, this was the closest he had ever been to a woman.

'What, blushing?' said the girl. 'I'll warrant that won't last long here. Anyway, I'm to Her Grace. As a maid-of-honour I must see to her morning clothes. I shall meet you at the sundial in the knot garden at two o'clock. Don't be late.'

And she had turned and gone without even so much as telling him her name.

'You understand your duties?'

Harry Norris's voice jerked him back to the present – away from pleasant thoughts of this afternoon's assignation.

'Yes, sir. And what are my tasks today?'

He held his breath lest Norris should give him something to do after midday.

'His Grace will be riding so you are excused until six. Then you must be present in the Chamber to await his return. I would advise you to find your way round the Palace. Get to know where everything is so that you can make your way about quickly.'

'I certainly shall!' said Francis.

'It really is high time,' he thought to himself, 'that I learned to find my way round more than just a Palace. I shall be a laughing stock if I don't. Anyway she called me the prettiest man in the Kingdom.'

And it was the word 'man' that pleased him, not the reference to his handsome appearance. However he spent a great deal of time, after he had dined, before a mirror in the Grooms' chamber, brushing his hair and peering at his chin to see if it needed shaving.

Promptly at two he was at the appointed place but after half an hour the girl still had not appeared and

Francis, rather tired of curious glances from fellow courtiers as he loitered ill-at-ease, was about to go when to his horror he saw Harry Norris himself coming towards him.

And as he drew nearer – Francis growing redder and redder – Norris thought that here he was, over twice young Weston's age, a widower, uninvolved in Court intrigues, and yet he could blush as easily as the youth who stood in front of him. Last month when he had seen Anne Boleyn at Hever Castle he had made a conscious and deliberate effort to cast off her spell; he had avoided even so much as looking at her. Had gazed at the ceiling, the floor, out of the window, anywhere, rather than see her face. And yet the sweet, haunting smell of her had been in his nostrils, the musical voice in his ears, the captivating laugh echoing in every room of the castle.

At night – sleeping a few feet away from the King, the other man who loved her to distraction – he had dreamed of Anne. The ridiculous thought that they might both mention her name had occurred to him. And then he had met her in Hever's rose garden, come across her unexpectedly, and gone as red – he a widower of thirty-two! – as young Weston was now. It had been his intention to tease Francis but the recollection of Anne Boleyn stopped him.

'Looking at the gardens, Francis?' he said instead.

'Er-yes, sir. Very well kept, are they not?'

'His Grace employs many gardeners,' said Harry. Out of the corner of his eye he had spotted Lucy, one of the several daughters of the Countess of Shrewsbury, hurrying towards them. He wasn't altogether surprised to see who it was. He would hardly have described her as a backward young woman and word had reached him that wagers were already being laid, amongst the younger and bolder of Katharine's ladies, as to who would be the first to attract the attention of young Weston. News of the boy's handsome appearance had preceded him to Court, probably brought in all innocence by the Queen herself.

'Have a good afternoon,' said Harry, with a very slight twinkle in his eye. 'And remember that you are on duty at six this evening.'

'Oh yes, Sir Henry,' answered Francis rapidly. He had also seen the maid-of-honour approaching and was in an agony of embarrassment.

'My betrothal to Ann Pickering really forbids this,' he thought.

But a second later he had forgotten all about Ann as the maid-of-honour curtsied before him and said, 'I didn't introduce myself to you this morning. I am Lucy Talbot, daughter of the Countess of Shrewsbury.'

'And I am Francis, son of Richard Weston. But you already know that.'

'Oh yes. Gossip travels very quickly in this Court. It is a veritable whispering gallery, as you will discover.'

She stepped back a pace and scrutinized him from top to toe. Aware that the Tudor livery of green and white suited him well, Francis set his hat at a jaunty angle and said, 'Do you approve, my Lady?'

'Aye, you're passing fair. You may walk with me in the gardens.'

He offered his arm and resting hers upon it, Lucy began to take him on a tour. Until this moment Francis had not quite realized the size and extent of Greenwich Palace. It was rather like three Sutton Places put together, with three quadrangles – known as courts – interconnecting each with the other. The last of these – Tennis Court – fascinated him.

'Does His Grace play tennis?'

'He loves the game.'

'Then I must challenge him.'

'Wait for him to challenge you, you forward creature!

Just let it be known to him that you play. You've a great deal to learn.'

She smiled up at him and said, 'You have, haven't you?'

Francis felt that wretched, uncontrollable shaking that had seized him whenever Ann Pickering was near.

'Why, you're trembling,' said Lucy. 'Is it the heat?'

'I think perhaps it is the after effects of riding. I came from Sutton Place only a day ago.'

'Wouldst like to rest a while in my chamber? It will be empty at this hour of the day – the other maids are all in the garden with Her Grace.'

So this was his moment then. 'I am being offered manhood,' thought Francis. 'Then for God's sake let me act the part.'

With a tremendous effort he controlled himself. 'Mistress Lucy, you are right,' he said. 'I do in truth have everything to learn.'

'How exciting,' she said and laughed so joyfully that it seemed to Francis the sound was taken up by all the gulls on the Thames as they hurried back to her apartments in the central block of the Palace, between Fountain Court and Cellar Court.

Just as she had predicted the room was empty.

'Suppose someone should enter?' said Francis.

'Then they must make a hullabaloo.'

And she turned a large key in the lock and left it in there.

'That is my bed,' she said, pointing to one of the four that occupied the chamber. 'Go and sit on it and I will bring you wine. Why, young Weston, you look doom-laden. This is an occasion for rejoicing.'

And with that she turned to face him so that he had no option but to kiss her as hard as he possibly could. However, he soon realized that there was more to it than

114

he had imagined, for her tongue, like a naughty little serpent, crept between his lips and touched his own.

'And that,' she said when they drew apart, 'is how they kiss at the Court of France. Do you like it?'

'I do,' said Francis and bent his head to practise this new-found art, while all the time aware that she was guiding him backwards till they both fell on the bed together. Then began such a tussle with laces and buttons and ribbons that Francis's brief spell of bravado vanished again. In the end he gave up, shaking his head in despair.

'Oh, you great fool, must I do everything for you?' she said laughing. And jumping to her feet, she began to undress in front of him. By the time she had reached her petticoats, Francis's doublet, hose and shoes were flying through the air in quite the most abandoned fashion for now there was to be no looking back. He had seen a woman naked for the first time in his life and if His Grace himself were to come through the door, he would have been unable to stop.

As she slithered on to the bed beside him he gave her another of the French Court kisses and then with her help was upon her and within her. As the world crashed and exploded round him he said goodbye to Francis Weston the boy for ever. Afterwards he said, 'But sweetheart, I may know little yet I do know that there should have been pleasure for you also.'

'Wait a while, young Weston,' she had answered with a saucy grin. 'We have the whole afternoon before us. Unless you are in a hurry.'

Years later, when he was condemned to die for a crime he had not committed – a crime involving just such a joy with a woman in bed – he thought back to that first day at Greenwich Palace and how he had straight away lost his virginity. He supposed if his judges had known that they would have called him even more lecherous and evil

115

than they did already. And yet there had been nothing but sweetness about the whole occasion. Lucy, the artless slut, with the warm mouth and eager body; he, the virgin boy, so happy to learn, so anxious to please. They had been like two exultant children as they spent those hours together loving the pleasure they were giving to one another. When half past five came and they had to part they promised to meet on the morrow and exchanged many tender kisses before Francis warily put his head round the door and then sped away, leaving his new-found mistress staring after him.

As he hurried along to the Privy Chamber he passed a prim looking young woman on her way to Lucy's shared room. She shot him a knowing glance and Francis suddenly felt as if he owned the world. He was on an equal footing now with everyone from His Grace down; he could listen to men's jokes in men's company and laugh in a man's world.

'Well,' said Mistress Elizabeth Burgavenny to Lucy, 'did you win?'

Lucy looked up. Her naughty face was still for a minute and then it crinkled into a smile.

'Aye,' she said, 'I did. And for proof here is a green ribbon from his livery. That will be five shillings for the wager, Bessie.'

'Lucy of Shrewsbury! This day you will have made yourself . . .'

She began to count on her fingers.

'Forty-five shillings. And you can remove that sour expression from your face for if you had got to him first, then you would be the richer.'

Lucy stopped suddenly. Forty-five shillings was a very great deal of money, enough to buy fine material for at least one new gown but something within her was sickened. She remembered the look on Francis's face; his trembling, his anxiety, his great delight in her. Momentarily she felt cheapened. Then she thought, 'But I did him a great service. I have made a man from a boy and anyway he will admire me in the new gown that will come from my winnings!' How simple it was to ease a conscience if one knew the way. She would ask him his favourite colour and the dress would be made in that. All was well again. She smiled a winner's smile at Elizabeth and stretched out her hand for the money.

In the Privy Chamber the six gentlemen-in-waiting, the four grooms and the page were awaiting His Grace's return. He had ridden with only a handful of courtiers that day, so his personal retinue were all there to greet him as he strode through the doors followed only by Henry Courtenay, the Marquess of Exeter, who was not only the King's first cousin but also his boyhood companion.

Courtenay's eyes swept briefly over the assembled men. They may well be the highest in the land – or the highest in favour – but they were responsible to him. He would not tolerate unkempt dressing, personal uncleanliness and, above all, any friction amongst them. The Gentlemen of the Privy Chamber were in a position of high privilege and the Marquess ruled with a fist of iron. One word from him to His Grace and a man could go out for ever.

Francis rose from a bow that he had practised painstakingly for months – ever since the King had first invited him to Court – to find Exeter's unblinking gaze fixed upon him. It raced through Francis's mind that, by some mystic power, the Marquess knew that he had spent the afternoon in Lucy's bed and was thoroughly disapproving. He felt a flush begin to creep up his neck. And it was the King who came to his rescue.

'Why, it's young Weston,' he said. 'When did you arrive?'

'Yesterday, your Grace.'

'And how are you settling down?'

'Very well, your Grace,' and Francis blushed scarlet.

Harry Norris thought, 'So Lady Lucy has won the wager. What wantons those girls are!'

'Excellent,' the King was saying. 'And now to dine.'

The old custom of all who lived at Court eating with the King in his Hall had died out over recent years. Henry himself had set the fashion for courtiers to dine in their own lodgings by constantly feeding in the Privy Chamber with his personal attendants – a custom he much preferred – and only using the Hall for banquets, masques, and other state occasions. In private he felt he could be natural; take off his shoes; listen to his musicians and singers; play and sing himself. And when he sang love songs he could let his mind wander over the miles to Kent, to Hever Castle, to Anne, each note of his lute seeming to say her name to him. And if the expression on his face should grow soft with love, then there were only his private Gentlemen there to see and each was sworn to obey the Marquess of Exeter's dictum. 'You will not be curious about anything concerning His Grace.'

Then if he was not in the mood for music there were other diversions. Sometimes they would sit back and listen to Will Somers's prattle; sometimes they would play cards – gambling all night and winning or losing vast sums. And this night it was to be Imperial and dice the King decided.

'You play Imperial, young Weston?'

'No, your Grace. I only know childish games which I played at home.'

'Then it's high time you learned. Come, sit with me. You shall be taught by the King of England himself and you will play the neatest card and throw the truest dice of all my Gentlemen before I've finished with you.'

And he put out his hand and ruffled Francis's hair affectionately. Francis knew that he should have felt a warm glow, a grateful happiness, at a touch from the hand of his anointed sovereign, God's divine choice on earth. But instead the most devastating shiver ran through him. Not the trembling that Ann or Lucy could cause but a ghastly, cold spasm as if he had been handled by something evil. It took every ounce of control he could muster not to actually shrink away from His Grace's fingers. The effort was so great that he broke out in a sweat. He experienced stark terror for the second time in his life.

His mind flashed back five years and he saw again St Edward's Well and the ghastly spectre that had looked at him with that wild empty stare. He had known with certainty then that he had seen a ghost. And now he felt the same ghastly chill. It was incomprehensible. The big, kindly King and that long dead woman; there was no sense to it.

Henry, seeing the boy sweating and shaking, was overcome with tenderness. To witness such evidence of emotion and loyalty was heartening in any circumstances. But with this child, son of his faithful servant Richard, it was doubly gratifying.

'What a good lad you are,' he said. 'I say, Henry – ,' this to his cousin Exeter, 'I'll warrant we've found the best page yet to enter the Chamber. We must watch his progress. He'll go far, you mark my words. Now, young Weston, to teach you the rules of Imperial.'

And so Francis sat down, gladly swallowing the wine that Henry Norris passed him, to play cards with Henry Tudor.

* * *

Anne Weston sat by an open window in Sutton Place, her head bent over the letter she was writing, her hand gripped firmly around the quill, the strokes of her pen quick and authoritative, belying the tremulous feelings she had within. For what woman – lest she be a widow – would dare take the matter of her daughter's marriage plans into her own hands? Yet what other alternative was there? To let Catherine endure further months of depression and loneliness?

Leaning forward slightly she looked down into the garden below. There sat her daughter, golden head bent over the embroidery with which she constantly busied herself these days, while Giles, who was never far from Catherine's side if he could help it, strummed on his lute singing as if his heart wasn't really in it.

'I am forced,' Anne thought, 'and Richard will just have to be made to understand. His tour of duty in Calais is a whole three months and I cannot see her go into a decline. If I can just get things begun – a meeting between herself and Arthur Culpepper. After that, of course, I can go no further. It is between Richard and the boy's stepfather to make the arrangements. But it would cheer her so.'

And so she went on making excuses to herself, knowing full well that Richard would not be pleased by her boldness in writing to the stepfather of Catherine's pre-contracted husband inviting both him and the boy to visit Sutton Place. But she had made up her mind and that was all there was to it. By the very same rider she would despatch another letter to Richard and he could puff and fume on the other side of the Channel to his heart's content.

She completed the letter and addressed it in her decisive hand. 'To Sir John Rogers, Bryanston, Dorset.' She pressed her seal into the hot wax and the Weston crest, brought back by one of Sir Richard's forefathers from the Crusades, stood out sharp and clear; a Saracen's head with open eyes and lolling tongue and, beneath, the words 'Any Boro'. It was family legend that the Crusader Weston had hacked off the man's head and had borne it on his lance in triumph, where – open-eyed in death – it had kept watch over him.

Now came the more difficult task of writing to her husband, but, thinking back to the previous evening, she proceeded with determination. It had been after the simple meal – which she and Catherine had taken to eating in a small chamber in the Gate House wing – and while Giles had been entertaining them with a few quiet songs, that she had first noticed tears running silently down her daughter's cheeks. The very silence of the weeping had been far more heart-rending than if the girl had burst out crying. It had cut Anne Weston deeply. Dismissing the Fool, she had crossed to Catherine and knelt beside her, cradling her into her arms.

'Why, my sweetheart,' she had said, 'what ails you? Are you unwell?'

'No, Mother, it is nothing.'

Anne had laughed.

'Catherine, that is the answer given by those who mean "it is something". Are you lonely, my darling? Is it that you miss Margaret and Francis?'

She had touched the raw nerve for now the tears came coursing hot and somehow sweet. Most delicately Anne had put her finger out and traced the pattern of one. How one suffered for one's children – all their upsets a hurt; all their joys a triumph.

'And is it that you, too, wish to leave Sutton Place? As a bride?'

'Aye,' came the whispered answer.

'But, darling, why did you not speak of this before?'

'I did not wish to leave you solitary. It is a very shadowy house at night.'

Now it was Lady Weston's turn to cry.

'But, sweetheart,' she said, hugging the girl to her, 'I can go to Calais with your father. The house can remain closed unless the family wish to use it. You kept silent about this for me?'

Catherine nodded her head.

'Oh, my dear goose. Tomorrow morning I shall write to Sir John Rogers about his stepson, Arthur. There was a contract with him when you were a child.'

The tears had stopped flowing and the china blue eyes were now fixed firmly on Anne's face.

'Do you know him?'

'I only met him once, very long ago. His real father was alive then.'

'What happened to him?'

'He died of some illness and then Arthur's mother was remarried to Sir John Rogers, who has a great and beautiful estate in Dorset. But she died in childbed shortly afterwards.'

'And you will write to him tomorrow?'

'Yes.'

A thought struck Anne Weston.

'Is it not your seventeenth birthday in two weeks?'

'Yes.'

'Then I shall invite them to come and stay with us for that.'

And so, explaining this scene as best she could to a man who could hardly be described as overladen with sentiment, Lady Weston completed her letter to her husband, sealed it down with a great show of determination and much pursing of the lips and gave it to her fastest rider.

'And be sure to deliver Sir John Rogers's letter well before you find a Calais-bound ship.'

The last thing she wanted was Richard taking it into his head to roar back and upset the arrangements.

Within eight days the rider had returned bearing with him a reply.

'Right honourable and my singular Good Lady,' she read, 'in my heartiest manner I commend me to you. It will give my stepson and myself the greatest good cheer to attend upon your daughter, Catherine, on her anniversary and we are, at this very time, preparing for the journey. Therefore, it is our intention to be with you and yours on 25 or 26 June according to the speed which your humble servants do achieve in the journey.

'May the Lord preserve your Ladyship and recommend me also to your good husband. At Bryanston this 17 day of June. Yours ever to command, J. Rogers.'

Sutton Place was at its best when full of people and now the usual hustle and bustle broke out. Lady Weston's sewing woman sent for two young girls from the estate to help her as a sudden order for three new dresses for Catherine and two for her mistress was given. The maids were out in force, cleaning and scrubbing; the kitchen lads polished till their knives and pots shone sun-like on the shelves; the ostlers swept out the stables and cleaned the harnesses and even the horses while they were at it; Giles of Guildford wrote three new songs – a labour of love, for had not Catherine always been his little darling? – and a chamber in the east wing that had never been used was nicknamed Sir John Rogers's room. Its large bed which had never been properly draped received yellow and red buckram hangings and a tester of yellow and green, and matching curtains were hung at the windows.

'It simply cannot be done in time, my Lady. I take pride in my work and I will not tolerate bad stitchery.'

The sewing woman's voice had risen to a tearful note but Lady Weston had calmed her down and sent for another four girls, known for their skills with the needle, to come up especially by cart from Guildford and stay at the mansion till everything – dresses, bed hangings, curtains and two new tablecloths for good measure – was completed to satisfaction.

At last it was the morning of 25 June – and a fine one at that – but by the evening a certain quietness was over the house as no sign of Sir John or Arthur Culpepper had appeared. Because of this delay the next morning saw servants, mistress and daughter at fever pitch. Catherine, who had worn blue the day before, decided on a new scarlet gown today, the very boldness of the colour giving her confidence. And though she walked moodily in the Long Gallery for most of the morning she saw at about noon, simultaneously with the gate housekeeper's cry, a cavalcade of riders appear from Sutton Forest.

As she sped down the staircase into the Great Hall her mother was hurrying up it and, meeting in the middle, they laughed and embraced rather breathlessly.

'Come, we must look composed,' said Lady Weston. 'Sit in that chair on the right of the Queen's fireplace. No, no, do not. For the sun will dazzle your eyes. There, with your back to the stained glass. Yes, that is a splendid effect. Your hair is like spun gold. I shall stay here and embroider. How does that appear?'

'Oh, Mother, most ridiculous,' said Catherine with a laugh. 'You're holding it upside down.'

The clatter of hooves was in the quadrangle and the sound of dismounting. With livery gleaming Giles Coke stepped smartly forward and swung open the great door known as the Middle Enter. There was a whispered conversation and then he announced, 'Sir John Rogers of Bryanston.'

Catherine was never to forget her first sight of her betrothed's stepfather for though he was quite old, about thirty-two or three, he had the face of an impudent scamp, an adventurer. And he had all the charm to go with it for he bowed before Lady Weston, kissed her hand and said, 'My Lady, how can I express my regret? My son Arthur was taken ill on the journey and had to turn back. That is why I was delayed. I was in two minds whether to accompany him but I decided to continue alone. At least we may meet and talk. Something I have been looking forward to since your letter arrived. And this must be his betrothed?'

And he bowed before Catherine who curtsied politely in turn, trying not to show her disappointment too greatly. But he must have sensed her reaction for he smiled and said, 'I know I am but a poor substitute for Arthur but I bring you his greetings and good wishes and on your birthday you shall have his gifts.'

'Oh dear,' said Lady Weston, quite put about, 'I do hope this visit won't be too dull, Sir John. My husband is in Calais – as I explained – and my son is at Court. There are only the two of us here.'

'And what better company could I ask for?' and he bowed again.

Anne thought, 'He is not at all what I expected. After all he *is* a man of estates and property, but he seems too – young. And far too . . . .'

She searched for the word in her head but the only one that suggested itself was 'naughty', and she rejected that angrily. But Giles Coke was stepping forward and leading Sir John to the chamber already named after him; while his retinue of servants were being shown their quarters by the yeoman and the butler.

His ablutions took him some while for the two women did not see him again until the midday repast at which he appeared, resplendent in an emerald green doublet, his dark, curly hair brushed and his face clean and glowing. He had very pleasant eyes, Lady Weston decided. Not so much grey as crystal in colour, yet not ice-like but warm and friendly and sparkling. She felt herself taking to him and wished that Catherine would say something. The foolish girl had sat with her eyes fixed firmly on her plate and hadn't uttered a word since the meal had begun.

' . . . and my wife died three years ago leaving me with my stepson, Arthur, who is eighteen now and a daughter of my own.'

For the first time Catherine spoke.

'What do you call your daughter, Sir John?'

'Alice.'

'I think that a pretty name. Is she a good child?'

'Aye, as good as any little maid can be who has no mother and is surrounded by servants.'

'And how old is she?'

'Three. My wife died in childbed.'

'Oh yes, my mother mentioned. I'm sorry.'

A ripple crossed Sir John Rogers's face as if he was on the point of making some remark but he merely said, 'Yes.'

Anne Weston thought, 'I'm sure that Culpepper woman he married was a middle-aged harridan. I am positive it was she I met at Court once and took a dislike to on the instant. I believe she had a sister-in-law called Joyce who married Lord Edmund Howard, Norfolk's brother.'

Aloud she said, 'Are you not connected to the Howards, Sir John?'

'My wife was. Her first husband's sister married the Duke's brother. But I make no such pretensions.'

So she was right. Joyce Culpepper had been a widow

with children when she married Edmund Howard and her brother's widow had also chosen a younger man. But how could such a disagreeable creature have managed to snare such a delightful person as Sir John Rogers? Anne Weston sighed. She supposed it to have been parental pressure, as usual.

Catherine was saying, 'Does Alice live with you, Sir John?'

'Of course. She is my jewel. I could not farm her out to my mother or sister. Are you fond of children, Mistress Catherine?'

Catherine went pink and said, 'Yes.'

Again Sir John looked slightly uncomfortable as he said, 'Then let us hope you and Arthur have a large family.'

Catherine lowered her lashes demurely and Lady Weston cleared her throat but Sir John seemed unaware that he was perhaps speaking a trifle too forthrightly.

'I drink to you, Catherine,' he said and he raised his glass to her.

That afternoon the fine June weather broke in a thunderstorm and Sir John, at his own request, strolled gently up and down the Long Gallery – which entranced him – talking to Catherine. Lady Weston, much to her chagrin, fell asleep in a chair and was unable to join in the conversation.

Preparing her young mistress for dinner that night Catherine's personal maid was astonished to hear her say, 'Meg, which of all my gowns makes me look the oldest?'

'The *oldest*, Mistress?'

'Aye.'

'Well I think, of them all, your night gown of black velvet which you had for the mourning when your aunt died.'

'But do I look pretty in it too?'

'What's all this about?' asked Meg suspiciously.

'Oh, we have Sir John Rogers staying here . . .'

'I know that. We've had nothing but his visit for the last two weeks.'

' . . . and he is very old and so is my mother and I didn't want to feel left out.'

'And what about young Arthur then?'

'He was taken sick.'

'Oh! So how old is this Sir John? I caught a glimpse of him and he looked lively enough to me.'

'Oh, I know not.' Catherine's voice was too casual by half, thought Meg. 'In his thirties.'

'I suppose that would seem like a man's dotage when you're only seventeen.'

But Catherine was already at her cupboard and impatiently pulling out the velvet night gown. And instead of a formal headdress suddenly deciding to wear her hair loose to her shoulders adorned only by an ornament made of pearls. As she brushed the pale gold locks till they shone Meg kept her thoughts to herself. However, any musing by either of them was rudely interrupted by a sharp knock on the door and Joan – Lady Weston's personal servant – walking in.

'Oh, Mistress Catherine,' she said. 'You're to go to your mother at once. She is most indisposed with an ague. I think we should send at once for the physician from Guildford.'

Catherine ran the length of the east wing from her own chamber – which had once belonged to Margaret and was quite large and grand – to that of the Master and Mistress. There she found her mother, colourless and covered with a cold, clammy sweat.

'Dear God,' she whispered clutching Joan's arm, ''tis not the Sweat is it?'

'Nay, for she has no pain at all, neither is she hot. This is an ague – a chill of the bones. But still we must fetch Dr Burton.'

'Catherine, Catherine,' her mother was calling feebly.

'Yes, Mother, I'm here.'

She went to her and sat down on the bed. Lady Weston stopped short, ill as she felt, on seeing this vision in black velvet.

'What? In mourning for me already? 'Tis only an ague, child. Why so sombre?'

'I thought the dress more – stately.'

Lady Weston shook her head against the pillows.

'All that to-do to get you three new gowns and now you wear one made two years ago. I don't understand you, Catherine. You . . .'

But her words were cut short by a violent fit of shaking. Catherine placed her hand on her mother's forehead and felt the dampness for herself.

'Mother,' she said firmly. 'I am sending for Dr Burton. Till he comes you must keep warm and still and Joan shall bring you a hot posset.'

Lady Weston struggled to sit up.

'But what of Sir John Rogers? Oh, this couldn't be worse. I shouldn't have written that letter. 'Tis a judgement on me.'

Catherine suddenly found herself very strong.

'Nonsense, Mother. You wrote out of kindness and nobody has a judgement against them for that. Sir John will be perfectly all right. With your permission I will adopt the role of hostess till your recovery.'

Lady Weston closed her eyes.

'Yes, yes, you have my permission. Maybe it's for the best. It will show him what a good daughter-in-law you will make.'

Catherine curtsied. It was not considered wise to kiss

the sick for everyone knew that the mildest infection could grow more serious and spread like wildfire amongst a household. Even a cold could lead to a coffin if one did not take all precautions.

But this was not the moment for speculating for there were important matters at hand. First, she despatched Toby to Guildford to wait upon Dr Burton's presence and then she sent Giles Coke to Sir John Rogers's chamber to ask if he would attend her in the Long Gallery.

John Rogers – standing in the shadows of the entrance – watched her silently where she sat at the Gallery windows for a good five minutes before he spoke. For once his rascal's face was set and serious as he looked at the gleaming head and delicately boned features; the small vulnerable body; the child-like hands plucking at the velvet night gown.

'You shall not be hurt,' he said silently.

From the gloom he called softly, 'Mistress Catherine, you summoned me?'

She rose startled, and curtsied.

'Oh, Sir John. I did not see you there. Forgive me.'

He walked towards her, the evening light shining into his face and into his light-coloured eyes so that they seemed to gleam. And tonight he wore a silver doublet encrusted with rhinestones. Nothing could have been more guaranteed to create an effect. Catherine, who had noticed a strange tightening in her chest and a numbness in her fingers ever since lunchtime, now felt her stomach lurch. She stared at him dumbly, admiration written plainly on her face for the world to see.

He laughed very quietly.

'You look as if you've seen a ghost, Mistress.'

'No . . . I . . . that is . . . I was thinking how much my

130

brother would admire your manner of dress,' she said lamely.

'If I said his good taste was echoed by his sister it would sound like conceit in myself. But it is true that your clothes enhance your beauty. First red and now black – dramatic choices indeed.'

Catherine did not know where to look. Blood was pounding in her ears and her cheeks were flushed.

She muttered the well-worn phrase, 'You do me too much honour,' and then took to gazing out of the window, her attention apparently riveted on some unseen object beyond the trees.

The scamp's face softened again, and he said matter-of-factly, 'But you summoned me, Mistress Catherine. Is there anything of importance?'

'Oh, yes. Of course. It is my mother, Sir John. She is sick with ague. I have sent for the physician from Guildford. She begs leave to be excused tonight.'

He looked concerned and thoughtful.

'I think perhaps it would be best all round if I cut my visit short,' he said. 'I will only be an inconvenience to you. I shall leave tomorrow.'

Her eyes were glistening suspiciously as she answered, 'Please do not, Sir John. My mother would be deeply distressed. She begged that your visit should not be interrupted. She implored me to ask you to stay.'

'God forgive me for the lie,' she thought. 'But he mustn't go yet.'

'God forgive me for being what I am,' thought John. 'But if I don't tread warily I shall seduce this girl.'

Now he bowed formally.

'I shall do whatever Lady Weston commands,' he said. They smiled at one another.

'Then farewell, Sir John, until we dine.'

It was two hours before Catherine joined him again

131

and when she finally arrived he offered her his arm and escorted her down the stairs and into the Great Hall where Giles Coke, without so much as a flicker at the lateness of the meal oversaw the serving of a great repast.

It rather amused him to note the way that Mistress Catherine sat at the head of the table, in her father's place, and Sir John – defying convention – sat immediately beside her, leaving the rest of the great board empty and ignoring the place set for him at the foot. Yet, after dinner, Coke was surprised to see that Sir John begged forgiveness and retired immediately to his chamber.

For the next five days, Catherine was busy in and out of her mother's sick room and it seemed to her, though surely she must be mistaken, that Sir John was avoiding her. He was there at mealtimes right enough, and spoke to her kindly and affably, but after that he would be gone, spending most of his time out riding or gambling with his manservants or playing the lute with Giles. Once, while her mother had been asleep, she had heard him singing – a light, pleasant voice – in the garden below and had crossed to the window to watch. The familiar lurch of her stomach that always accompanied a glimpse of him had taken place.

'Dear Holy Mother forgive me,' she had said silently, 'because I am sure that I love him for he is not really old at all – I only said that out of foolishness. And now he is destined to be my father-in-law and I am in such agony of spirit.'

On the evening of the fifth day as Meg brushed her hair before dining she suddenly burst into tears.

'Hey, Catherine' – the old and familiar servants were excused from formality at certain moments – 'what is the matter, pretty chuck? It's that Sir John, isn't it?'

The weeping girl nodded.

'Dost love him?'

Catherine had flung her arms round the servant's waist and buried her face in her apron. There was no need for reply.

'Then tell him, sweetheart, tell him. He looks a pretty fellow to me. He may have a saucy face but there is no evil in it, do you understand me?'

She felt Catherine nod against her.

'Then be brave. He will know the right thing to do. What's the point of marrying the son if you love the father?'

'Stepfather!' came a muffled voice.

'Well then.'

Catherine's round blue eyes stared up at her and for a moment Meg saw a distinct look of Sir Richard in them.

'I shall tell him this very night, Meg. It will be better than going on like this.'

Despite her determination, during the meal she was strangely quiet and after a few desultory questions and answers about Lady Weston's health, they fell to eating in silence. It was as the fruit was being served at the end of the dinner that she said to him, 'There is something I wish to say to you, Sir John. So tonight, unless it upsets you, I would prefer to let Giles the Fool sing to us and not dismiss him.'

He looked at her curiously. His feelings about her – in one way so clear, in another so confused – had led him to keep out of her way as much as possible during the visit and he thought wryly about the nature of man and the division between love and lust. Was there ever true love between two adults, he wondered, or was it merely the call of the poor body glossed over to make it acceptable to the soul? He shook his head for he did not know the answer and Catherine mistook the action.

'You would prefer otherwise, Sir John?'

'No, no – let him sing.'

She lost courage a little when they were actually seated in the Gallery. She had had the fires lit and two chairs placed comfortably. Giles, on her instructions, had tucked himself discreetly away in the dimness so that only his voice could be heard. All other servants had been dismissed so it was Catherine herself who poured John Rogers's wine. But she found herself unable to speak and they sat in silence again, listening to that melodious voice pouring out its heart with love. For had not the Fool always loved her and now he suffered sitting, as he was, in the half dark and seeing her with another man.

Every ounce of his melancholy was coming forth. His Romany heart wept for his ugliness and his age and his station in life which doomed him for ever to worship silently the ground upon which she walked. And to the couple before the fire the music was cajoling and pleading so that as Catherine's hand stole out to take Sir John's, his at the same time was reaching for hers. Her look of wonderment as this happened met that of such ardour in his eyes, that in a second he was kneeling at her feet. And then after showering her fingers with kisses he had pulled her to stand up and was holding her against his heart, which she could feel was suddenly beating fast.

And he had swept her up in his arms and was carrying her before she could say a word. Catherine knew that this was the moment when she should start protesting, beg him to put her down, call for Giles to help her, but instead she signalled him to stay where he was for a languorous feeling was affecting her limbs and she did not want it to stop. Worse still, she wanted to proceed, to be kissed on the lips by Sir John, and let him play the entire game of lovemaking with her.

And so it was that she found herself naked in his bed and felt the unkind pain of the loss of her maidenhood turn into a rhythm that finally erupted in a strange sensation. She lay in the darkness against his chest and he said, 'I have broken all the laws of hospitality. I deserve death at your father's hands.'

'Oh Sir John, do not speak so. I love you. I wanted this.'

But he would not listen and in the darkness said, 'Catherine, I must tell you the truth. Not only about myself but also about Arthur.'

Suddenly child-like she said, 'Is it a good story?'

'Aye, that it is. A tale for a winter's night. Let me light the candle.'

And in the Long Gallery, curled like a dog before the remains of the fire, the Fool slept. And in his sleep he sobbed and in the firelight the marks left by the tears glistened on his cheeks. For he had seen his beloved go to womanhood and knowing that was what she desired, he had said nothing. And the walls absorbed the sound as he wept with the hopelessness of it all. And in centuries to come those sensitive enough could still hear him as he cried for the loss of his one true love.

7

It was the dream again only this time it was worse than ever. It began in exactly the same way with that agonizingly slow progress across the quadrangle, but on this occasion when the door of the Great Hall flew open and Mistress Anne Boleyn came into view the girl was dressed in deepest mourning and had a black veil draped over her, making her almost appear headless. The old woman in the Long Gallery was the same but it was in that strange banquet that things grew more sinister, for instead of letting the servants shut the door in her face Anne Weston walked into the room and up to the great chair at the head of the table.

'Speak to me,' she demanded of the man sitting there, the man they called Getty. 'Where is Francis? You've hidden him, haven't you?'

In the usual unnerving way all the guests looked through her as if she were not there, so she tapped the host on the shoulder but he seemed not to notice. Then, suddenly, Giles was in the room with her.

'Don't worry, Mistress,' he said. 'I'll tumble for them.'

'But will they look at you, Giles? They can't see me.'

'That's because they don't want to, my Lady.'

And then he began to dance round the room and she saw with horror that the little jester's head on the end of his stick was not a replica of Giles's face but of Francis's. Furthermore it was alive because it was shouting 'Help! Help!' It was so revolting, seeing her own son as a doll, a miniature, that Anne Weston screamed herself into wakefulness.

She was in the great four-poster with the sarsenet and tawny curtains, in the Master's chamber of Sutton Place – and she was alone. Richard was in Calais, Margaret was with Walter at Haseley Court, Francis was at Greenwich, and Catherine . . . . Well, she had not seen her since the morning she had left Sutton Place with Sir John Rogers. To be strictly accurate she had not even seen her then for there had been nothing but a note lying by her – Anne's – bed. The wretched girl must have crept in in the darkness and left it. Lying now on her fear-dampened pillow Anne could remember the words by heart.

'My dearest Mother,

I will never forgive myself for leaving you while you are still ill and had not Dr Burton assured me that it was nothing serious, I would not be quitting Sutton Place. I know that you will find it hard to pardon me but I am going to Bryanston with Sir John, there to be married in his chapel to him and not to Arthur who was born lunatic and has grown worse with the passing of years and from which terrible fate he has delivered me. Always your loving daughter. At Sutton Place this second day of July, yours to command, Catherine.'

Anne had sent a rider of course and he had come back with a long face. The few hours start they had on him had been enough. They had been married by Sir John Rogers's own priest the previous day.

'And has the marriage been consummated?' asked Lady Weston, not feeling in the mood to beat about the bush.

'Aye, my Lady, he bedded her forthwith as soon as the wedding feast was done.'

'Then there's scant chance of an annulment.'

'My Lady . . . .'

The rider had hesitated. He was a leathery-looking

young man, as if the saddles he constantly besat had become one with him.

'Yes?'

'My Lady, I do not know that you should press for it. Mistress Catherine seemed content and begged with me to plead on her behalf. She desires nothing more than the blessing of you and Sir Richard. And the story of Master Arthur Culpepper's madness is terrible. The Steward told me all of it. It would seem that he enjoyed torturing things. Sir Richard would not have allowed Mistress Catherine to marry him, that's certain.'

So Anne – after taking advice from Joan, Giles and Giles Coke – had written her daughter a cool note. Nothing more, naturally. It would not be fitting to pardon such a marriage too easily.

Unfortunately her recent illness had left her weak for travel and therefore it was impossible for her to sail to Calais. So she was faced with the prospect of living alone and though, during the day it was enjoyable enough, it was at night that her torment started. For the recurring dream was becoming more and more frequent. As usual, when the master was absent, Joan had slept on a trussing bed in Anne's room but this night – when the dream had been at its worst – she had slept in her own chamber for fear of giving her mistress the cold which was starting to form on her chest.

'Oh God,' Anne thought. 'This dreadful nightmare. How it haunts and pursues me. There is something terribly wrong I know. But what *is* it? I must have help!'

It was already first light and a thrush sitting in the beautiful elm tree that grew near her bedroom window was beginning to call those first thrilling notes that would set the whole dawn chorus off into their pagan hymn to the unknown day. And, of a sudden and for certain, Anne knew what she must do. She must go immediately to the mysterious house in Cordwainer Street and seek the help of Dr Zachary. And then on to Greenwich Palace to see for herself that all was well with her son and at the same time to pay her respects to Her Grace.

Full of purpose now she rose from her bed and drew back the curtains. Pools of reassuring light formed on the bright Turkey carpet; the night of terrors almost vanquished. One more thing was to be done – the throwing open of the windows and the letting in of the clean morning air. And as she did this Anne noticed Giles on the distant lawn. Though he was far away she could see that he stood in one of those dark green circles that inexplicably formed in gardens and meadowlands. She knew it was widely believed that these were where the midnight fairies danced. There were those – intelligent people amongst them – who thought that the mortal world was shared by a whole host of unseen creatures; subjects of Oberon and Titania and the Elf King. And she, who most certainly believed in magic and spells, was inclined to feel there might be truth in it.

Giles, as a Romany, was quite definite in his views. To him they were always there, ever watchful. Ready to help or hinder the mortal in his predicament depending on how one had treated them. She had caught him one night putting milk outside the kitchens of Sutton Place.

'Giles, what are you doing?' she had asked and had thought to herself that here was a treat for Robin Goodfellow.

'It's for a poor hedgehog, my Lady.'

'Nay. You'll not deceive me. 'Tis for one of your invisible friends.'

He had given her a strange look; half mocking, half reproving.

'Only invisible to some, my Lady.'

'Then do you see them, Giles?'

'Would you believe me, whatever I answered?'

The reply had silenced her; at that moment Giles's funny crinkled face had had an expression of great dignity. As she descended into the Great Hall an hour later she saw him just about to leave by the Middle Enter.

'Giles,' she called out, 'I am going to London. Toby will accompany me and Meg, too, for Joan is ill. I shall leave the care of all in the hands of Giles Coke and yourself.' Then she added, 'Thank you for the good spell.'

He started guiltily and said, 'How did you know, my Lady?'

'I saw you from my window. What exactly were you doing?'

'I was calling up the tutelaries.'

'They are the fairies who guard families, are they not?'

'Yes, my Lady.'

With the dream so fresh in her mind the answer was disquieting.

'Do we need protection, Giles? Is there something you know?'

Again, that blankness in the tumbler's eyes; the air of deliberate innocence.

'I don't understand, my Lady. I always ask the tutelaries for their care.'

Why the evasiveness? The man was being deliberately uncomprehending. And why this chill of fear in herself? When the dream had plagued her before, Dr Zachary had told her she was seeing the house as it would be in time to come. But now this explanation seemed incomplete. Anne Weston knew at that moment, standing in the Great Hall of her mansion, that there was something sinister hidden amongst its splendour.

* * *

Zachary Howard was sitting in his father's sumptuous lodgings in Greenwich Palace, talking earnestly. It was not often they had time together as father and son, for the secret of their relationship had never been revealed and so the opportunity to converse closely was something they both relished. The Duke all the more so, for looking at his son as he moved and spoke he would see an expression or gesture to remind him of the boy's mother – his true love who had died in agony. Sometimes it was so vivid – a look in the eye, a turn of the head – that his heart would constrict. After all these years the memory of her still moved him and there were nights when he would wake thinking he could hear a snatch of her strange, sad song. And then he would weep to know it was only a nightingale that called.

Of his three children Thomas Howard loved Zachary best. But there was more than love between them; there was respect. Norfolk the King-maker – leader of the great Howard clan – plotted his political course on a grand scale and feared no man except the King. And constantly behind him stood the tousle-haired figure of his natural son. For it was he who consulted the stars on the Duke's behalf, read the ancient cards, looked at that strange, crystal glass that always seemed blank when Norfolk picked it up and stared into it.

And today he was particularly glad that his 'witch boy', as he secretly thought of him, had come to see him. For the Duke was troubled by a persistent rumour that his spies were bringing him regarding his niece, Anne Boleyn. A rumour that – if it were true – might bode trouble on an unprecedented scale.

He hadn't approved, of course, when his sister Lady Elizabeth had married Thomas Boleyn of Norfolk. A puny upstart – just a glorified merchant when all was said and done. And it was he – the Duke – who had obtained places for the two Boleyn girls at Court when they had returned from France. And fine thanks he'd received for his pains. Mary nothing but a great trollop lolloping in and out of the King's bed and Anne dismissed over the Harry Percy affair. But they *were* his nieces and the fact that their mother had died and Thomas had re-married some Norfolk bumpkin couldn't remove the fact that Howard blood ran in them – they were part of his mighty family. And now this disquieting murmur – that his younger niece, Anne, had the King so in love with her that he was beginning to question the legality of his marriage to Katharine. And it was to Zachary he had turned and for a week now his son had been closeted in that gaunt house in Cordwainer Street, consulting charts and setting out those frightening cards with one to represent Anne, another His Grace and yet another, the Queen.

'And what did it all tell you, my son? Surely to God it is not as serious as they say.'

The square face that turned to him suddenly seemed very like his own, the line of the jaw as hard and as tough as any of the Norfolks.

'It is as serious and more, Lord Duke my father.'

For once Thomas failed to smile at the form of address that Zachary always used.

'What is going to happen?'

'My cousin Anne Boleyn is destined to become Queen. Nothing can stop her.'

'But she is only a girl, Zachary. And not even pretty. Mary is the one with the good looks.'

'Be she the ugliest hag in Christendom, her power is enormous. She could make any man she chose fall in love with her.'

'Jesu, is she a witch?'

The words were out before the Duke had had time to

think. He could see the glower on his favourite son's face almost before it settled there.

Thomas thought, 'He's angry. He hates talk of sorcery.'

And Zachary, yet again, saw in his mind's eye the fragile head of his mother dropping forward as the scarlet flames leapt at the great pile of wood and straw beneath her feet.

'Forgive me.' The Duke's enemies would not have believed the gentleness of his expression. 'Remember, I loved her too.'

Zachary smiled and patted his father's hand. 'I know, I know,' he said. 'You have proved that in your goodness to me, Lord Duke my father. But we speak of cousin Anne. I do not know if she is a mistress of Satan – that has not been revealed to me. But in everything I see her might. It is shown in her life chart, in the Tarot cards, in the crystal. Your niece will sit upon the throne of England, sir.'

'But what of the Queen? Is she going to die?'

'Her fate is terrible. Divorce, misery and exile. She will die alone and friendless.'

'God's head,' said Thomas Howard. 'You are sure?'

'I swear it. I was given the meaning quite clearly. The most tremendous force in the Kingdom lies in the form of Anne Boleyn.'

The Duke of Norfolk sat shaking his head. If anyone else had told him this he would have laughed him out of the room. He did not see at all how it could come about – and yet to back up his son's prediction were the facts that the King visited Hever frequently, that the upstart Boleyn had been created Viscount Rochford and that secretly it was said the King had raised the matter of the validity of his marriage to Katharine – for had she not been previously married to the King's own brother?

'But there is more,' Zachary was saying.

'More?'

'Aye, because of Anne many men will die – great men some of them. Why this is not yet clear. But one thing is certain. She herself will meet a brutal death. She will plunge from the pinnacle to the depths that lie beneath.'

The Duke saw that his son was trembling and another wave of tenderness swept him. Because of his mystic gift he sometimes forgot that Zachary was still young; still vulnerable to fears and emotions that a man leaves behind when he passes forty.

'Why do you shiver?' he asked. 'You don't know Anne, do you? Surely she had left Court before you arrived.'

'I saw her once when I was with my tutor. I looked particularly, for I knew her to be my cousin. You are right, Father, she is not pretty. She is beautiful. And as to her death, there is – oh merciful Christ – there is the possibility that it could be by fire.'

'Dear God,' thought the Duke. 'I think the boy has some feeling for her himself. And after seeing her only once! The wretched girl is a witch and will die as befits one.'

And at that moment a great dislike for his niece Anne Boleyn was born in Thomas Howard's heart; a dislike that was never to leave him. To see his son disturbed, to hear that great men would lose their lives, to be told that Queen Katharine, a woman he had always liked and vaguely pitied, was to die in misery was too much for him to stomach. He made a resolve at that moment to oppose the climber Boleyn's girl as best he could. But he must be subtle. He had no wish for his head to be one of those that rolled and this put a new thought into his mind.

'Zachary, am I to die because of Mistress Anne? You may be honest with me.'

'No, Lord Duke my father. That is not your fate.'

The amber eyes were staring into his fixedly and Thomas felt uncomfortable.

'Do not gaze at me so. What is it you have to tell me?'

'It is you, Father, who will pronounce sentence of death upon her.'

There was total silence in the room. With a shaking hand Norfolk poured wine.

'It is you – who lost your love in the flames – who will condemn her to burn.'

And with those words the great Dr Zachary put his head in his hands and wept. Howard sat motionless, stunned by what he had just heard. The incredible story was too much to comprehend. And then came the kind of thoughts that make born survivors the breed of people they are.

'At least *I'll* live through this. And if Boleyn's daughter is to bring havoc in her train then I'll not quibble if indeed *I* am he who dooms her.'

He saw Zachary wiping his eyes, noticed the whiteness of his face beneath the thick black curls.

'My son,' he said quietly. 'If it is decreed that these things will happen, then we must bow to fate. I would not willingly condemn another to die but if it is writ that I shall be Anne's judge then so be it. You must not torture yourself with this. It is already obvious to me that there is some strange attachment in your heart for Anne Boleyn. Therefore it follows that if I am to condemn her your hate will turn upon me. I want you to swear now that when the storm begins you will remain loyal to me regardless of what it is my destiny to do.'

'Lord Duke my father,' Zachary said. 'I know that I wept like a child just now and it is true that the very sight of Anne stirred my soul but you have been good to me. I owe you my life in every way. I give you my oath, in my

145

mother's name, that if you should kill Anne the Queen with your bare hands I will still remain your liege man.'

'Then there is love and peace between us?'

'Always,' said Zachary.

It took Anne Weston two days to reach the house in Cordwainer Street for she broke her journey overnight. And it was in the late afternoon of the second day that she finally arrived, only to be told by the girl who answered the door that Dr Zachary had gone. Anne could have wept. Long journeys were no joy to her and to find the man she most urgently desired to see not there was frustrating to say the least.

'What are your instructions, my Lady?' asked Toby. 'Do we proceed to Greenwich now to see Master Francis?'

'No, we'll spend the night at The Holy Lamb and then if Dr Zachary has not returned in the morning, Meg and I will go to the Palace by water and you can bring the horses down and join us there.'

But persistent knocking at the door the next day only brought the slattern's face to an upstairs window shouting that Dr Zachary had not come back. There was nothing for it but to make for Greenwich. Hiring a boatman at the reaches just beneath the Tower of London, Anne and Meg set off.

The Thames was in an exuberant mood. A light wind was ruffling the water and it seemed as if the whole population had turned out, either for business or pleasure, to make the most of the sunshine and the breeze. The river was crowded with skiffs and wherries and the privately-owned barges of the noble and wealthy. One such, covered with brightly coloured flags, proclaimed a bridegroom and his attendants making their way with much merriment to a church down stream. Alongside rowed another barge crowded with musicians blowing wind instruments with a goodly sound. In the midst of the confusion Anne Weston saw Thomas More in his black barge, deep in conversation with a companion and typically oblivious of the noise around him. She called to him for they had once lived near each other in the village of Chelsea, but her voice was lost in the wind and the general hullabaloo. A barge of the King's household, clean and fresh with its crisp green and white Tudor colours, went past crowded with young retainers. They raised their caps to the bridegroom and some shouted ruderies were exchanged between the two vessels; all in good part, however. Anne suddenly felt how exciting it was to be alive.

At the water steps of Greenwich Palace she saw the barges of both the King and Queen riding at their moorings and also that of the Duke of Norfolk. So the royal household was in full complement and somewhere amongst them was Francis, no doubt enjoying himself to the full and quite forgetful of the fact that it was several months since he had seen his parents or Sutton Place. And she was proved quite right. For as she walked with Queen Katharine, after the midday repast, towards Tennis Court she quite distinctly heard his voice amongst the shouts and general clamour. But to her astonishment he was not one of the spectators but actually playing and his opponent was His Grace himself. And Francis, so fleet of foot at fifteen, was giving the King a hard game. Each point was being strongly fought for and the monarch was in a lather of sweat.

Anne was surprised and yet not, in the way of all mothers, at the change in her son. He had left home a boy and now she saw a young man – taller, more firm of muscle and with the childishness gone from his face. Looking at him objectively she felt sure that some girl must have succumbed to his charms for he truly was the

147

most handsome creature; so beautiful in bone structure and colouring that it seemed impossible that half the female Court was not in love with him. And a certain change in his bearing, even while he played tennis, told her that her son's innocence was a thing of the past. She wondered who it was who shared a bed with him. Or perhaps it was more than one. Her mind shuddered away. A part of her still wanted him to be her sweet, untainted boy.

Feeling someone gazing at him he looked up and was so surprised to see his mother that he missed the next ball and the King, with a slashing stroke, won the match.

'Well done, young Weston,' His Grace was shouting.

As Francis ran towards Anne she hoped that he wasn't being too familiar with the King but was reassured by the fact that Henry himself joined them, wiping his face on a towel.

'You have a fine son, Lady Weston. The most amusing Page of the Chamber ever to serve. Why this imp has taken money off me at dice and cards already.'

And Henry was laughing in the hail-fellow-well-met way of his that Anne never quite liked. She dropped a curtsey and said, 'I hope that my son is doing nothing to annoy your Grace.'

'On the contrary, madam, I envy you your boy.'

And just for a brief minute the King's eyes filled with tears and Anne remembered that had Henry, Prince of Wales, lived he would have been exactly the same age as Francis.

And she felt a warm feeling of reassurance. His Grace was looking on Francis as if he was that long dead infant come to life. How wonderful indeed that her son should have found such great favour at Court.

That evening, playing cards with the Queen in Katharine's apartments, she said, 'I am so happy, your Grace, that Francis has settled in well. He seems to have become quite a man. I hardly recognized him.'

From behind them there came a muffled but quite distinct giggle. Katharine raised reproving eyes and Anne looked round. Working on their embroidery with an air of studied innocence were maids-of-honour, apparently not listening to the conversation of the two older women. But Katharine was too quick for them and shot them both a freezing glance.

'Who are they, your Grace?' asked Anne in a lowered voice.

'One is Elizabeth Burgavenny and the pretty one is Lucy Talbot, daughter of the Countess of Shrewsbury.' A smile played round Katharine's lips. 'She is quite friendly with Francis, I believe.'

Anne gave the young woman another, more scrutinizing glance.

'Talbot, Talbot,' she said aloud. 'Was it not Lady Mary Talbot that young Harry Percy married?'

'Yes, one of her elder sisters. It was said that he was pre-contracted to her and that was why he could not marry Mistress Anne Boleyn. Do you remember the younger Boleyn girl?'

'Distinctly,' said Anne.

Later that night, she was escorted to a bedchamber – the evening's card play done – by Lady Lucy, the picture of demure goodness. But the downcast eyes and folded hands did not deceive Anne Weston for a second. Here was a born seductress – little wonder that Francis had changed! She only hoped that he would form no foolish attachments – that there would be no repetition of the Harry Percy affair. She had just heard from the Queen that the couple were already separated; that Lady Mary had returned to her father in a wild fury and had declared herself her husband's bitter enemy. Remembering Harry

Percy's face as he held Anne Boleyn in his arms that night three years ago, in the gardens of Hampton Court it went through Anne Weston's mind that perhaps the marriage had never been consummated. That perhaps his love for Anne had been so strong that it had rendered him incapable of ever taking another woman. Or perhaps, if that was far-fetched, Mary Talbot had found it impossible to live with Anne's ghost, for ever haunting her husband in his waking, in his sleeping and in the marriage bed. Whatever it was, it must have been a most daunting experience for the bride to have left, expressing loathing, within three years.

And it was with her thoughts totally engrossed with the intangible Anne Boleyn that Lady Weston rounded a corner in Greenwich Palace and ran straight into the dark figure of Dr Zachary. To say that she was startled was to minimize her emotions. She could only think that it was pre-destined that they should meet at that moment and she said without preamble, 'Oh, Dr Zachary I must speak to you; I have so much on my mind.'

His answer was both apt and unusual.

'Is the silence of Sutton Place beginning to murmur?' he said.

8

It was a crystal morning, the sky unclouded and the March wind blowing the wild early daffodils. In the midst of their vivid carpet stood a contrastingly sombre beech tree, on a low bough of which, quite alone, sat Anne Boleyn. As always, her natural grace adapted to her surroundings; her green velvet skirt draped to the ground as if she had pre-arranged the folds, her black hair flew out loosely on the breeze. Her gaze was turned towards the Thames, breathing in the sweet river air, and on her lips was a smile of undisguised triumph for Mistress Anne had achieved her objective. After four years she had been reinstated at Court as one of Katharine's ladies; four years which, at times, she had thought would never culminate as she wanted. For she would only return on her terms – with the monarch of all England begging and pleading for her to be at his side.

She thought, 'If only I could have been Harry's Countess. I loved him so greatly and I will never and can never love like that again. And Wolsey broke our match at Henry's instigation. How much I despise the King and his man of God.'

And the expression of discomfiture on Henry's big, bland face when she refused a gift or did not reply to a letter or was in a capricious mood, gave her pleasure. For had not he, through Wolsey, reduced Harry to tears? Harry, who had held her in his arms and kissed her and asked her to share his bed, even though she had timidly refused. And now people wondering why she constantly rejected the King, thought she did it to keep his interest sharp. If only they had known that to see the look of sorrowful disappointment in his eyes was the breath of life to her.

It had all started as a terrible game. Her first bitterness after she had been sent home in disgrace, separated for ever from the man she loved, had been against Wolsey. But it hadn't taken her long to burrow out the truth. She may have been only sixteen years old but when the King had come calling at Hever, she had known. Everything – instinct, intuition, sixth sense – had pointed to Henry VIII wanting her for himself, tiring of her poor, silly sister and desiring another Boleyn girl for his bed, at the cruel expense of her love for Harry Percy. But the sport had begun; to see how far she could push the two most powerful men in the land. For what had she to lose?

And now sitting amongst the daffodils and feeling the wind blowing freshly against her skin she thought with supreme pleasure that her triumph had been far in excess of her original intention. The King had actually fallen in love with her and she was in the strongest position of all to inflict the little hurts that can make each day a misery to a lover. Not only that but her web was growing closer to Wolsey. He had described her as a 'foolish girl' to Harry.

'We will see,' she said aloud.

Only one thing troubled her. What move next? Her prime objective – to punish Henry and to be brought back to Court in triumph – had been achieved. But now she was at a crossroads. She could either become the King's mistress or . . . Or what? Fade into obscurity when Henry eventually grew tired? Or dare she go for the highest place in the land? Could she, dare she see if Henry would divorce Katharine and marry her?

The thought was so utterly stimulating that Anne threw back her head and the cloud of black hair flew as she laughed aloud. How wonderful at nineteen to be able to sit in a tree like a forest creature, and make decisions as to what scheme one would venture next with the King of England.

And that was how Francis Weston first saw her; glowing with pleasure and exuding the vitality of utter confidence. He thought that she was the most arresting girl he had ever come across. Almost unreal, an air of something like magic about her.

At that moment they were probably the two most self-assured people at Court. She for the sweet taste of power in the mouth of one so young, he for the knowledge that he was the most handsome man in the King's service even, some said, in all England.

She laughed again as she saw him staring at her and called out, 'Don't be afraid, sir. I have not really lost my wits. It is the March wind that has made me into a March hare.'

Francis bowed.

'Francis Weston, madam.'

She jumped down from the tree and stood facing him, her great dark eyes alive with some secret joke.

'How very formal. Then I must be as well. Anne Boleyn, Viscount Rochford's daughter,' and she dropped a small curtsey.

At once the name was familiar to Francis. Had he not overheard his parents discussing her some years ago? Yet all he could recollect of their conversation was that she had six fingers on one hand. Without deliberate intention his eyes swept downwards and he saw, for a split second, a protuberance growing from the little finger of the left before the girl tucked it into her long sleeve. Knowing that she had seen him looking he felt embarrassed but Mistress Anne went on talking as if nothing had occurred.

'And what are you doing out so early, Master Weston?

Should you not be attending His Grace in the Privy Chamber?'

How did she know his position at Court, he wondered?

'His Grace rode at dawn, madam. I have already waited upon him.'

'Then you are free to talk to me?'

Francis bowed.

'I am at my Lady's command.'

For some reason he was not at ease with this young woman. Usually he was at his best in female company, more than aware of the effect of a glance from his vivid eyes, but this girl was different. He sensed a power and determination that would be utterly unswayed by a look from a saucy courtier.

'You have not told me why you are abroad at this time. I'll wager half the Court is still asleep.'

He wanted to say, 'And what of you? What kind of woman sits in a tree and laughs at the world an hour after first light? Or at any hour for that matter?'

But he was too well schooled in courtly behaviour to voice such a thought and answered, 'I came here to run, madam.'

'Run?'

'Aye. His Grace often chooses me to oppose him at tennis play but I have yet to win a match.'

'So how does running feature, Master Weston?'

'The King is a better player than I, my Lady. But he is not nearly so fast. Therefore it seems to beat him I must outrun him.'

He felt the brilliant eyes turn on him and looking at her saw a thoughtful expression on her face.

'To beat him I must outrun him,' she repeated quietly.

'That is what I believe.'

Once again he heard her extraordinarily exuberant laugh.

'Why, Master Weston, I'll warrant you're right,' she said. 'Come, I'll race with you. Let us each pretend that the other is His Grace.'

She picked up her skirts in one hand, shouted 'Go' and was off towards the river before he could collect his wits. And that was the picture of her he was often to see through the years to come – hair streaming and skirts flying as she sped through the daffodils, the sound of her voice echoing back on the wind. It was only by pushing himself to the limits that Francis managed to pass her, for she had made a good start and was extremely light and swift on her feet. As she breathlessly came into second place she held out her right hand to him.

'A bold victory, Master Francis,' she said, 'but as you said, the King is not so fast.'

Francis thought, 'There is some hidden meaning in this. What does she really think?'

But she was an enigma and her face unreadable. Suddenly very curious, Francis asked, 'Will you be staying at Court, Mistress Anne?'

'Aye, for a long time,' she answered and her small white teeth showed as she smiled at him. 'I think you have helped me decide that.'

'I, madam?'

'You have just given me some very good advice.'

Francis gave up completely trying to understand. The girl obviously delighted in speaking riddles which were impossible to fathom. What he was thinking must have shown in his expression for impulsively Anne put her hand in his and said, 'I shall need friends at Court, Master Weston. I was there some years ago but I – left. Will you be one of them? I would be so glad of your help.'

She was instantly transformed from a rather vexing creature in to a nymph of charm and sincerity – a changeability that was to grow more and more pronounced in later years. Warm and friendly like this she was irresistible. Francis raised her hand to his lips.

'It will be an honour, madam.'

'Good. Now go to your running. I shall sit in the tree again and play the lute.'

And as he ran to and fro, sometimes imitating the quick moves made on a tennis court, he heard behind him notes of music and a voice full of sparkling cadences, yet husky and thrilling. He turned and waved his hat to her, because, for all her strangeness, he liked her though he found it difficult to decide whether she was plain-featured or uniquely beautiful.

Eventually he grew tired and, returning to the tree, his face streaked with sweat and out of breath, he said, 'I will bid you adieu, Mistress Boleyn. Unless you wish me to walk with you back to the Palace.'

'No, I will stay here and enjoy the morning.'

'Then I hope to have the pleasure of seeing you very soon.'

He bowed and walked some distance away. When he was sure that she could no longer see him he stripped off his clothes and dived into the river for the smell of his exertions was about him and no member of the Privy Chamber must be in the least unclean and unpleasant. The Marquess of Exeter had personally thrown poor William Carey out to wash only a few days before.

The water was cold and he stayed in for only a few minutes, drying himself with his shirt and rubbing some wild lavender into his skin. Anne, who had climbed one branch higher in order to get a finer view of the landscape stared at him in fascination. She had never before seen a man naked. Once, when she had been very young and both nursemaids ill, she remembered her mother – Lady Elizabeth – washing herself and Mary and George

156

together. She had looked at her brother in awe, thunder-struck by the difference between him and herself, and had received a blow on the ear for doing so. And now here was this beautiful young man – blissfully unaware that she could see him.

She thought, 'Harry would have been like that; firm of flesh and hard of muscle. If only I had gone into his bed, even once. Just to have known the feel of his body, skin against skin.'

But too late for regrets. They had married Harry to Mary Talbot with disastrous results and now it was up to her to take revenge for his and her own ruined life. She thought of the King's body – the first signs of corpulence just appearing, despite all the hard exercise he took. And as her dark eyes steadily watched Francis dressing she thought of his words. 'To beat him you must outrun him.' Yes, she'd do that all right. She would run and run until the Queen's crown was put on her head and Henry Tudor would know – if he didn't already – what it was like to physically ache with frustrated longing.

Half an hour later – very much as she had expected – she heard a voice behind her say, 'Oh, my little love, what are you doing? You could fall. Why have you climbed so high?'

Without turning round she replied, 'From here I can see from the Palace to the Tower. Climb up, Henry. Climb and look at your kingdom.'

And as she heard his heavy frame heave on to the lower branch she picked up her lute and strummed the strains of a Norfolk air – a harvesters' song of thanks for the grain. She thought how apt it was, for was not she beginning to reap her own particular crop? As she felt the King's lips on her neck she still did not turn and it was as well for him that he could not see the cruelty of her smile.

* * *

For once Harry Norris was alone. The King's Esquire of the Body sat in his little-used apartments more than a little drunk and intending to get fully so. For what he had feared had finally happened. Anne Boleyn had returned to Court and now it must surely be only a matter of days before she granted the King the ultimate favour. And the very thought of it made the man considered rather dull and boring by many of his fellow courtiers rise to his feet and begin to pace the room, silent tears running down his face. It was precisely at this desolate moment that a knock came on his door; nothing, he thought, could have been timed worse.

'Wait,' he called out but his voice was muffled and Francis Weston, standing on the other side, misheard and walked straight in.

'Good God, Sir Henry! Are you ill?'

'Yes,' said Harry wildly. 'I have the ague. I am sweating.'

'The strangest sweat I've ever seen,' thought Francis. 'The man's in tears.'

'Let me help you to your bed,' he said aloud.

It suddenly seemed to Harry that all he wanted in the world was for someone to care how he was feeling.

'It's this damnable ague. Oh dear Christ!' he muttered.

And then, standing there, in front of a sixteen-year-old boy, Harry – to his bitter shame – burst into uncontrollable weeping. It was a wretched moment for them both. The older man disgusted with his lack of control; Francis embarrassed to see someone, whom he had always looked upon as middle-aged, in such a pitiable state.

'Yes, Sir Harry,' he said awkwardly. 'Ague can play the devil's own tricks. Perhaps you should rest.'

And he took the older man by the arm and laid him on his bed, drawing the coverlet up over him. Then just as he left the room he heard it. There was no doubt in his mind at all. Into his pillow Harry Norris groaned one word – 'Anne.' For no reason – for it was a most common name – Francis was certain that Sir Harry was referring to the strange creature he had met that morning. She of the black hair and eyes and unconventional ways.

As he left the room and walked slowly along the corridor his face bore a puzzled look. He was sure that there was something going on – and all connected with the girl – but he could not imagine what it was. He pondered about it all day. Throughout a desultory game of tennis with William Brereton and still while he hurriedly changed his clothes in prepartion for the evening's activities.

'Be sure you're on duty in good time,' Brereton had shouted as they ended their game. 'His Grace has guests for an informal supper.'

'Who are they?'

'I don't know.'

But even though he arrived punctually at five o'clock, Francis found the place already in uproar. The barber was at work on His Grace's beard and Henry Norris, looking pale and dreadful, was supervising preparations for the King's bath.

'Francis, pour in these oils!' he called.

Without thinking, Francis exclaimed, 'God's head, this is a great to-do,' only to be rewarded with a black look from that raven of a man, Exeter.

'Hold your tongue, young Weston.'

But as he and Francis collected the King's glittering doublet of red jewel-encrusted velvet from the Yeoman of the Wardrobe, William Carey whispered to him, 'It is only my sister-in-law and her brother.'

Francis gaped.

'I would have believed it royalty from the preparations.'

William smiled a little sadly and shook his head.

'They haven't a title between them,' he said.

The King's musicians had already arrived and were playing one of His Grace's own love songs by the time Henry was satisfied with his appearance. He emerged from his bedchamber, perfumed and sweet smelling, and stood before the great fire that had been built to combat the March night. Yet within all that splendid apparel there was only a mortal man Francis thought. For the King's hands were trembling and the diamonds and emeralds on his fingers flashed a million anxious reflections as he toyed with his glass.

From the door Roger Ratcliffe announced, 'Mistress Anne Boleyn and Master George Boleyn' and Francis, as he bowed, thought, 'So it *is* the girl.'

If she had bribed the Yeoman of the Wardrobe, she could not have chosen an outfit more cleverly designed to blend with that of the King's. From top to toe she shimmered in cloth of gold but in the slashes of the long sleeves glowed crimson – an exact replica of the colour and stuff of His Grace's doublet. The effect was breathtaking as she slowly curtseyed before him and then let him raise her and move her to stand by his side.

At last Francis knew the answer to the mystery. He may yet be young but he could recognize blatant adoration when he saw it and the King's features almost seemed to burn with joy as he looked at the girl. And glancing swiftly at Norris – in control now but still white lipped – Francis caught a fleeting glimpse of the same look.

'Gentlemen,' said the King, 'may I present Lord Rochford's daughter Anne and her brother, George. They will be joining us at Court. I ask that you make them heartily welcome.'

Mistress Anne curtsied most prettily and said, 'I look forward to friendship with you all.'

It was a friendship destined to kill four of the men who stood in that room and who paid their respects to her.

It occurred to Francis as he cantered through the last of the trees and caught his first view of Sutton Place that he had never seen the house so sombre. A pall of grey cloud hung over it, giving it a desolate appearance and the tower of the Gate House was swathed in mist. He had never thought of the mansion as an unhappy place but it struck him now that it had a decidedly menacing appearance.

Inside, the atmosphere was no better. His father stood in the Great Hall staring into a dismal fire, the only sound that of wet, spitting logs and the rain beating against the windows. On hearing Francis enter he looked up and even the pleasure of seeing his son again could not remove the gloomy aspect from his usually expressionless face.

'Well, my boy, well,' he said, attempting a smile. 'How is life at Court? You have grown taller.'

Francis went to embrace him and for once Sir Richard did not move quickly from the contact but held his son tightly for a moment or two. This, in itself, was enough to convince Francis that something was wrong.

'Is everything all right?'

'No, your mother has taken to her bed. She's been there for the past three days.'

'Is she ill?'

'There is nothing wrong with her body. She's taken leave of her senses! She has consulted some wretched astrologer in London and believes this house to be accursed. There has been nothing but weeping and wailing ever since. I could smite the fellow's head from his body.'

Francis's mind immediately leapt to Dr Zachary. He had no doubt whatever that his mother had consulted him on her last visit to Court. However, he decided to say nothing. The grim set to his father's jaw convinced him that Sir Richard's threats were real enough and that there might well be an argument of tremendous proportions brewing. He – Francis – knew Dr Zachary hardly at all, only noticing him as a tousle-headed figure who frequented Court from time to time. Nonetheless, he had come to the conclusion that he was the son of Norfolk himself, not merely a lowly bastard of the clan. Laughing at himself for displaying some of his father's diplomacy Francis simply made a reproving sound and shook his head while Sir Richard made an irritable movement, kicking one of the hissing logs with his booted foot.

'God's head! Sometimes she sleeps and sometimes she lies awake without speaking. Go to her and see if you can get this rubbish from her head, Francis. A Viking curse! That sorcerer preaches Paganism!'

'Viking?'

'King Knut's niece Edith is supposed to have cursed that disused well near the ruin of the hunting lodge.'

Instantly Francis felt a clammy sweat. Something he hadn't thought about for months was there again, crystal clear in his mind. The apparition writhing on the ground, the hollow-eyed stare it had given him.

'Christ!' he said involuntarily.

His sudden pallor seemed to infuriate his father beyond all reason.

'What!' he bellowed. 'You too! Have I sired an idiot? God's mercy, Francis, if you encourage your mother in this I'll beat you personally.'

Francis thought, 'Nothing changes. He shouted and struck me all those years ago when I saw that dreadful thing. Now he is exactly the same.' The gloom of the day seemed to have stolen into Lady Weston's chamber for it was almost entirely in darkness. Francis, with great purpose in his footsteps, strode to the windows and drew back the hangings. In the grey light that crept in he saw that his mother was awake and peering over the counterpane to see who had entered.

'Why Francis!' she called. 'How very glad I am to see you.'

With a great inner resolve to do his utmost to raise her spirits, Francis said, 'Father tells me that Dr Zachary has upset you.'

Lady Weston fell straight into his trap.

'Yes, my interview with him was disturbing.'

So Zachary *was* the culprit. Francis resolved to have words with him as he braced himself for a show of bravado.

'He's only young, Mother. Looked upon by many as a charlatan.'

'I thought of him as highly regarded in Court circles.'

'By the gullible, perhaps. Anyway, how could he know of a Viking curse? It was all so long ago.'

'Apparently there is a tale written down by a chronicler of that time. A man who witnessed the event and entered a monastery through fear of what he had seen. It is still in existence in the Abbey's papers.'

'And Dr Zachary has actually seen it?'

'Yes.'

Francis sat silently. It was difficult to think of an answer for, so far, there had been no mention of crystal or star gazing. Nothing that he could make fun of as a magician's artifice.

His mother was speaking again.

'Francis, Giles the Fool told us a little of the story when you were a child. This place wiped out the Bassett family but I thought at that time it was they who were cursed.'

'Perhaps they were. Perhaps that is the explanation.'

'I fear not. Dr Zachary told me the rest of the history. There is too much evidence.'

And then Francis sat in a state of mounting tension as Lady Weston spoke of a tale so bizarre that he found himself shaking. Again and again the vision of that spectral figure at the well came into his mind and the whole chamber seemed full of shadows as the story unfolded.

After the death of the homosexual Hugh Despenser on the gallows, the old manor house where he had once consorted with his lover King had fallen into disrepair and though Edward III had given the Manor of Sutton to the Woodstocks – the Earls of Kent – they had not chosen to take up residence there.

'Despite this,' said Lady Weston, 'an immediate evil fell upon their line. Both the Earl of Kent and his brother died without leaving a living heir and Sutton passed to their sister, Joan.'

But though Joan, the Fair Maid of Kent, lived on and married three times her eldest son Thomas was beheaded, leaving no children, and his brother died shortly after inheriting the estate.

'It is always the heir who is in danger, Francis.'

With two brothers dead and childless the estate now passed to Joan's daughter who had married into the Beaufort family. Immediately a sinister destiny enveloped them. John Beaufort, the Earl of Somerset, died young after inheriting Sutton and then his eldest and his second son followed him. His third son Edmund was killed at the Battle of St Albans shortly after inheriting the estate. Edmund's closest son, the new Lord of the Manor of Sutton, was promptly beheaded on the battlefield after the Battle of Hexham and his two younger brothers were both killed at Tewkesbury. There was no male heir. It had happened again. Death and destruction, childlessness and the fall of another mighty house.

'Do you realize, Francis, that this land has destroyed four great families – the Bassetts, the Despensers, the Woodstocks and the Beauforts? It could destroy the Westons too.'

'I hope to God not. Did Zachary offer you no advice? Surely something can be done to ward off this malevolence.'

For the first time Anne Weston smiled.

'Yes, he gave me amulets for all of us – even for Margaret and Catherine. But for you he sent something most special. A charm that came from his mother which is most powerfully protective. Pass me that wooden box.'

From it she took a golden chain on which hung a strange blue stone, the like of which Francis had never seen before. And in the stone, carved by what means he could not imagine, was a symbol vaguely resembling an eye.

'How much did he charge you for this?' Francis asked, taking it in his fingers.

His mother looked at him reprovingly.

'He charged me nothing for the amulets – even yours, which was precious to him.'

Francis immediately felt ashamed of himself. Norfolk's dark-haired bastard had done him no harm and yet he had tried to demean him. And as Francis held the ancient talisman into his mind flashed a strange picture of a fair-haired girl wandering through a cornflower field and at her side a dark child, picking a posy for her and running; running with his bare feet, feeling the freedom of the wind blowing through his black curls.

'Romanies,' he said aloud.

Lady Weston looked at him curiously but Francis said no more. He slipped the chain around his neck and against his skin the gemstone felt warm and vibrant, not cold as he had expected. With a great sigh of relief Anne Weston jumped from her bed.

'Now you are safe,' she said.

Francis smiled.

'Mother, was all this moaning in the darkness a ploy? Was it done to make me wear this amulet?'

The blue eyes, so like his own, gave him a knowing glance.

'It wasn't making *you* do so that worried me most. But to get your father to put one on was hard work indeed.'

Francis's infectious laugh filled the room. The thought of impassive Sir Richard, the seasoned political campaigner and climber, actually agreeing to wear an amulet to ward off the evil eye struck him as comical. And he was still smiling as he descended the staircase to the Great Hall where Sir Richard was hunched before the miserable fire. He looked up as he heard Francis approaching.

'Well, how is your mother?'

'Greatly recovered, sir.'

Francis's eyes began to crease at the edges but his face had an innocent air as he said, 'It seemed she wished me to wear a talisman to protect me from the curse and that was at the root of her distress. Of course, I agreed. I realize, Father, that you do not approve of such foolishness and would not consider such action yourself but I trust you will forgive me.'

Sir Richard shifted uncomfortably in his chair and his eyes looked directly into Francis's. Under scrutiny his son felt his lips begin to twitch.

'God's head!' roared Sir Richard.

Francis collapsed into a laughing heap. And then he was off at great speed with Sir Richard in full pursuit, up the stairs and down the Long Gallery, too fleet of foot for the heavier built man to catch him up. By the time his father had panted into the Gallery, Francis appeared to have vanished into the air and look as he might Sir Richard could not find him anywhere.

Eventually he gave up and went to his wife's chamber to find her dressed and Joan attending to her. Francis, after listening to the quiet for a long time, lowered himself out of the largest chimney breast, somewhat darkened by soot and grinning like a blackamoor.

A few days later Sir Richard and Lady Weston left Sutton Place for Calais though Sir Richard was opposed to leaving Francis as master of the house.

'But truly, Master,' said Giles Coke, 'what mischief can he get up to on his own?'

But they were all to be surprised for on the afternoon of the third day after his parents' departure, a message came through from the Gate House that four visitors had arrived. Francis, who had been practising tennis strokes in the garden, hurried to wash the sweat off and change his shirt, and by the time he descended into the Great Hall, he could hear the laughter and chatter of three men and a woman. Even before he turned the bend in the stair and could actually see them, he knew who the girl was. The melodious voice of Anne Boleyn was unmistakable.

The afternoon sun was pouring through the stained glass windows and a nimbus of rose was around that black, silky head as she turned to greet her host. Francis often thought about her looking as she did at that moment, glowing in the reflected light and with some inner lustre of her own.

Standing with her and all looking towards him were her brother George, her cousin Thomas Wyatt, the courtier poet, and another of her cousins – Sir Francis Bryan.

'My parents are not here,' said Francis and then felt foolish and boy-like, for he had spoken too quickly, had blurted almost.

'We know,' Anne answered and she gave him a slow, sweet smile. 'We came to see *you*. We have ridden from Hever this very day.'

That evening they dined in the Great Hall very resplendently. Giles Coke as Steward, standing in watchful attendance, could not help but admire his young master for the skill with which he played host. But it was the girl who really caught and held his attention. Frankly, he thought her ugly, preferring plump, soft women. To his way of thinking her chest was too flat, her neck too long, her nose too sharp. Admittedly she had a fine pair of dark eyes and thick hair but that wasn't enough to warrant the amount of admiration she was receiving.

Looking from face to face of the four men present Giles could see that they were all entranced with her. Even her own brother obviously found her amusing and interesting, though he was the only one who was not sitting forward in his chair hanging on her every word as she chattered away.

But then as he silently observed her, Giles quite suddenly saw her fascination. It was her very animation, her sheer vitality, that was so captivating. To his mind she looked as if she would always be able to amuse, to cheer a man if he came home exhausted. And there was something else – but he could not grasp it. It was too intangible a quality. The only way that he could think about it was as a kind of mysteriousness. She looked as if she knew things that ordinary people might not be able to comprehend. And when he saw her in this light, Sir Richard's Steward understood that she could be mistaken for beautiful because she dazzled the eye so much that it was impossible to see what she really looked like at all.

And after dinner when the company had retired to the Long Gallery where, good servant that he was, he stood partly in the shadows so that his presence should not be obtrusive and she took up her lute and sang, he, too, felt her power creep over him. It was during the lyrical love duet that she sang with her cousin Thomas that Coke had the strange experience of stinging behind his eyes. Why, he had not wept since he was a boy and now here was this girl making unknown emotions rise in him and choke in his throat. Small wonder then that Francis was gazing at her in wonderment, that Wyatt was obviously in love with her, that Sir Francis Bryan shot her brilliant glances from his grey unblinking eyes.

Francis, flushed with wine and a certain self-importance, was speaking '. . . but the house is supposedly built on accursed land.'

Four pairs of eyes fixed themselves upon him.

'Sutton Place cursed?' said Wyatt.

'So it's said. And the old manor house before it. Edward the Confessor's wife laid a spell of evil at a well which is on our property.'

'An intriguing thought,' answered Thomas, his poet's imagination captured by the idea of pale queens long dead uttering words that could reverberate long after the speaker had crumbled to dust.

'And is it true?'

Beneath his shirt Francis felt the amulet warm against his chest. Unconsciously his hand stole up to touch it.

'I don't know,' he said.

Anne shivered despite the heat of the fires.

'*Who* knows what destiny has in store for us?' she said.

Bryan's voice, so quiet that it was unnerving, was speaking. 'Who indeed.'

And he smiled though Francis saw that the grey eyes

never moved. He wondered if the man had something wrong with him that he blinked so little.

Anne rose to her feet.

'Gentlemen, I beg your forgiveness. I am tired after so much travelling. I bid you goodnight.' And she was gone before anyone could answer.

In the sudden silence Francis Bryan turned his unnerving gaze on George Boleyn and Thomas Wyatt.

'I am told that we are away from Court at a stirring time. It would seem that His Grace is most seriously considering whether his marriage to Her Grace is truly legal.'

'Oh!'

George's closed face, rather like Anne's in its dark quality, did not alter. But Francis, too young yet to have learned the art of dissembling, stared open mouthed.

'But that is ridiculous,' he said. 'They have been married for years.'

'Eighteen to be precise,' answered Bryan drily. 'Longer than you have lived, Francis. And long enough for a man – even a King – to grow bored.'

He looked directly at George who remained impassive and merely raised his shoulders slightly in reply. It was Thomas Wyatt who said, 'Yes, it's true. It is a tightly kept secret but His Grace was called to trial at York House on May 17 to answer the validity of his marriage.'

'But who would dare do such a thing?' said Francis.

The other three burst out laughing, though not unkindly.

'Listen, Holy Innocent, nobody would. Therefore it's obvious that His Grace himself is behind the whole thing. He wants to be free of Katharine.'

Francis sat with his mind in turmoil. He remembered the looks he had observed passing between the King and Anne; thought of the way Henry sang while she played

170

the lute; remembered how his fellow courtiers had stirred when His Grace, in full public gaze, had selected Anne for his partner at the May masque for the French ambassadors. God's life, he had been slow witted! He had realized that the King was infatuated but that it should be more serious than that he had not even considered.

Despite the four fires it seemed to grow suddenly cold in the Gallery.

'How strange that the King should choose May 17,' he said. 'That was the day on which my father was granted the Manor of Sutton.'

George appeared to have been affected by the chill too, for he trembled.

'I feel as if that date reminds me of something,' he said.

It suddenly seemed to Francis that a black spiral was whirling towards him down the length of the Gallery. Something terrible and formless and – inescapable.

9

The Holy Lamb in Cordwainer Street was, considering both the time of day and the temperature outside, practically deserted. Two old men sat supping in one corner, so bored with each other after all their years of companionship that they could no longer be bothered to speak and they, apart from one young farmer come to the City to sell produce, composed the entire custom.

Outside, the almost empty midday street was vile with the smell of rotting garbage and filth, for no efforts had been made of late to do anything about clearing it. It was the summer of 1528 and the heatwave had brought in its wake an evil epidemic of the Sweating Sickness. With the knowledge that one could wake in the morning apparently quite well and be dead by evening, so quickly and violently did the symptoms appear, many of the citizens had left London and those that could not remained in their houses.

The King had sped from Greenwich to Waltham and Anne Boleyn had left for her father's home, Hever. She had more reason than most to be afraid, for one of her own servants had indeed caught the illness. Cardinal Wolsey had left York House for The More and the Duke of Norfolk had gone to Kenninghall Castle. Francis Weston, seeing the Court breaking up and going out of London, had thought it expedient to head for Sutton Place.

But there were some who had not been able to make their escape in time. Sir William Compton and Sir Edward Poyntz, old established friends of the King, were dead and

William Carey, husband of Anne Boleyn's promiscuous sister, was at this very moment gasping his way out of life. And in the forbidding house next door to The Holy Lamb, Zachary Howard lay alone in a dark room, wrapped in as many blankets as he had been able to find, pouring sweat from every part of his body. His dark hair normally so wild clung to his head damply, his eyes were closed with exhaustion, but before he had been forced to take to his own bed he had made up a huge pitcher full of sweet-smelling liquid, following a remedy taught to him by his mother. The only thing missing was fresh raspberry leaves but in their place he had substituted honey, roses and foxgloves.

As he lay, now, constantly sipping the brew and remembering in his fever how his mother had wandered unconcerned amongst the sick and dying pouring her herbal remedies down their throats when the Sweat had come to their small village in Norfolk, he knew that he must go on drinking. Knew that even if his arm could scarcely lift the jug he must not let his body dehydrate, for that meant certain death.

And all that afternoon he had battled to live though at one point he had grown so feeble that he had lapsed into unconsciousness and his hand, reaching out to take some more fluid, fell limply over the edge of the bed. It was then that his mother came to him.

'Zachary,' she said. 'Wake up!'

He opened his eyes and wasn't at all surprised to see her. She had aged not at all and in her fair hair she had woven a garland – a little coronet – of forget-me-nots.

'Zachary,' she said again, 'do you hear me?'

'Yes, Mother.'

'You must drink, little darling.'

She had called him that when he had been very young and he wondered if she knew that he was a full grown

173

man now, knew that she was dead and had come from whatever place she rested because he was not far from death himself.

He felt her small hand, like the touch of winter, on the back of his neck as she raised his head and helped him to drink. The whole room seemed to be blurring now, closing in on him and growing darker. And then he floated up and looked down on his body which lay like an abandoned cloak on the bed.

'Am I dead, Mother?' he asked.

'No. But you are near it. So you must fight to return to life. But first I will let you see something.'

And, as clearly as if he was in the room with him, Zachary saw his father, the Duke of Norfolk, drenched in sweat and panting for breath.

'Oh my God,' he said. 'I must go to him.'

'Zachary, this is two weeks hence. You will have time to get strong enough for the journey. But first you must conquer the space between you and your body. Go back!'

He tried but he was too weak to cross the distance.

'I can't.'

'Zachary, you must.'

He looked at her and saw her blue eyes shining almost fiercely.

He placed his square, strong hand – so like his father's – into her frozen fingers and was amazed by the strength of her grasp as she began to pull him down towards that shell of himself, that thing which had once been he and which he could see was already assuming the ghastly pallor of death.

'I don't want to,' he said.

'And let your father die without your help?'

Now there was a loud thudding and he realized that it was his heart pounding. His mother brushed her lips against his and was gone.

Two hours later Dr Zachary woke shivering. The fever had passed and the Sweat was over. Raising his head he finished the last of the brew then, pulling the blankets closely round him, he fell into a natural and peaceful sleep. He wondered, as he closed his eyes, if he had been delirious and dreamed of his mother but the next morning when, weak as a cat, he got out of bed to relieve himself and change his night shirt he found a single forget-me-not on the floor. So she had come!

From that moment Zachary set about the business of making himself strong enough to travel to Norfolk as quickly as possible. Even though he knew that his father could not die – for was he not destined to read the death sentence to Anne Boleyn? – nonetheless he could not let him suffer. He must make the journey to Kenninghall as soon as he was fit to mount a horse.

The wretched girl who worked for him had run out of the house the second she had seen the Sweating Sickness start and had obviously decided not to return. So he was hampered by having to look after himself, something he found difficult in his debilitated state. However, the old woman from The Holy Lamb, having heard a rumour that the 'magician' was sick with 'the Sweat' timidly knocked on his door – presumably to see whether he was dead or alive – and gave him a one-toothed smile of genuine gladness when, after much effort with the bolts, she saw him standing in the doorway pale and drawn but obviously cured.

That very day she sent him a coney pie and a steaming dish of roach, together with pigs' pettie toes, cheese and wine. And though he could not eat much of it the next morning he found his appetite returned and breakfasted on salt herrings and ale. At midday he had oysters, ribs of beef and sheep's feet and that night dined on capon. On the following day he paid her the bill and gave her good money to clean his house for him in his absence. Then, packing the herbs and medicaments he would need for his father into his saddle bag, he listened with an emotion approaching that of a released prisoner to the sound of his horse being led round by a lad from the stables nearby.

And then off to leave the stench of London behind heading for Chelmsford before nightfall, for he must cover forty miles a day to get to the Duke by the time the Sweat came upon him, and this over villainous roads, some little better than cart tracks. His few stops were to drink ale at midday and to pick from the meadows the fresh flowers and leaves he needed to complete his potion. Otherwise he rested himself and his horse at wayside inns only after the sun had gone down and he could no longer see his direction.

The stretch of Roman road beyond Chelmsford had helped him to speed up but the last twenty miles from Thetford to Kenninghall were over mud tracks, baked hard and cracked by the heatwave. The horse picked its way carefully and Zachary's heart gave a lurch of fear, for the turrets of the castle were in sight and he knew he must brave his way past his father's second wife, Elizabeth Stafford, daughter of the man whose death on the block had given Richard Weston the gift of Sutton – Wolsey's old enemy, Stafford, Duke of Buckingham. Not only she but also the Duke's twelve-year-old son – Zachary's half-brother – had to be reckoned with.

And much to Zachary's surprise it was the boy himself who came to the Gate House to see just exactly who this jackanapes was that demanded audience with his father so urgently, refusing to move and saying he was from Court. Yet as soon as he entered the room the twelve-year-old Earl of Surrey was stopped short for there, beneath a mop of hair as black as a raven, were the familiar Howard features; the broad nose, the pointed chin, the deep-set eyes that he himself bore. There was no doubt in Surrey's mind that he was looking at a bastard of their family and, very probably, his own father's son. Then the thought occurred to him that as this man was about ten years older than he, it would be he – the stranger – who would have been Earl of Surrey, had he not been fathered outside wedlock. All these ideas only pushed the boy – already precocious – into a more aggressive approach than he had originally planned.

'Well?' he said.

'I have come to see the Duke of Norfolk,' answered Zachary.

He thought, 'If ever a wretched brat needed a beating, one stands before me now. No wonder the Duke is bedding down the laundry maid.'

For his father had admitted to him on the last occasion they were alone that he was seeking solace in the warm arms of the laundry girl.

'Though she is simply to satisfy my body, Zachary – Elizabeth being such a cold creature. I have loved no woman with my heart except your mother.'

Zachary brought his mind back to the present.

'My father is sick with the Sweat and cannot be disturbed. Who are you?' Surrey was saying.

'Dr Zachary, His Grace's own physician. He sent me to attend the Duke.'

Surrey's jaw dropped. This was an answer he had not expected.

'Do you bear a letter from His Grace?' he said.

Zachary drew himself up to his full height and glowered at his half-brother.

'It is not customary for the King's physicians to be doubted by anyone – particularly small boys. Now, my Lord of Surrey, permit me to pass – on the instant! Do you wish me to return to London and tell His Grace that the Duke of Norfolk died because his own son prevented my entering?'

Zachary made his face grow dark and his eyes gleam in his head – a trick he had learned when dealing with Court cynics who tried to deride his gifts. He bent down so that his eyeballs were on a direct level with Surrey's.

'Or do I smell a plot?' he said suspiciously. 'Perhaps it is your wish that your father should not recover? Perhaps you have mighty ambitions for one so young? Perhaps I should report to His Grace that the senior Duke of England's life is threatened at the hands of his own son? Villainous wretch! Stand aside!'

And he shouted at the top of his voice, 'Hold fast, Lord Duke! Help is at hand.' And, swinging his saddlebag violently in the direction of Surrey and catching him a well placed blow in the ribs, he charged out of the Gate House and across the lowered drawbridge and into the castle itself.

There he bellowed at a frightened servant, 'Dr Zachary – the King's principal physician. Come to cure the Duke. Take me to him at once if you value your life.'

And so within moments he was in his father's bedchamber where to his horror he found that all the windows had been thrown open and the Duke was lying uncovered on his bed sweating profusely.

'Close the windows and light a fire immediately!' he said to the trembling servant; but before the man could move a cool voice spoke from the doorway.

'Who are you and what are you doing?'

It was the Duchess of Norfolk staring at him icily. Zachary bowed low.

'Your Grace, I am Dr Zachary. The King's physician.'

'Oh? I have not heard of you.'

'I am recently appointed, madam. Perhaps since your last visit to Court.'

As the Duchess rarely went to London this lie was easy enough but still she looked at him with deep suspicion. Through her mind was going the idea that this man was a bastard of the clan for Zachary's similarity to the Duke was growing more pronounced as he grew older.

From the bed the Duke's breathing could be heard as an ugly rasp and without caring for the consequences Zachary rushed to his side.

'Madam,' he said, 'you *must* let me care for him. I realize that it is difficult for you to entrust the life of your husband to a stranger but I promise you that if I fail to save him you may have me taken in chains to London. For God's sake, your Grace, I am no poisoner!'

From the lower regions of the castle the Earl of Surrey's voice could be heard shouting for his mother. Fortunately the words were indecipherable.

'Your decision, madam?' said Zachary urgently.

'Oh, do what you will,' she said impatiently. 'But if he dies you will answer for it before His Grace.'

With a swirl of his cloak Zachary was on one knee before her, raising her hand to his lips. For no reason that she could ever fathom Elizabeth Howard put out her other hand and touched his head. If only she were able to feel the love that he obviously did for the man who lay dying on the bed; if only the bitterness caused by her father's intolerable execution had not eaten her soul like a canker; if only all her future years were not doomed to be a sea of 'if onlys' as she progressed from resentful middle age to rancorous senility.

So a great roaring fire was lit in the hearth which, combined with the heat outside and the closure of the windows, turned the room into a veritable furnace. The Duke was wrapped in coverlet upon coverlet and as these

179

became drenched in sweat they were changed for dry ones and throughout the night Dr Zachary, dressed only in shirt and hose, held the Duke in his arms and poured into his mouth some strange, sweet-smelling potion that he had prepared himself with pestle and mortar in the castle's kitchens.

Elizabeth Howard, too, kept vigil. Sitting alone in the castle's Great Hall, her hands working ceaselessly at her embroidery, stitching without really seeing. The stranger's arrival had brought too many feelings, long suppressed, struggling to the surface of her mind. She knew that she could never love Thomas – the husband who lay upstairs fighting for his life; that she had been obsessional in her devotion to her father; that her relationship with her son was one of both love and hatred. Love, for producing a boy who could perhaps emulate his grandfather; hatred, because he was posturing and selfish and lacking in the qualities she held dear.

And as dawn came up throwing its grey pallor on to the stonework she faced the thing she dreaded most of all. Taking a mirror she stared joylessly at that which she detested – the onset of age. Bags of puffy skin were visible beneath her eyes and lines appeared when she smiled – though that was a rarity these days. The sad droop of disappointment had made its mark round her mouth and her skin had lost all its triumphant bloom looking pale in the cruel morning light. Elizabeth let out a great sigh which summed up all her life and expectations in one sound.

Then wearily she ascended the stone spiral and went into her husband's vaulted chamber where the fire still blazed despite the mist that lay over the Norfolk land promising another day of scorching heat. On the bed she saw the Duke swathed in coverlets but breathing normally and sweating little and still holding him in his arms, though he was fast asleep, was Dr Zachary.

Elizabeth stood in the doorway and looked at them. There could be no doubt. The two faces so close together were conclusive proof. She wondered who the mother had been and momentarily envied her. She, who had gained Thomas's love while he had been young and eager and had produced a child so lively and so colourful; while her own destiny lay bound up with a husband who had probably never loved her, a son headstrong beyond his years and a daughter ambitious beyond reason. And at the end of it all – what? How pointless the brief span seemed. Elizabeth Howard turned away and went to her chamber to weep for the futility of her life.

Somewhere in the depth of sleep Zachary heard her go for he woke startled. In the silence of the chamber he heard his father's regular breathing and, placing his hand on his forehead, felt only the minimal dampness that meant the crisis of the illness was past. Putting his head on the Duke's chest he listened to the lungs and heard no ominous sound of stored fluid. So fate had fulfilled itself. The Duke of Norfolk would live to play his part in the great destiny of England.

Quietly, Zachary prepared to leave and the morning haze still lay over the land as he took his last glimpse of Kenninghall Castle, the turrets bright in the still-hidden sun, the smoke from the Duke's solitary fire hanging motionless in the air. Everything pointed to it being another glorious day.

'And it is said the Lady Anne lies within an inch of her life though her father is over the worst and George Boleyn, when I left him, had certainly recovered.'

Henry Knyvett, on leave from the King's temporary Court at Hundson Manor, was staying at Sutton Place. A

181

close friend of Francis's, he had made the Sweating Sickness an excuse for not travelling as far as Norfolk to stay with his family whom he found staid and too restrictive for his liking.

'Then let us hope the inch shortens,' said Anne Weston.

Nobody answered her and the silence grew uncomfortable. Yet in houses all over the land, belonging to both the nobility and the ordinary people, sentiments like hers were being expressed by those who had heard the news that Anne Boleyn was near to death. For the truth was out. The King may speak of an uneasy conscience, say that he questioned the legality of his marriage but nobody was deceived. He wanted to marry Thomas Boleyn's black-haired daughter and discard Katharine like a worn-out garment.

'And worn-out she is,' said those who were young and cruel and followed the rising star of the house of Boleyn.

'But that's no excuse,' answered Katharine's supporters. 'Her Grace has been a good Queen to us and suffered much. It would be a wicked thing to do this to her now. Let him take the whore for his mistress, just as he did her sister.'

And of those who remained silent and held their peace the great majority, from Cardinal Wolsey down, hoped in their secret hearts that the wretched girl would not recover and that there would be an end for ever to this terrible fevered longing that held the King in such torment. For surely such an agony of love could not be bringing him any happiness?

Now Francis said, 'I pray that Anne lives, Mother. She is a good friend to me and I am fond of her. You like her, Henry, I know.'

He turned to Knyvett, who had no intention whatsoever of being drawn into a family argument and mumbled, 'I – er – have formed no opinion of the lady.'

Francis snorted and it was at this point that Sir Richard came in.

'Whether Mistress Boleyn lives or dies is not our concern. And you, Francis, should not speak to your mother in that manner.'

'But I merely pointed out that I liked Anne. Where's the harm in that?'

The logic of this seemed to pass clean over Richard's head for he answered, more loudly, 'Look to your behaviour, Francis. You will not think yourself so grand if you end up with a whipping.'

'God's head,' said Francis. 'I am seventeen years old and have been at Court for three years. Grant me, please, the honour of thinking I have some intelligence.'

Henry Knyvett was now staring fixedly into his wine glass and it was Anne Weston who tried to put an end to the argument.

'Please, Richard, Francis. We have a guest. Let us speak of pleasant things.'

But Francis was in a ridiculously stubborn mood and seemed determined to swim against the tide.

'Well, you started it, Mother, if I may say so,' he answered.

'You may not,' said Sir Richard and his hand shot out across the table and hit Francis round the ear. Without another word his son rose and stormed from the Great Hall. Henry Knyvett thought, 'Jesus, I came here to get away from this sort of thing. And here they are going at one another like tom cats in an alley.'

Aloud he said, 'Er – if you will excuse me, Lady Weston, Sir Richard. I think I will take a short walk before sunset. I have a slight headache – nothing to concern yourselves with. Er . . .'

Lady Weston began to apologize for Francis's behaviour.

'Oh, 'tis nothing,' said Knyvett, making things much worse. 'My father is much stricter than Sir Richard. A veritable bully at times.'

He then went bright red, tried to drink his wine in one draught but choked on it so that it came running out of his nose. He could hardly remember an occasion when he had been more acutely embarrassed.

'Do go, Henry,' said Anne, putting him out of his misery. 'Find Francis and smooth him down.'

With a sigh of relief Knyvett bolted from the Hall to the accompaniment of Richard muttering under his breath, 'What a great ninny! No wonder the boy is growing up into a no-good wastrel. He thinks of nothing but sports and gaming. Utterly selfish, that's his trouble. There ought to be a war. That would make him a man.'

'I am glad there is *peace*, Richard. I have no wish to see Francis killed. Think when you speak.'

The widely spaced eyes regarded her coldly.

'I do think, wife. And that is why I should advise you not to make public your dislike of Anne Boleyn. Many years ago we saw the first signs of the King's love and you know, as well as I, to what point it has gone.'

'Is she his bedfellow?'

Richard shook his head.

'If she had consented she would have lost him. The great thrill with the King is to hunt his quarry. But do not underestimate her. The day may come when those who now speak against her might go in peril of their lives.'

'But surely,' she said, 'His Grace cannot dispose of Katharine. The Pope would never give the nod to an annulment.'

'Strange things happen,' answered Richard slowly. 'I intend to keep my mouth shut and wait.'

'Well, I shall remain loyal to the Queen. She has been my friend since she was a girl.'

Richard reached over and patted her hand. One of his rare smiles crossed his face.

'You are a good woman and constant, Anne, but you must wear the mask of Janus. There is no danger in that foolish boy, Knyvett, but there might be those only too glad to report that the Westons of Sutton Place are opposed to the Boleyns. In any event you would not wish to fall out with your son.'

'Do you think he is enamoured of her himself?'

'I don't know,' he answered thoughtfully. 'It is possible, I suppose. I think, in any case, it was clever of you to occupy the time he is forced to be at home because of the sickness by inviting his betrothed. He was greatly smitten with her but memory fades quickly when you are young and it must be three years since he last saw her.'

'A good three years.'

Richard smiled.

'Then let us see how Mistress Ann Pickering can pit her strength against that of Mistress Boleyn.'

So it was with some trepidation that the Westons waited in the Great Hall and, in a repetition of her arrival three years before, heard Ann's escort crossing the cobbles.

Francis thought, 'I am dreading this. I have changed so much. And even though Lucy Talbot is now married I have shared a few beds since, and Ann Pickering is just a child of fifteen. The whole affair is doomed to disaster I fear.'

But the Cumberland heiress once again took him by surprise. Instead of the formal opening of the door to her Steward by Giles Coke, it was she who appeared as the door swung open.

'Oh, dear Westons, how I have missed you,' she said and in a totally unconventional manner she flung herself first at Lady Weston, then at Sir Richard, who was given a smacking kiss on the cheek which completely took him unawares, and then finally at Francis.

'You have got very tall,' she said, 'and I, so my serving maids tell me, have developed a chest.'

'My dearest Ann,' remonstrated Lady Weston, 'one does not speak of these things before gentlemen.'

'Oh,' came the answer, 'doesn't one? That comes of my being an orphan and living so far away from Court. Francis, you will have to teach me everything that the maids-of-honour do. Then I can have pretty manners.'

As usual, try as she would to look demure, a mass of red hair was descending from her headdress and one of her ribbons was undone. And at the same time she was gazing at Francis with her meadow blue eyes wide with laughter.

He bowed very formally.

'Mistress Pickering,' he said.

She was definitely mocking him as she curtsied and said, 'Master Weston.'

Then suddenly she looked serious – or as serious as was possible for her.

'I will try to behave well,' she said, addressing all three of them. 'I am just so unused to company.'

Francis thought, 'I am acting absurdly. I am trying to look like a courtier merely to impress. What an idiot I must seem to her!'

He said, 'I think the way you behave is charming.'

Then he realized that he sounded patronising for she shot him a tremulous, anxious glance. The memory of how much he had loved her three years ago came vividly back and he longed to take her in his arms and kiss away the small hurt he had just given. But he had no opportunity to be alone with her.

Throughout dinner at which Henry Knyvett, who gazed at Ann almost without ceasing, was present she avoided

Francis's look, staring at the ceiling, the floor, anywhere, rather than catch his eye. And after the meal, which seemed to go on for ever, Giles entertained them and though Francis might move restlessly in his chair Ann sat stiffly, her hands folded in her lap, her eyes never leaving the action of the Fool.

Immediately the entertainment was done she stood up and said, 'I hope it is not rude of me if I ask to go straight to my chamber. The travelling has tired me more than I realized.'

And with a formal curtsey to Sir Richard, Francis and Henry she was off accompanied by Lady Weston. Knyvett let out a great sigh.

'God's head, Francis, you are a lucky dog,' he murmured just low enough for Sir Richard not to catch the words. 'You should see what my family have singled out for me. I'll swear that her eyes look two different ways at once. I'll not go through with it, even if I'm forced abroad. But yours is a veritable angel. I wish I stood in your shoes.'

And how could he know, poor guileless creature, that one day he would. That when Francis's body lay in its tragic box – no true coffins for those who had offended against the King – and the young widow was desolated with grief, it would be to his clumsy kindliness that she would turn. And that when that day came he would think of these words, uttered in innocence, and weep for his friend's death. Look at the cloud of red hair lying on the pillow beside him, raise a lock to his lips while she slept, and realize that none of this glory would have been his but for an accident of fate. And then he would feel guilty in his happiness as Ann would stir in her sleep, and wonder if the hand that stole out was searching for him or for Francis. Sad Henry Knyvett – the last man alive to consciously wish harm to another – was fated to win his greatest prize through the destruction of a friend.

Francis was saying, 'Yes. I have been fortunate. And now through my own foolishness I have offended her. Tomorrow, Henry, I would like to ride with her alone. Will you forgive me?'

'Of course. But if you should tire I would be happy to look after her for you.'

'I think there is little chance of that.'

Yet the next day when the family – who rose and breakfasted early at the wish of Sir Richard – were again assembled she refused to look at him once more, other than for formal morning greeting. Francis decided that he must act.

'Mistress Ann,' he called to her as she was walking away with his mother.

She affected not to hear so he ran up behind her and took her arm by the elbow.

'Mistress Ann, will you ride with me? I would like to show you Sutton Forest. Please!'

As he said the last word in the most earnest voice he could muster he slightly increased the pressure on her arm and was rewarded by a rose pink blooming in her cheeks. Lady Weston had tactfully gone on to the kitchens and Henry had made a rather clumsy exit in the direction of the garden, so Francis was able to speak more freely.

'Forgive me if I have displeased you,' he said. 'Tell me what is wrong.'

'I will when we are outdoors,' she answered. 'I am happier in the air and the freshness than I am in houses.'

So they walked round to the stables and he lifted her on to his best mare.

'Come on,' she said. 'I am used to a gallop.'

And off she went at great speed through the parkland and towards the towering forest, a young hound leaping behind her and Francis pushing his horse to the limit to keep up. At length she slowed her pace and looked over her shoulder for her companion who was a good quarter of a mile behind. Her headdress had fallen off completely now and he saw as he approached the glorious hair burnished by the sun and the creamy glowing skin.

'You are even more beautiful now that you are grown,' he said. 'I am so glad that you are going to marry me.'

Rather to his consternation she burst into tears.

'What's this, what's this?' he said, dismounting and then lifting her down to stand beside him. 'Don't you wish to be my wife? Would you have the contract broken?'

Her eyes were like rain wet flowers as she looked at him.

'No, it is not that.'

'Then what, sweetheart? Do not cry so.'

He wiped her cheeks with his shirt sleeve for he had no handkerchief with him and knowing her usual state of disarray he doubted very much that she would have one.

'It is just that I cannot be free with you.'

Francis was more than perplexed.

'I don't understand you, Ann. Who are freer than husband and wife?'

She turned away from him and looked back over the parkland from which they had just come. In the distance the hound could be seen desperately trying to catch them up.

'I feel like that dog in your presence,' she said. 'I know nothing, Francis. My mother died in childbed, my father followed her seven years later. I was brought up by servants and was able to run freely on my estates in Cumberland. I am a country girl but I could see yesterday that you are a man of Court. You have good manners and stylish behaviour. I will for ever be pounding behind like that animal. It is not my way to adopt airs. I like to behave directly. How can I do that with you? You will think me the greatest bumpkin on this earth. Not fit to be taken anywhere. Oh, I can curtsey and dance and play the lute – very badly, I may add – but I do not know how to converse politely.'

'Then converse rudely for all I care,' he answered. 'I think you are the most endearing woman I have ever met.'

The hound panted up to them and fell at her feet exhausted.

'Do you want me to do that to prove I mean it?' said Francis and before she could answer he had done so and was kissing her shoe. She dropped down on the ground beside him, as artless as a child.

'Will you kiss me now?' she said.

'Only on one condition.'

'And what is that?'

'That you will always be like this – completely free with me. If you want a kiss, say so. If you want me to bed with you, say so. If you are with child, tell me. Let there be no barriers between us. Let us have a love that is never spoilt by cynicism or artifice.'

And with that he kissed her full on the mouth, putting his tongue between her lips and drawing as close to him as he could the soft warmth of her body. And while he held her so near his hands explored her.

'Is that courtly behaviour?' she asked, rather surprised.

Francis laughed.

'No, darling. It is man's behaviour. Only done between those who are intimate. Let me kiss your new grown chest.'

And together they undid the top of her green damask gown so that she was naked to the waist. He gently bent his lips to the roundness of her breasts, caressing first one and then the other.

'Lest the other one be jealous.'

'And would you like my hands on you, Francis? Is that what lovers do?'

'Yes,' he said and taking her hand he guided it within his hose.

'Ah, I know what that is,' she said, 'for I have a black stallion in Cumberland and when he is with the mares he produces the same.'

Francis laughed. 'Men pride themselves on being well made in that place and to be compared with a stallion is a great compliment. Thank you.'

And they fell to kissing once more, fondling each other until Francis finally said, 'May I love you now? The stallion is desperate for the mare.'

And it was then that Ann sat up slightly and said, 'I have the most wonderful pain which I know will not be satisfied until we couple but I feel that we should not.'

'Why, sweetheart, why?' said Francis, slipping his hand within her skirt.

'Because,' she answered, 'your father – who is my guardian after all – told me that we must wait another two years before we marry and if you make love to me and then I am sent away I shall be like a child deprived of sweetmeats and may run wild amongst the stable lads. It would be better for my peace of mind if I do not know what lovemaking feels like.'

Reluctantly he had to agree.

'But you will let me kiss you and touch you each day like this?'

'Oh yes, yes,' she said, 'as often as you like. But we must stop short, Francis. You can work off your feelings on the mares at Court, no doubt. But I shall have no other stallion than yours.'

He was amazed by the combination of beauty and sensitivity in such a young girl. Releasing her gently he

191

gazed at her, taking in every detail of the red-gold hair, the cornflower eyes, the clear, glowing skin.

'My Rose of Cumberland,' he said. 'I am the luckiest man on earth and I shall worship you till death.'

A cloud went over the hot sun and they both shivered.

'Don't speak of that ever again,' she said, 'for when you die my heart will die with you.'

He held her close and said, 'Come, let me dress you, sweetheart. I cannot kiss you any more without forcing you to love me. I am only a man after all.'

'And the most handsome in England, so I've heard it said.'

'Who could know that? 'Tis only Court foolishness.'

'Perhaps, but I like to think it is true. It is good for my conceit.'

'Then think it. For I know I have the prettiest betrothed.'

'Shall we have beautiful children, Francis?'

'Aye, a houseful. Boys and girls and twins. I shall keep you well occupied, madam, for I shall never be able to keep out of your bed.'

She wrinkled her small nose and said, 'It sounds delightful. Do you swear that our life together will be like that?'

'I swear it,' he said.

And so, in their innocent happiness, they slowly walked their horses back to Sutton Place unaware of the sinister forces gathering against them.

As with all those who have the gift of second sight the certain knowledge that a particular event has taken place occurs when the clairvoyant expects it least. And so it was that Zachary Howard, taking his time about returning to epidemic-ridden London, was sitting contentedly in the sunshine outside an Essex tavern when he became clearly aware that his cousin Anne Boleyn was sick with the Sweat. And because he had seen her from afar and loved her he knew that he must go to her – even though she, like his father, was not destined to die.

And he fell to considering the strange role that life lays down for each individual. How many people should be in a certain place at a particular time so that a sequence of events may be set in train. How strangers may pass one another, never knowing what other progression could have come about if they had stopped for a moment to speak. How he, with the gift inherited from his mother, was still merely an instrument of providence; simultaneously all-powerful and yet powerless. It was difficult indeed to know the future and act in the present. But so be it; that was his fate. Almost with an air of resignation he mounted his horse and followed the pilgrim's path to Kent.

In her father's home, Hever Castle, Anne Boleyn lay in the darkness and thought, 'If death comes to take me now, I won't resist. I don't care any more. The King writes letter upon letter. He sends his physician, Dr Butts, to cure me. He smothers me with overwhelming love and yet I feel nothing for him. And now I am caught on a tread-mill for Cardinal Campeggio is being sent by the Pope to try the case of the validity of the King's marriage.'

And in the stillness of her chamber she felt the springing tears well out of the corners of her eyes and down onto her pillow. She was compelled to swim with events for having used every device to attract the huge ego of the monarch, so that she may hurt him, pinch his soul, barb his self-love, the situation had gone out of control. What had started as revenge for the ruining of herself and Harry Percy had grown into a monstrous snowball. And if she tried to break free now the King's reaction would probably be only to love her more. For she no longer bothered to behave particularly well in front of him – sometimes being downright ill-tempered if the mood so took her. But the King – oaf – as she very secretly thought of him – only responded by showering her with further gifts and love letters.

'Oh yes,' she thought, 'it would have been so much better if I had died of the Sweat. Better for all the country.'

But then there was still Cardinal Wolsey – he who had reduced Harry to tears and referred to her as a 'foolish girl'. He still sat, fat and proud. But growing more and more worried! To see him toppled would be very satisfying.

And with that she dried her eyes and called out for her serving maid to draw back the hangings and tidy her bedclothes. But as the afternoon light filled the chamber she saw that it was not her servant but her cousin Jane Wyatt – Thomas's sister – who was in the room.

'Why, Jane, have I been sleeping?' she said. 'How long have you been here?'

'I rode over this morning. How do you feel? You have become even thinner.'

'Aye, a veritable bag of bones indeed. If the King were to see me now I wonder what he would think.'

Jane, who had inherited some of her poetic brother's imagination, had a none too pleasant mental picture of Henry crushing her friend's fragile body beneath his in an ecstasy of lust. She wondered if Anne had yet shared His Grace's bed for, close a companion as she might be, it was not the way of Mistress Boleyn to discuss such matters. Her eyes always had a slightly secretive look and her face could indeed grow dark if she were ever pressed to reveal information.

'A curious girl,' thought Jane, 'not like other people. I wonder if she has any weaknesses at all.'

If she had been in the room but five minutes before and witnessed Anne weep for her lost love she would not have credited what she saw.

'I think, Anne,' said Jane, answering her earlier question, 'he would love you if you were almost a skeleton. His Grace worships you to the point of distraction.'

Anne nodded gloomily.

''Tis true enough.'

Jane laughed and said, 'They say he is bewitched by you.'

Anne made a contemptuous sound.

'They can roast in hell. They would ruin everything. I will not tolerate they, Jane. As far as I am concerned it is I who count.'

Jane Wyatt thought, 'How dangerous she is. She cares for nobody but herself. Poor Queen Katharine!' And then a ridiculous idea came into mind for she caught herself thinking 'poor King Henry'!

To lighten the atmosphere she said, 'There is a very odd young man downstairs who says he wishes to see you.'

'Oh?'

'He states his name is Dr Zachary and he is sometimes at Court where he believes you may have noticed him. He looks a veritable rag bag to me. A great mass of hair and a black cloak and exceedingly travel stained.'

She did not add that as she had walked past him in the small Hall at Hever she had never in her life felt such a wave of power emanate from anyone. So strongly had it affected her that she had turned to look at him again, breaking the rules of good behaviour, only to find a pair of strangely beautiful amber eyes smiling at her.

Anne frowned for a second and then laughed.

'Oh, the astrologer. Yes, he is very popular. He reads the stars for many at Court. It is said he is related to my mother's family – the Howards. Though a bastard, of course.'

'Will you see him?'

'Why not indeed? Brush my hair, Jane, and wash my face. Let us find out what he wants.'

'I sent a servant to him for he looks as if he's travelled far.'

'Good. I think this could be amusing for I'm sure that he is a fraud.'

Inexplicably Jane was annoyed.

'Why should he be? Truly, Anne, I think at times you are too harsh.'

The black eyes flickered over her cousin but without malice.

'Yes, I suppose I am,' she said wearily, leaning back against her pillows. 'But it is the world that makes us so, Jane. We are all born in as guileless babes. It is life's cruelty that is the great corrupter.'

Jane was silent. She simply did not, and knew that she never would, understand her black-haired cousin who could make men fawn at her feet and yet had no particular good looks; who seemed so exuberant and yet so sad; who was a strange mixture of so many things that it was hard to find out what she was really like at all.

She picked up the thick tresses in her hands and started to brush them. The bones of Anne's skull showed as the hair parted across the middle.

'In that small space,' thought Jane, 'is the subtle brain that will decide the future of England. Dear God, it looks such a little thing!'

She was glad when the knock came to the door to disturb her disquieting thoughts.

'Enter,' called Anne, and there in the entrance, looking

somewhat cleaner than when he had first arrived but still rather wild, was the young man Jane had met in the Hall. He bowed.

'My name is Dr Zachary,' he said.

'Yes, I have heard of you,' answered Anne. 'You are an astrologer and soothsayer I believe.'

'I have the gift of second sight. And I do read the stars. But that was not why I came, Mistress Anne. I am also a herbalist and I know you have been sick with the Sweat. I have brought a tonic to strengthen you. For that is all you need now. Dr Butts has done well, for you were perilously ill at one point.'

'And how do I know it is not poison?' said Anne laughing. 'I have numerous enemies now that the Cardinal comes from Rome to question the legality of His Grace's marriage.'

Many men would have looked furious but Zachary merely shrugged his shoulders.

'Whether you drink it or not is entirely your decision, Mistress. I made it to help you but there are those incapable of accepting help when it is offered.'

'Come,' she said, 'I did not mean to offend you. Pour me a draught, Jane, and I will take it now to show my good faith. Sit down Dr Zachary and forgive my rudeness. As you know, I have been ill and I forget myself.'

Aware that his eyes were following her every move Jane Wyatt took the leather bottle that Zachary handed to her and poured a good measure into a glass. The liquid was clear and golden and smelt of wild flowers. Anne drank it in one mouthful and almost immediately her eyes seemed to grow heavy with sleep.

'Well, astrologer,' she said, 'I feel rested even now. My limbs are getting heavy.'

'In a few minutes you will fall into a deep sleep,' he said. 'And when you wake I want you to drink some more. And when you wake again I want you to repeat the action. In this way you will sleep for four days. After that you must eat as much strengthening food as you can and then you will be able to return to Court in August, when the sickness will have left London.'

The pupils of Anne's eyes were dilating as she looked at him but she said dreamily, 'And what is to be my fate, astrologer? Will I return in triumph?'

'In great triumph, mistress. To your own house in the Strand, with gardens that go down to the riverbank.'

'How well that sounds. But what then, Zachary, what then?'

She was practically asleep.

'In five years time,' he whispered, 'the crown of England will be put upon your head.'

Her eyelids fluttered but there was no other indication that she had heard him. Her breathing was deep and even and she seemed in a sound sleep. Zachary read Jane Wyatt's mind and laughed.

'Nay, I did not poison her,' he said. 'I am a cousin of hers and I once thought I loved her.'

Jane blushed and cursed herself for a fool.

'Yes, you are right,' he said. 'It was when I saw you that I knew I loved her no more. For you are so familiar to me. I have often seen you though until this moment never with my actual eyes.'

'I don't understand,' said Jane.

'Perhaps this will explain,' answered Zachary Howard and taking her in his arms he gave her a kiss of such passion that she would have fallen down if he had not been holding her.

'Will you be my wife?' he said.

'Happily,' answered Jane, quite regardless of the fact that less than an hour before they had been total strangers.

* * *

The Sweating Sickness had passed and from various temporary residences the Court was reassembling.

Zachary, after tarrying in Kent a few days with Jane Wyatt, had returned to Cordwainer Street in the middle of July even though the pestilence was not quite over. Before he left he had persuaded her into marriage by Romany rite, taking her into the forest that surrounded Hever, drawing blood from both their hands and then binding them together. Even while the handkerchief was still on them he had consummated their love out there in the Kentish woods, the sun on their naked bodies, her cries of pain and pleasure mingling with the call of the birds. And he, like a wild creature himself, carnal and thrusting until she was finally his.

'Tell Mistress Anne that you will come with her to London as a member of her household,' he said, as they parted on the edge of the wood, he leaning down from his saddle to kiss her.

'And if she does not agree?'

'She *will* agree.'

Riding back to her father's house, her virginity gone, her hand still throbbing from the nick that Zachary had made in it with his knife, the gently raised Jane Wyatt wondered if she had taken leave of her senses.

The King, accompanied by George Boleyn and a few other courtiers, set forth from Hunsdon Manor at the end of the month when he was utterly sure that the Sweat had passed.

He thought, 'Each step of this beast brings me nearer to my sweetheart who, vexacious creature, refuses me still. And yet I will not break my vow to myself. I would rather stay celibate than have another woman.'

Aloud he said to Henry Norris, 'Harry?'

'Yes, Your Grace.'

'You are a widower. Have you ever had long spells of – er – abstinence?'

'Yes, Your Grace. I once waited three years before taking a trollop.'

'And did you find – forgive me – that the celibacy had affected you in any way?'

'No, Your Grace. I was a little uncontrolled, that is all.'

Both Norris and George Boleyn, riding within earshot, knew exactly what this was all about. The King had not made a nocturnal visit to Katharine's apartments for nearly two years and Norris, in his privileged position, knew for sure that Anne Boleyn was refusing Henry her bed. George grinned to himself.

'So he fears losing his potency,' he thought. 'He'll go madder than ever to have Anne if that's in his head.'

At Sutton Place, Francis and Ann Pickering were locked in an intimate embrace. She was glad that they were in the house with people around them for today, as they were saying farewell, she felt she might have given in and in fact was about to do so when she was saved by the sound of Lady Weston's approaching feet. Francis made a headlong plunge to hide under the bed.

As the door opened Ann was to be found sitting nonchalantly enough before the window striving as usual to get her red curls into some semblance of order. Lady Weston, however, was not altogether fooled for her quick eye had noticed a slight movement of the bed's hangings.

'Oh, Ann,' she said in an extra loud voice, 'if you see Francis tell him to come at once. His horse is saddled and ready and he must start off now to reach London before nightfall.'

'Yes, Lady Weston,' the girl answered, rising and bobbing a curtsey.

As soon as the door closed Francis reappeared, somewhat dusty.

'Did she suspect?'

'Aye, so go quickly.'

So with one last kiss they went separately to the courtyard where Ann, running to the top of the Gate House tower, waved and waved till he had vanished into a black dot.

And so – with Queen Katharine stitching patiently away at her embroidery; the King striding restlessly through the corridors; Cardinal Wolsey working into the hours before dawn on The King's Great Matter, as the separation from the Queen had come to be known; the Duke of Norfolk taking up residence in his London home and listening with an appreciative smile to his son Zachary's description of his Romany wedding; and Francis Weston running around the tennis court with Henry Norris – the actors were in place. All of them waiting for that little dark girl to leave the woods and fields of Kent and take the dusty road to London – and to destiny.

10

'He's dying,' said Dr Burton flatly. 'There is nothing I can do for him. He may live another month, two perhaps.' He shrugged his shoulders and shook his head. 'That's the way of it.'

Anne Weston sat down more hurriedly than she had intended.

'But why? He has had such a healthy life. Most of it out of doors till he came to live with us. How could a man like that be struck down?'

Dr Burton looked at her, sighing slightly.

'God in his mercy alone can know, Lady Weston. Who is to say why cankers eat away at a man apparently hearty, while others of puny, bloodless mien are spared. All I can tell you is that death is at work in your Fool, madam, and that he must prepare his soul for immortality.'

'Poor Giles, he has always been so harmless.'

'It is never easy to lose a good servant,' said Dr Burton, matter-of-factly. He had long since dismissed emotion when it came to his work. As a youth, shortly after taking the Hippocratic Oath, he had wept for the dead, rejoiced when a sickly babe survived, felt personal gratification for every cure that resulted from his care. But now he had changed. It was impossible to maintain personal involvement with one's patients and remain of balanced mind. The best he could hope for was to learn more. Eleven years before – in 1518 – the College of Physicians had been founded and he had been one of the first to join. There, pooling his knowledge with others, he had

202

realized that if he was to serve he must look on the human race as so much meat; dissociate himself from suffering the better to alleviate it.

'He was more than a servant, he was a friend.'

Dr Burton made a tutting sound and reached into the wooden chest that his servant carried for him on his visits.

'Let him drink this physic three times daily. It will not help the disease but it will soften the pain. As the end draws nearer I will strengthen the compound.'

'God's life, what a cold-hearted creature the man is,' thought Anne. 'He speaks of death as another would talk of ending a visit. Yet in a hundred years,' she pondered, 'who will know what I was? Or who will care? And though Giles of Guildford – known as the Fool – gave pleasure to so many with his capers and singing he'll not be remembered or wept for by those that are yet unborn. Oh, how wickedly shallow is the whole stuff of creation.'

'. . . and keep him in bed,' Dr Burton was saying. 'The more he rests, the more slowly the disease will spread. His days as a Fool are over, I fear. Best to look for a new one.'

'Aye,' she answered wearily. 'I'll inform my husband.'

'In Calais, is he?'

Dr Burton was now making the small talk of all practised physicians as they prepare to leave.

'No, his Treasurership ended last Michaelmas. Had you not heard?'

'In truth I hadn't, Lady Weston; I so rarely see you. A hardy family.'

She smiled albeit faintly, for her thoughts were full of Giles. 'No, he is now Under-Treasurer of England and has returned to Court.'

'Indeed, indeed. A great honour for Sir Richard. Please

pass on my congratulations. Well, his statecraft will be needed. These are turbulent times.'

Even country doctors like Burton knew that the Pope's Legate – Cardinal Campeggio – had arrived in England during the previous autumn to hear the case for the annulment of the King's marriage. It also seemed to him, though he was no Court politician and had no experience of state matters, that the Cardinal must have received instructions from a higher authority to procrastinate. For it was only now – the summer of 1529 – that the Legate Court was finally in session. Furthermore, so rumour said, Mistress Boleyn had been sent from her fine lodgings to Hever Castle in a bitter mood. Dr Burton smiled thinly. What men would do for the urge within them to possess a woman. He wondered if the King ever *did* obtain his desired end and marry Mistress Anne, whether he would find her so different from the Queen when he got her between the sheets. Younger, thinner, more vivacious – yes. But actually *different*?

'Will you call again next week, Dr Burton?' Lady Weston was saying.

'If it will make your mind easy, madam. But there is nothing I can do in truth.'

It was with a sad heart that she sat in her little chamber in the Gate House wing after he had left. Sutton Place without Giles was an unbearable thought. And yet, she supposed, his strange weakness of late had put the idea in her head that one day they would have to do without him. But not so cruelly soon for the man was not old. Why, his face hadn't altered at all since the day she had first met him. But then people with those crinkly, ugly looks seemed timeless. She had always imagined, without consciously thinking about it, that Giles had not changed since he was a child. And the idea of a little boy with bright blue eyes, big teeth and hair cut as round as a basin made her smile despite all.

The knock on her door made her jump a little for she was far away. Back in Sutton Park, by the ruins of the old manor house, one summer's day eight years ago, watching a strange figure come striding out of the woods with all its worldly goods on its back. Giles, the strolling player, the Romany storyteller, come to look over the new Lord and Lady of the Manor.

'Come in,' she called.

And there he was. Dressed and risen from his sick bed, his face still bearing that awful parchment colour it had had for the last few months. But for all that attempting his toothy grin.

'Giles!' she remonstrated. 'What are you doing? Dr Burton left the strictest instructions that you need to rest in order to . . .' Her tongue slurred slightly over the deception, '. . . to make a quick recovery.'

He put on the blank expression that he always adopted in any kind of difficulty. Only this time at the back of his eye was a 'very-well-if-you-must' look.

'Well, my Lady,' he said. 'It is difficult for me to lie still in any sort of comfort. I am, by nature, a restless creature and in truth I am more unhappy lying down – unless I am drunken or asleep, of course – than standing up. Therefore if my Lady would permit me to sit when I am weary . . .'

Furious with herself for her thoughtlessness Anne motioned him to the chair opposite hers.

'. . . then I think you will find that I will recover better. Standing or sitting is my preference, my Lady.'

Anne hesitated.

'But Dr Burton did say . . .'

'Ah well, that was for his usual kind of patient, my Lady. We Romanies are a different breed.'

205

There was a silence. Anne could, as his mistress, order him to stay in his chamber but in God's name if the man was dying surely he should be allowed to do what made him happiest.

'If it makes you content, Giles, then you may stay up. But promise me that you will take rest if you feel like it.'

'I give you my word, my Lady.'

Their eyes met fully and each knew that the other was aware of the truth but was afraid to speak, nicety and convention standing in the way, though Anne, as a staunch Catholic realized that it was her duty at some point soon to suggest that Giles saw a priest, whilst rather dreading the reaction.

'Then all is well,' she said.

'Is it, my Lady?'

So here it was. He was going to come out with it. He was too close to the earth and life's secrets to be fooled. He had probably known months before Dr Burton. Poor, brave little Giles.

'Please, my Lady, can we deal straightly?'

'Yes,' she said quietly.

'The physician – good man though he is – can do nothing for me. There is a growth inside me that is eating my life away. So, my Lady, I am asking you – as a kind mistress and a friend – to do two things for me so that I may leave in peace.'

'And they are?'

'To let me see Mistress Catherine again. She has not been in Sutton Place since she ran away with Sir John and I have grieved for her that Sir Richard's anger still rages.'

'And the other?'

'I would like, before the end, to see that mighty sorcerer Dr Zachary. Master Francis told me that he is spoken of as having Romany blood and that he is supposedly the greatest astrologer in the land. How much I would like to meet him.'

Anne sat silently. To call Dr Zachary from Court presented little difficulty – but to go against Richard's orders and write to Catherine! And yet what a wonderful excuse. And then she felt sickened with herself for looking on a man's death as an 'excuse' and 'wonderful' at that. Yet how she longed to see her daughter again. What a bitter three years during which Catherine's pleading letters had grown less and less frequent and had eventually stopped. Naturally, there had been great pleasure in visiting Margaret and Walter, though this happiness had been slightly marred by the loss in January of Margaret's longed-for first child after a pregnancy of only three months. Yet for all she knew she could be a grandmother. Perhaps Catherine had produced a living child and had not even told her. Anne Weston made up her mind.

'I shall write to Catherine today, Giles,' she said.

'And what about Sir Richard's anger, my Lady?'

'Sir Richard will have to bear it like a man. To be alienated from his own flesh is ridiculous. He will have to bend with the wind – something at which he is most adept.'

'Aye, when it suits him, my Lady.'

Normally she would have reprimanded him for criticizing his Master but in the circumstances she let the remark pass.

'And I will try to contact Dr Zachary for you.'

Giles kissed her hand and then held it against his crinkled cheek for a moment. She felt the warmth of his tears and it was too much for her. Abandoning all convention she put her arms round him and wept.

* * *

It was 23 July and the Legatine Court in Blackfriars was packed to the doors. Looking round him carefully, Richard Weston's apparently unconcerned eyes took in and made a mental list of all those who had turned out to hear the judgement on the annulment of the King's marriage. For this was to be the day. As soon as the King arrived Cardinal Campeggio would announce the verdict.

In the centre of the room was the now empty high seat in which the King would shortly take his place and below it was a great chair for the Italian Cardinal. Next to it was Wolsey's place. Richard thought how uneasy his patron, already seated, looked. Folds of skin hung where the face had once been full and fleshy and the body that had been so proudly stout now seemed swamped by its great red robe. Just behind him, his thick lips whispering constantly in Wolsey's ear while his eyes darted round the room non-stop, sat the man who had always appeared to Weston the epitome of the word commonplace, Wolsey's secretary Dr Stephen Gardiner. But today he seemed to have a new vigour about him – as if he was drawing life from his wilting master.

'A man to be watched,' thought Richard.

He turned his attention from the clerics to the peers of the realm. Those to be noted were surely the ones absent, for nearly every coronet in the land had turned out on this, the day of all days, when history would be made, when the King of England's marriage might be declared null and void in the eyes of all-powerful, ever-present Rome.

Thrusting well to the fore, of course, was the master of self-advancement Thomas Boleyn, Lord Rochford. Today his broad face bore a strained expression and his large dark eyes – so similar to those of the skinny chit who was at the very core of this whole charade – stared ahead of him broodingly. Richard was secretly delighted. He hoped that within minutes the smug fool's hopes would be sent packing, and those of his daughter with him.

Slightly to Boleyn's right and studiously ignoring him sat his kinsman the Duke of Norfolk. He seemed to be one of the few people in the hall not overawed with the magnitude of the occasion for he sat back in his seat, one leg crossed over the other, his face all smiles as he talked to his coterie of followers. One in particular caught Richard's eye for he had not seen him at Court before. A man of about thirty-five with dark, curly hair and unusually brilliant eyes that seemed to shine like crystal. Richard watched him murmuring something into Norfolk's ear and then, to his astonishment, they both looked directly at him. Without revealing any surprise Richard bowed his head to them and they responded, though neither of them smiled at all.

At the witness table, just in front of the stall where the Court were crammed in like sheep, sat Charles Brandon, Duke of Suffolk and the King's brother-in-law. Bearded and powerful he looked now like a smouldering lion. A King's man to the last, he had given evidence some days previously that on the morning after Queen Katharine's marriage to Prince Arthur he had seen the bridal sheets stained with virgin's blood; that she had been the Prince's true wife in every consummated sense, a fact that Katharine vehemently and on oath had denied. Which was lying, Richard wondered. Could a good and pious woman like the Queen be forced into deception to save her daughter the stigma of being called bastard? Or was Brandon's memory conveniently at fault? Or could the blood have been from a scratch or caused by Katharine's moon cycle? Richard fairly and squarely put his money on Brandon as the liar. He was so deep in the King's pocket that he would sell his grandmother to infidels to help him.

Weston's gaze moved on to the Marquess of Exeter,

poised like a bird of prey on the edge of his chair and doing precisely the same as Richard. Taking stock of everyone present and, no doubt, making mental notes of any misbehaviour among the younger courtiers; dark eyes observing everything and closed face revealing nothing. The man was a veritable night stalker!

Following Exeter's look Richard found himself staring straight at Francis.

'God's life,' he thought, 'that boy will die owing money to tailors.' For his son stood out amongst his cronies in a beautifully cut and made doublet of emerald green with golden stitchery.

'And they're little better,' Richard thought. 'Like a bunch of prancing peacocks all of them.'

Though he had to admit, with a grim sort of half-pride, that Francis was far and away the best looking and best dressed of all. He scrutinized the little gang closely. The obvious leader – as brother of the King's light-of-love – was George Boleyn. He, too, seemed under a strain for if the verdict should go against Anne his family's ambitions would be dealt a severe blow.

'Though they would wriggle back,' thought Richard. 'That girl's hold on the King is quite extraordinary, unnatural almost.'

On George's left sat his cousin Thomas Wyatt and on his right another cousin, Francis Bryan.

'The clan is out in force,' thought Richard humourlessly. But it was Francis's obvious intimacy with them all that set him thinking. He had forgotten how long ago he had learned never to ally himself to a shooting star but to wait until it blazed into a comet. His father, Edmund Weston, had taken a calculated risk by backing Henry Tudor against Richard III, a gamble that had paid off handsomely. But to back the house of Boleyn, at this stage of the political game, seemed to him stupid in the extreme. They were very far from out of the wood.

But there was his son laughing and joking with them and beside him young William Brereton – probably about a year older than Francis – was holding forth in a manner more suitable for a Court masque than a Court of Law. Richard moved his gaze round and his eyes alighted on Sir Henry Norris looking unusually stern and set-faced sitting apart from the younger set and staring straight in front of him. He put Norris's gloom down to the atmosphere of general tension and would never have guessed that the man was racked by his usual agony of spirit, half of him praying that Campeggio would find against the King so that the glorious inhabitant of the woods of Hever might never be able to marry His Grace; the other half cursing his jealousy and wishing that his royal master, who had always been so good to him, might have his way.

The courtroom rose to its feet as Cardinal Campeggio tottered in. The little Italian, with his long white hair and beard contrasting wildly with his scarlet robes, looked like a grotesque. The limping, caused by his terrible affliction from gout, ridiculed what should have been a majestic figure. Richard had wondered at first if the ailment was diplomatic; yet another ploy to delay the Court proceedings – for he was convinced that Campeggio's agonizingly slow journey to England and the subsequent seven-month delay before the Court was convened were all part of a deliberate plan being masterminded by Rome. But after seeing the Cardinal near to and looking for himself at the swollen joints and the afflicted eyes, he had come to the conclusion that the condition was genuine but a useful adjunct to the general delaying process. Was it a stroke of genius on the part of the Pope to send a Cardinal whose health was so frail?

The King must have been watching from the back of the Court because the second that Campeggio had gasped his way into his place, the trumpets rang out and Henry – striding as if his very walk was a veiled insult to the Legate – was crossing the courtroom and taking his seat in the high chair. There was a general hubbub of people seating themselves but the King, looking more anxious than Richard ever remembered him, was already flashing a jewelled hand at his Proctor as a signal for the proceedings to begin.

Rising to his feet the Proctor said loudly, 'My Lord Legate, all the evidence in the case has now been heard. What is your verdict?'

He sat down and from every man present there was total quiet as with painful slowness the Cardinal hauled himself from his chair.

'Your Grace, my Lords, gentlemen,' he said in measured and deliberate English, 'today begins the vacation in Rome, therefore I am unable to continue with the hearing. I adjourn this case until the first day of October. Thank you,' and he fell back into his seat amidst a totally stunned silence. Richard Weston himself did not believe what he had just heard and it was obvious that nobody else in the packed and over-hot hall did either.

Then came the reaction. White lipped, the King rose from his chair and just for a second Richard wondered whether he might be about to smite the Cardinal; but, without even looking at him and speaking to no one, Henry thrust his way out of the courtroom and vanished from view. With his exit the storm broke. From everywhere came cries of 'No, no!' and 'Give us the verdict.'

And above them all roared the Duke of Suffolk's voice as he crunched his fist down on the table before him, 'By the Mass, now I see that the old saw is true, that never a

Cardinal or Legate did good in England.' And he was off on the heels of his brother-in-law the King.

Oblivious of the commotion all round Campeggio busied himself with collecting his papers and tidying up his things. But beside him, Richard noticed, Cardinal Wolsey had taken on a ghastly grey pallor and his head had slumped forward on to his chest. Despite the chaos, Richard was able to get a glimpse of Rochford – or Boleyn as he still thought of him. The man was white to the gills. Just for once Weston allowed himself the luxury of a display of public emotion. He grinned.

Francis's clique were all crowded round George Boleyn, presumably offering their condolences in the face of this monumental defeat. Sir Henry Norris and the Marquess of Exeter were already leaving to attend upon the King. But Richard, in no particular hurry to be gone, let his eyes wander once more over the gouty little man who had caused this violent reaction. Was that a hint of a smile on the lips or was he merely wincing in pain? Richard admired nothing more than coolness and at this the Cardinal was obviously the master for he hobbled off clumsily yet with a deliberation which suggested nothing had happened at all. One would never have thought that he had just won a triumphant – and immensely insolent – victory for the Church of Rome.

Richard caught himself thinking, 'Counter move that, upstart' as Thomas Boleyn, trembling with rage, went to join his son.

He was so lost in his thoughts that he did not see the Duke of Norfolk approaching and was startled when a voice at his elbow said, 'A round to the Pope, was it not? The vacation in Rome! God's life, one must almost admire the impudence. But how are you, Weston? You seem to have resided in Calais these three years past.'

Richard rose and bowed and then noticed the brilliant-eyed stranger who had obviously been talking of him was standing by Norfolk's side. The two men were bowing formally to each other as the Duke said, 'Sir Richard, I would like to present a kinsman of mine – Sir John Rogers of Bryanston. He tells me that he is most anxious to meet you.'

It was twenty days since Anne had written to Catherine – twenty days of waiting anxiously for a rider bearing a reply and twenty evenings of disappointment as the sun set and nothing had happened. Dr Zachary, on the other hand, had responded quickly and there had been high hopes when the horseman carrying his letter had come to the Gate House. Giles had made his way there across the quadrangle meeting Anne, who had come through the house, in the porter's lodge. But one look at the seal had been enough.

'This is not from Catherine, Giles,' she had said.

His face, through which the bones of his skull were now showing clearly, had seemed more gaunt than ever but had cheered slightly when she said, 'But 'tis from Dr Zachary. He will attend upon us within the next three weeks.'

After twelve days had elapsed her fears for Will the rider had grown. Every road was riddled with cut-throats and she felt it possible that he might never have reached Dorset. On the other hand he could be there and attempting to persuade Catherine to reply. Anne dithered round Sutton Place unable to decide whether to write again, to despatch a search party to look for Will, or to do nothing. Each day caught her saying, 'Shall we wait one more day? Perhaps tomorrow there will be an answer.'

And then, just as she was growing desperate and was on the point of writing and sending the new letter with four men for safety's sake, Joan had come running to her saying, 'Giles is wild with joy, my Lady. He says that Mistress Catherine – I mean Lady Rogers – will be here as the sun goes down tonight.'

'Has Will returned without my knowing?'

'Nay, madam. He says he has had a dream.'

Standing before her, Giles looked embarrassed and rubbed one of his shoes against the calf of the other leg. He appeared greatly like a child asked to sing before assembled company.

'Now what is this about a dream, Giles?' asked Anne.

'It was a prophecy, my Lady. I saw – as I slept – Mistress Catherine's cavalcade come to the Gate House with the setting sun behind them. And I knew it would be today.'

Anne looked at him uncertainly. He was a dying man and should be humoured and yet she did not wish him to build up his hopes for naught.

'Then I will order the cooks to prepare some extra food for tonight but Giles . . .'

'Yes, my Lady?'

'. . . it shall not be *too* much for it was . . .'

'Only a dream. Aye, my Lady, I know. But I shall be content with that.'

And he had walked off in a more sprightly fashion than she had seen for weeks. By six o'clock that evening she doubted whether an iron bar would have held him down. He loitered round the porter's lodge to such an extent that eventually he got in the way and was asked rather curtly if he would leave. Presenting himself before Anne, wearing the doublet that Richard had brought him back from Calais and which Giles considered to be high fashion par excellence because it had been stitched in France, he looked at her like a whipped spaniel.

'Roger has sent me forth from his lodge, madam. He says he tripped over me at every turn.'

'Then Giles, watch from the Long Gallery. Or from the Gate House tower. You'll not be underfoot there.'

He smiled, his funny face almost back to the look it had borne before the disease gripped him.

'I'll to the tower, my Lady.'

Despite all Anne found her own footsteps taking her towards the far windows of the Long Gallery from whence one could see for such a good distance. And though she pretended to be embroidering and though Joan and Meg, who came to join her, pretended as well all three of them kept shooting little glances at the window until eventually they all three caught each other looking simultaneously and burst out laughing.

'What three fools we are,' said Anne, 'to sit here because of a dream.'

'Ah, but it was a Romany's dream,' answered Meg, 'and they do count for more than the dreams of ordinary folk.'

Anne smiled at her.

'So they do, so they do,' she said.

'My Lady, quick. Oh, my Lady.'

It was Joan kneeling up on the window seat, her stitching dropped to the floor, her back an arc of concentration. In a second the other two women were beside her and there could be no doubting what she had seen. The sun *was* setting over Sutton Place and a cavalcade of riders with a litter – which indicated beyond doubt the presence of a woman – was coming out of the trees.

'It *is* her,' shouted Meg, laughing and crying at once. 'I know it. It is my lady, Catherine.'

The stone spiral staircase that connected the Gallery with the Gate-House wing was alive with the sound of their merriment as Anne and her two serving women raced to the entry arch. And there could be no question, for leading the group was Will – the Westons' own rider – and peeping out of the curtained litter, looking very pale and tired, was Catherine's anxious face.

Anne began to run forward, calling out, 'My sweetheart! My sweetheart!' And Catherine, seeing her, shouted back 'Mother!' throwing back the curtains of the litter as she did so. And it was then that Anne stopped short in amazement for Catherine was more than great with child – she was enormous.

'Oh, my darling,' said Anne. 'How could you travel in that condition?'

'Mother, I had to because of Giles. I'm not too late, am I?'

'No, dearest. Look he's coming.'

And with his face almost split in half with a grin the Fool was hurrying towards them as fast as he could. But he, too, was halted by the sight of Catherine's swollen belly.

'Oh, Catherine,' he said, 'did you journey thus for me?'

'Aye, aye, you old hobgoblin. Now for God's sake help me down for I have such a pain in my back.'

And as she walked slowly through the Middle Enter and paused looking about her after all the years away, the waters in which her baby was living suddenly gushed out and she stood, with a look of astonishment on her face, in an ever growing pool.

'Oh, Mother,' she said, 'the jolting must have started the wretch off. I had thought I would at least get here safely.'

'Is it your full time?'

There was anxiety in Anne's voice for the chances of an infant born prematurely were slight indeed. Catherine patted her stomach reassuringly.

'With that great swelling you should know the answer.'

Her mother put her arms round her – as best she could.

'What a magnificent gift you have brought! My grand-child will be born at Sutton Place.'

'Yes.' Catherine's face contorted slightly. 'Now may I go to my chamber for I think he starts to shift?' And then a naughty grin crossed her face. 'No, I think it better if I go to Sir John Rogers's chamber. Let the fruit of his labours see its first light there.'

'Can I play the lute for thee, Catherine?' said Giles, ridiculous but anxious to please.

And she was kind.

'Yes, for a little while. You may sit outside the door and when I want you no longer you must go.'

'Aye, mistress.'

He kissed her hand as her mother led her up the staircase, with Meg supporting her on the other side and Joan following behind with a mop as more of the water trickled down. Over her shoulder Lady Weston called to Giles, 'Send Giles Coke to Guildford for a midwife and for Dr Burton, too. Hurry!'

But in fact there was no need for speed for once settled comfortably in Sir John Rogers's bed where, she thought very privately, he had taken her virginity away and now his child would be born, Catherine did not go into labour at once and was able to eat an excellent supper of pheasant. So Giles merrily played his lute in the corridor outside and the midwife – a clean respectable farmer's wife who had a way with new mothers – had time to take a good repast of trout, lamb and game pie.

It was at about eleven o'clock that Catherine did eventually start to feel the mighty waves of childbirth and throughout that night she exerted herself with all her strength. Symbolically it was with the dawn that the midwife's big, gentle hands eased the slippery little body

218

away from its mother's and it was Dr Burton, who was in the room to attend the newborn, who said, 'You have a fine gentleman here, Lady Rogers. A very goodly young man.'

'A boy?' said Catherine, leaning back exhausted on her pillows. 'Then let him be called Giles.'

'I'll tell your mother the glad tidings,' and the midwife hurried out to break the news to a Sutton Place that had not slept that night. And within minutes tankards and glasses were being raised to Master Giles Rogers, while Giles the Fool wept with joy and Lady Weston held her first grandchild in her arms, looking at him fond-eyed and making the noises that grandmothers had made for centuries before her and would continue to do for centuries to come.

'And I hope, Sir Richard, that that has allayed your dislike of me.'

Sir Richard Weston and Sir John Rogers were sitting in The Green Man Inn at Richmond on the very first stretch of their journey to Sutton Place.

'It has, Sir John,' said Richard.

He had drunk more than was customary and as a result was feeling mellow. Furthermore, through some grand irony, he liked the company of the son-in-law whom he had spent the last three years bitterly ignoring, and had grown completely tired of attitudinizing over his daughter's elopement so all he said was, 'Do you love her?'

'Very much. It has been a good match. And now that we meet at last, Sir, I will sign a contract with you assuring her of my money and estates in the event of my death.'

Richard, suddenly generous, answered, 'And I shall give her a dowry.'

John Rogers laughed. 'A little late for that, Sir Richard. Make a settlement on your grandchild instead.'

'You have a child?'

'No, not yet. But when I left her to come to Court she was great with it.'

'Then let us pray for her safe delivery. It is not fitting for a man to have reached my age and be without a grandchild.'

'Aye and she'll make a kind and good mother for she has treated my daughter, Alice, like her own these past three years.'

They arrived at Sutton Place during the afternoon of the following day and John supposed that thoughts of his imminent fatherhood were heavily on his mind, for he could have sworn that on the calm summer air was borne the cry of a very young baby. But Sir Richard had heard it too and shot his son-in-law a surprised glance saying, 'What was that?'

'It sounded like an infant's cry.'

Without another word they simultaneously broke into a gallop to cover the short distance to the Gate House. And there was the porter coming out to meet them, his face wreathed in smiles.

'Welcome home, master. Welcome after so many years, Sir John.'

'Is there a baby here?' asked Richard.

The porter's grin spread wider.

'Aye, Sir. Your grandson – Giles Rogers.'

Richard had never seen a man move so fast as Sir John did now. He was off his horse, running across the quadrangle and into the house in what seemed to be one stride. And his great shout of 'A son! A son!' echoed and re-echoed round the terracotta brickwork of Sutton Place's courtyard. Giles Coke, hearing the din, began to open the Middle Enter but had only swung the door half ajar before Sir John shot past him and, pausing only to say 'Where are they?' had started to run up the stairs to the east wing.

'In your old room, Sir,' Coke called after him.

And that was where he found them. Catherine's round blue eyes huge with amazement at seeing him there and the baby, who bore an amusing likeness to Sir Richard, asleep in his cradle and looking rosy-cheeked with the obvious good health that every parent so anxiously sought for, for did not thirty out of every hundred children born never reach their first birthday? Leaning over John picked up his son who gave a milky yawn and continued to sleep.

'Oh, my darling,' he said to Catherine, 'how well you have done. What a fine boy you have given me. Was it difficult for you?'

'A hard night's work,' she answered.

'I wish I could have been here. But why did you travel so near the end of your time?'

And then she told him of the evil growth that was gnawing at the life of Giles the Fool and how, terrible though it was to say it, this had been the final spur to her mother and had ended the silence and enmity.

'I suppose there is nothing that does not have good in it somewhere.'

'But it is wicked to say that about death.'

'Sweetheart,' said John, 'I think Giles would gladly have given his life to see you happy again. And you have amply rewarded him by naming our son for him. He will go in peace.'

'May I stay here till the end comes? Dr Burton says it can only be a matter of weeks now. And besides the babe is too small to travel at present.'

'We shall *both* stay – for your father, I believe, has

taken a liking to me at last and would enjoy a spell of my company.'

Catherine sighed. 'What a turnabout it all is.'

'Aye, the wheel of fortune is never still. It is a good thing we cannot see what lies ahead.'

'Ah, but there are those who can, John. Dr Zachary, a great astrologer, is here in the house and he has cast a horoscope for our son.'

'And?'

'He is to be a famous sailor and fight for a Queen of England in a mighty sea battle.'

'So His Grace will have no male heir then?'

'It would appear not. He also said that we would have another son and three daughters.'

John laughed.

'Good God, then you'd better hurry up and rise from your childbed, woman. It would seem I have a great deal to do. It is a relief that there are many rooms at Bryanston.'

'That reminds me of something else he said.'

'What was that?'

'That one day – in the centuries to come mark you – there will stand on the site of our house a building which will house many children who have gone there to learn. Isn't that strange?'

'Perhaps it is a place that likes the young,' John answered.

That night at dinner served in the Great Hall with Sir Richard and Lady Weston, Sir John Rogers and Dr Zachary present, Anne Weston turned to the astrologer and said, 'Dr Zachary I am most concerned that Giles will not see our priest. I would dearly like him to make a confession and receive the last rites. Can you not persuade him?'

The sorcerer's tousled head shook.

'No, my Lady. You see he is a true Romany – full-blooded. He believes in many things, including Lord God, but there are so many other aspects of his creed – the old gods, the unseen people, powerful magic – that the teachings of Mother Church are not acceptable to him.'

'But I would not like to think of him in hell.'

Dr Zachary smiled.

'A truly pure soul like his will have no battle. You believe that God is all seeing and merciful, do you not?'

'Yes.'

'Then His Goodness will extend to a poor Romany who never hurt another creature in his life.'

'You are certain?'

'I am. But to ease your mind I will speak to him of the sacraments.'

'I have heard said that you have Romany blood, Dr Zachary,' said Anne.

'Yes, it is true.' A look of pain crossed the astrologer's face momentarily.

'And Howard blood for sure,' thought both Richard and John. Having been so recently with the Duke at Blackfriars, the resemblance between Howard and the sorcerer was doubly noticeable.

As if reading his thoughts Zachary said, 'There are many rumours about my origins – all greatly magnified I assure you.'

But later that night, in Giles's chamber, the Fool knelt before him and kissed his hand.

'I think you are twice blessed, Dr Zachary,' he said. 'For I feel that you have the mingling of Romany and noble blood. Am I right?'

'Yes,' said Zachary. 'A secret known to none but yourself, and safe with you.'

'Aye,' said Giles, rising slowly to his feet. 'I shall keep

it for the few hours left to me – for it is to be tonight. You know that, though?'

'Yes,' said Zachary in the Romany tongue. 'And it will be as you would wish it?'

'Yes,' Giles answered in the same language. 'I shall return to the earth as I must. The stars must be my canopy as I die. There can be no four walls about me.'

'Are you in pain?'

'Greatly so. The physician's dose is of little value.'

'Here.' Zachary produced a bottle from the depths of his cloak. 'This will ease your departure.'

'Is it poison?'

'It is the elixir of death – and yet of joy. When you have drunk it you will sleep as you have never slept before. Take it as you lie beneath the moon, as it is our birthright to do.'

'And must I see the priest?'

'Yes, it will please the good woman. I shall call him secretly to you now. Rest a while for you have a long journey to make.'

So the Westons' cleric was awakened from his slumbers and bustled to the Fool's chamber to give him the last rites and hear his harmless confession. He felt uncomfortable throughout as if he were intruding upon something secret and a little beyond him, for all the while the black-cloaked figure of Dr Zachary stood motionless by the door watching as Giles received the final sacraments. There was an uncanny atmosphere in the room, the like of which the priest had never before experienced. He had done his Christian duty for the Romany but he was uneasy in his mind. There was something, dare one use the word, almost pagan about the two of them – the Fool and Lady Weston's strange young guest. He was so disturbed that he took a nip of strong ale before he went back to sleep.

Giles opened his eyes.

'Dr Zachary – Master – it is time now.'

'Is it? Then I will help you, my friend.'

'I beg you pass me my bag of tricks. I wish to leave my things behind. The stick with the Fool's head is for the baby, the box of coloured stones for Lady Weston, the handkerchief for Sir Richard and my lute – my lute is for Catherine.'

From round his neck he took his amulet.

'That is of great power. An old woman who lives by those sacred stones at Salisbury gave it to me. I shall leave that to . . .'

But he did not complete the sentence. He looked instead at Zachary and said, 'Who shall I leave it to, Master? For the curse of Sutton will strike one of them, won't it? Who is most in need of this?'

'Give it to Francis,' Zachary said softly.

The Fool wept.

'No, not he. Will he be cut down in the flower of his youth?'

'It is so destined. But if I can fight the malediction by my power then it shall be done.'

'Will you add my amulet to help him? Will you put it round his neck yourself?'

'It shall lie beside that of my mother which he already wears.'

Giles knelt before Zachary.

'Give me the Romany blessing for he who is about to die.'

And Zachary repeated the strange chant that he had so often heard his mother croon over the sick and dying and which had been one of the many pieces of so-called evidence that had led to her being branded a witch.

'And now farewell.'

Giles picked up the bottle of elixir.

'I will walk with you as far as the Gate-House arch.'

And so they went out together into that incredible night, beneath a firmament blazing with the ice-cold mystery of the stars. And as he walked across the court-yard Giles looked for the last time at the dark outlines of Sutton Place that lay like a sleeping cat in the stillness. How good it was to feel his soul uplift, to know that soon in the deepest part of the forest he would lie upon the ground and drift into eternity. He looked once again at the mansion house.

'Spare Francis,' he said.

But the stones made no answer.

11

It seemed, that winter of 1529, that all England had frozen. From November onward the earth was hard with frost, the trees white and crisp with rime, the lakes and rivers sharp with ice. It was so cold that the long-awaited snow would not fall and the disgraced and humbled Cardinal Wolsey – exiled from Court – shivered pitifully as he knelt in prayer on Christmas Eve.

'Oh merciful Jesu, I have done my best for His Grace. I was not a plaything of Rome as he suspected. I would have sacrificed half my wealth to obtain the King's annulment for in it lay my future security as well as His Grace's desire.'

And he thought of the faces of his enemies – particularly the Dukes of Norfolk and Suffolk – as Cardinal Campeggio had adjourned the Legatine Court in Blackfriars last July. He had known then that the knives would be out for him and that the sharpest and most deadly of all would be wielded by a woman – Mistress Anne Boleyn; the night crow. That black, dark appearance, those strange cold eyes, that sallow complexion. Ugly, repellent creature! How the King could even find her attractive, let alone entertain an adoration that surpassed ordinary love, was beyond his credibility. And the unnerving way she had of watching him – Wolsey. Her face, when he had caught her unawares, bearing a look that had frightened him even then. It was as if she bore some bitter grudge against him. But for what reason? He had once called her a 'foolish girl', many years ago now, when he had dismissed Harry Percy from his service and broken the betrothal between them. But surely . . . It was all so far in the past. And though he had never liked her he had hidden it cleverly enough. Yet he knew for certain, though others may prate their delight at seeing a man once so high brought so low, that behind his downfall lay that instrument of darkness – Thomas Boleyn's daughter.

A cold gust swept through his meagrely furnished private chapel and he drew his robes even more tightly round him.

'God, make me warm,' he prayed, like a child.

Oh, Holy Mother, so alone and so desperate – everything gone. Stephen Gardiner – the man whom he had considered his friend and ally – turned coat and became chief secretary to the King; all his pensions, money and property stripped from him; the great seals of England removed. He had been lucky to escape with his life. But the greatest hurt of all had been that of His Grace riding off with the night crow without even bothering to say farewell. Riding out of his life – he, the monarch, whom Wolsey had genuinely loved and worked for. Now the Cardinal was tasting – and it was gall in his mouth – the lesson of humility. He rose, achingly, from his knees, and went to dine alone.

Not many miles from where he sat chewing on a small piece of turbot and drinking some rough red wine – for his appetite had all but gone these days – dinner was being served in Sutton Place, though admittedly the high table was empty and it was the servants who sat in the Great Hall. Under the supervision of Giles Coke – and with the full permission of the absent Sir Richard – plates of pike, gurnard, tench, conger-eels, lampreys and chines of salmon were set down. For this was a fast day – on Christmas Eve no animal flesh was to be consumed. However, there was ale in abundance, and much raucous jollity; coarser language and jokes filling the air than would ever dare have been voiced had the Master and Mistress been present. And eventually it came round to the toasts. First – for it was as pleasant to draw the honourings out as long as possible as it was an insult not to drain one's tankard – came the Master. Then, amidst a lot of cheering, the Mistress – Anne's popularity with those who worked for her was heartily endorsed. Then the young Master. Mistress Margaret and her husband, and Mistress Catherine and her husband coupled with the names of baby Giles Rogers – for had he not been born within these walls? Finally the King and Queen. Tankards were raised and then a voice called out from the direction of the kitchen lads, 'Aye, good Queen Katharine. We'll have no Nan Bullen for England.'

Giles Coke frowned as more voices joined in.

'No upstart for us.'

'Long life to Queen Katharine.'

'May Nan Bullen rot.'

'Silence,' shouted Giles, standing up the better to be seen. 'The toast of their Graces.'

As the tankards were raised he remembered her coming to Sutton Place in the summer, two years ago. Recalled, by momentarily closing his eyes, that magical quality of hers, how she had made him cry when she sang with her cousin Thomas Wyatt. He hadn't known then what he – what all of England – now knew; that His Grace was in love with her and wanted a divorce in order to marry her. But Giles was one of the few of the common people who could understand. Silken black hair and tilting eyes; a nightingale.

In the Great Hall at Bryanston – decorated with boughs of holly, sprigs of mistletoe and garland upon garland of greenery, the meal was over and Sir John Rogers's Fool was entertaining. At the top of the table sat Sir Richard, then Margaret, while Walter Dennys sat beside Lady Weston. John's daughter, Alice, now nearly seven, sat open-mouthed on Margaret's knee – overawed with the joy of Christmas Eve and the pleasure of twelve more days to come – while Master Giles, now two, sat on his mother's lap and chortled at anyone who smiled at him.

Margaret, her arms clasped tight round the little girl, glanced enviously at her sister's belly which was for the second time growing great with child. Since her own miscarriage at the beginning of this year there had been no sign of a baby and the flux that followed the moon's cycle had come upon her with infuriating regularity. But she had one ray of hope. She had visited Court that autumn, for her father was grooming Walter – now totally grown out of his spots and only stammering under extreme provocation – for state duties. Whilst there her mother had insisted that she see an extremely odd young man called Zachary.

'Sweetheart, he is not only an astrologer but a herbalist. He may be able to give you something to help you.'

And so he had – a bottle of clear liquid that smelt strongly of raspberries.

'And when shall I take this?'

'In the middle of your cycle – at Christmas time.'

'At Christmas time?'

Zachary's eyes had crinkled.

'Aye.'

'Why then?'

'Because everyone is relaxed with the great amounts of food and wine.'

'And what has relaxation to do with it, Dr Zachary?'

'A very great deal, Lady Dennys.'

'But surely that is old wives' talk?'

Dr Zachary had laughed.

'Do I look like an old wife?' he said.

230

So, not feeling too confident but prepared to try anything, Margaret had wrapped up the bottle well so that it should not break on the journey from Haseley Court to Bryanston. And Walter, catching her eye now over the dining table, knew what she was thinking and gave her a wink.

Zachary, spending Christmas Eve with Jane Wyatt in his house in Cordwainer Street, also remembered it suddenly and smiled.

'Why are you laughing?' she said sharply.

'About a potion I gave to a young woman to take at Christmas in order that she may conceive. I'll warrant her husband will be wrecked by the end of the twelve days.'

Uncharacteristically Jane burst into tears and said, 'I wish you would give me something to abort, you damnable sorcerer.'

Zachary looked at her in astonishment.

'Sweetheart, what ails thee? You are not with child?'

'I believe so. You have treated me as your wife ever since that wretched Romany wedding I was fool enough to enter into. And now that I am maid-of-honour to the Lady Anne and residing at Court you've had me in your bed at every opportunity. I hate you, Zachary. I'm not married in the eyes of the Church, state or my family and now my belly swells.'

He was beside her in a second and holding her tightly.

'Then we must journey to Kent as soon as the twelve days are past and gain your father's consent to a marriage by priest.'

'He will never give it. He wishes me to marry into the nobility.'

Zachary laughed.

'He will agree I promise you.'

Jane wiped her tears on his handkerchief.

'Will all be well, Zachary?'

'Yes.'

'I hope Anne does not notice my swelling. She has become very proud since the King has given York House to her and they are totally refurbishing and extending it. They are even knocking down the neighbouring houses to give her a deer park. Did you know that?'

Zachary nodded.

'It is a great irony that it should be one of Wolsey's dwellings. How sweet that must taste to her.'

Jane looked at him blankly. Many of the things he said meant nothing to her and now he was muttering, 'And Wolsey is but the first of many to fall. Anne, the Lady of bitterness.'

Jane, misunderstanding, said, 'Aye, I believe the King's sister felt great bitterness when Anne sat above her in the Queen's chair.'

'This was at the banquet following Thomas Boleyn's elevation to the Earldom of Wiltshire?'

'Yes.'

Zachary looked thoughtful. His father had been present and described the scene to him. On the day after the investiture which had raised Anne to the title of Lady Anne Rochford and George to that of Viscount Rochford – the King had given a banquet followed by a masque. And she had sat above the highest women in the land, including his father's wife. It had not gone down well. Suffolk had quite literally muttered into his great beard that his wife was the King's sister and should not be seated below 'that arrogant Boleyn woman'. While Zachary's father, Norfolk – though hardly in love with his wife – still considered that she took precedence over the daughter of a newly-created earl.

Just down the river from Zachary's home at Greenwich Palace the Lady Anne Rochford was holding her

Christmas Eve in great pomp. Fast day it might be but she had contrived, with her usual style, to make every dish of fish look exciting and little delicacies of shrimps and oysters had been set at each place round her table. The King had left her now to do his duty and pay his respects to Katharine, who had her apartments on the floor below, and was stolidly chewing her way through her meal with the few courtiers who had remained faithful to her.

'I shall be glad when York House – or Whitehall Palace as it is to be called – is ready,' said Anne to the many resplendent people gathered round her. 'Greenwich is not really – convenient.'

A ripple of laughter broke out for they all knew what she meant – Whitehall Palace was to have no apartments for Queen Katharine. It would be the home, exclusively, of Henry and Anne.

'I wonder if she'll go to bed with him when they get there,' thought Francis, for it was rumoured by all and sundry that the Lady Anne was still a virgin despite the gifts, money and, now, her own palace, that the King had bestowed on her.

And Anne thought, 'I have outrun the King until I am exhausted and the only weapon left in my armoury is my body. I am nearly defeated though none of these grinning dolts would credit it. I sit at the pinnacle of my power and I am no nearer marrying him than I was when he first fell in love with me. The Pope has almost beaten me. And now what options have I? To be his mistress all my life? Or worse, to be cast off when he grows bored with me? How easily that could happen! And now, I suppose, my original purpose is finally achieved for I have done what I set out to do. I have fully avenged Harry Percy and Anne Boleyn – or the poor shadows they once were – for Wolsey is struck low and will go even lower, and the King is tormented by love for me. So here I am with a cause with which I never started out – to become Queen of England. And I can see no clear way in which that is ever likely to happen. I am like a pet bird sitting in a cage of its own devising with the only way out blocked. And to think it all began as a girl's game of revenge. Dear God, what have I done?'

Tears were a luxury that Anne Boleyn rarely allowed herself but now the sheer magnitude of what lay before her, together with the realization that she had gone too far to turn back combined to make a solitary trickle run down her cheeks. Seeing that Francis Weston had noticed it she dashed it away.

'And what of you, young Weston?' she said, for she had long ago learned that in order to defend oneself one must attack first. 'What of your betrothed? I hear it is over a year since you have seen her. And did I not spy you sporting with a maid-of-honour the other day?'

Francis looked sheepish.

'Yes . . . no.'

'And what does that mean?'

'I have not seen Ann since the summer of last year but she was ill on one of the occasions when I was to visit her and on the other bad weather stopped me leaving Court.'

'Bad weather?' said Anne, innocently widening her eyes.

'And no, I was not sporting with a maid-of-honour. We were discussing a wager that we had had on a certain hound.'

'And the hound's name would not have been Francis Weston?'

'Indeed not,' he said, all righteous indignation. 'I have missed Ann greatly and we are to be married in May next year.'

'Married,' said Anne Boleyn and Francis thought he could hear a slight sigh in her tone.

And far away in Westmorland Ann Pickering sighed too. Killington, her manor house, was colder than most, set bleakly as it was in the land of towering peaks and mighty lakes. But she had chosen to winter there for her Cumberland estate – inherited from her mother – was at Moresby and exposed to the cruel winds of the Irish Sea. In summer one could ride one's horses across mile upon mile of white sand all belonging to her, and this was where she intended to bring Francis after they were married – if she could get him away from Court long enough! It was like a paradise in the warm months but now she had shut the house up – with only a handful of servants to weather the bitter chill.

But it was freezing at Killington too and after a brief meal in a small private chamber with her Steward, her butler and her two personal maids, Ann retired to bed early, leaving instructions that some of the kitchen lads must sleep in the Great Hall to make sure that the fires stayed in all night. For on Christmas Day she always gave a banquet for everyone from the estate and all must be warm and comfortable. She wondered how it would be possible for her to keep up this tradition after she had married.

In fact she had been giving a lot of consideration lately to her future life in general and Francis in particular. Her sixteen-month parting from him had not helped her peace of mind at all. It was unfortunate that she had been sick with a fever on one of the occasions when Francis had been due to come to Cumberland but the tale of bad weather precluding him during his other leave she had thought flimsy. And because he had asked her always to be free with him she had written and told him so. After a long while a letter had returned and he had admitted the

235

truth. He had been so involved in so many various gaming sessions – dice, cards, bowls and tennis – and with so much money at stake that he simply could not afford to leave Court. It was then that she had realized that, beautiful and kind though he was, he was also a compulsive gambler. But that he loved her she had no doubt. His letters – scarce though they were – were always full of tender phrases and reassurances. And yet could a man like that remain faithful? She thought of his hot pursual of herself and was sure that in sixteen months total celibacy would have been impossible. The stallion would undoubtedly have found a mare – or two! Ah well, as soon as winter released its grip and the weather made it feasible for the arduous journey to be undertaken, she would leave in her bridal entourage. And then, Master Weston, watch out! She may be no Court lady but she was capable of feminine trickery.

Ann Pickering smiled to herself as her maid helped her into bed on that bleak Christmas Eve, drawing the coverlets up round her mistress and then kissing her on the forehead, for the girl had been her own jewel ever since she had been born. She bent to throw more logs on the great fire and said, 'Why do you smile, chuck?'

'Because tomorrow we start our twelve days of merriment. And when that is over all we have to do is wait. And then one day, you know how it is Peg, we will hear the earth tremble with spring.'

'Hear it? Nay, you can't hear it.'

'But you can. It is a whisper somehow amongst the hills and the valleys listen and shoot up their flowers. And then on the wind you can smell it and one's blood gets a wild fever. Has your blood never been wild, Peg?'

'Aye, aye, when I was young. It is good that you are to be married soon for only a man can cure that wildness.'

'Yes,' said Ann, 'and I have the most handsome man in England.'

'Oh, he'll cure you all right,' said Peg softly as she left the room.

Christmas was over; the plays and masques for Twelfth Night done, the last of the revellers abed. The usual hustle of Greenwich Palace was somewhat subdued that morning of the 7 January, 1530, but already on his way there, sitting in the cabin of his barge and wearing a fur-lined cloak to protect him from the snowstorm that was hurling into the Thames' grey water, was the outlandish figure of Zachary Howard. On his head he wore a hat entirely made of fur which he had bought from Sir Richard Weston's trading ship and which had come from some wild place beyond the sea. For covering his hose he had donned a pair of purple stockings to keep his legs warm. To make the extraordinary picture complete he carried a woman's fur muff over the top of his gloves. As a man of fashion Dr Zachary was a Court joke. But he rather played on this knowing that his swirling cloak and generally eccentric appearance enhanced his reputation as a mystic and astrologer.

But to the Duke of Norfolk, waking with the effects of wine-supping still pounding behind his eyes, an apparition like a grizzly bear standing at the foot of his bed and saying, 'Lord Duke my father, wake up!', in an urgent tone of voice, was not at all amusing.

'Zachary,' he said irritably,' what in God's name are you doing here? Go away!'

And he turned his head back into the pillow. But to his annoyance Zachary sat down in a chair by the window and the Duke could feel, even though his eyes were closed, that amber gaze boring into him. In the end he gave up and raised himself into a sitting position, groaning very gently as he did so.

'Well, what is it?' he said. 'Zachary, I do not care to be disturbed like this. What do you want with me?'

His son's eyes were fixed on him and Thomas Howard was reminded of the time – so many years ago now – when he had placed the box containing the boy's mother's ashes in the Norfolk family vault. Then he had felt reluctant and now he knew that, once again, his bastard was about to persuade him to some course of action in which he would have no real desire to participate.

'Go on,' he said wearily.

'My wife is pregnant,' said Zachary flatly.

'Wife?' exclaimed the Duke. 'Oh, that Wyatt girl. But Zachary, she is naught but a mistress. Romany weddings are not legally binding.'

Zachary got up, his cloak dropping to the floor, and stood with his back to his father. Anyone else would have looked ludicrous in such bizarre clothing but there was something about the astrologer that defied laughter. He had an inner dignity that rivalled that of any statesman of the day.

Norfolk said, 'Come, come, Zachary. Those words tumbled out more cruelly than were meant. So Jane carries your child?'

Still without turning Zachary said, 'Lord Duke my father, I wish to marry her according to the rites of the Church. And her father will not consider me a suitable match. It is imperative that you tell him who I am.'

Now the Duke sat up sharply.

'But that is a secret that we agreed should never be spoken. Anyway there is old, bad blood between Wyatt and myself.'

For at Bosworth the Howards and the Wyatts had

238

fought on opposing sides. The Duke's father had supported Richard III and Howard's grandfather had fallen in the battle; disgrace and the Tower had been the Howard reward and it was only the brilliance of Thomas's father as an administrator that had won him his freedom and restored the family to its former splendour. Sir Henry Wyatt, on the other hand, had been imprisoned for calling Richard III pretender. And old memories still cast their shadows.

'Father, for once the truth must be said. And now that Wolsey has gone you are, next to His Grace, the highest ranking man in the Kingdom. Sir Henry Wyatt will not readily oppose you.'

'It is not easy to speak of one's bastards to an enemy.'

It was a rare occurrence for Zachary to lose his temper but now he did. He turned from gazing out of the window and his eyes were wild with anger.

'God's blood, my Lord Duke, have you no sense of proportion? Richard III must be dust and yet you speak of enemies. And you, as a man in a man's world, dare not mention the bastard of your youth? Wouldst have your grandchild born out of wedlock as well? Where is the sense in all this?'

And he snatched up his cloak and left the room calling out, 'I'll to Maidstone and plead my cause myself. Jane shall not suffer humiliation at the hands of anyone for she is a good and kind-hearted girl. Goodbye, Lord Duke.'

Thomas Howard fell back on to his pillows. In his imagination he could see Zachary striding out of the palace and boarding his barge, hunching his shoulders against the cold. He loved his son so much that he could even visualize the scowl on his face, the way those black curls would squash as he pulled that ridiculous hat down to cover his ears.

'God damn all,' said the Duke of Norfolk, rising from his bed. 'If I take to horse now I can get to Maidstone before him. Will, Will, . . . !' – his principal servant came hurrying into the room – '. . . get out my warmest riding clothes – and quickly. It would appear we have an urgent journey to make.'

The roads were hard with frost, which in some ways made the going easier, and the cold seemed to have discouraged the cut-throats. Despite this, Norfolk took the precaution of riding with three armed men as an escort. Now that he was President of the Council of England he would be an even more attractive target for robbery and probably murder. But despite his good intention and hard riding, a blinding snowstorm at Wrotham Heath halted his progress and he was forced to take shelter in an inn. Though anxious to reach Wyatt's home before dark, Howard had to admit that the enforced stop was extremely comforting and it was with just a shade of reluctance that he saw the snow ease away and, casting a longing look at the fire, got into the saddle once more.

But the delay had been enough to give Zachary the advantage for his son must have continued through the blizzard. As darkness fell over Kent the Duke saw a familiar figure coming towards him from the direction of Allington Castle. There could be no mistaking the unconventional dress nor could there be any mistaking the desolated droop of the shoulders and the miserable attitude of his head.

'Zachary!' he called out.

In the gloom he saw his son peering to see where the voice was coming from.

'Over here.'

Visibly cheered Zachary trotted his horse to where Howard had halted his party.

'Lord Duke,' he said, kissing his father's hand, 'I knew you would come.'

'The crystal ball, no doubt,' answered Thomas drily.

The impish face was suddenly creased in a grin.

'No. Just good judgement on this occasion.'

The Duke motioned his guard out of earshot and then said, 'What has happened? Did Wyatt show you the door?'

'More than that. He thrashed me for giving his daughter a great belly.'

And for the first time Howard noticed that the boy sat on his horse with obvious pain and that there was blood running down from a cut on his head. Now it was his turn to lose his temper.

'God's life,' he roared, 'I'll have that bastard in the Tower on some trumped-up charge. He shall answer for this. By Christ, he will!'

And spurring his horse into a gallop he took off, shouting instructions to his servants to take Zachary to the nearest inn and attend to him. Allington Castle lay another three miles away but it was pitch black by the time he arrived. The drawbridge had been pulled up for the night but the Duke, sweating with rage despite the cold, stood up in his stirrups and screamed, 'Open up in the name of the King of England. Lower this bridge, do you hear me?' until eventually the porter's frightened face appeared at a window calling out, 'Who's there?'

'The Duke of Norfolk, Lord President of the Council of England.'

With a great rumbling the drawbridge descended and Thomas Howard's horse thundered across it and into the courtyard.

'Where is Sir Henry Wyatt?' he demanded tersely.

'He dines, sir, and cannot be disturbed.'

'Oh, can't he,' said Howard. 'Tell him the Duke of Norfolk is here and demands an audience. At once!'

And with that he strode into the castle in the wake of scurrying and terrified servants.

Sir Henry, when he found him, was sitting alone at his dining table in one of Allington's smaller chambers. Without so much as a formal greeting the Duke sat down immediately opposite and said, 'How dare you thrash my son, sir? How dare you? The King's Grace shall hear of this, I can promise you.'

'Your son, my Lord?' said Wyatt, half rising.

'Yes, my son, sir,' answered Howard, pushing him down again.

'You mean that rag bag who was here earlier? That creature who has robbed my daughter of her virginity? Yes, indeed, His Grace shall hear of the matter.'

'Listen,' said the Duke, grabbing Wyatt by the collar of his coat, 'your damnable daughter is being offered marriage by a Howard. You should consider yourself honoured. A small country knight to be allied with the most powerful family in the land. God's head, you are most fortunate to get such a match for the wretched girl.'

Wyatt's eyes tightened.

'But he must be a bastard. Surrey is your heir.'

'Even the King has a bastard,' retorted the Duke. 'Have you forgotten Henry Fitzroy? Well, you have just laid hands on Zachary Fitzhoward and I've a mind to lay a charge of assault against you. I feel His Grace will not be unsympathetic.'

'But what of Jane's child? He has made her swollen in the belly, did you know that?'

'Of course I did,' snapped the Duke angrily. 'That's why he wishes to marry her. As for dowry and settlement we do not require them. It is I who shall settle estates and money on her. Does that satisfy you?'

An unreadable expression was beginning to creep over Sir Henry's face.

'If – I repeat *if* – I consent to this union you will accept my daughter as a Howard?'

'Yes, yes.'

There went any final hopes that the Duke might have of ever mending the breach in his marriage – but to the Devil with it.

'And contracts shall be exchanged between us?'

'Yes, damn you,' said Thomas. 'And for your part I want the wedding to take place within a week. Also you shall buy my son a great gift to compensate him for the injuries that you have inflicted upon his person. And now I am going to dine. Prepare your best chamber, Sir Henry, for tonight the Lord President of England sleeps beneath your roof.'

'One final thing.'

'Yes?'

'My daughter has a good position at Court.'

'In the retinue of *my niece*, the Lady Anne Rochford. I shall have her released from that as soon as I return. Send your other daughter, Margaret, in her place. Now speak no more or I might anger.'

And with that the Duke of Norfolk fell to feeding leaving Sir Henry Wyatt in a state bordering on nervous collapse.

It was in early March that Ann Pickering first heard what she always thought of as the stirring of spring. At last the relentless frost and snow had cleared and she was able to take her favourite horse out for the gallop they both needed. And it was there, on a hill overlooking the village of Kendal, that it happened. Turning her face into the weak sun she suddenly felt tremendously aware of all the sounds of the earth.

'Listen, it's spring,' she said.

Her Steward laughed at her. She had always had this fancy ever since a small girl.

'I hear nothing, mistress, except the birds. They're twittering a little more.'

'Yes, that's part of it. But the hills are singing to one another.'

'That's just the wind echoing round.'

'Oh, Seaton, you really can't hear it, can you?'

'No, mistress, perhaps there are only some of us allowed to do so.'

'Now you're humouring me.'

But she knew and she felt the stirring within herself; as if somewhere deep inside a spring brook, that had been frozen for the winter, broke free of its crystal gaoler and began to gush forth, gathering speed as it flowed towards the wild flowers that grew along its bank.

'Come, we must go home,' she said.

'Tired already, mistress?'

'No, not tired. In fact the opposite. But there is so much to be done, Seaton. I am to be a bride in May and there are only six weeks left till I depart.'

'But your sewing women are well ahead, are they not? I saw your wedding gown being stitched only the other day.'

'It's not that. I have to say goodbye to Killington – and to Moresby. And all my friends from childhood. And then there are the practical things – the packing of the goods I shall take with me to Sutton Place.'

Seaton was silent for a moment, then he said, 'You won't come back here to live then, mistress?'

'No, it is not possible. My future husband is a courtier – a favourite of the King. How could a man like that live here?'

'But how could a country girl live at Court?'

He had known her for so many years that he could say such things.

Ann looked thoughtful and then she turned her wide blue eyes on him.

'Seaton, I think Master Francis is the kind of man that I could lose if I did not stay close by. Please don't misunderstand me. He is not a bad man – just easily distracted.'

Seaton thought, 'What a wise brain lies in that head of seventeen years. She'll bring this colt, Weston, into a good running rein.'

But he had reckoned without one thing – the flaw in the diamond; Francis's total inability to sense danger, utter ineptitude in realizing when a situation was worsening and only a change in course would avoid disaster. It was as if the political awareness of two men had gone into his father leaving none whatsoever for the son.

It was the middle of April when Ann finally set out with her suite; her maid Peg, several other women servants and various men of her household who would conduct her to Sutton Place and handle the enormous amount of baggage that was going with her. As the winding entourage finally rounded a corner in the grassy track and Killington Manor was lost to view she turned her horse and galloped back for a last glimpse.

'Don't worry,' she said to the house in which she'd been born, 'I'll bring Francis to see you if I have to drag him by the hair.'

Three weeks to the day later Francis set out from Greenwich Palace to become a married man. He was nineteen, the sun was out and he had never felt more pleased. In the last week he had beaten the King at tennis on four separate occasions, winning four angels per game – very high stakes indeed. Added to this he carried on him the

King's wedding present – £6.13s.4d.; not to mention the three new shirts and pairs of hose as an extra gift. And his tailor, Bridges, had made him such a fine white doublet with silver threads and buttons and decorations of drop pearls for his wedding day, which was now only one week away. Small wonder that a song rose to his lips as London was left behind and he and his man servant stopped at The Wheatsheaf at Esher to drink some midday ale.

Looking across at Wolsey's now empty residence, which was visible from where they sat, Francis wondered how the Cardinal fared in his diocese of York where he had at least retained the title of Archbishop. Just for a moment a thought went through his head about how devastating it must be to fall from a favoured position to nothing. He had heard that the Cardinal now wore a hair shirt and lived most modestly but, greatest degradation of all, the man who had been the 'other King' had been forced to take to his heels and make an undignified exit north on being told by his Steward, Thomas Cromwell, that the Duke of Norfolk had threatened, 'If he go not away, I will tear him with my teeth.'

'I should dislike more than anything to lose favour,' thought Francis. But small chance of that. Why, the King had embraced him most fondly earlier this morning when he had left Greenwich Palace and on the previous evening Anne Boleyn had brushed her cool lips against his cheek and wished him great joy.

'Will you not come to my wedding?' Francis had said.

'Aye, I might,' she had answered with one of her strange smiles. 'Would you welcome me?'

'Of course.'

She had laughed then, putting her head back so that her long, slender neck had suddenly looked frail and vulnerable. She was so small and thin and yet so mighty

246

that there was something disquietingly unreal about her. Francis sometimes had the ridiculous notion that they would all go to sleep and wake up in the morning to find that Mistress Boleyn – or the Lady Anne Rochford as she now was – had never existed at all. But he didn't like those thoughts. They led him down paths to sinister recesses in his mind where dark things lay.

Unconsciously, as it so often did, his hand stole up to feel the amulet round his neck which had now been joined by the carbuncle that Giles had left behind for him. And that was another nasty idea – that somewhere in the thick forest Giles lay rotting. For Dr Zachary had assured the Westons that their Fool had returned to the wild to die. Francis stopped his train of thought and ordered more ale. This was no mood to be in with his wedding only seven days off.

Yet a frown was to return to his face once more as he came within sight of Sutton Place for there, distinct against the sky-line were two riders at full gallop and the great mass of red hair streaming out from behind one of them told him that it was his betrothed, Ann, and that she was accompanied by a man.

He had not seen her for nearly two years and he couldn't in all honesty say that he had spent his time pining – for gambling, drinking and whoring were pursuits guaranteed to deploy the concentration – but now a totally unreasonable jealousy swept over him. He dug his spurs into his horse's side and sped forward to catch the riders up. The thud of the approaching hooves must have caught Ann's attention for he saw her look over her shoulder, heard her joyful shout and watched her rein her horse round. She hastened towards him but her companion merely halted and stayed where he was. As Francis drew nearer he saw that it was Henry Knyvett.

'Oh Francis, Francis,' she was calling. 'You are here at

last. My household came ten days ago. I thought you were never going to arrive.'

Francis was surprised with himself. Instead of greeting her lovingly he said, in quite the most churlish manner, 'Well I see that you've been kept amused.'

Ann looked amazed and then she followed his eyes which were fixed firmly on poor Henry who, fortunately, was too far away to hear what they were saying.

'God's life,' she exclaimed, 'don't you start any stupidity, Francis! The days have been boring enough without your company. And Henry arrived at his house in East Horsely for *your* wedding before you – the bridegroom! Did you expect me to sit like a nun when he invited me to ride? I suppose you have spent the last few days in virtuous prayer rather than leave Court to join me?'

He suddenly felt utterly foolish but decided to battle on.

'I am a courtier,' he said grandly. 'I cannot leave His Grace's side willy-nilly. I have been busy.'

'Oh, no doubt,' she retorted. 'The King would need your opinion on matters of state, of course. I hope the entire monarchy does not collapse in the few days that you have taken off in which to marry me. Now go to.'

And she wheeled her horse once more, called 'Henry' to the bemused Knyvett and went off so extremely fast that both men were left staring after her. Henry trotted over to where Francis sat, gazing after the vanishing figure of his betrothed.

'Francis!' he said extending his hand. 'I left Court two days ago. How did you get on with that last tennis match? It was still being played as I departed.'

Francis lowered his voice to a guilty murmur which was quite unnecessary for Ann was by now a mere speck in the distance.

'I won,' he said, 'but don't mention it in front of Ann

for she has just rounded on me. She feels I should have been here sooner.'

Henry thought, 'Had I such a woman to marry nothing would have kept me from her. Francis Weston takes his luck to the limits sometimes. I am only grateful that that hideous creature my father had selected for me died of the Sweat.'

And then he crossed himself for such thoughts were evil even if they happened to be true.

'I think,' he said mildly, 'that you are fortunate indeed, Francis, to have Ann Pickering. I thought it when I first met her and I think it even more now. She has grown into a full-fledged beauty and you will have to work hard to keep her at your side.'

Francis decided to vent his spleen on his unfortunate friend.

'How dare you?' he said. 'I love her dearly.'

'Then show it you doltard,' answered Henry and headed his horse off in the direction of East Horsely. Francis could not remember ever having seen him angry before.

Sutton Place was swarming with servants and guests for the great occasion of the marriage of the son of the house and Francis, after a vain attempt to find either of his parents, was about to retire sulkily to his chamber when he ran into his brother-in-law, John Rogers.

'Ah, there you are,' John said. 'We wondered when you would be arriving. 'Tis all hurly-burly here. Catherine is with your mother going through great lists of food. There are enough victuals in the place to feed the Court, I'll swear.'

'Did you . . .'

But Francis's voice was drowned by the musicians starting their practice in the Great Hall.

'Christ!' he bellowed furiously. The day, which had begun so brightly, was fast turning into a tragedy.

'Come and drink with me in the Gate House wing,' shouted John. 'It is less like the Tower of Babel.'

And he tactfully led Francis away and bolstered him up with some of Sir Richard's malmsey.

'You know, Francis,' John said, 'you have a beautiful bride who will bring you a great deal of property and prosperity, yet your father told me that you stayed on at Court to play tennis! Don't you think that rather stupid?'

'His Grace would not have been pleased if I had left before the games were done.'

And there was an element of truth in the answer. Sir John raised his eyebrows, unconvinced.

'Go and wait for her with the porter. This is no way for the nuptials to begin.'

So, as Ann Pickering walked her horse through the Gate-House arch, to her astonishment a figure jumped out before her and brought her to a stop.

'Please get down from the saddle, sweetheart,' said Francis.

'No I will not!'

'Then, my darling, you force me to join you.'

And without further ado he jumped up behind her and, putting his arms round her, took the reins and turned the tired animal out towards the woods again.

'Francis, what are you doing? Dismount at once.'

'I cannot do that, Ann, because I must kiss away your anger with a foolish and jealous lover – as soon as we're out of sight of all those eyes in Sutton Place.'

Ann went through the motions of struggling but, in truth, it was rather enjoyable to be pinioned by Francis's arms and to be squashed against his chest. So much so that she turned her head to look at him and then they found that they could not wait to kiss one another. Gratefully the horse came to a stop and grazed.

The next few days were filled with what seemed like a non-stop procession of guests arriving for the wedding. Walter Dennys appeared from Oxfordshire on his own, for Margaret had become pregnant at Christmas and dare not risk the babe by travelling. Sir William Weston – Richard's younger brother and Lord Prior of the knights of St John of Jerusalem in England – arrived with all due pomp for he was the premier Lay Baron in the House of Lords and acted accordingly. But for all his dignity he had been a tough and brilliant soldier and had been created a Turkopolier while still a young man – even before the Siege of Rhodes when the Knights had eventually capitulated with honour to the mighty Suleiman.

During the following day several other senior members of the Weston family arrived. First came Mabel Dingley, Sir Richard's sister, accompanied by her husband, Sir John, and her son, Sir Thomas, with his wife Isabella. It seemed to Ann Pickering that she was suddenly surrounded by an enormous group of people – all related – and she would have felt small and isolated if it had not been for the constant presence of Francis by her side.

Early in the morning of the next day more of the Dingley family arrived, followed shortly by Anne, Lady Verney – Richard's youngest sister, but already a widow. Her son Francis Verney – after whom Francis Weston had been named – joined her that evening accompanied by his tiny wife, Eleanor. Though barely five feet tall she was the mother of twin boys – lusty thirteen-year-olds – who had accompanied their parents in order to play their part in the wedding ceremonial. However, they, apart from seven-year-old Alice Rogers, were the youngest present. All the infants had been left behind. There was not a parent in the land not fully aware of the dangers of

251

travelling and anyone under six was considered safer with his maid and wet nurse. So Lady Weston was deprived of the pleasure of seeing Catherine's six-week-old son, Richard. And Giles Rogers, too, had stayed at home in Bryanston.

That night, at a banquet in the Great Hall – the conversation being shouted over the noise of the musicians – Francis said to his father, 'Sir, Ann and I have been discussing something of import.'

'Which is?'

'That we feel it would be easier for all if we called her by her father's private name for her – Rose. There are so many Annes in our family. Would you be disagreeable?'

Sir Richard was about to answer but his brother William's voice boomed across, drowning even the sackbuts.

'A splendid idea. I like to know who I'm talking about. It has always been my hobby. Talking – and thinking, of course – about people. And nothing spoils that more than not knowing who is who. Now at the Siege of Rhodes against Suleiman the Magnificent – what an incomparable warrior that man was! – there was a very beautiful girl called Rose. An infidel, of course, but very beautiful.'

And he stared into his glass, lost in reminiscences. Francis wondered if – holy knight though he was – the tent curtains had parted during that long hot siege and Sir William had seen the honey-skinned Rose standing there. And if he had felt those long shapely limbs wrap themselves round his as her soft laughter had rung out on the warm night air. Even old and revered uncles must have had their day.

'You're right, Francis,' Sir Richard said, smiling indulgently at his brother who was still lost in pleasant thoughts. 'Three Annes in Sutton Place are quite enough.'

He patted his widowed sister Anne Verney's hand. 'Shall we all drink to Rose Pickering?'

Goblets were lifted as they chorused 'Rose Pickering'. But Sir Richard's words about three Annes might well have been an omen, for the next day the contingent from Court arrived and there in their midst, riding a jet black horse and dressed in shimmering gold – an exciting and dramatic choice – was the Lady Anne Boleyn herself.

Anne Weston gasped.

'I cannot have that woman in my house, Richard. She has betrayed my friend, the Queen. I cannot speak to her.'

Her husband turned to her with a very straight face.

'Anne, you must. She is a friend and guest of Francis's but more than that – far, far more – she is the power that will be followed now that Wolsey has fallen.'

'You sicken me, Richard. That is all you think of – power and which is the right camp to follow. Have you no thoughts of loyalty? You throw away Katharine and Wolsey as if they were wornout shoes.'

'And that is precisely what they are,' said Richard quietly. 'Wife, you want a husband who keeps his head upon his shoulders, do you not?'

She nodded, dumb with chagrin.

'Then listen to me. I know what I say.'

'No doubt, no doubt! But none the less I hate this political chess. However as it is Francis's wedding I shall receive her. But by the Holy Mother do not expect cringing and crawling from me. Mistress Anne – I mean the Lady Anne . . .', she made a contemptuous sound, '. . . and her brother the Viscount – prize parvenus that they are – will receive the minimum courtesy from me. But I am sure that you will more than make up for it!'

And with a great deal of rustling of her skirt and over-loud footsteps she swept from the room.

The arrival of the Duke of Norfolk and Henry Knyvett completed the wedding party. And Anne Weston, looking round the Great Hall on the wedding eve, had to admit that, despite the ill-will she bore against some present, the company was more sparkling and elegantly arrayed than those invited for Margaret's wedding.

Again and again she felt her gaze drawn to the Lady – Anne Boleyn – whom Sir Richard, with an eye to a new patron now that Wolsey was toppled, had put to sit in the place of honour. Observing her closely she saw that though her clothes and jewellery were now expensive and she had painted her face, yet those great dark eyes had an almost tired expression in them – as if she had travelled a million miles and was weary of all things. Just for a split second Anne Weston felt sorry for the woman who was rocking the monarchy to its foundations. It seemed to her that Anne Boleyn was no longer a free soul but driven by some relentless force.

Ann Pickering thought, 'I don't like her. Not at all. She is remorseless. And bitter too. A dangerous combination. I wish Francis were not so intimate with her.'

And she had such a strong feeling that Francis must be protected from the Lady that she shifted uncomfortably in her chair.

The wedding morning dawned brightly and quietly for everyone kept to their own apartments in company with their servants as they dressed themselves for the ceremony. A few people broke their fast early in the Great Hall but the majority ate in their own chambers. Only Walter Dennys, who had been up since before dawn with Sir Richard's gardeners, was working hard. He had supervised the weaving of greenery into the musicians' galleries with several devices of knotted flowers and down the walls of the Hall trailed garlands of roses, columbine, gillyflower and violets both wild and tended. With his own hands he had made a chaplet of white roses for the bride's head.

In the darkness, Sir Richard's cook and his lads and maids had been working all night long and now the sides of beef, whole sheep, geese, capons, swans, peacocks, herons and pheasant were ready. There were two dozen different kinds of pie, shrimps, oysters, salmon and a dozen other fish. But the finest work was the decorated boar's head and the confectioner's sugar love-tree from which hung delicacies shaped as hearts, rings and lovers' knots.

'And how many dishes for the first course, Barnard?' asked Lady Weston.

'Sixty, my Lady.'

'And the second?'

'Eighty.'

'And the third?'

'One hundred, my Lady. This is the finest feast we have ever prepared.'

'And all to be served on our best crystal dishes.'

'All but the boar's head which is to be borne on the great silver platter.'

Anne Weston left the kitchens and went to her chambers to be dressed by Joan.

At exactly midday the wedding party assembled in the Long Gallery. This comprised Francis and his entire family except for his young twin cousins Nicholas and Charles Verney who had another role to play. As soon as the other guests from Court had joined them they set out to walk in a laughing, merry mob to Sir Richard's chapel which lay in the west wing of the small inner court. And as soon as Francis, flanked on either side by his mother and sister, appeared at the top of the staircase, the musicians in their bright liveries of crimson and gold, jammed together in the two galleries above the Great

Hall, burst forth with the most cheerful sound. A melodious blend of sackbuts, lutes, kytes, crumhorns and viols filled the air.

In her chamber Rose Pickering heard the music and her heart began to thud. She was already dressed in a gown of white satin, puffed with cloth of silver and trimmed with yards of lace into a crystal and pearl coronet. Now, on hearing the noise, Peg put the delicate chaplet of white roses round the headdress and stood back to admire her charge.

A knock came at the door – it was the bridegroom's man come to take her to the chapel. And Francis had chosen Henry Knyvett. Rose saw that he was moist-eyed.

'What Henry, tears?' she said. 'This is a day for rejoicing.'

'Oh Ann – Rose,' he answered, 'It is you that has moved me. I shall always be your devoted friend.'

And making a great effort and rather unceremoniously wiping his eyes with his sleeve, Henry offered Rose his arm and led her towards the Great Hall. As they reached the staircase Nicholas and Charles Verney, her two 'sweet boys' clad in blue satin and with sprigs of rosemary tied round their sleeves, stepped forward to complete her escort. The musicians, pouring sweat, played as though their lives depended on it as the bride descended into the Great Hall and out through the Middle Enter towards the chapel.

Francis was already standing at the altar before Sir Richard's priest, clad in gorgeous new vestments especially for the occasion, and as she walked slowly down the centre aisle through the dense crowd that packed the small building Rose saw him steal a surreptitious glance at her. She already cared for him so deeply that she dare not meet his gaze but lowered her eyes as they knelt together waiting for the long and exhausting ceremony to begin. But when at last it was over and they rose as man and wife Francis took her hand and led her, at the head of the whole procession, back to Sutton Place for their wedding feast.

It seemed to him that they would never be alone. That the moment that he had been waiting for since he first met her, would never come. The enormous banquet that his mother had so painstakingly planned was constantly interrupted by singers and musicians, to say nothing of Sir Richard's new Fool – a thick-set Spaniard with a good singing voice but little else to commend him. He hovered round the bride rolling his dark eyes and making rather bawdy jokes which eventually could no longer be taken in good part.

'Be gone,' hissed Francis, 'or God's life, I'll bloody your nose out of all nick.'

At last the moment came. Rose was led upstairs by the female guests. Then Francis was removed and amongst a welter of lewd jokes, digs in the ribs and nudges was undressed and put into his night shirt and led to the newly decorated chamber which he and his bride were to occupy.

She was waiting for him, sitting up in the big four poster, a demure white nightdress buttoned to her throat and a night cap on her head. With shouts of 'Good Sport' and 'Go to it, lad', Francis was put in beside her and Lady Weston herself drew the curtains round them. Everything appeared to become quiet but Rose saw Francis give her a wink and put his finger to his lips. Cautiously he put his head between the curtains and then there was a cry of 'Out, Out,' and a great deal of scuffling. Peeping, Rose saw that William Brereton and George Boleyn were the offenders but were leaving unceremoniously with Francis's foot helping them on their way.

He locked the door and then quite unselfconsciously

peeled off his shirt and stood naked before her in the candlelight. And to his great joy she responded by getting out of bed and removing first that silly lace cap, so that the magnificent red curls came tumbling down, and then her nightdress. At last he was able to see her as he had always wanted – without clothes to hide the sweetly-made body.

'Does the stallion wish the mare?' she said.

'For the rest of his life,' he said.

She laughed with pleasure and rolled into the middle of the great bed. And Francis, full of wine and lust, set about the joyful task of consummating his marriage.

12

The sound of the sea as it swayed its way back and forth across the silver sands of Moresby seemed like that of a pleasured cat to the almost sleeping Francis. He lay flat on his back, his shirt beneath his head for a pillow, his nakedness facing the sun. Beside him lay Rose in a similar posture though with a wide-brimmed hat – borrowed from one of her gardeners – covering her face, for the freckles that Francis found so endearing were considered ugly blemishes by a Court that had tended to worship the fair until the dark beauty of Anne Boleyn had arrived in its midst.

To lie thus, naked with one another on an open beach – albeit Rose's property so there could be no fear of prying eyes – was an act that would have horrified the majority of married people. But to this couple, who had sworn always to be free together, it was a natural part of their life. In fact they had just made love, not bothering even to hide behind the rocks and revelling in the freedom of sun and sand. And now they dozed, side by side, Francis's hand gently stroking the very slight rounding of Rose's belly.

The marriage had been an unqualified success – in fact Francis had surprised himself at what a good husband he had made. It had never occurred to him for a second that any part of the perfect relationship he enjoyed with his wife had been entirely due to her efforts and, in some ways, sacrifice. If anyone had told him so he would have looked first astonished and then angry. He sincerely believed that he had been blessed by Heaven – that the wife chosen for him by his parents was that magical thing known to only a fortunate few, his soulmate.

And now that sweetly growing stomach! Had there ever been a man more fortunate? Raising himself on one elbow, he gently leant over and kissed it. Beneath her straw hat Rose stirred lazily. Francis tickled her slightly and then went back to sleep. Looking at him through the holes in the straw Rose thought, 'The most handsome man in England! And how very much I love him. But what will he do without me when this babe comes? He is so good-natured that he could be led into any mischief.'

She had always known that he was weak, of course. Known almost from the first time she had seen him when she had been a very young girl. And during their summer courtship in the year of the Sweating Sickness she had decided that, however much she disliked it, she must stay by his side at Court if their marriage was to be the experience of joy that she desired so much. And in order to do this she must get a place, for there was no room in the royal residences for wives and husbands who were not attached to one of the retinues.

So, when her marriage had been only one day old and before the Lady Anne Rochford had had time to depart from Sutton Place, Rose had been to see her. She could remember the occasion vividly. Anne Boleyn, as most people still thought of her, was seated alone at the far end of the Long Gallery gazing distantly out of the window. She had looked up as she had heard the approaching footsteps.

'Ah, Mistress Weston,' she had said – and Rose had had a slightly pleasurable sensation at being addressed by her married name – 'how goes it with the bride?'

'Well, my Lady,' Rose had answered, dropping a polite curtsey.

Now she must dissemble in order to secure her future

happiness for once again the dislike of Anne was welling within her. Those strange dark eyes that could smile till the moon turned blue but would always bear resentment in their depths; that disfigured hand which she concealed so cleverly; the mystical power she had over men. For a second Rose had examined her conscience. Was it jealousy that made her dislike the Lady so? But she had no time to think it out for Anne Boleyn was looking at her with a question in her eyes.

'Madam,' Rose had said, 'I have to come to ask you a great favour. I would like a position in your household.'

Anne Boleyn had not replied, merely looking at the girl in an oddly blank manner.

'The point is,' Rose had continued, 'I love Francis very dearly and I do not wish to be parted from him. As a Gentleman of the Chamber he must stay with His Grace so, therefore, my Lady it is up to me to obtain a position at Court.'

'How old are you?' Anne Boleyn had asked.

Rose had thought it a curious question but had answered, 'Seventeen, my Lady.'

'Seventeen,' thought Anne. 'I was sixteen when they took me from Harry.' She smelt again the heavy blooms of that midnight garden at Hampton Court, heard Harry Percy murmur, 'Anne, my love witch', felt the big, gentle hands hold her against him. Would he never leave her? Must he always haunt her as she did him? Would it always be he who kissed her and caressed her when it was, in fact, the King? And when she finally yielded up her body – as one day she must – would it be Harry Percy who would slip between the sheets with her and take away her virginity? If she convinced herself hard enough could she step into the realm of fantasy and even enjoy the lovemaking of Henry Tudor? For if she were to cry 'Harry' at the height of her pleasure His Grace would not

261

suspect – would never know that he was but a substitute for the man she had once desired and would always love.

'You may have your place, Mistress,' she said to Rose. 'You may return to Court with your husband as my maid-of-honour. I will speak to His Grace about your sharing apartments with Francis. I am sure he will be agreeable.'

So, her love of the country sacrificed for her other love, Rose had gone to live at Court and watched, with growing concern her husband's ineffectual life style and incessant gambling.

'It is too much,' she had said after three months of silence. 'What is the matter with you? Your gaming is like an illness.'

'But, sweetheart,' he had answered, 'that and sporting pursuits are the only things I do well. I am no statesman like my father.'

'But surely you could try.'

For the first time she had seen the obstinate streak that Francis kept well concealed.

'Has it occurred to you, Mistress,' he had said, 'that I might enjoy these pursuits? And what harm do they do, pray?'

'They are so useless.'

'Is not your embroidery and your riding useless? What great matter lies in your activities? Put your house in order, Rose, before you start to rebuild mine. Good day to you.'

And he had gone off. She had not seen him again until dawn when he had come to bed flushed with triumph and wine.

'God's mercy, where have you been?' she had asked.

'Playing dice and beating the King,' he had said shortly.

'How much did you win?'

'Forty-six pounds.'

Rose fell back on the pillows with shock. Her husband

had just taken from the royal purse twenty-three times as much as his annual Easter and Christmas reward. And in one game!

'Francis, you should not push His Grace so far.'

But Francis was already asleep.

After that she had decided to let the matter rest. It was the nearest they had come to an argument since their marriage and it was perfectly clear that nothing would change him. It was as he said. He was happy in his way of life and it seemed harmless enough. And she had to confess that she was proud of him as he ran nimbly round the tennis court, trouncing all challengers. Admitting defeat, Rose dropped the subject and they returned to their blissful and loving existence.

And now it was June, 1531, and they had come to Moresby to belatedly celebrate their first wedding anniversary.

'Rose?'

She hadn't realized, deep in her thoughts, that Francis had woken up.

'Aye?'

'Let me love you again.'

She raised her straw hat to look up at him impudently.

'Do you never grow tired of it?'

'Never. Do you?'

'I'd be in a pitiable state if I did.'

And the thrust of his body seemed in her mind to become one with the sounds of the sea and the earth; the harmonious blending of everything that nature had ever intended.

That night in bed they held each other tenderly, too tired for any further love and yet still desiring to be close. And it was as they lay thus that she felt a stirring in her womb – as if a butterfly had opened its wings within her.

'He stirs, Francis,' she said. 'The babe stirs.'

263

And in the darkness she heard him sob with joy and held him tightly against her. For what malice lay in such a man? Weakness and frivolity were diminished to their correct stature beside such goodness of heart.

'I tell you,' said the Duke of Norfolk to Zachary, 'that this hypocritical situation in the Kingdom cannot go on much longer. Somebody or something will crack under the strain. Hey, hey, hey, my pretty beauty, thou wouldst not cry for thy grandfather?'

This last remark addressed to his granddaughter, Zachary's child by his wife, Jane. After the Duke's nocturnal visit to Allington Castle the wedding had proceeded with great despatch, so that a perfectly legitimate baby had been born six months later. And now here she was, nearly a year old, and bearing a most uncanny resemblance to Zachary's mother.

'It is sickening to behold,' Zachary agreed, smiling fondly at his wife who was distracting the child with a toy of silver bells.

'I don't know how my niece has the gall to do it.'

'Or the Queen the tenacity not to crumble.'

For all three – Henry, Katharine and Anne were still living under the same roof. Wherever the Court went, moving from one palace to another or on royal progress, so did both the women. Moreover the King and Queen visited one another every few days and on state occasions Katharine appeared as the ruling consort.

'If only the work at York House was completed so that Anne could move in. That would be something. It is like some damnable farce being played out. I truly believe, Zachary, that public opinion is hard against the King and his . . .'

He hesitated over the word. It would have given him the greatest satisfaction to say 'great whore' for his unnatural dislike of his niece grew with each passing month, and as for that crawling father of hers . . . But he knew that Zachary still had a regard for her whilst Jane – now openly accepted as the Duke of Norfolk's daughter-in-law – had once been one of Anne Boleyn's ladies. Howard reflected briefly that the Lady had very few women friends, the two Wyatt sisters apparently the only exceptions.

Zachary ignored the incomplete sentence.

'There will be a break very soon now. The situation is coming to its climax.'

'Poor Katharine, poor Katharine,' said the Duke shaking his head. Anyone else might have considered the possibility that it would be Anne who would go down but not so Howard. He believed only too well in his son's prophecies and was certain that Boleyn's daughter was destined to become Queen before she fell out of the King's favour.

'Zachary,' he said suddenly, 'will I outlive His Grace? Does danger lurk for me after the death of Anne?'

It was something he had never asked before and his son gave him a solemn look.

'By a cat's whisker you will. But you have many enemies, Lord Duke my father. Be advised by me. As the King lies dying, have a fast horse at hand so that you may flee to Kenninghall. In that way you will survive.'

'Ho hum,' said Howard, but he had grown a little pale.

'Will you dine with us, my Lord?' asked Jane coming back into the room with the child Sapphira, who had been removed for making too much noise.

'No, my dear. The Court moves to Windsor tomorrow and I have a great deal of preparation still to do. Come, let me kiss this poppet.'

The girl was handed to him and he lifted her high and then held her so that her small arms were round his neck.

As he embraced her fondly she distinctly whispered 'Thomas' into his ear. It quite chilled him and he thought about it a great deal on the ride back to Greenwich Palace.

Having waved him out of sight the family turned back into their large and comfortable new house. Standing in the open country, it was still only a few miles from Greenwich Palace, which suited them well for Zachary could easily ride or go by water to Court. And those who wished to consult him privately could journey to him without difficulty. Rather to Jane's surprise her father had given the house to them for a wedding gift. But then the whole business of her sudden marriage to Zachary had puzzled her. She could never understand why her father had given his consent at all. Sometimes she wondered if Zachary had put a spell on him.

'Oh Sapphira,' she said, putting her daughter in a tub of water for her wash – a job she loved doing herself – 'what a strange, lovely man is your father!'

'Oh indeed he is,' said Zachary from the doorway.

Jane laughed and splashed water at him.

'That will teach you to pry,' she said, as a good handful wet his unkempt locks causing him to shake his head like a dog.

'I'll teach you manners tonight,' he said. 'Now hurry up. I'm hungry.'

Sapphira began to cry, standing up in her tub and holding the edge of it in her fists. Zachary went over to her and bent down so that his eyes were completely level with hers.

'Be gentle, sweetheart,' he said, and she stopped at once.

'You've a goodly way with the little maid,' said Jane.

'Well, I've known her a long time,' he answered.

Jane shrugged her shoulders. As happened so often

with her husband she had no idea at all what it was he was talking about.

It was their habit during the summer to walk about their gardens after they had dined and this particular evening, as they stood watching the sun descending into the river, the sound of oars came to them on the breeze.

'A visitor?' asked Jane.

'Aye,' said Zachary sighing.

And as they watched, the barge of the Lady Anne Rochford came into view.

'Why, it is Anne! What can she want at this hour? A consultation with you, I suppose.'

'I fear so. Yet it is not like her to ask for help. Something must have gone wrong.'

Jane stepped forward to greet her cousin with a kiss noticing, as she did so, how unusually pale Anne Boleyn was and how strained her expression.

'Dr Zachary,' said Anne without preamble, 'I must speak with you urgently. Something very strange has taken place. I do not wish to offend you, Jane, but I can stop for no social chit chat until I have talked privately with your husband.'

Zachary made a small bow.

'Then if my Lady would be good enough to follow me.'

And he led her to the top floor of the house. Just as in Cordwainer Street, he preferred to work in the attic for it was there, so he said, that he was nearest to the stars that ruled all their lives.

'Well, Lady Anne,' he said, 'what is it that disturbs you so deeply?'

'This,' she replied, and from the depths of her cloak took a book and flung it on the table where lay his crystal scrying glass, his ancient cards and his astrologer's charts. Zachary bent to examine it. It was a loathsome thing. There was no doubt in his mind that it was the product of a black coven for it prophesied the future in the most terrifying manner. One page, crudely marked with a hand-written H, showed the King looming mighty overall. Another, marked K, showed the Queen howling with despair and wringing her hands; and yet another – and by far the most sinister – depicted Anne herself, her bloodied head lying at her feet.

'Where did you find this?' he asked.

'It was left in my bedchamber. By what agency I know not.'

'Did anyone else see it?'

'My principal maid-of-honour, Nan Saville. She was greatly afraid.'

'And so should you be, Lady, for it is a wicked thing.'

He looked Anne straight in the eye but other than her unusually pale countenance she showed no fear. It ran through Zachary's mind, not for the first time, that she might not be entirely unfamiliar with the dark power.

'Why did you come to me?' he said.

'Because though I declared it to be just "a bauble" to Nan I am in truth affrighted. Zachary, am I to die? Can you do nothing to protect me?'

'I can start by committing this to the fire to which it belongs.'

He picked the book up in one hand and took a candle in the other but before he could touch one of the pages with the flame it seemed as if the whole room started to vibrate. A cabinet containing glasses, jars of herbs and his pestle and mortar suddenly flew open and the contents began to crash upon the floor. The crystal hurled itself through the air and smashed through one of the windows and his cards hurtled round the room as if in the midst of a great wind.

Anne Boleyn cried out, 'What is happening?'

But Zachary did not answer. White to the lips, he had

snatched his dagger from his belt and was scratching a great circle on the floor-boards and then another within it. As if in retaliation the big clock, which stood in the corner of the room, lifted up and propelled itself directly at him.

'*Sator arepo tenet opera rotas*,' he began to chant and threw himself down as the clock landed on top of him.

'Get into the circle,' he shouted to Anne. 'For Christ's sake get in!'

Like one in a trance, she obeyed. Struggling out from beneath the clock's weight, Zachary snatched up some vervain and dill from the mess of broken herb jars that lay on the floor. Then screaming at the top of his voice, '*Salom arepo lemel opera molas*', he fought his way to stand beside her.

'Draw the pentagrams,' he commanded passing her his knife, and saw that she knew at once what he meant. He had no time to ponder the significance of this for between the two circles, struggling all the time as if he was buffeted by a gale, he was spreading the herbs.

'*Sator arepo tenet opera rotas*,' he repeated again, but to no avail. The maelstrom continued as he sought sanctuary beside the half-fainting Anne in the very centre of the four pentagrams. Standing there, supporting her in his arms, he was aware that he was witnessing demonic frenzy of the most unbridled force and knew that if either of them dared move out of the protection he had made they would be as good as dead. And powerful though he might be he had no idea as to what he should do. His magic was not strong enough to combat the fury that had been unleashed.

Chairs were smashing themselves against the walls and his table was lifted up and then dropped thunderously on to the floor. Zachary had never tasted terror before but now it was like salt in his mouth. He had closed the circle with his dagger after he had gone in and knew that nothing, however strong, could touch them there but he could only watch impotently as the violence threatened to consume the entire room.

'*Salom arepo lemel opera molas,*' he said again desperately and then – to his horror – he saw the door begin to open.

'Jane, keep out!' he yelled. 'Don't come in for the love of God.'

But it was too late. His wife stood in the doorway, her eyes wide with fear and disbelief, and struggling and screaming in her arms was Sapphira.

'Take the babe out. Go away!' he shouted again as a great cloud of evil sulphur filled the room. But Jane stood transfixed, her mouth open to shriek but the sound caught in her throat somewhere. Her arms must have lost their strength for the child slithered down to the floor and began to crawl amongst the broken glass and spilled herbs that by now were littering the entire room. Seemingly unafraid of the objects flying past her Zachary saw his daughter stretch out her tiny hands and begin to play with the herbs.

'Sapphira,' he called out.

She looked across at him standing helplessly in the magic circle and it seemed that those eyes were so familiar. She gave him a little smile and said, to no one in particular, 'Begone'. And then she put one small finger in the dill and wrote '+ JHS +'. There was a sudden and total silence and, lying where it was on the floor, the evil book burst into flames and was no more. In the amazing stillness that followed Zachary looked at his daughter and bowed. It was the bow of an acolyte to a master, the acknowledgement of superiority. He knew that he stood in the presence of the greatest power of them all.

* * *

Because of Rose's condition Francis insisted that she made her journey from Moresby back to Windsor – where the Court had moved for the summer hunting – in a litter, with him riding beside her. She grumbled a little, for she was an excellent horsewoman, but his look of genuine anxiety as he said, 'But, sweetheart, it is for the sake of the babe', so touched her heart that she gave in and they left two days earlier than they would have normally done.

'And we will tell the Lady Anne that you wish to retire at once from her household.'

But at that Rose's face took on a determined expression that Francis knew only too well.

'Not yet, darling, the rounding is still very small. I shall stay at Court until it grows unsightly.'

'But why? You like Sutton Place. Why not rest there till the child is born?'

'Because I enjoy the Court in summer; the hunting and the progresses. I shall retire in the autumn.'

'I don't understand,' said Francis.

They arrived at Windsor Castle to find yet again the situation that had made not only the English Court a veritable swarm of gossip but had also set those of Europe chattering. Queen Katharine was established in her apartments with her retinue; the Lady Anne in hers; the King, looking more strained than even his oldest servants could remember, strode between the two sets of lodgings.

But it was in Anne Boleyn herself that Rose at once noticed a difference. Those deep, mysterious eyes carried a new expression – defiance, coupled with something else. As she got out the Lady's velvet hunting gown on the first morning after her return from Moresby, she puzzled about it.

'Did you enjoy your leave, Mistress Weston?' Anne was asking, as one of the maids brushed the thick, lively

271

hair that hung down the length of her back and which made Rose think of a black waterfall.

'Yes, my Lady. It was very pleasurable,' and she walked up behind Anne, the gown draped over her arms, and stood looking at her in the mirror. Anne caught her gaze and it was then that Rose decided what this new quality was in the Lady's eyes. She looked haunted. As if she had been to hell and back but had emerged from the ordeal with a grim determination to proceed at all costs.

'Why do you stare so?' said Anne. 'It is supposed to be unlucky to gaze upon another in a mirror.'

'Nay, madam, that is for old wives,' Rose answered. 'I was thinking how beautiful your hair looked.'

It was a half-truth but it seemed to satisfy the Lady well enough.

'Aye,' she answered, 'fear of the unknown is for fools and old women. Are you superstitious, Rose?'

'Sometimes, madam. Sutton Place is supposedly cursed. Did you know that?'

'Yes, Francis told me some years ago.'

As always when Anne Boleyn mentioned Francis, Rose felt that strange stirring resentment that she could not control. His familiarity with the King's love annoyed her. So she was none too pleased when Francis announced in bed that night, 'The King leaves for hunting long before first light tomorrow and he has asked me and a few others to join him. I think we will be away several days.'

'Is the Lady going?'

'I suppose so. His Grace has not actually said much about it. He seemed – reserved.'

'She has not mentioned anything to me.'

'That reminds me. The King has written to my father and he wants you to deliver the letter to Sutton Place personally.'

'Me? Why not send a rider?'

'I don't know, Rose. Something strange is afoot.'

'In what way?'

'I have no idea. Rose, I must sleep or I will never get up in time to leave.'

She lay awake for a little while wondering about it all but was deeply asleep when Francis hauled himself out of bed and dressed by candlelight. He kissed her into half wakefulness.

'Goodbye, sweetheart. I'll join you in a few days. Perhaps at Sutton Place.'

'Why there?'

'You ask so many questions. Take the letter to my father. I'm sure that contains all the answers.'

Rose went back to sleep and dreamed of Anne Boleyn's Breton greyhound Urian – an animal she personally detested because of its evil nature – putting its head back and howling without stopping. But to her horror when she woke she found that the sound was real. From some distant chamber came a cry of such anguish that it seemed hardly human. Running into the corridor still in her night attire Rose met Margaret, Lady Lee, another of Anne's maids.

'In God's name, Margaret, what is that dread noise? Is somebody dying?'

Even Lady Lee, who as Thomas Wyatt's other sister had been a childhood friend of Anne Boleyn, looked sickened as she said, ''Tis Her Grace.'

'What ails her?'

'The King left with great stealth in the early hours of this morning and the Lady Anne rode with him. He did not say farewell to the Queen and she says she knows certainly that he has left for good.'

'*How* does she know?'

'Intuition, I suppose.'

273

'If she is right then it is scant thanks for twenty-two years of faithful marriage. My heart bleeds for her.'

'Rose, how can you say that and still serve the Lady Anne?'

'I can say it and I do. I would not abandon a beast thus.'

And red in the face Rose stormed back into her chamber. It was only then that she saw the letter addressed to 'Sir Richard Weston, Sutton Place' and by it a note from Francis reading, 'Dearest Wife, I love you. Remember to deliver this *in person* and immediately. Yours in good health but sleepy, Francis.'

The letter seemed to be of such urgency that she forgot, temporarily, about the babe and had a horse prepared with her side saddle. The grooms hoisted her up and adjusted her foot in the stirrup then, with her long blue skirt flying out beyond the animal's flank, she went off with all speed through Windsor Forest and Woking and on to Sutton Place.

Sir Richard and Lady Weston were both in residence and the arrival of their daughter-in-law found them in the gardens where they were examining some new shrubs given to them during the previous autumn by Margaret and Walter to celebrate the birth of Margaret's son – another Richard.

'My dearest,' said Anne. 'What a wonderful surprise. What are you doing here? I thought you were with Francis at Windsor.'

'I was until this morning but His Grace has written in urgency to Sir Richard and for some reason wished me to deliver the letter personally.'

'Richard, you must open this letter at once,' said Anne, as he approached them. 'I burst to know its contents.'

Muttering to himself about 'confidential matters', Richard nonetheless obliged.

'It is quite straightforward,' he said having scanned it. 'The King is hunting round Windsor and wishes to make this his first stop. He will stay at his hunting lodge in the great forest tonight and will be here tomorrow – July 12.'

'And how many people are with him and who are they?' said Anne suspiciously.

'He says about a dozen altogether.'

'*Who are they?*'

'His Grace, some courtiers, Francis – and the Lady Anne.'

Rose thought that Lady Weston might explode with anger.

'Then I shall not be in Sutton Place when they arrive,' she said, her face scowling like a child's. 'While the Queen remains deserted at Windsor, I'll be no party to it. If he wants to parade his trollop around he may do so but if she comes under my roof she will not find the mistress of the house here to welcome her.'

Even Richard looked shocked. 'Mind your tongue,' he said.

He could not have spoken worse. Anne stamped her foot and said, 'I shall be gone within two hours. First to see Catherine and then on to visit Margaret. I do not know how long I shall be. Months, probably.'

Sir Richard looked after her vanishing figure and shook his head as she ran into Sutton Place.

'She has always been very devoted to Her Grace,' he said, and it was the nearest tone to apology that Rose had ever heard him adopt. 'She met her when Katharine first arrived in England, you know. While Queen Elizabeth of York was still alive. Anne was one of her ladies.'

Rose said, 'The Queen is very distressed, Sir Richard.'

Richard said, '*Life* is greatly distressing, Rose. Often men and women can be grievously wronged through no fault of their own. The Queen's fault is that she grows old and cannot give the King an heir and her second fault is that the King fell out of love with her. But those are not defects in themselves.'

'Yes. But why is there no law of compensation?'

'If I knew the answer to that, my dear, I would have solved the riddle of life's essence. For we are all at the mercy of circumstance. I pity the Queen, of course I do. But there is nothing I can do to help her. No violent protestations on her behalf, no grand gestures like the one my wife has just made, will alter the facts. His Grace desires Anne Boleyn. And one day, I expect, he will grow tired of her too. And then the treadmill will start again and nothing any of us can do will help *her*.'

'You will always weather the storm, Sir Richard,' said Rose.

'Only by sitting perpetually in the crow's nest, my dear.'

She laughed.

'I wish I had your brains, Sir.'

'I think in a way you have, Rose. I certainly feel happier about Francis since he married you.'

'I love him.'

'And he you, butterfly that he is. My dear, for his sake will you act as hostess when His Grace and the Lady arrive? It will not be a great number and Giles Coke will advise you.'

'Of course, I will.' She turned to go into the house to see if she could help Lady Weston but stopped short and turned back to Sir Richard. 'Do you like the Lady?' she said.

'It is expedient to do so at this time.'

'But really – in your heart?'

'In my heart she does not exist, Rose.'

She said, 'I see,' and went on her way into Sutton Place.

By five o'clock Lady Weston, declaring loudly that she would rather spend the night at the Angel Inn in Guildford than another minute under 'this wretched roof', had departed. And Sir Richard and Rose dined alone in the small chamber.

At about six o'clock the next day the royal party appeared, the grooms dragging two stags, three does and various hares, rabbits and smaller game. Rose rapidly had the lads remove the kill to the kitchens so that His Grace could dine off his own fresh meat that night.

The King seemed in an extraordinary mood, veering from the over-hearty – laughing too loudly and slapping his male companions on the back – to the nervous; uneasily moving his shoulders and looking about him with an almost furtive expression on his face.

The Lady Anne, on the other hand, appeared elated. Her dark eyes sparkled with inner excitement as if she had just won a round in a game of which she had been growing tired.

And as Rose held the bowl and towel for the Lady to wash herself in the privacy of her chamber, Anne asked, 'Can you keep a secret, Mistress Weston?'

'I believe so, madam.'

'Then hear this. When His Grace rode away from Windsor yesterday morning it was the end of his marriage. He plans to order the Queen out of her apartments before he will return to the Castle.'

Rose tried to keep her face as impassive as Sir Richard's as she answered, 'Where will Her Grace go?'

'I don't know. Probably to one of Wolsey's residences now that he is dead and gone.'

'Dead and gone! How sweet those words are,' thought Anne. 'And Fate played into my hands totally for when he was arrested last November it was Harry – Harry Percy – who went to take him. I wonder if he thought of me as he said the words "high treason"; if he remembered how that monstrous churchman killed our love?'

Rose Weston was saying, 'It is strange that the Cardinal died on his journey to the Tower. As if he was never meant to go to the block.'

Anne gave her a chilling glance.

'Yes, that was a pity,' she said.

And that night at dinner in the Great Hall – with Katharine of Aragon's device still blazing defiantly from round the fireplace – Anne was indeed treated as if she were already the monarch's wife. She was the first to tread upon the great red carpet laid down for Henry's feet and she sat at the head of the table on the King's right hand. Rose, sitting on his other side, was only thankful that Lady Weston was not present. Whether deliberately or otherwise, it was now openly flaunted that the King had left his wife for good and that the girl attendant to the King's sister, Mary Rose, was set firmly on her course to the crown matrimonial.

And how she was fawned upon. 'Would my Lady like this? Would my Lady like that? Would my Lady sing for us?' And Francis one of the worst offenders too. Rose wondered how much longer she could endure this never-ending meal watching her husband with eyes for nobody but the Lady and all the while this gnawing pain deep down inside her body. A pain that refused to be ignored and refused to go away however much she shifted position. And that she dared not do too much, for one did not move uneasily in one's chair when acting as hostess to the King of England.

At last it was over and it was time for the Fool. Pablo the Spaniard replaced the musicians who had been playing in the galleries throughout the feast. Rolling his dark eyes he went on one knee before the Lady and burst into a sensuous song from his native land; a song which conjured up pictures of vine-covered balconies, court-yards in which fountains played and lovers met in the half-dark. It must have been from just such a land that Princess Katharine had sailed to marry Prince Arthur of England. Had such a thought struck His Grace also for he was frowning slightly? Or was it that he disliked the swaggering Fool as much as Rose did? Whatever the reason he clapped his hands and called out, 'Hey, fellow, let's have a more cheerful air. This is no night for melancholy.'

Bowing Pablo changed rapidly to one of His Grace's own compositions. And his ploy proved right for now the King was smiling again and reaching out to take the Lady Anne's hand.

Rose, seeing the room through what seemed like a mist, was to have one last impression before she lost consciousness. She saw the satisfied smile that flickered slightly round Sir Richard's lips and knew that he had decided on his new patron; she saw the King, his features blurred, his status reduced to that of an over-large school-boy because of his obsession; she saw Francis, amused and adoring, gazing at the girl who was to hold sway over them all.

It was as well that she found herself unable to speak as she lurched up from her chair or she might have cried out what she really felt, 'Curse you, Anne Boleyn.' But it was not to be for Rose, who had always thought of herself as one of the strongest people alive, country-bred and resilient, was swooning down and down into darkness. And the pain, which had turned into a searing agony, told her that the babe was going to leave her – that the child created in love by Francis was destined never to be born.

13

She was like a flame, shimmering from the top of her gleaming head to the satin shoes on her feet. Since first light Anne Boleyn's ladies had been up and about her apartments at Windsor Castle preparing their mistress for the most important day, as yet, of her life. And now she stood before them clad in a short-sleeved surcoat of crimson velvet furred richly with ermine, her skin glowing from the scented oils they had rubbed into it, her hair glittering with a woven cascade of diamonds. It was the 1st day of September, 1532, and she was about to be created a peeress of the realm, the first time that such an honour had been bestowed upon a woman in England.

She was fat and puffy and middle-aged, unfashionably dressed from the threadbare headdress to the sensible, worn shoes on her feet. Since early morning Queen Katharine had been up at her pathetic little court at The More – a former residence of the dead Cardinal Wolsey. Two of her few serving women – by order of the King her establishment had been reduced to absolute minimum – had risen with her. They had done their best with her but no artifice could disguise the darned morning gown, the face pinched and lined by the yielding up of hope, the white straw-like hair straggling out from beneath her coif. It was the 1st day of September, 1532, and the Queen of Castile's daughter had no honours left except her title and the goodness of her humbled spirit.

* * *

It seemed to Rose Weston as she stood and surveyed Lady Anne that she had never disliked the woman quite so much as she did at this moment. Everything about her was too triumphant, too radiant, too gloriously illusory. She longed to smack that clever, dark face saying, 'Here! This is for Queen Katharine, and this is for my dead babe, and this is for my husband who wastes his life under your spell. And this is because you are too proud by half for anyone's good.'

But such thoughts – and there had been a lot of them since the child had miscarried – must be dispelled. If Francis were to be protected – and it appeared to Rose that he grew more indolent with each passing day – then she must play the game of double face. After the loss of the child, over a year ago now, she had returned to Anne's service as soon as Dr Burton had agreed. But in some totally illogical way – and she knew deep within herself that it was unjust – Rose had blamed the Lady for the aborting of the babe.

Dr Burton had looked at her rather narrow-eyed when she had persisted about the cause of the baby's loss.

'Who is to know, Mistress Weston, exactly what determines these things? The hard ride probably did not help but yet we cannot lay the blame entirely at its door. But why don't you retire from Court life, reside at Sutton Place? You will soon conceive another child, I'm sure.'

'Then there is nothing permanently wrong?'

'Nothing, I assure you.'

'And I may rejoin Francis at Court?'

'Yes – but why, madam?'

'He needs my company,' Rose had answered vaguely.

'He'll tire of it fast if you stifle him,' Dr Burton had thought as he had turned and wiped his hands on a towel. But he had kept his ideas to himself. A determined young woman, that. Why waste one's breath?

And, sure enough, Francis *had* resisted Rose's tightening yoke and she, aware of the cooling of their bond, found Anne Boleyn a most convenient figure to carry the blame for all. But now she smiled a sycophant's smile and murmured complimentary remarks in chorus with the other maids-of-honour.

Yet even while they looked at her Anne's mind went back precisely one month to an evening in August when she had walked with the King alone in the gardens of Hampton Court.

'I will go on no longer like this,' he had said abruptly, his voice suddenly different from the usual gentle tone he used to her. She had roused herself from a dream-like state for it seemed to her that somewhere a blackbird was singing 'Harry, Harry' and in her mind she was walking again with her lover . . . oh God, could it really be eight years ago? . . . beneath these very trees, smelling these very flowers.

'Henry?'

She had turned to look at him genuinely unsure of his meaning but something at the back of that cold, blue Tudor eye had sounded an alarm in her brain. She, who could do anything . . . anything . . . with him, was in danger.

'Don't pretend not to understand me,' and his tone had contained the same harsh quality, 'or have you forgotten that I am a man as well as your King?'

And that turn of phrase had frightened her as well. 'Your King.' Only once before had he spoken to her in such a manner and that had been when she screamed at him that they would never marry, that she had sacrificed her youth for nothing. He had suddenly, then, told her to be silent and the next day her uncle of Norfolk had come to her privately and advised her to watch her tongue, that

His Grace had complained that Queen Katharine would not have spoken to him with such impudence.

'I warn you, niece,' Howard had said, 'that you do not lead a charmed life.'

And something in the way he spoke had sent the same thrill of unease through her as she was feeling now.

Instinctively she had done the right thing. She had put her right hand with its long delicate fingers on the King's arm and said, 'Your Grace, have I displeased you?'

As always he had capitulated.

'No, sweetheart, no. I realize that you are a virtuous woman . . . a good woman . . .'

And then he had gone rambling on about his age, about sexual frustration, about his desire for her being a constant torture. And something within her told her that this was the end of her carefully guarded virtue, that the trump card which she had waited to play so long, which had gained her so many points in the royal marriage game, was about to become the joker of the pack if she did not use it soon.

'But, darling . . .'

She must make one final attempt for once he had taken her virginity, crushed her frail body beneath his mighty frame, what power had she left? Her cherished mystique would be gone. She would cease to be an enigma and become an ordinary flesh and blood woman.

He had turned to look at her with that eagerness which another woman with another man would have found touching and pleasing but which merely, because he was and always would be an oaf in her eyes, served to annoy.

'Darling, if I should have a child. Let us face facts. Our marriage looks no nearer than it ever did. I do not wish to be another Bessie Blount.'

He winced slightly. 'Bessie Blount.' The coarse name

283

for Elizabeth Tailbois – mother of his bastard, Henry Fitzroy, Duke of Richmond.

'I have already thought about that,' he said, a fraction too eagerly. 'I think, my sweetheart, that I owe you a great honour for your patience with me. I want to elevate you to the peerage – in your own right. Then if there should be a child . . .'

He did not complete the sentence. There was no need. He was telling her that any offspring of her body would be born to a title. She felt total desolation. He had no intention of marrying her. He was tired of the whole long dreary process. She was to be fobbed off with ennoblement.

But then common sense prevailed. If that were the case why had he rid himself of Katharine? Why had he gone so far, suffered so much, in trying to obtain a divorce? Anne Boleyn had braced herself. She knew that her relationship with her sovereign was at a crossroads. She must grant him his victory or lose him for ever yet, in giving in, she may well forfeit the crown which now seemed the only thing worth going on for. With all her old charm she had managed her infectious laugh.

'As my Lord wishes,' she said. 'On the night that I am elevated I shall also be elevated to your bed.'

'I must wait till then?' he had answered, but lightly with only the slightest suggestion of an edge in his voice.

She had given him a flirtatious glance.

'It would be the first time that His Grace would have taken a peer of the realm to his bed, would it not?'

Her look was enough to set his blood pounding. He had crushed her in a wild kiss, his hands grabbing at her breasts, her thighs. Still laughing she had pushed him off and for what seemed like the millionth time he had accepted it. Rejection had become a habit with him now.

'The date will be the first of September,' he had said. 'Mark it well, my Lady Anne.'

And now it was here and she knew that the Court, already assembling in the Presence Chamber to witness the ceremony, was buzzing with gossip. Was the Lady's supremacy over at last? Was the peerage the equivalent of a pension? Or was this yet another mark of the King's besotted adoration? And at the centre of all these questions she stood in her apartments – a small, dark figure, clad in vivid red – and knew none of the answers herself.

Rose Weston, Margaret Lee and Nan Saville were curtseying before her, their faces expectant.

'Yes?' she said absently.

'Is my Lady satisfied with her appearance?' ventured Nan.

Anne Boleyn slowly turned to look at herself in the mirror. A sloe-eyed nymph, her hair sparkling with diamonds, gazed back at her. She and her reflection stared solemnly at one another.

'No smile on such a great day, madam?' said Lady Lee, who had known her longest.

Anne pulled a wry face like that of a little girl's, totally at odds with the splendour of her apparel.

'No, no smile,' she said.

In the Presence Chamber Henry, attended by the Dukes of Norfolk and Suffolk, shifted impatiently in the chair of state. Today he was raising his love higher than than any other woman in the Kingdom – with the exception of one. That dowdy figure in The More still stood between him and his desire, and disgrace her and demean her as he might the fact remained that she still bore the title of Queen. He found himself wondering what she was doing now – sewing, no doubt. And for some ridiculous reason he remembered how she used to mend his shirts. Why think of that with the distant trumpets telling him that Anne was already approaching? He sniffed a little and Norfolk hearing the faint sound looked at him and thought, 'God's life, what a dance that vixen has led him. And yet for all her ill-temper she is now to receive this extraordinary honour. I don't think I have ever disliked anyone so much in the whole of my life.'

The door of the chamber was thrown open amidst another clarion burst of sound and the entire Court rose. Norfolk watched Suffolk, the King's brother-in-law, as he heaved himself to his feet. Into that beard of his he was muttering and though the words were not audible it was not hard to guess his feelings. But the French Ambassador was smiling and the members of the Privy Council, although solemn as befitted their estate, were certainly not antipathetic. The Weston clan – Sir Richard, his two sons-in-law and that idle boy of his – were a mass of smiles. And small wonder, for the old man and the son were much in the Lady's faction. Looking around him Norfolk played for a minute a guessing game of 'They love her, they love her not', all judged by the expression on faces.

But his attention was drawn once more to the doorway where a magnificent procession was beginning to move slowly forward. First came Garter King-at-Arms holding the patent of nobility in his hand and immediately behind him came Norfolk's own daughter, Lady Mary Howard, carrying a crimson robe of state over her left arm and a golden coronet in her right hand. Norfolk smiled. He could hardly credit that he had sired both this demure, neat-tressed girl, walking so beautifully and proudly, and the wild-locked Zachary. But the fact remained. They were both his. He saw Mary's eyes flick up for a second and glance at Henry Fitzroy, the King's bastard. He was unable to see the response for the young man was standing behind him, but he imagined – if the lad was anything like his father – he had given her an unabashed grin. He was right. The delicate skin had coloured a little and she was gazing firmly in front of her once more.

But now it was the moment they were all waiting for. Anne Boleyn, walking between the Countesses of Rutland and Sussex, and followed by her attendants and many of the highest ranking women in the land, was making her slow progress towards the King's chair. Even Norfolk drew in a breath. With her skin translucent, her eyes huge, her black hair flowing loose, it seemed as if a creature of legend had come into the room, as if a fairy maiden was amongst them. And vivid against her apparent fragility the voluptuous crimson of her gown was shocking. Mentally Norfolk bowed to his niece. Dislike her, hate her, do what you will, she had more grace and style and sense of occasion than any woman he had ever seen.

As she approached the royal chair and even while she walked Anne made three deep curtsies and finally, arriving before Henry, knelt at his feet. Garter handed the patent to the King, who in turn gave it to his secretary, the Bishop of Winchester – none other than Dr Stephen Gardiner. Just as Richard Weston had thought, the man had climbed high since the disgrace of Wolsey. Clearing his throat the Bishop began to read the charter.

At the appropriate moment the King rose most solemnly, wrapped the robe of state round Anne's shoulders and placed the delicately wrought coronet on her brow. She remained kneeling before him while Gardiner droned on. But the Court was already crackling with a silent excitement. The words 'lawfully begotten' had been omitted from the ancient wording. If the Marquess of Pembroke – as the Lady had just been created – gave birth to a bastard it would be entitled to her dignity and estates.

So that was it! Her enemies exchanged knowing glances. He would never marry her now. She was being cast off with second best and any child that His Grace might father was already being provided for. In the pro-Boleyn camp there was equal concern. Was this the end of the rise to power of their Lady? Or was it just another stepping stone?

Anne, still kneeling like a postulant, was aware of it all. She summoned up every ounce of her mighty will. They would read nothing in her expression as she rose to face them. And now the test had come for Secretary Gardiner was finally silent. The King himself was helping her to her feet, handing her both the patent of nobility and another granting her £1,000 a year for the rest of her life. It was done.

Looking to neither right nor left but straight into Henry's eyes she thanked him most humbly for the great honour he had done her. Then with her head held high and adorned with the gleaming circlet and the flashing brilliants, she backed, turned and left the room – her train carried by Nan Saville. The trumpets rang out again as she and her attendants departed, leaving the Court with no idea as to her innermost thoughts.

'What does it mean?' whispered Margaret Lee as they followed the new Marquess out.

'I don't know,' answered Rose Weston. 'I'll see if Francis has any idea. He is . . . close . . . to her.'

Margaret shot her a glance but made no comment.

Inside the Presence Chamber the French Ambassador leaned over to Suffolk, the King being safely out of earshot, and asked precisely the same question.

'She's done for,' said Suffolk gleefully. 'She's probably pregnant and he's paying her off. And I for one will be glad to see the back of her.'

'Not so loud for God's sake,' said Norfolk intervening.

288

'The place is ridden with spies. Anyway you're wrong. That one will sit on the throne, mark my words.'

Suffolk guffawed but admittedly lowered his voice.

'The Duke has a bastard who reads the future in the stars, Excellency,' he said. 'I'll swear he knows if a man breaks wind in the next county. Between them they've got us all mapped out. That's right, isn't it, Thomas?'

Howard looked down his broad nose.

'My son is not infallible,' he said. 'But he seems to have knowledge of what is to be and has been proved right in the past.'

The Ambassador appeared interested.

'I would very much like to visit him,' he said. 'I have always been rather fascinated by such things. Perhaps you would be so kind as to arrange for me to meet your son, Lord Duke.'

Suffolk puffed a bit as he said, 'It is all rubbish in my opinion. Scrying glasses and mystic cards! 'Tis for old women and goose girls. Begging your pardon, Ambassador.'

De la Pommeraye raised his shoulders in a gesture so Gallic that it set Norfolk grinning.

'Everyone is entitled to their view, my Lord of Suffolk. But I would be the last to poke fun at the unknown. And in truth my King has his own astrologer attached to the Court.'

'Ah well, he's French,' said Suffolk, as if that explained everything, and went off muttering.

'I think my boy will be present at the Marquess of Pembroke's banquet, Excellency,' said Norfolk. 'I will perform the introduction there.'

De la Pommeraye bowed.

'Too kind, my Lord. I may probably ask him the future of England as well as my own.'

He laughed but his eyes were alert, unjoking.

'I doubt very much that he would tell you.'

'But I take it, from what you have said, that Madame la Marquise will become Queen despite today's strange ceremony.'

'I only gave my opinion,' answered Norfolk.

But the Frenchman was too quick. It was not entirely for his diplomatic skills that the French King Francis had made him Ambassador to England at the time of the greatest upheaval the country had ever known.

'Ah, but my Lord Duke,' said de la Pommeraye bowing once more. 'I am quite sure that your astrologer son has advised you. You would be foolish indeed if you had not asked him and that, sir, you are not. Good day to you. I must speak with Dr Gardiner – a man who progresses, no?'

And he was gone in a whiff of perfume and flash of rings.

By two o'clock that afternoon the Castle was quiet. Mass had been heard in St George's Chapel in front of His Grace, the new Marquess, however, keeping discreetly to her apartments. And now both the King and his love were resting in their separate quarters; both aware of the night that lay before them and both, in their completely different ways, afraid.

Henry thought, 'God's precious life! It must be six years since I have performed the act. Six long years.'

And he remembered with a shudder how terrible it had been towards the end with Katharine. How humiliated he had felt, how emasculated, as that part of him, the stature and performance of which preoccupies the mind of all healthy males, had failed to respond at all. Jesu, how he had sweated with a dread of impotence. And then that whispered fearful consultation with his principal physician, Dr Cromer.

'But, may your Grace forgive me, is all well with . . .
with . . . any other lady?'

'There is no other lady,' he had answered shortly.
'Only the Queen.'

How could there be anyone else when he was already
possessed utterly by that little dark daughter of a Kentish
knight?

'I see.'

Dr Cromer had fingered his beard thoughtfully. He
was in the most delicate situation of his life. One false
move and he might end up in the Tower and yet his duty
lay to his patient, be he King or ploughman.

'Your Grace,' he started again, 'is all as it should be
when your Grace is . . .er . . . perhaps . . . er . . .
thinking?'

'Thinking?' repeated Henry.

'Oh God, how can he be so obtuse?' thought Cromer.

'Thinking . . . pleasant thoughts.'

'He must understand me now, he simply must!'

'Oh, I see.'

Henry grinned at him. He could be very charming,
very boyish when he chose to be.

'Yes, Dr Cromer. All is well with me at those times.
And also when I kiss . . . a certain person.'

'Then, your Grace, I fear the fault lies with Her Grace.
Forgive me, Majesty, but I must speak the truth.'

What a relief to be able to say those words and what
an even greater relief to see the King smile.

'Then I shall not fail when the "certain person"
consents?'

'You need have no fear, your Grace.'

But how could Henry have known that the 'certain
person' would keep him waiting year in and year out. So
that now he would lie in his huge bed and pray that
tonight when she was finally beside him he would be

capable of doing what he had so often dreamed about. Taking her – and roughly too – repaying her for the thousand times she had refused him. If he had been a less sensitive creature than he was, he would have begged a physic from Dr Cromer or even from that quack Zachary – Howard's natural son. But had he done so he would have announced to the world that the consummation of his love for Anne was near. And she was too beloved, too cherished, to be subjected to even a breath more gossip. He must put his trust in everything he held sacred paramount of which, may God forgive him, was his love for Anne.

She, when the ceremony was done, had asked her maids to strip her of the heavy garments of state and now lay upon her bed in naught but her white petticoats, the crimson robes so beautiful and yet so burdensome hung away out of sight. She longed to blurt out, 'What is it like to lie naked with a man? Come tell me the truth?'

But how could she? She who represented the future of England – God willing and if her nerve held out and if today's ceremony did not herald utter rejection – speak thus to any of her women? But as Rose Weston drew the heavy curtains over the windows of her bedchamber she forced herself to an intimacy entirely against her nature.

'Mistress Weston, you once told me that you loved Francis dearly.'

'Yes, my Lady Marquess?'

She sensed the stiffness in the reply and wondered, yet again, at her inability to make friends with her own sex.

'Tell me . . .'

'Yes, madam . . . ?'

Rose wasn't making it at all easy for her.

'Is there beauty in married life?'

'Yes, madam,' came the reply, and now she sensed the iciness in the voice and wondered what she had done to

292

give ill-humour. She sat up on the bed and looked at her maid-of-honour.

'I meant no offence,' Anne said – humbly for her.

'No, my Lady!'

The curtains were almost drawn now.

'Will that be all, my Lady?'

'Yes,' said Anne, suddenly bone-weary of everything. 'Yes, that will be all.'

How pleasant it was to sink back into her pillow and by the very act of closing her eyes shut out the entire world. If only she need never more open them. How much easier for all the mummers in her particular drama if she could step out now. Katharine could have her beloved Henry, the wrangle with Rome could end honourably, the people of England could cease their muttered hatred. Nan Bullen, Marquess of Pembroke, could slip quietly into the earth which made her.

'Go,' she said aloud but it was not to Rose Weston – it was to herself.

'As madam commands.'

Anne was too beyond hurt to hear the bitterness in the reply.

Francis did not become consciously aware that Rose was nowhere about the Castle until much later that afternoon. Having met Nan Saville and learned that the Lady had long since retired and the maids-of-honour dismissed he began, in a half-hearted way, to look for her. But during his search he ran into his brother-in-law Walter Dennys and challenged him to a game of chess – sporting pursuits being forbidden on the Sabbath – and this whiled away another hour or so. By this time it was too late to seek Rose out for he was on duty to attend His Grace at supper.

'Tell Rose I sought her,' he called to Walter as they parted company.

Honour had been satisfied – he had gone through the motions of trying to find his wife. With rather a heavy heart he set out for his chamber to change his clothes for the evening and it was there that he found her lying in the darkness, awake but unspeaking, curled round like a babe her knees to her chin.

'Ann,' he said, so startled that he called her by her proper name.

'If you look for your mistress,' she answered, 'she rests in her own apartments. Why not go to her? She speaks of the beauty of marriage!'

A bitter laugh followed this statement and a move to turn her back. Like all gentle people Francis, when he did lose his temper, did so like a rainstorm.

'God's blood, Rose,' he shouted, 'that is the most treasonable and unjustified remark. Do you know what you are saying or have you lost all that remains of your failing wits?'

She sat up and screamed at him, 'Wouldst call me a lunatic, you wicked man?' And then she was on her feet and running towards him, raining blows on his head and face.

'Rose, stop. Stop!'

But she would not, hurling cuff upon cuff at his unprotected head.

'Jesus, woman, you *are* mad!' he said and picking her up off her feet he threw her on to the bed where she suddenly burst out crying and lay panting and shaking like an injured animal.

'I never want to see thee again,' Francis shouted. 'You are not the woman I married, do you hear!'

And snatching up his clothes he left the room only to be attacked himself by a violent fit of trembling which persisted spasmodically throughout the evening and the quiet supper that His Grace was giving for a few carefully chosen friends.

Sir Richard, of course, noticed it at once and though no expression crossed his face he drew his son on one side as soon as the musicians started to play.

'What ails you, Francis?' he said. 'You're shaking like a girl.'

'It is Rose, Father. I believe she has gone clean out of her head.' He lowered his voice. 'And to make matters worse she has taken some passion against Lady Anne and rants opposition to her. If it should reach the King's ears I fear for her safety.'

Sir Richard's lips twitched downwards very slightly.

'Then she must be removed out of harm's way at once,' he said. 'If I take her to Sutton Place at first light can you persuade the Lady Marquess that Rose was struck ill during the night?'

'Easily enough. But what ails her in truth?'

Walter Dennys spoke from behind them.

''Tis the loss of the babe.'

'But that was over a year ago.'

'It matters not. Margaret was never right after she aborted until she was pregnant again. She c-c-cut down her favourite shrub for no reason!'

John Rogers, joining his brothers-in-law, added, 'If you speak of the women's mopes 'tis true enough, Francis. Send her to Sutton Place and then give her the only cure I . . .'

'. . . believe in plenty of babies . . .' continued Francis.

'. . . to keep the wives quiet,' finished John.

'A basic philosophy,' said Sir Richard shortly.

'But a good one. Good evening, gentlemen. I go to play cards.'

He bowed first to his father-in-law and then to Francis

and Walter, the pearl in his ear bobbing over his black-clad shoulder.

'Now, Father, take that pursing from round your lips. You know full well that you like him, rogue or no.'

But any further discussion was brought abruptly to a halt, for the King was rising from his chair and with him, as formality demanded, the assembled company followed suit. Henry's eyes were shifting in the oddest manner from one guest to another as if he dared not look directly at anybody.

'Lords and gentlemen,' he said, 'I regret that I am weary after today's ceremonial. Pray excuse me. Please continue the evening.'

And he was gone, followed by Henry Norris and the other Gentlemen. But once in the King's private apartments, with one of his characteristically abrupt changes of mood, Henry Tudor became irritable. The monarch who had only that very morning been magnificent in stately splendour was now issuing crisp orders at such speed that his serving men were in some difficulty to know where to begin. Simultaneously he wanted a scented bath, his barber, his finger nails cleaned and a newly-made night shirt.

And even as he gave instructions he thought, 'She will not come. I know it. She will spurn me even at this stage.'

And there was almost relief in the dreaded idea. Relief that he would not have to prove himself after all. But with the relief there was hurt; hurt that after everything he had done, every humiliation he had suffered – why, had he not cast off Katharine who had loved him so humbly? – Thomas Boleyn's daughter would reject him as nothing more than a lump of middle-aged flesh.

Henry Norris thought, 'God's sacred life, but it is here at last. I have lived through this night a million times in my imaginings and now it comes. She is going to repay him.'

And he set his look – blank, uncaring eye; ready-to-smile mouth – and wondered why Francis Weston glanced at him oddly. But then came the surprise that he had not anticipated. As the Gentlemen of the Chamber were dismissed for the night the King said, 'Harry, you will sleep in the ante-chamber as usual.' He had waited, been prepared for a casual dismissal, but this . . .

'So I'll to bed.'

Norris stood nonplussed. The preparations, the agitation, the general air of unrest had led him to certainty; certainty that before this night was through his life would be in ruins, his obsessive love for Anne betrayed. But now he was being bidden to perform the ritual of searching for the King's enemies. Dared he hope that, yet again, the Lady had refused? But with that thought came the sobering conclusion that she could not, for her own safety, deny the King much longer. He – Norris – knew, of all people, that Henry's temper had been growing shorter and shorter of late. If ever he had seen a frustrated and worried man he saw one now in his sovereign.

He managed his usual combination of an easy smile and business-like approach as he went through the motions of inspecting the royal bedchamber, even stooping to peer beneath the colossal bed. Straightening up he said, 'All is well, your Grace.'

'Then I bid you good night.'

Norris bowed and backed through the doorway.

'Sleep soundly, your Grace.'

As he quietly closed the King's door he saw that Henry had already blown out his candle.

At Windsor, in similar fashion to many of the royal residences, Norris did not actually sleep in the royal bedchamber but in an ante-room outside. Now he walked into it and lay down on his bed, fully clothed. As his mind churned over the day's events and he visualized that crimson figure as it knelt so meekly before the King – was it only this morning? – he wondered for the millionth time how so delicate a body could house such an indomitable will. And then he became aware of a feeling of impending disaster that he could not describe but which kept him staring sleepless at the ceiling until long after the moon had risen.

At Sutton Place – her face silvered into a sleeping mask by the same moon's ascendance – Anne Weston dreamed again. Once more she stood outside the mansion but this time it was not in the violent sunset but in a wild and cruel night with a black-clouded moon leaping in the heavens. Again that feeling of being completely alone, of fear, of loss. And as if to mourn for her the wind soughed in the trees like a chorus of chanting voices. The atmosphere was repellent. She knew that the land feasted greedily on something inhuman; that kindness and joy must for ever be denied it. As she stared at the house Anne felt the bleakness of death reach out and claw her soul.

Gliding like a night walker she moved silently across the ground and felt no shock or surprise at seeing that the Gate-House wing and Tower no longer existed; that she could see straight through what had once been the quadrangle to where the moon blazed in the firmament of the windows. Breathlessly she found that the Middle Enter stood waiting open for her, while beyond it the house yawned like a devouring grave.

Now she was acting under compulsion. She would gladly have turned away, never to learn what Sutton Place wanted to show her, but she was thrust forward. She moved silently through the door and stood, looking about her, in the Great Hall. Coming towards her from the far end, walking like ghosts, their eyes blank and staring were her daughter-in-law Rose and Henry Knyvett. Francis was not with them and Anne was amazed to see that they appeared to be a family for Rose held a baby in her arms and behind them came two other little boys and a girl. It was the largest of the children that caught her attention, however, for though he had Rose's red hair his face was that of Francis.

The strange group drew near and passed so close to Anne that she could have reached out her hand and touched them but she dared not for they still stared ahead in that unseeing manner, hardly seeming to breathe. They moved like the walking dead and she was relieved when they went noiselessly out of the door and were gone.

Now her feet turned towards the west wing – to the kitchens and pantries. And from there she ascended a stone spiral staircase to the store rooms above. But now all was changed and different. Where she had once laid apples to keep for the winter months, stood an elegant bedchamber, furnished in a style quite strange to her. And against the far wall was a large four poster bed, its hangings turned to silver by the moonlight.

She had no wish to cross to it, to draw back the curtains and look within, but she had no control over what happened – she was as powerless to resist as a child. Soundlessly she opened the hangings. Lying so close together that they could have been one, were a man and a woman. He, dark-haired and delicate featured had his arms round his beloved, his sleeping hands relaxed and resting on the pillow, while round one of his fingers he had woven a lock of her hair. And what hair it was. Like a silver cloud bursting forth round a face so perfectly boned and structured that Anne drew breath. She knew that she must be looking on one of the most beautiful women ever born. And yet, fearfully, it reminded her of someone. Oh God, surely not that frightening old woman who appeared in her nightmares? But it was. That such splendour could degenerate made Anne feel faint. And the man, as if hearing her exclamation in his sleep, flicked open his large, heavy-lidded eyes and looked straight at her. But it was obvious that he did not – or could not – see her, for he merely kissed the perfect mouth that lay beside his and slept once more.

And now the room became like a vortex, whirling and misting before Anne's eyes. Trembling, she clung to one of the bedposts but that was melting in her grasp. Beneath her feet the floor undulated and looking down she saw that the carpet was changing, turning into a different texture and colour even while she watched it and the room too was transforming. The shape and the windows remained but the furnishings had altered and, once again were of a type quite unknown to her. Another bed appeared in a different place from the last and in it a man – bright-eyed, with something of the robin about him in the way he looked around so sharply. Then, startlingly, he began to speak aloud, though no one except she was there to listen.

'Damnable house. Why can I never sleep here? Night after night listening to that bloody clock chiming. And the quack's sleeping pills useless. I really hate this place. If it weren't for Mollie I'd go tomorrow. Though a fat lot of help she's being at the moment. When I told her about the White Lady – what a bloody cliché – she looked amused.'

Then he began to shout in a highly belligerent manner, 'Are you there, White Lady? You really enjoy haunting me, don't you? Oh yes, I've seen you. You're everywhere, aren't you? In the Long Gallery, in the Great Hall, in this room with your bloody apples. Do you enjoy trying to frighten people?'

Despite every wish and instinct Anne found herself walking towards him and as she did so a beam of moonshine came through a crack where the curtains were not properly drawn. The man looked straight at her and his face was livid in the half-light.

'Don't touch,' he screamed. 'Go away.'

Anne stared at him helplessly and then came the sound of approaching footsteps. A woman hurried in saying, 'What is it, Alf? Can't you sleep?' And a man, standing in the doorway, said, 'Can I get you anything, Lord Northcliffe?' The man in the bed replied, 'It's that accursed White Lady.' And then the room began to whine and vibrate again. And once more it was changing its furniture and contents while maintaining the shape and windows of one of Sir Richard's store rooms.

And Anne was to witness the most macabre thing of all. Through the door two men were pushing an extraordinary wheeled chair in which was slumped a very old man dressed in what she took to be sleeping clothes. And as they lifted him out and laid him on top of yet another bed she saw that he was dead for his hand swung limply down and one of the men had to lift it and place it carefully beside the body. Then they went out, leaving her alone with the corpse. Fearfully she crossed over and stood beside it. And as she looked into his face she saw that the dead man was the occupant of the great chair that stood at the head of the table set for the bizarre feast she had attended so often in her nightmares.

'Who are you?' she said aloud, and it seemed to her then that he sighed his final sigh in that treacherous moonlight. And as she put her hand out to touch the lifeless face the moon went in and she was alone with him in a void, a dense blackness through which she was falling and falling.

Anne Weston woke to find that she had walked in her sleep. Somehow she had managed to traverse the Great Hall and make the difficult ascent to the store rooms in the west wing. She stood in the very room of which she had dreamed and saw that there was nothing there at all, only the crisp smell of last year's apple harvest.

It was just as Henry Norris was finally drifting off to sleep that he heard a sound and was instantly awake again. Cautiously he opened his eyes and gazed in amazement at what he saw. In the doorway dressed in a gown of silver brocade, her moonlit hair glistening with jewels, stood Anne Boleyn. She began to cross the room towards the King's bedchamber.

'Madam . . .' whispered Norris urgently.

She smiled at him – the strange, haunted smile of one who must go to fulfil her destiny.

'It's all right, Harry,' she said.

But Norris was too good a courtier. He jumped from his bed and went before her to the King's door. Opening it he called out 'Sire!' into the darkness.

'Yes, Harry?' answered the King's voice.

'The Marquess of Pembroke, your Grace.'

From inside the room Norris heard Henry give a great sob. It was the sound of a man at last at the end of a long and hazardous journey. Like a girl in a dream Anne Boleyn crossed the threshold and closed the door behind her. There was silence everywhere.

14

The autumn wind was blowing briskly from the sea and Zachary Howard sniffed like a hound as he caught his first sight of the misted outline of the French coast. His dark curls gleamed with the crisp salt that the spray brought in its wake and the black cloak he wore billowed out, transforming him into a creature of the air as he turned to stare again at Calais – that small piece of English territory that lay, to the French's chagrin, in a key position on the French shore.

The letter summoning him had been short but to the point.

'By command of the King's Highness you are to attend the Court of Calais there to exercise your arts for the enjoyment of Our Most Royal Brother of France.'

The signature had been that of His Grace himself, and it had been dated October 21, 1532, and sent from Boulogne.

Zachary grinned a little. The French Ambassador had been as good as his word. He had returned to his own country to negotiate the great meeting between his sovereign, Francis I, and Henry VIII but had not forgotten to mention his amazement at the skills in divining both past and future displayed by the Duke of Norfolk's bastard. And so now he was summoned like a performing bear to do his tricks – as they considered them – for the monarchs of England and France.

His grin ceased. He who had spent so many years studying all that he could of the unseen power and splendour of the universe and meeting in his quest things

303

dark and terrible, as well as those of goodness and light, did not care to be reduced to the status of a tumbler. But nobody who wished to keep his head would refuse a royal summons to this particular occasion. For was not Anne Boleyn, Marquess of Pembroke, to be presented in all her newly acquired splendour to the King to whose first wife, Queen Claude, she had once been maid-of-honour? Henry seemed determined to win the world's approval for the woman considered by many as nothing more than a calculating whore and he was starting with his old rival for the leadership of Renaissance Europe – the sovereign lord of France.

Zachary turned briefly away from the ship's wooden prow. He knew, without her even giving him so much as a word, that Anne now wished desperately to conceive a child, saw this as her only hope of getting Henry to marry her and escape for ever the iron fist of Rome. And with this very thought in mind he had placed in her personal travelling chest some bottles of the elixir he had given to so many barren women, remembering how his mother had picked the fresh raspberry leaves from the fields of Norfolk and added to their compound a pitcher of clear water that had been left overnight in the centre of a sacred ring of trees where, it was said, Freya had once made love to Odin. A pagan belief but, nonetheless, Zachary too would make the journey there about four times a year and leave many such pitchers while he kept vigil in the nearby woods. And sure enough nearly all the women who had bought his panacea had borne a healthy child within the year.

And now the great Lady herself would drink the humble recipe and put her hand to her belly and wish that the future King of England might take life in there. And Zachary knew, with sadness, that that was one thing he could not do for her – that Anne Boleyn would never bear a living son. And that she would not live to see her daughter grow and ascend the throne and become one of the mightiest monarchs England was ever to know. He sighed and went below deck; sometimes he found his gift of clear sight too much to bear.

Rather to his disquiet Zachary discovered, as the ship slid quietly into its moorings, the cold-eyed Francis Bryan waiting to greet him on the quayside. The unblinking stare that had upset so many of Bryan's fellow courtiers was now being bent upon the astrologer as he descended the rope ladder and felt, for the first time in his life, the soil of France beneath his feet. Unsmilingly Bryan gave a perfunctory bow.

'A pleasant journey?' he said in a tone that indicated he cared not a whit nor a jot what the answer might be.

'What?' said Zachary, feigning deafness.

Bryan was forced to repeat the question but Zachary merely touched his ear and shrugged his shoulders, rolling his eyes round at the same time so that he appeared totally imbecile. Gritting his teeth Bryan gave up and gestured towards the two horses that stood tethered nearby. But Zachary simply gave an idiotic grimace and went lolloping off in the opposite direction.

'God damn you,' said Bryan and rapidly mounting went in pursuit of the black cloaked figure who was by now striding purposefully towards the more evil-smelling and disreputable part of the harbour.

'Dr Zachary,' he bellowed, catching up with him. 'You are going the wrong way. Will you please mount, sir, and follow me.'

He was rewarded with a beaming smile and a 'You are addressing me, sir?'

'Yes,' said Bryan exasperatedly.

'Do I know you, sir?'

'God's life, I am Francis Bryan. You have seen me at Court oft enough.'

Zachary peered at him shortsightedly.

'Why, you are Francis Bryan,' he said.

Bryan's usually expressionless eyes were glinting.

'Enough of this game, Dr Zachary. Remember that I have the ear of the Lady. She is my cousin.'

Zachary's features transformed into a look that made Bryan go cold.

'The Marquess has many cousins,' he said.

For a second Bryan did not comprehend but then he remembered that Zachary was the natural son of Anne Boleyn's most powerful uncle – Norfolk himself.

'And one day,' Zachary continued, 'she will be betrayed by one of them who will be known for ever more as the Vicar of Hell for that very deed.'

'You speak of me, astrologer? God's mercy, if I had my way you'd be burned at the stake.'

But even as he finished speaking the blow to his stomach had knocked him from his horse and he lay gasping for breath amongst the filth of the Calais cobbles.

'Never,' hissed his assailant, his amber eyes frightening to see, 'never say that again in my presence if you wish to live.'

And without another word or even a glance Zachary mounted Bryan's horse and galloped off leaving Sir Francis to lie where he had fallen, blood gushing from the corner of his mouth.

It took Zachary only a few minutes to find the Lantern Gate – the principal entrance to the fortress town – and giving his name to the host of guards who protected it he found himself escorted to richly appointed quarters in the Beauchamp Tower. Obviously the French King must have spoken of him with enthusiasm to Henry for he was being treated as a man of rank and estates by being given such privileged lodging, for crammed within the houses and dwellings of the fortress were some 2,400 people and 2,000 horses. Zachary considered himself more than lucky not to find himself with the less fortunate members of the Court who were sharing over-crowded rooms with resident citizens.

Having visited the Tower jakes, washed the sea salt from his skin and allowed a servant to unpack his few clothes, Zachary lay on the bed and closed his eyes. He had left Dover – whence he had journeyed from Greenwich on the previous day – at dawn's first light in order to catch the tide and now it was past noon. That, combined with the unusual exertion of a street brawl, was enough to make him feel suddenly lacking in energy.

He awoke to hear a gentle knocking on the door and to discover that it was already dusk. Guilty that he had slept longer than he should, Zachary called out to the visitor to enter and was pleased to see Francis Weston standing in the entrance to the bedchamber. Observing him closely Zachary wondered if there could be anyone in the Kingdom to rival this beloved plaything of Henry and Anne.

At twenty-one Francis was in the full glory of his physical development without any of the disfigurements that the passing years must inevitably inflict on him. His body was slender but strong with exercise, his hair gleamed like gold thread, his eyes were clear and unmarked – as yet – by his late night drinking and gambling activities. And marriage had matured him without making him old. He was lively and bright yet considerate. Small wonder that the King and the Lady Marquess treated him rather as one would a delightfully spoilt pet.

'Dr Zachary,' he said, smiling and bowing, 'I am so glad that you have joined us. All is to-do in the fortress for His Grace and King Francis only arrived this morning from Boulogne. The cooks and lads have worked until they will sleep on their feet, I'll swear. And tonight is the first of the great banquets to which I have come to invite you.'

Zachary sat up and stretched and then shook his head several times. He reminded Francis of a dog that had slept well but was now preparing itself for the chase. And he was obviously already alert for he said, 'And how goes it with the great meeting? Is the Marquess pleased?'

Francis pulled a wry face.

'In honesty not really,' he answered. 'None of the French royal ladies will meet her. They say her reputation . . .'

'So King Francis is alone?'

'He is here with the King of Navarre and other nobles – but no women.'

'And is the Lady hurt by this?'

Francis laughed.

'God's head, no. She is so strong I doubt that anything could disturb her.'

Zachary thought, 'How little you know her! You live almost within her pocket, see her every day when you are at Court, and yet you have no idea what goes on behind those eyes. One quick laugh, a clap of the hands, and you are deceived.'

Noncommittally he said, 'One can never tell with women.'

Francis smiled and said, 'How is your wife?'

'With child. As round in the belly as a rosebud.'

It was an unfortunate turn of phrase for Francis sighed deeply and answered, 'I wish my Rose would bloom.'

Zachary said, 'I feel sure that she will soon. But I shall read the ancient cards for you before I leave Calais. It is something I have always wanted to do.'

Rather to his surprise Francis said, 'Why? Why me in particular? Is it because of Sutton Place?'

Zachary hesitated and in that revealed too much.

'It *is* cursed, isn't it?' Francis went on and his hand touched the amulets that he wore beneath his shirt.

'Yes, yes,' Zachary answered, turning his head away. 'It is evil land.'

'And there is nothing that can be done?'

'When my little maid – my daughter – is older we will attempt an exorcism.'

'Your daughter?'

'Aye. She is a great magician. I dare say no more and I beg you to keep a still tongue lest she be branded – witch.'

The word seemed torn out of him almost against his will.

'But she is only a child of two,' Zachary went on. 'Her body could not sustain the onslaught. I must wait till the moon has started its mysterious cycle within her. Then her powers will be at their greatest.'

Francis stared at him.

'But that could be another ten years or more.'

'Yes. But listen to me – never take my mother's amulet and Giles's enchanted stone from round your neck. They have mighty strength.'

'So I *am* in danger?'

'They will protect you until Sapphira is ready. Now worry no more. Everything will be done to combat the spell. Think of the child that is to come. Here.'

And Zachary crossed to the small wooden chest that he had handled himself throughout the journey and, unlocking it, took out two bottles of the liquid that he had prepared in order that the Lady Marquess might conceive.

'What is this?'

'I gave some to your sister Lady Dennys, and did she not bear a son?'

Francis shook his head with amusement.

'Dr Zachary, your doing is in everything.'

The familiar imp-like grin spread across the broad Howard features.

'Hardly so. I believe your brother-in-law Walter played his part. As you must too.'

Francis was smiling.

'I'll have no patronizing from you, sir. I'll warrant you're not much older than I.'

'Half a dozen years perhaps but I am old in wisdom.'

'Well, Methuselah,' answered Francis, 'the message from His Grace that I was told especially to deliver is . . . do you want the actual words?'

'Yes.'

'Tell that *boy* of Tom Howard's not to wear a hideous cloak to the banquet and to get a brush through his hair.'

Zachary bowed his head.

'Answer to His Grace that the cloak will be reluctantly discarded but the hair presents difficulties. On the rare occasions that my wife attacks it she meets with little success. Furthermore I have no brush.'

'A servant will bring one,' said Francis. 'I will not offer to lend you mine! Farewell until eight o'clock.'

It was dark by the time Zachary left the Beauchamp Tower and took to the cobbled streets of that extraordinary citadel – the walled and apparently impregnable fortress town of Calais. He had never in his life seen anything quite like it. Within the great outer bulwark of bastions and towers were row upon row of narrow streets in which lay houses, churches, shops, a Guildhall, an Exchequer, a large market, a castle and the usual collection of inns and brothels. But all encased in a mighty stone embrace. As his horse walked slowly forward towards the

Staple Guildhall where Henry VIII was in residence and the banquet was to be held, Zachary stared about him in amazement.

It seemed that from every window of every house there hung a flag for the night was alive with swirling pennants depicting the lions of England and the fleur-de-lys. And at regular distances along the walls of the sloping and strangely-shaped buildings lighted flambeaux had been placed, so that the many members of the Court swarming forth from their various lodgings to attend upon the King's Highness and his Royal Brother of France, could see their way clearly in the October darkness to the Guildhall which stood, like a medieval merchant's palace, festooned with banners and ornamented outside with a great carpet which had been woven by that very Staple of which the Guildhall was the hub.

And once within, Zachary felt that surely he had stepped into a dream for no artifice of craftsmanship or design had been spared in order to seduce Francis of France into accepting – perhaps even adoring – the King's most precious jewel, Anne Boleyn. The walls of the banqueting hall were completely covered with silver patterned tissue and in order to disguise the joins a master goldsmith had created waterfalls of gold filigree encrusted with brilliants and pearls. Light was thrown on to the great dining table by twenty branches of candles – ten of gilt and ten of silver – suspended from the ceiling by chains worked in the same metal. The effect was devastating. Zachary, raised in the hedgerows until he was ten and after that leading a relatively simple life, was overwhelmed. And with the human quality that stopped him from being in any way a frightening figure, he was glad that his wife Jane had insisted upon him taking a new, though rather violently coloured doublet to France and that he had obeyed the King's request and left his cloak behind. To be eccentrically dressed at the Court in London was one thing but here, amidst so much splendour, it would have been ridiculous.

Charles Brandon, Duke of Suffolk, watching Zachary come in turned to Norfolk and said, 'God's precious blood, Tom, here comes your bastard looking for all the world like a quince. And why is his hair so strange?'

'I believe he has been fighting with a brush,' said Norfolk, laughing despite himself. 'But say nothing to him, Charles. By his standards he is cutting a fair figure.'

Brandon guffawed into his beard.

'God preserve us all. Look at these preening peacocks. And for what? Just so that Henry can flaunt his . . .'

'If I've told you a thousand times,' hissed Norfolk, 'keep your voice down.'

'I said it to him in England,' answered Brandon. 'It is costing too much and might involve us in God knows what kind of treaty with France. And he sent me packing then. Because it's all to please her. She was determined on this meeting. And being given Katharine's jewels for the occasion. I assure you, Tom, my stomach is a-heave over the whole affair.'

'It is outrageous,' agreed Norfolk. 'But she's kept quiet; stayed here in Calais while His Grace went to Boulogne. You must admit, Charles, that she is behaving well.'

'Aye, well and furious no doubt. And she's not coming tonight either. God knows when she's going to meet King Francis. I wonder what game she's playing with us all now.'

And he stumped off irritably leaving Norfolk free to go and speak to Zachary who was advancing towards him in a doublet and hose of such vivid yellow that Howard's eyes jumped in his head through looking at them.

'Lord Duke my father,' said Zachary, bowing.

'My dear boy. You had a safe crossing?'

'Very fair, my Lord, very fair.'

'But already in trouble I hear. Sir Francis Bryan makes loud complaint to all who care to listen that you gave him a mighty blow in the stomach and then stole his horse.'

Zachary grinned delightedly.

'Aye, 'twas a wonderful moment to see him lying on the ground – all his puff blown out.'

'And what quarrel has he with you, pray?'

'None to speak of but I care very little for his manner. He is a friend to no one but himself, mark my words.'

Norfolk sighed.

'Is he to be avoided, Zachary?'

'As much as possible.'

'I will add him to the list,' said Norfolk, a trifle wryly.

But the voice of Thomas Wyatt – Anne Boleyn's poetic cousin and Zachary's brother-in-law – was interrupting their conversation.

'The heart doth fear, the eye doth wince. Is't mortal man or is't a quince?'

'Exquisite,' said Norfolk gazing down his nose. 'Very clever, Thomas.'

Out of the corner of his eye he could see his son beginning to scowl and knowing His Grace's stringent views on unruly behaviour, he hastily added, 'We greatly appreciate your couplet to Zachary's clothes. It *is* to Zachary's clothes, is it not? To be honest I find your verse so witty that I sometimes cannot understand it at all. Farewell.'

And taking his bastard by the elbow he led him away before any further exchange could take place. It was a relief to hear the English trumpeters blare out the call that meant King Henry was approaching, and an answering call from their French counterpart sent the monarch striding directly to the door of the Guildhall to greet King Francis. As the minstrels struck up in the large,

313

decorated gallery the French King and his entourage came into the room and the Duke saw Francis I's eye flit quickly over the gathering, presumably to catch a glimpse of the Lady Marquess. But he was to be disappointed. Anne was being as good as her word. There was no sign of her and no place had been laid for her between those of the two monarchs at the glittering banquet table. Instead of trying to make her presence felt the woman for whom all this magnificence, this conferring of sovereigns, had been designed, appeared to be content to keep quietly to her apartments, her beautiful dresses and Queen Katharine's jewels lying unused.

Norfolk observed as Francis of France whispered something into the ear of the King of England and then he saw them both look across in the direction of his son. He saw, too, the look of amused incredulity that spread over the face of the world-weary Frenchman. No doubt his Ambassador had described an oddity but he still had not been prepared for anything quite like Zachary. The Duke caught himself wishing that dreadful doublet and hose at the bottom of Calais harbour. And now to make matters worse the two Kings were walking towards them and, very slightly, Francis's lips were twitching. Every protective instinct in Norfolk flew to the surface but there was little he could do. The entire Court was looking on for they had all heard of the interest shown by the French monarch in the renowned astrologer from England.

Yet it was with an extraordinary dignity that Zachary bent to kiss Francis's hand and, as he stood up, look directly into the French King's face. Just as many years before the architect da Trevizi had felt energy and power emanate from the rumple-headed figure before him, so now did Francis. For to stare deeply into Zachary's eyes was to sense the presence of things unseen, figures swathed in mist, shadows that moved silently, the distant murmur of voices from an empty church.

'You have great knowledge,' said Francis slowly. 'Will you share some of it with me?'

Zachary dropped on one knee.

'My knowledge is there for all that genuinely seek, Majesty.'

Francis nodded his head.

'Thank you, astrologer,' he said.

As he rode towards Sutton Place from his home in East Horsely, Henry Knyvett thought, 'You are a fool to yourself. She is a married woman – has been for two years now – and yet you cannot resist the flimsiest chance to seek out her company. This obsessive love is good for nobody.'

But even as these ideas were going through his head he was, quite unconsciously, pushing his horse on even harder, for news that Rose Weston had left Court and was living at Sutton Place in poor health had reached him only the day before, on his return from visiting his father's estates in Norfolk. It had come, of course, from his principal servant.

'They do say, master, that she is badly sick with the mopes and has been ever since she lost her babe!'

'But that was over a year ago, wasn't it?' Henry had answered, starting to remove his travel-stained clothes in readiness for the great pitchers of hot water and wooden tub that had been brought into his bedchamber.

'Aye, master, aye. But women are funny creatures. Some can go quite strange in their minds with that sort of thing.'

Henry had paused in the middle of taking off his shirt.

'In that case I'd better visit Sutton Place tomorrow,' he had said and then realizing that his servant was giving him a look that could only be described as knowing he had added making, as was usual with him, the matter far worse, 'Her husband would expect it of me. He is with the King in Calais at the moment.'

'Oh, you'll be nice company for her then. No doubt she's lonely in that great house.'

Henry had felt his neck and cheeks growing uncomfortably hot.

'Of course if Sir Richard and Lady Weston are not in residence . . .'

'Oh they're there, master. But you'll be a young person for her. I think it is your duty to go.'

Poor Henry had given him a grateful look.

'That is how I see it, Rob. As a friend of Master Francis I am obligated.'

His servant had sighed.

'It will be a Christian act of kindness, sir.'

He had turned his back and bent over the tub, testing the water's heat, so that his blushing master should not see his broad grin.

And now Knyvett was in Sutton Forest and about to ride clear of the last of the trees and see Sutton Place come into view. In the crisp October air the motionless trails of smoke from the chimneys hung above the garden's scarlet leaves like upward pointing pennants and the terra-cotta brickwork glowed with all the mellowness of an autumn field after the harvest was long gone. Knyvett fractionally slowed his mount. Could Sir Richard's mansion ever fail to capture the imagination of even the dullest of mortals? For that was how he considered himself – stolid and boring above most men – and yet each time he saw Sutton Place his heart lifted a little. And that had started even before he had first seen Rose and fallen in love with her. But now the thought of her being in the house, forlorn and depressed, made him hurry on again, his heart thumping in his chest.

He was received in the Great Hall by Lady Weston, Sir Richard being out riding. It struck Henry that she gave him an odd glance and when Rose came down the great stairs and offered him her hand to kiss he was quite certain that the older woman was staring at them strangely.

Anne thought, 'It is so like my dream. The two of them together without Francis. I wish he hadn't visited her – somehow it frightens me.'

But then her usual good sense prevailed. Of all the men on earth Henry Knyvett must surely be one of the least harmful and kindliest natured, quite incapable of betrayal or of wooing a friend's wife . . . The idea was out of the question.

'You'll dine with us, Henry?' she said.

'I would be delighted, Lady Weston. But, with your permission, may I take Rose riding? I thought the air might do her good and . . .'

His words vanished in a gulp and he knew that he was blushing again.

'Yes. Yes, of course.'

But there was hesitancy in her voice and a chill of fear in her blood. Henry picked up the intonation.

'Of course, if you thought the exercise might be too much for her I . . .'

It was not like Anne Weston but she answered, with an edge in the sound that surprised even herself, 'Yes, it probably would tire Rose too greatly. Dr Burton has instructed her to take life quietly.'

Rose said, 'Then Henry can walk with me in the Long Gallery. I promise you I shall sit down if I feel unwell.'

Once out of earshot she said to Knyvett, 'I think my mother-in-law is in the sullens over something. Perhaps she and Sir Richard have fallen out.'

'Possibly it is my arrival. In truth she did not seem pleased to see me. I felt I had caused her annoyance.'

Rose laughed.

'Oh, Henry, how could anybody be annoyed by you? Why you're as amiable a fellow as ever breathed.'

'How dull that makes me sound. I do not wish to be dull, Rose.'

She wanted to say 'You're not' but the words hung on her lips for, in truth, that was how she always thought of him – like a faithful but not over-bright hound. And now he was looking at her as if he were indeed a dog, his eyes anxious and earnest with the need for reassurance. Rose lied.

'You could never be dull, Henry. Why, your kindness makes you sparkle. You are like a diamond in your friendship.'

He suddenly raised her fingers to his lips and kissed them and in that split second Rose knew for certain that he was in love with her, knew why Lady Weston had been uneasy and knew in her heart that if she stayed away from Francis for any length of time it would be all too easy to bask in the great torrent of adoration that was now flowing towards her from this steadfast man, as different from his friend Francis as lead is to quicksilver. Gently she took her hand away.

'I think I might return to Court soon,' she said.

'But are you well enough? What of Dr Burton's instructions?'

'Dr Burton has already strengthened me with his physics. He is just being a little over cautious I think.'

'You – miss Francis?'

She turned to look at him.

'Yes, Henry, I do. I think perhaps one doesn't realize how deeply one loves a person until one is apart from them. Have you ever felt that?'

318

'Yes,' he said and turned to look out of the window at the end of the Gallery.

'I think I behaved foolishly when I was at Court last. I should not dwell in the past. I will have other children.'

'I am certain of it.'

And what he would give to father them; he imagined a jolly little son, stocky like himself, and a daughter as pretty as Rose.

'It was jealousy that caused it, Henry. I was jealous of the Lady.'

He turned round from gazing out at the parkland. 'God's holy life, jealous of her? But compared with you she is ugly.'

Rose laughed.

'Now you are being polite. There is nothing ugly about the Lady. Men admire her I assure you.'

'That is something else. She has a set of followers . . .'

'Of which Francis is one.'

Knyvett thought, 'Now I could sow a seed of doubt that would stay for ever in her mind and in that way I could win her – if not in marriage at least in the bliss of her bed.'

But how could he put down all that was natural in him? His overwhelming honesty rose to the surface and he said, 'Francis likes her, it is true. But you need have no thoughts of his loving her. Why, he would as soon lose his life as lose you.'

'Is that really true?'

'In the name of our Holy Mother, it is.'

'But he was in a fury with me when I left Court and I haven't seen him from that day to this.'

'I saw him before he embarked for France and he was perfectly affable. You have nothing to fear.'

She put her hand out and touched his arm.

'Thank you, Henry,' she said.

'You know that you will always have a friend in me. Remember that, Rose. Whatever happens I will always be here if you should need me.'

She smiled at him.

'And if you take a wife would she be my friend too?'

'Despite my parents' anxiety I have no plans for marriage – unless she looks like you.'

'Flatterer,' she said and ran the length of the Long Gallery, the song that had been silent inside her for months suddenly rising to her lips.

It was three days since Zachary had arrived in Calais, three days during which he had worked hard and diligently. On the morning following the first of Henry Tudor's banquets he had presented himself at the Exchequer – where the French King was in residence – and after a wait of only a few minutes had been shown into a chamber in which Francis was seated at a desk, working on state papers. He had looked up as Zachary had come in and then risen to greet him.

'My dear young friend,' he had said in French, 'I welcome you with pleasure. The pursuit of learning – all kinds of learning – has always fascinated me.'

Zachary had bowed and had been unable to resist a trick of *léger-de-main* which he had taught himself in order to impress the older ladies at Court – apparently of their own volition his crystal scrying glass and the mystic cards had appeared in his hands.

Laughing, Francis had applauded.

'Deep pockets in the cloak, no?' he had said.

Zachary had nodded and smiled.

'But I feel that the rest of your skills are a greater mystery to mankind. Tell me how you came to have these powers.'

Zachary shook his head.

'Majesty, I cannot answer. From the time that I first understood my mother would speak to me of the hidden secrets of life and because I was her son and she had passed on to me her gift of seeing clearly, I knew at once the things she told me. Then my father sent me to a learned man who not only taught me how to read and write and educated me in Latin and Greek but showed me how, as the mighty stars march their way through the heavens, they influence the lives of kings and men.'

'So I could not learn your arts?'

'After many years' study, your Grace, you might well learn the secrets of the firmament but to be able to hold this scrying glass in your hand and to know by its very feel what inevitably must be played out, that I doubt.'

Francis smiled and motioned Zachary to a chair.

'And will you tell me my destiny?'

'Certainly.'

'Even if it be bad?'

'By the rhythms surrounding you I know that nothing bad awaits your Grace. But let me look more deeply.'

And the King of France watched as Zachary's face softened into a dreamy stillness, the crystal glowing against the blackness of his cloak. Eventually he spoke.

'Your Grace, you will be remembered for ever not for your brilliance in war – for the suffering of war is rapidly forgotten – but for what you give the world through your love of the arts. You have already encouraged and invited to France one called Leonardo . . .'

'Da Vinci?'

'Who has gifts beyond the understanding of ordinary men and two mighty painters, known as Raphael and Titian, will fulfil their greatness through your patronage. Because of this, mankind will be for ever in your debt. And by the great laws of reward your own life will always be colourful and exciting and you are, and will be, the lover of many women. In fact one of them is the most beautiful woman in the world – although she never smiles.'

Francis laughed. His exquisite mistress Diane de Poitiers – also destined to be the lover of his son – not only never smiled but made a point of showing no emotion whatsoever.

'To smile or frown, laugh or cry, makes lines appear on the face,' she had said to him once, gazing at the flawless reflection in the mirror before her. 'You, Francis, have altogether too cynical an expression. You are becoming wrinkled and will die young. I intend to stay looking as I do at this moment.'

And she did. There were rumours at the French Court that she practised magic in order to achieve the miracle but all she did was stare at those who said it with her wide blue eyes, giving no hint of what she thought. Somehow Diane de Poitiers had discovered the secret of eternal youth and she kept it, whatever it was, hidden behind a closed and mask-like expression.

Thinking of her words Francis said, 'Will I die young?'

'No, your Grace. Nor will you be extremely old. You will go at the average age for such things.'

'And what of my destiny here in Calais? My Royal Brother Henry wishes me to approve his marriage to Madame la Marquise but something in me hesitates. Will she become Queen, Zachary? Where will it lead?'

For the first time Norfolk's bastard raised his eyes and looked at the French King. His face still bore the same faraway look but something in his manner had sharpened.

'Majesty, I made a vow on the ship as I crossed to Calais that I would not discuss the future of England with you.'

'But I only wish to know about the Lady. If I tell

322

Henry to marry her and take his joy while he can will I be committing a sin in the eyes of God and Church?'

'Your Grace, I will say this much. Whatever you advise our King to do the course of events will be the same. The Marquess will wear the crown of the English Queens and there's an end to it. You must advise what you feel is right in your heart.'

'Then I will tell him to marry her. No man – particularly a King – should be deprived of sons.'

'So be it.'

'But why does she avoid me? I have not seen her since I arrived. Why does she keep to her apartments?'

Zachary's face transformed from that of a mystic and wore instead the look of a naughty schoolboy. He put the scrying glass down on the table.

'Your Grace, I do not need the aid of divining instruments to answer you that. The Lady is quite capable of not appearing at all. She plays games with men – all men. Even mighty Princes. She will greet you when she deems fit.'

Thinking of Diane de Poitiers, Francis sighed.

'Why are women so strange, Zachary?'

'If I knew that, Majesty, then I would be the most powerful magician on earth.'

They laughed together and the Frenchman said, 'How lucky Norfolk is to have a son such as yourself. I have not enjoyed the company of another man so much since . . . I cannot remember when. Will you spend the day here so that we can converse longer? Or are you busy with your own affairs?'

Zachary bowed.

'I would be privileged, your Grace. My natural conceit always relishes speaking with one who appreciates what I do.'

And so they had spent the time discussing every subject, the French King himself throwing logs on the crackling fire that combated the chill late October wind of Calais so that they would not be bothered by the plod of ministering servants. And just as it had been on the previous day it was dusk when Zachary went out into the streets of the fortress and made his way back to the Beauchamp Tower. But this time he did not attend King Henry's banquet but instead stayed up all night studying, by the light of as many candles as he could find, the life chart of Francis I. The long and complicated process was made no easier by the fact that all his learned books, with the exception of one, had been left at home in Greenwich. So it was from this one tattered volume that he had worked until it was broad daylight again and he had finally fallen asleep, long after the clock had struck the hour of noon, his head on the table in front of him, resting amongst the papers that showed that the great constellation of Virgo had been ruling the heavens when the son of an obscure cousin of Louis XII had struggled into the world at Cognac and had, by virtue of his determined personality, become King of France. The life pattern of Francis I was complete. All that was left to do was to copy it out in neat hand.

And this he did when he awoke again at six o'clock, before shaving his face, washing himself and putting on a fine doublet of black embroidered with sparkling silver threads – an unexpected gift from his father, Norfolk, which had been waiting for him on the previous evening with a note begging him to wear it to further state banquets 'if you would show your father love and respect'. Zachary was only too pleased to do so for it was made of choice stuff though the colour he considered very dull.

'And what of the Marquess of Pembroke?' he asked

the servant who was helping him. 'Did she attend upon the King last night?'

'No, Dr Zachary. They say she won't appear at all. That she smokes with fury.'

'Because of the French Queen?'

'Her and the other great ladies of France. None of them would shift to meet her.'

'Yes, I know.'

'Do you think she'll come out of her apartments?'

Zachary's smile beamed at him.

'I don't think she would miss the opportunity for a cage of apes.'

But when he arrived at the banqueting hall he saw that once again the royal cup bearers of both England and France stood side by side behind the two chairs of state – no place had been prepared for the Lady.

'Well?' said his father, apparently appearing from nowhere and muttering right into his ear.

'She will come tonight.'

'You're certain?'

'Absolutely. It is the third evening.'

'So?'

Zachary patted Howard's arm.

'Three is a very important number in magic, Lord Duke my father.'

'And what does the Marquess know of magic?'

Zachary pulled a face and shrugged his shoulders.

'Enough to bewitch a King.'

'Are you saying she is a mistress of Satan?'

His son was suddenly very straight-faced.

'No, I am not. She is a mistress of subtlety and charm and cleverness. That is all.'

'But would you swear that she is not familiar with the black arts?'

In Zachary's mind he was back in the mayhem of his

room in Greenwich, saw again the evil book depicting Anne Boleyn with her head at her feet, envisaged the terror that raged when he tried to destroy it. He had thought then that Anne knew more than she had said, had cut the pentagrams into the floor rather too readily for a novice.

'Well, would you?' the Duke repeated, looking closely into Zachary's face.

'Father, do not press me. I know not and that is the truth.'

Norfolk pursed his lips and nodded apparently satisfied with the reply and further conversation was halted by the call to dine. Zachary found himself seated next to a very pert young woman who gave her name as Rosamund Banastre and informed him that she was a daughter of Lady Banastre.

'And you are the famous astrologer from England, are you not? Do not look surprised. Everyone has heard of you, even us poor bumpkins whose fate is to dwell in this benighted town.'

'You find Calais boring? I would have thought it quite the hub of activity.'

'Aye at times like this it is exciting enough. But can you imagine *living* here. Everybody knows the business of everybody and there is nobody to meet unless there be important visitors from England. I swear by God's holy blood that I am destined for an early grave through sheer despair. Wilt read my future Dr Zachary and see if I am doomed to die a maid?'

And with this she gave him a most unmaidenly glance that for no reason made him feel exceedingly hot. He looked away hastily and found himself the subject of four hostile stares. His father's legitimate children – Lady Mary Howard, soon to be married to the King's bastard, and the Earl of Surrey, only sixteen years old but already a married man – together with their respective partners, were subjecting him to an ice-like scrutiny. In fact his half-brother Surrey's wife Frances, only sixteen herself, went so far as to poke the tip of her tongue out at him. Henry Fitzroy, Duke of Richmond, due to marry Zachary's half-sister before the year was out, contented himself with an unblinking glare.

'Who are those people,' came Rosamund's voice, 'that they dare gape at you so?'

'Acquaintances from Court,' said Zachary and rising to his feet he began smiling and waving and bowing with such wild and exaggerated gestures that the quartette was finally forced to look away.

'But surely that was the King's son the Duke of Richmond?' Rosamund went on, leaning against Zachary's shoulder.

'Aye, aye, we're old friends.'

'It would please me so greatly to know all these people. I envy you Dr Zachary. Are you a married man?'

He turned to study her properly. She was a very pretty girl – round-bosomed and golden-headed – with the look of a bed romper in her eye. Zachary gave her a wink and said, 'Aye, but my wife is in England, is she not?'

'And I am here.'

'Indeed you are,' said Zachary and slipping his hand beneath the shadowy protection of the table cloth he put it round her waist, which was quite pleasing to the touch, and squeezed.

'Ah well,' he thought, 'I have been faithful to Jane for two years – nay nearly three if I count the time before I married her – and it is the destiny of every man alive, lest he be plain beyond measure, to roam abroad sooner or later. Therefore I shall do it with a good grace and a pleasing smile as did my father before me.'

And he raised his goblet to Thomas Howard who was

deep in conversation with his boon companion, the King's brother-in-law, the Duke of Suffolk.

'You drink to your father? 'Tis said openly here that you are the bastard of the Duke of Norfolk.'

'And it is true, madam.'

His eyes were alive with light and for a moment Rosamund Banastre wondered if she had taken on more than she could readily control. Then she thought, 'By God's blood and body, 'tis better than rotting with idleness.'

Their hands had just joined beneath the table when a clarion of trumpets announced the entrance of the masquers. With his fingers entwined Zachary watched with the half interest of one on the first stages of desire, more aware of the pressure of Rosamund's breast teasing against his arm than he was of the dancers. Yet the four young women dressed in crimson and green were pleasing to look at and he was just about to relax totally and let the rest of the evening swim into a daze when one of the eight masked dancers that were following the four maidens caught his attention. Her face may be hidden beneath a lacy gold and red disguise but he knew at once by the turn of her head and delicacy of tread that Anne Boleyn had finally arrived – that her self-imposed retreat was over. With her arm extended and moving in perfect time with the music, she made her way towards the table where the two Kings sat side by side. Nothing of her features or her cloud of hair could be seen beneath the mask which stopped short at her neck, resembling more a fantastic visor than anything else.

A quick look at Henry's face – besotted and smiling – gave everything away. He was party to the plot. But Francis I obviously had no idea what was really happening as the Lady touched him on the shoulder and asked him to dance. He rose most gallantly and at this the other eleven women accompanying her all begged a partner from the top table. As Henry stood up to join in it was a signal for every man in the room. All but the very oldest turned to the woman next to him.

'Mistress Banastre,' said Zachary, 'nothing would give me greater pleasure than to step forth with you though I must confess that I am not as adept a dancer as you might wish.'

'Dr Zachary,' she replied, 'to partner you in any pursuit would be pleasurable.'

And dropping a curtsey she moved off nimbly to the strains of a galliard. Zachary thought that he had never seen so fair a company as, all enmities and intrigues temporarily forgotten, the Courts of the Kings of England and France joined together in the liveliest dance of the times. Henry VIII, however, did not take a partner but weaved amongst the dancers and with much laughter began systematically removing the visors from the masquers – leaving Anne and the French King till last. As her mask came off she curtsied to the ground, humbly raising Francis's hand to her lips. The whole droop of her shoulders and curve of her back suggested the postulant. In that one gesture she put paid to any rumours Francis might have heard that she was naught but an over-bearing strumpet. With her jewel-bound tresses still draping over his hand he raised her to her feet and in that one move she transformed into a regal gold-clad figure with diamonds blazing at her throat. One look at the King of France's face was enough to show that he was completely captivated. Anne raised her head and tilted her eyes as she and Francis laughed together.

'So that is the famous Marquess,' said Rosamund. 'I have never seen her before. That was a very clever idea to go to the French King masked. Do you think she thought of it?'

'Without a doubt,' answered Zachary.

Amidst a great deal of panting and noise the galliard ended and the gentler strains of a pavane started up.

'When their Graces leave then so shall I,' said Zachary, continuing to dance. 'I lead a quiet life – am naught but a Romany lad – and am not used to such wild rollicking.'

'And where will you go to, poor bewildered country fellow?'

'To my bed in the Beauchamp Tower. And what of you?'

'My mother is at home with a quinsy and the house is full of lodging courtiers. I find it crowded. Wouldst brighten my life and read my future?'

'Most gladly,' he said.

He thought, looking at her, that he had never wanted anything quite so much as to go to that round tower room and fall on to the bed with her but was wise enough to know that, though he might tumble into glory with many an eager-mouthed damsel, he would never desert, nor wish to, the sweetly-mannered girl who sat at home in England, expecting his child.

But these ideas were not in his head when there came a gentle rapping at his door and Rosamund's impudent face appeared round the opening.

'I thought I would never get here,' she said. 'The streets are swarming with the homeward bound.'

'Did Thomas Wyatt see you?'

'No. Only Francis Weston – he was coming into the Tower to place dice.'

'He's quite safe. He's more devoted to the gaming board than to women. He'll say naught.'

'Why do you fear Wyatt?'

'He is my wife's brother and has none too great a love for me at the best of times.'

'God's body, you're not the type of man who talks

330

incessantly about his wife, are you? If that be the case I shall go. There is nothing worse.'

'Aye but there is,' said Zachary, throwing his head back in a guffaw.

'And what is that?'

'One who says you remind him of his mother.'

Rosamund clapped her hands with delight and giggled.

'Come, great astrologer,' she said. 'Show me all your magic arts.'

But despite her words it was she who set to, undressing him with skilful fingers and tickling him till he collapsed in a heap of loud and joyful laughter. And then what romping as his tousled head all but vanished between her breasts and they shouted teasing merriments at one another.

In the room below Francis Weston and Sir Griffith Doon paused in their game and looked up.

'What was that?' said Sir Griffith. 'Did you hear a cry?'

Francis winked.

'It's nothing that need concern us. I believe Dr Zachary is consulting the stars on a maiden's behalf.'

Griffith roared.

'God's head, is that what he calls it?'

'It's gone quiet now.'

'I think we should drink to their health.'

And the two men raised their glasses in silent salute while upstairs Zachary and Rosamund ceased their funning and settled into the delightful sensations of ravishment.

As the coldness of grey dawn came at last to the fortress town all was still. Zachary slept curled like a cat round his new mistress; in the King's bed Anne Boleyn lay open-eyed listening to his snoring and wondering if this night she had conceived a child; King Francis smiled in his sleep as he dreamed of Diane de Poitiers; the Duke of Norfolk drank a potion for indigestion. And Francis Weston slumbered deeply and peacefully, the dice still clutched in his hand.

15

It seemed to Rose Weston cuddled next to Francis in a safe warm sleep, that the voice calling in the distance was part of the pleasurable dream she was having. In the dream the baby, which she was now certain was growing inside her, had been born and was toddling with her through the Great Hall at Sutton Place. She had just lifted him up to see the colours of the stained glass windows when Lady Weston shouted to her. At first Rose could not hear the words but they grew louder and louder and she wondered why her mother-in-law was saying, 'Wake up, wake up. Come along, it is most urgent that you get up. Rose, please wake.'

And then the Great Hall faded away and she felt Francis's back against hers, saw the hangings of their bed – one curtain drawn back – and Nan Saville leaning over her, shaking her anxiously by the shoulder. She realized, with a slight sense of disappointment that she was in the Palace of Whitehall and that the baby was still a tiny seed as yet unmoving within her.

Upon Francis's return from Calais – delayed by a whole two weeks as continuing storms in the Channel made it impossible for the Court to attempt the crossing – she had written at once to the Lady saying that she was now well enough to resume service and asking permission to go back. So Rose's first glimpse of the husband from whom she had parted on bad terms two months previously had been as he had ridden through the Gate-House arch of Sutton Place, sent to escort his wife to London. They had met in the Great Hall.

'Well, madam,' Francis had said, bowing to her, 'do I find you in better spirits?'

She had answered, ignoring the question, 'Do you remember once, before we were married, that you told me to be free with you in all things? You said to me, "Let us have a love that is never spoiled by cynicism or artifice." I think those were the exact words you used – do you recall them?'

'Yes.'

He was looking at her as she spoke, thinking that her eyes – abrim with earnestness – were like flowers; that he had forgotten quite how her hair could glow like the fire of evening.

'Then I am asking you now to put aside all dislike of me. I could not help myself. I lost all good cheer when the babe aborted. Francis, love me again as you used to – please.'

Much to his shame Francis's debonair manner was ruined by sudden tears that came gushing down his cheeks without warning.

'Don't, sweetheart, don't,' said Rose, pulling him close to her and burying her face in his doublet. 'I would not upset thee were I to be given all the world.'

Francis rubbed an impatient hand across his eyes.

'What a milksop idiot you must think me. It is just that I care for you so deeply that my feelings are a curse as well as a blessing. Apart from you I am miserable and when you are angry it is even worse. I would do anything then to prove that I no longer love you and yet I cannot. I believe I am tied to you by an invisible thread. I know I am a useless wastrel. But in love for you I am the thriftiest wretch living.'

And he kissed her with such desperation, wet cheek upon wet cheek and the salt of her weeping running into his mouth, that he was suddenly on fire with longing.

'Get to your bedchamber,' he whispered. 'The matter is urgent.'

'Why?' she answered, her naughty grin beginning to spread across her face.

'I've not had a woman these two months past.'

'Nor I a man.'

He looked down at her his tears all gone, as merry as a monkey now.

'Then, you poor lonely woman, let me show you some tricks to make you marvel.'

'Learned in Calais?'

'No. Taught me by a little married trollop.'

'Oh?'

'With hair as red as sunset and eyes like the meadows of Cumberland. Do you know her?'

'Probably,' said Rose and laughing they went to their bed and it was on that afternoon, even without Dr Zachary's elixir, that Francis had once again made her pregnant.

And now she was waking into a cold January morning, the father of her child still asleep beside her and Nan Saville hissing, 'Be quiet, let Francis sleep on. The matter at hand is most secret.'

As soon as her feet were on the floor and before she could even slip an extra robe over her night attire Nan had taken her by the hand and led her out of the room with her finger to her lips indicating that they must move in total silence. Once within the ante-chamber Nan said, 'You must dress at once – a good stuff morning gown.'

'But why? It is still dark. Has morning broken?'

'Aye, it is gone four o'clock.'

'Nan, what is happening? Where are we going?'

Rose's bemused eyes had taken in the fact that not only was Nan already dressed but that her face was freshly painted.

335

'We go to the Marquess.'

'At this hour?'

'Yes. We are to attend her.'

'For what?'

'At her marriage.'

'Her marriage?'

Rose was aghast. As far as she knew there had been no dispensation from Rome and Queen Katharine was still His Grace's legal wife.

'Yes,' repeated Nan tersely.

'But why like this? In such secret! In the dark!'

Nan turned to look Rose squarely in the eye.

'Because the Prince of Wales grows in her belly. The matter can be delayed no longer.'

Rose shook her head incredulously. So it was over. The final blow to the honour of Katharine, daughter of the Queen of Castile, the ultimate achievement for Anne, daughter of a Kentish knight, was to take place at the time when more souls took flight from their earthly shells than at any other span of the twenty-four hours. It would be in blackness that Anne Boleyn would finally reach her goal; the blackness that, to Rose, surrounded the whole extraordinary affair.

Standing there in her nightdress in that bleak January, in that palace of sleepers, she shivered.

'You're cold,' said Nan. 'Come, I'll help you dress.'

But it was not that which had made her tremble. It was the presentiment that anything so sombre, so stealthy, could only end in something equally sinister. Without knowing why Rose made the sign of the cross.

'God protect us,' she said.

Nan gave her a strange look but echoed, 'Amen.'

Twenty minutes later Rose was dressed and the two women, hand-in-hand, had left the apartments allotted to the Westons and were making their way through the main corridors of the recently-built Whitehall Palace towards the west turret. There they climbed a spiral staircase until they came to a room at the top that Rose had not realized even existed. So this strange attic was to be the marriage place of England's new Queen!

A makeshift altar had been set up complete with crucifix and rich plate and Henry Norris, white as a dead man, was lighting the candles as Rose and Nan came through the door. The three of them apart from Thomas Heneage – another of the King's long-serving and trusted gentlemen – were quite alone.

'At what hour were you summoned?' Heneage asked, breaking the unnerving silence in which they had all stood regarding one another.

'The Marquess told me last night to be up and ready by four and to wake Rose Weston and bring her here. What of you?'

'Sir Henry woke me. Until then I knew nothing of it.'

Norris, still with the same deathly expression, said, 'His Grace gave me my instructions after supper yesterday.'

Rose said, 'Does anyone else know of this? Did you bring the altar plate unaided, Sir Henry?'

'Myself and Thomas – nobody helped us. We four are automatically sworn to secrecy. You realize that?'

'But who is to perform the ceremony?'

'Dr Lee – one of the chaplains. Even now a guard will be waking him and sending him here.'

Rose was longing to ask if the Pope had finally found in favour of His Grace, agreed with the contention that the marriage to Queen Katharine had never been legal and issued the papal bulls pronouncing the annulment. But she dared not. One look at the straight faces round her compelled her to silence. She felt that to utter a word would be like blaspheming in church. And the same constraint seemed to have fallen on everybody else for they all four stood in the same uncomfortable quiet again, carefully avoiding each other's gaze, as they awaited the arrival of the royal bride and bridegroom.

A heavy and purposeful tread on the stair announced the presence of the King as effectively as the trumpets which usually preceded him. And the rapid flinging open of the door told the two Gentlemen of the Chamber that he was in an impatient mood, wedding day or no wedding day. He stood for a moment looking them all over and muttering, 'Yes, yes,' under his breath. Then he said in a voice that sounded unnaturally hearty, 'A bitter morning, is it not, for Harry of England to take a bride?'

Nobody answered and the King went on, 'What, all struck dumb?'

Henry Norris gave a choking swallow and it was Thomas Heneage who said, 'The coldness is countered by the warmth of our hearts, your Grace.'

'Well said, Thomas, well said. But where's the Marquess? Did you wait upon her, ladies?'

'No, your Grace,' answered Nan. 'She told me to come directly here with Mistress Weston.'

The King huffed a little but made another determined effort to hide the unease that was obviously gnawing at him.

'Madame Anne is as unpunctual as the rest of her sex,' he said and gave a laugh so false in sound that the quartette of courtiers shifted their feet and shot sidelong looks at each other. It was a relief to hear the rustle of silk and smell the slightly heady scent that always seemed to accompany her and see Anne Boleyn standing in the doorway silently watching them.

Wolsey had once described her as a night crow but this morning she looked like a changeling. The dark clothes she wore made her seem thinner than ever and the bones of her chest and wrists were scantily covered by flesh.

Her eyes were enormous and her hair, brushed as smooth and as shiny as raven's feathers, hung loosely about her face and shoulders. She appeared such a will-o'-the-wisp, such a child, in the flickering and feeble candle light that it was difficult for Rose to imagine that a baby dwelt in that delicate body. In fact it was difficult to imagine Anne Boleyn even being subject to the moon's monthly cycle let alone the intimacy of a man's passion. Particularly that of the King. He towered over her and seemed to loom all round her and the thought of him overpowering Anne's body in the act of lovemaking was revolting to Rose, who had never known anything but the suppleness of Francis in her bed.

But any doubts that anyone had voiced about the King's love for the lady, any thoughts that he was buying her off with a peerage, could be firmly scotched. Despite his present disquiet he looked at her adoringly and said very simply, 'You do me much honour in wedding me.'

In reply Anne curtsied but said nothing. Her face was enigmatic, unreadable. She could have been the most confident or the most frightened bride but no hint showed. It was only the enormously dilated pupils that betrayed her. She had reached her moment of ultimate triumph and was terrified at arriving there.

And it was into this extraordinary scene that the chaplain Dr Lee walked.

'Your Grace, I . . . I . . . Forgive me, your Grace. I have just been aroused from my bed and told to come here,' he stuttered, his eye running over the altar and wondering what he was meant to do at this unholy hour in this ridiculous attic.

'Very good, Dr Lee. I am pleased to tell you that you are about to conduct the ceremony of marriage between the King of England and the Marquess of Pembroke.'

Rose watched Lee's expression as it became frozen

339

with disbelief. She could almost hear him praying, 'Oh God, not me. Not me chosen to act against the Pope. God, can you hear me?'

His elongated face like that of a silly horse, complete with many teeth set in higgledy-piggledy style about his jaw, was growing longer by the second and his mud-coloured eyes were giving a plentiful showing of white. He opened his mouth to speak, thought better of it, closed it again, and ended up by saying, 'Hum, hum' and staring into space. On any other occasion this would have been enough to send Rose into convulsive giggling but the King's flint-like stare stopped everyone in their tracks.

'Did you not hear, Dr Lee?' he said, his voice so gentle that it sent a shiver through the unfortunate chaplain's skinny frame. 'I am asking you to celebrate a nuptial Mass – now. There are four witnesses present, there is an altar and communion plate. What more do you require?'

There was a moment's intense silence then Rowland Lee found his voice.

'Your Grace, forgive me, but I am by the rule of my conscience as well as that of Mother Church forced to ask you this question. Has His Holiness granted you dispensation? Has your marriage to Queen . . . I mean to Katharine your wife been dissolved?'

'Yes,' said Henry.

'But the papers . . .' answered Lee agonizingly.

'Are upon me.'

And Henry tapped his chest as if something were stored in an inner pocket of his doublet.

Dr Lee saw his way out of the dilemma and grabbed it with the determination of a doomed man sensing the chance of reprieve.

'Then in that case, your Grace, I am allowed by the authority of the Holy Roman Church to perform the ceremony.'

Everyone looked at the King but he made no move to produce the papers, merely taking Anne by the hand and leading her forward to the altar.

'Then begin, sir priest, begin,' was all he said.

Dr Lee, mopping his brow surreptitiously, moved into the place of the officiant and there in the darkness of that comfortless attic Anne Boleyn became the wife of Henry VIII. The whole business contrasted so starkly with the richness and colour of their love affair that Rose was reminded of the final spark after an exuberant sheet of flame. It seemed that nobody in the room – not even the priest, bride or groom – could quite comprehend what was actually happening for, the ceremony over, the King rose to his feet and said in a business-like voice, 'We must leave here separately. Too many people on the stairs at once would rouse attention. You are, by your fealty to us, to speak no word of this. Dr Lee you go first, then Her Grace the Queen, then Mistress Weston followed by Mistress Saville. You, Henry and Thomas, clear up here and depart. All of you are to walk in silence.'

They all stared at him owlishly and it took Rose a full minute to realize that 'The Queen' meant Anne Boleyn. With an effort at collecting herself she curtsied and kissed Anne's thin white hand. Beside the gleaming gold wedding ring the deformed finger – not hidden for once, twitched with a life of its own. It fascinated Rose horribly and she was glad when Dr Lee took the hand in order to give his kiss of loyalty.

A few seconds later and it was all done. The chaplain had departed, Anne had followed him and now it was Rose's turn to descend the winding spiral down to the main body of the palace. As she moved into a long corridor lit by flambeaux, which led her away from the west wing, she glimpsed Anne's swiftly-moving figure just disappearing in front of her. And then she heard a sound which made the hairs prickle on her body. From the darkness before her came a laugh. A laugh so deep from the throat that there was nothing in it of purity or humour. It was a cry of malice, of victory, of vengeance. It was a sound not of the mortal world.

Rose was still shivering when she climbed back into bed beside Francis. He, half waking, turned and flung an arm across her, muttered 'You're cold' and holding her against him, went back to sleep. But Rose lay awake until the first reassuring shafts of light fell on her face and the hours of the night stalkers were at an end.

Spring came late to Sutton Place that year and the great horde of daffodils that turned one of the many lawns behind the house into cloth-of-gold were slow to show their delicate faces. At night the wind howled down the Long Gallery and all four fires were needed to contrast the blistering conditions, while the logs in the fireplace in the Great Hall spat and crackled like gunshot. Reflecting the light of the flames as brightly as it had done on the day it was first painted, Katharine of Aragon's emblem – the pomegranate – seemed to draw all eyes of the family, gathered together for the spring hunting, involuntarily towards it.

'I sigh for the Queen,' said Anne Weston. 'What kind of existence can it be at The More? And they say that she is to be moved soon to the manor at Ampthill. Always a little less comfort if you notice.'

'That is not all that is said,' John Rogers answered. 'At Court last week I was told, on the best authority, that His Grace has secretly married the Lady already.'

'What!' exclaimed Lady Weston. 'But that would be bigamy. He is still husband to Her Grace.'

'Not in his eyes,' said Sir Richard drily. 'It is rumoured

that the Marquess's brother Rochford has already been sent to France to inform King Francis of the match.'

Rose felt herself growing wretchedly hot as everyone turned to look at her.

'But Rose you were at Court until a month ago. Did you hear anything of it?'

'Surely it's untrue,' said Margaret. 'Even His Grace would not dare marry without dispensation.'

'Unless the Lady were p-p-pregnant,' answered Walter.

'Let Rose speak,' said Sir Richard over the top of them.

'I know nothing,' she said far too hastily, more than aware of her father-in-law's expressionless eyes appraising her.

'Nothing?' he repeated, smooth as an old panther that had not lost its skill to stalk. 'How strange, sweetheart. Do you think the Lady was hiding anything from you? She can be quite a mistress of deception when she so chooses as all well know.'

Rose looked frantically from face to face. Sir Richard, as usual, was totally unreadable – he could have spoken in good faith; Lady Weston was aghast and anxious to hear anything that Rose could add; Sir John Rogers was cynical, amused – as if he thought Rose knew a great deal more than she was saying; Walter Dennys was his usual honest and perplexed self; Margaret seemed interested but, as always, had the slightly preoccupied air of one constantly planning a grand design in topiary or water garden; while Catherine's eyes were as round and as china blue as they had been when she was a child listening to a tale from Giles the Fool.

'Well?' said Lady Weston impatiently.

'I know nothing,' repeated Rose nervously. 'There are always rumours about the Court. You know that, Sir Richard.'

'Aye, I do. But this one seems to have gained some substance. Perhaps through its very persistence.'

'It is said that she was secretly married to the King in the presence of two of his gentlemen and two of her ladies,' John Rogers put in, the diamond in his ear sparkling as he turned to look at Rose even more squarely.

'But if the marriage was so secret how do people know this?' she countered.

'Perhaps one of them talked,' he said and leaned back in his chair.

'But that's impossible,' came out of her mouth before she had time to think.

Rogers gave a short laugh.

'They were all too trustworthy, were they?'

Rose fought back tears.

'I don't care for your manner, John. That is not what I meant. I meant . . . well, yes in a way I did think that anyone who served the King or the Marquess could be trusted.'

Catherine entered the lists.

'You are clever enough for two, Sir John! I'll warrant if Francis was here he'd have you on the floor for the bully you are. Don't address Rose in that jackanapes tone or by the Mass I'll leave this house and you in it.'

'Catherine, that will be enough,' he snapped in reply.

'Oh will it? I . . .'

'Please do not quarrel at my table,' pleaded Lady Weston as the Rogers launched into a verbal battle of viperish content.

'This is t-t-too bad!' said Walter, his voice deafened by the shouts.

'Catherine, remember where you are,' tried Margaret, more loudly.

344

'By the living Christ, you are the worst shrew in the Kingdom,' bellowed John.

'And you the most prancing, overblown peacock that ever thrust forth a shank. Aye, and a spindle shank at that!' ·

Rose burst into a spectacular fit of weeping and not to be outdone the Westons' favourite hound put back its head and let out a blood-curdling howl.

'God's blood – silence!' thundered Richard in a voice that would have been audible in Guildford. 'You popinjays, you urchins! Do you think I fought at Bosworth before you were even born to have you air your paltry squabbles in my house? Be quiet John Rogers, and you Catherine. Rose, dry your eyes. Now listen to me you bunch of snivellers. It matters not a damn from a tinker whether the Lady is already married or whether she isn't. The fact is that His Grace is determined to have her for wife regardless of the Queen, the Pope and the Devil. And when this is made public the country will divide and families will divide and heads will roll. And one family that will *not* divide is that of Richard Weston, Knight of the Manor of Sutton. We will stand united behind the King and whatever he chooses to do. I trust that my meaning is more than clear? And if there are those in this Hall who do not agree, then let them leave now.'

He stood with his fists on the table looking around him. Nobody moved even to breathe and after a full minute's silence he seemed satisfied.

'Very well. Sir John, Catherine – you will apologize to my wife. Rose, I think you are tired and Margaret will escort you to your bedchamber. And I will get on with my food. An excellent pie, Anne, excellent.'

And he tucked into a vast helping of mutton and pastry accompanied by a dish of shrimps.

The fire in the Great Hall grew low, the hounds lay

sleeping, their heads between their paws, and softly Sir Richard's Fool strummed his lute. Everything was very calm again as those in the mansion prepared for the night. Only Rose tossed uneasily in her bed, missing Francis's presence and feeling the newly-awakened baby moving inside her.

The next day saw the wind dropped and the sunshine and freshness of late March at its most exciting. John Rogers and Walter Dennys rose soon after dawn to ride with their hounds and were amazed to see their father-in-law, as tough as old leather, already in the stables. The far apart eyes regarded them as brightly as ever, only a fainter tinge in the pigment giving away the passing of sixty-seven years. But his back was as straight as it had always been and his frame still lean. For his age – and he must have been one of the oldest men still serving the King actively – he was quite remarkable. The three of them were soon mounted and galloping away in the direction of Windsor accompanied by Sir Richard's huntsmen, the two younger men knowing quite well that Sir Richard would probably be the least tired when they returned to Sutton Place after nightfall.

The women of the house, slightly subdued after the quarrel of the previous night, rose late and took a leisurely breakfast in a small chamber in the Gate-House wing and it was then that Catherine, gazing out of the window at the bright sky and small hurrying clouds, suggested a ride.

'But I dare not,' said Rose. 'Last time it caused me to abort.'

'Then we will walk,' Margaret answered. 'I am most anxious to study the trees. Where shall we go?'

'To the old ruins. Where we first met Giles the Fool. Do you remember, Margaret? All those years ago! Poor

Giles, I miss him when I stay here. Do you remember that day, Mother?'

Lady Weston sat in silence. Catherine was speaking of an incident that she could never forget. The moment when she had first heard the legend of the curse of Sutton. She could see him now striding towards them through the forest, his hair cut as round as a basin, his toothy grin visible from yards.

'Dear Giles,' she said. 'He was a good servant.'

'Joan was telling me that he haunts the Long Gallery. That those who are sensitive can hear him weep. Is it true?'

'Joan is getting old, Catherine – as indeed are your father and I – and she dreams her dreams these days.'

'Then it is her imagination?'

'I have never heard him but then perhaps I am not receptive to such things. But I would like to think that part of Giles remains with Sutton Place – even if it is his tears.'

They all sat silently for a moment thinking of the little man who had meant so much to them in different ways. Then Margaret said, 'Come, we shall be weeping if we think too much. Let us breathe the morning while it is still young.'

So the three young women set out alone except for Jacob and William – two of Sir Richard's lads – who were to walk behind them and see that they came to no harm.

Leaving by the Gate-House they turned west and headed off through the meadowland to where the trees grew more thickly in that part of the forest where Edward the Confessor, a gaunt and desolate King, had ridden in the chase hoping, by the very speed of his mount, that he might forget he was nothing in the eyes of others – neither a proper male nor a lover of men.

'Do you remember Giles's story, Margaret?' Catherine

was speaking. 'How this belonged to King Edward. His hunting lodge is still here, Rose. You can make out the shape of it even now.'

'It was a great tale,' said Margaret. 'It is a pity that there is a notion of the land being accursed. That was wrong of Dr Zachary. He should not have told mother.'

'But surely the architect da Trevizi was reputed to have seen a ghost. Isn't that how it all started? Do you remember him, Margaret? I always thought his eye was at full gape for you.'

Margaret blushed and said, 'His eye was at full gape for any woman – old or young. But I longed for him and there's the truth of it. He held my hand once and I thought I would faint. He had very beautiful fingers, you know.'

Catherine laughed aloud.

'Such talk from a respectable woman whose life is devoted to gardens, children and curing Walter's stammer! Wouldst take a lover, Margaret?'

'Indeed not.' Margaret's cheeks were very red. 'Walter is a very satisfactory husband.'

Catherine pursed her lips and shook her head.

'Who would have thought it! Like the old adage, I suppose. Still waters running deepest. I personally would like to have a lover to see what it is like.'

'But surely Sir John . . . ?'

'Oh, he's a lusty enough fellow. I've no complaints on that score. It's simply that I would like to compare him with another. Don't look so worried, Margaret, there's scant chance. I am constantly with child.'

She patted her belly.

'Not again!' said Rose.

'I think so.'

'God-a-mercy, does the man never cease?'

'No, never. It seems that my trollop's nature combined with his lusts have turned me into a brood mare.'

And Catherine grinned, her eyes as wide and fresh-looking as ever greatly at odds with her self-confessed sensuality.

'Lower your voices,' said Margaret. 'The lads are all ears.'

Catherine and Rose smiled but did as they were asked and after a few minutes more the party came within sight of the overgrown stones that had once been a saint's hunting lodge.

'And there beyond,' said Catherine pointing, 'are the ruins of the manor house. Look at that arched window. I wonder who stood there and gazed out. The house passed through many famous hands before it fell into decay.'

'Why was it left to rot?'

'I don't know. I think there was a scandal. Probably Hugh Despenser and his lover King. The Despensers were the last to live there.'

'My history is poor. Which King was that?'

'Edward II. The one who had a red hot poker up his . . .'

'Catherine, please!' said Margaret. 'You have become so coarse.'

'And you so respectable. It's true about the poker. I was merely giving Rose a history lesson. Was I not, Rose?'

And she burst into fits of laughter. Margaret made her face very straight and said, 'I'm surprised you've never been here, Rose. Why is that?'

'Francis would never bring me. He says he doesn't like it. That the place is haunted.'

Both sisters turned to stare at her.

'Haunted? He's never said that to me.'

'Nor me.'

'He just muttered something about the curse. He believes in it you see.'

Catherine and Margaret looked at one another in surprise.

'You don't?' Rose went on.

'I wouldn't go that far,' Margaret said. 'I believe that some places can be unlucky. But in truth Sutton Place has never brought any of us ill fortune.'

'Father hasn't got his longed-for peerage.'

'But Catherine, you could hardly say that that was due to a curse.'

They were walking forward as they talked and it was then that Rose saw the glint of water in the long grass.

'Is that the old well? The one where the Viking Queen laid the spell?'

'Yes, that's it. It's so overgrown that one could easily fall in. We should ask father to send a scyther down. Be careful.'

But Rose was hurrying forward apparently fascinated by the thought of a watering place so ancient that a kinswoman of the warrior Knut had probably trodden where she now stepped. And there it was, concealed by the long wild grass but still clearly a well. Kneeling down, she began to pull at the undergrowth with her hands and the cold clear water came into view, freshly gurgling up from the earth's heart. Cupping her fingers she bent over to drink and was instantly swept by a bitter chill that engulfed her like a mist. With teeth chattering and body shaking she looked up to see that the day had grown dark. And then looming beside and yet over her, screening out the sun, stood a shape. A shape without form or definition. A grey, swirling nothing that somehow she knew was female. And as she looked at it, her body rigid with fear, it threw itself on the ground beside her, writhing and contorting, and from somewhere in its depths came a terrible cry.

Rose wanted to run, wanted to scream, but she was numb. Her body had ceased to obey her brain's commands. She could only look on, sickened, as a featureless face turned towards hers and she found herself staring into completely hollow eye sockets. As she fainted she heard one coherent word, 'Edward.'

She was only a few yards away from her sisters-in-law but they had turned back to observe a merry red deer that had jumped out into the clearing behind them. They both moved their heads together at the strange gurgling sound that came from the direction of the well.

'Rose!' shouted Catherine and started to run for Francis's wife was lying waist deep in the water, her face submerged. Only the spread of her skirts – which had caught in the opening – stopping her from completely falling in.

'Help,' screamed Margaret. 'Jacob, Will, quickly.'

Jacob, a great ox of a man with a diminutive reasoning power that prevented him from rising any higher than cleaning lad, passed them all as he sprinted forward and picked Rose up bodily. Her head hung backwards over his arm, her headdress drenched and hanging to one side, revealing wet strands of hair clinging round her face. Her eyes were closed and she seemed not to be breathing. He looked helplessly down at her, not sure what he should do.

It was Will, only fifteen years old but bright as gold, who tilted her right over and thumped her back till the water poured out of her lungs and on to the ground. And as she gave a frightening gasp and drew in a deep choking breath she coughed and spluttered as some more water spewed from her mouth.

But Margaret and Catherine had stopped where they

stood, staring not at the girl's struggle back to life but at the sinister red patch that was forming on her skirt between her thighs.

'Dear God, Margaret, she's aborting the babe. She's bleeding.'

'Straighten her up Jacob. Put her on the ground,' Margaret called.

But even as she ran to her sister-in-law she knew that it was too late. The blood was beginning to gush forth, obscenely staining the delicate blue of Rose's dress.

'Oh God's mercy, she'll break her heart,' said Catherine bitterly.

She watched with anguish as the life blood of her brother's child drained like a sacrifice into the earth round the well.

Zachary thought, 'I have never seen a woman look quite so ill. Whatever the Tarot tells me, whatever I see in the crystal, I must choose my words more carefully than I have ever done. I think this girl's sanity lies in the balance.'

Across the table from him sat Rose Weston, her body thin, her face drawn, the cloud of hair that had once shone, dull and lifeless.

'My mother-in-law told me that I must see you, Dr Zachary. She believes that you will be able to help me – if anyone can, that is.'

Even her voice had lost the light laughing sound that had once been one of its attractions.

'Can you tell me all that is wrong, mistress?'

She smiled wryly.

'You sound like Dr Burton but he treats bodies. What do you treat Dr Zachary?'

'To say souls would be fanciful so I shall reply that I treat nothing. If by my gift of clear sight I am able to help those in need then I suppose you could say that I assist the human spirit. Does that answer you?'

'I did not mean to give offence. It is just that I feel I have been to hell.'

Zachary took the scrying glass between his hands.

'Lady Weston told me that your child aborted by the old well known as St Edward's. A haunted place, I fear. Did *you* see anything?'

But already he knew that she had. His body was going as cold as hers had been on that morning two months ago when she had almost lost her life and vibrating from the crystal was a terror so great that Zachary muttered beneath his breath a spell to ward off the evil eye.

'Yes, I saw something,' she was answering. 'And Francis did too, you know. Years ago when he was a child. It was the same thing. A woman – a terrible woman – a face without eyes. Is it she who laid the curse?'

'Yes,' said Zachary shortly. 'I believe you saw what is left of the anguish of a long-dead queen.'

Beneath his touch the scrying glass was pulsating with life.

'Am I now accursed, Dr Zachary? I nearly died of drowning. Will it happen again?'

'No, madam.' Now he picked carefully over what he had to say. 'It is the land itself that is under evil influence.'

'And those who own it?'

'Obviously they must be involved.'

Rose looked at him, her eyes those of a fanatic in an unnaturally white face.

'There is only one other thing I want to know. Will I ever bear a living child?'

He stared at her with a gaze that was already growing dreamy.

'Put out the cards for me, mistress. I will tell you what they say.'

But he was hunching over the crystal, his wild hair drooping forward putting his face into half shadow. The visions that came to him as he sat transfixed were very much what he had expected. Violence, death and menace totally engulfing Francis Weston's future. And the Tarot confirmed his fears – the Tower, the Reaper, the Moon. But still one thing eluded him. He was not sure exactly how Francis was to meet his death.

'You will be with child four more times, Mistress Weston. And each time the child will live and grow to adult life. In two years' time your first son will be born.'

'So Francis will be safe.' She sighed with relief and a very faint imitation of her once captivating smile appeared. 'I can just see him with four children, Dr Zachary. He will cease to be a boy then I think.'

The flash of clairvoyance that had been escaping him suddenly blazed with unpleasant clarity. He saw Francis, a headless corpse, lying in the straw of the scaffold, saw him thrown into a communal grave with faithful Henry Norris. But on what charge? With a great effort he turned his concentration back to Rose who was saying, 'Is it true? You are not just telling me this to please me?'

He managed a smile and said, 'I assure you, you will bear four living children, mistress. Three boys and a girl.'

She got to her feet and he realized with relief that she was going to ask no more. She had heard all she wanted and was weaving for herself the strands of the future.

'Mistress Weston,' he said, also rising, 'may I offer some advice? Forget the horror of what you saw and heartily enjoy this next year. Though you do not think it, it will be a very happy one if you decide to make it so. Do not shut yourself up in Sutton Place. Go to Court, take part in the Lady's coronation. She will not spurn a loyal retainer in her moment of splendour. Be carefree and light-hearted, madam, I beg you. Time is flying for us all.'

'I shall,' she said. 'Now that I know I will safely have children I can be merry again. Francis is to be made a Knight of the Bath on Coronation Eve, you know. He is well-loved of the King and Queen.'

After Rose had gone he sat in silence for a long time, the room growing dark and the only sound coming from Sapphira who had entered and was quietly playing with his herbs and pestle and mortar.

'A savage world, my daughter,' he said eventually.

The three-year-old, without looking at him, answered, 'But still with beauty. Despite the killings there are madrigals.'

As he so often did when his amazing child spoke, Zachary shivered.

16

Francis thought as he stepped aboard the barge that was to row him up the river to the Tower of London that the Thames had been transformed. The waterway used by the Court and the population as their main thoroughfare now looked like a painting of the city of Venice, for the river that was normally a workaday mixture of merchants, travellers and fishermen was as resplendent and crowded as the Grand Canal during a carnival.

At the head of it all, pulling on its moorings like an eager pup, rode the Queen's barge – the arms of Katharine of Aragon which had once decorated it obliterated beneath the freshly painted emblem of Boleyn. And behind it, waiting expectantly for the moment when she would emerge from Greenwich Palace, an escort of barges rested on their oars forming part of a floating retinue that would escort Anne Boleyn into the city for her Coronation. Above each vessel the flag of the owner furled in the early summer breeze and every member of the Court vied with his neighbour in providing elaborate decorations of flowers, bunting and bells, and brightly coloured musicians. In fact the noise was dreadful for each barge had its own set of players all engaged on different tunes. Added to this the constant firing of gun salutes, the tinkling of bells as the swell lifted the ships where they rested mixed discordantly with the shouts of the Court one to the other. The only thing that was quiet was the crowd.

Francis found their silence almost unnerving as he leant over the rail of the barge especially set aside for those who were to receive knighthoods of the Bath on Coronation Eve. From the vast flotilla that lay behind the official procession – and he reckoned with his eye that there must be over two hundred assorted craft – there was hardly a sound except for the cry of a baby or shout of a child. The citizens of London had come to look at the woman who had usurped Katharine's throne but not to cheer her on. It was an uneasy feeling to watch them as they sat in their overcrowded vessels, sullen and gaping. He thought that he had seen crowds at executions in a more cheerful frame of mind.

But for all their hostility nobody could detract from the sparkle of the water, the clearness of the sky or the brightness of the sun. Anne, in her usual extraordinary way, had managed to pick the finest day of the year for her water pageant. And at that moment Francis had no regrets about the enormous bill that he was running up with his tailor Bridges – though there was scant chance of paying it off unless he had an extremely lucky win – because it was good to stand in the sun and know that it was shining on his hair and his new silver doublet, picking up the gleam of the crystals and other brilliants that were embroidered in the fabric, and to catch the eye of a maiden recently arrived at Court and give her a wink that made her look away. And then still to be looking and give her a grin when she glanced back again. It was the stuff of which living was about and Francis was happy to be young and breathing in the strange dank smells of the river, drinking the wine that was passed to him, and feeling the warmth on his neck. He wished that he could ensnare the pleasure for ever and feed from it when he was old and dried out and beyond anything but mumbling.

But a fervent salvo of cannon brought his attention back to the present and the crowd of people gathered outside the palace. Looking carefully he saw that there was a stirring amongst them. Anne Boleyn was about to make one of her carefully timed entrances.

She had chosen cloth of gold for the occasion and her hair was straight and long, the blackness woven with cascading jewels – an old but attractive artifice of hers. Her train, as she walked slowly forward to embark, was carried by four of her ladies one of whom was Rose Weston. Francis had seen her briefly that morning as they had hurried round their shared apartments, anxious to get dressed and go their different ways. A quick kiss on the cheek had been their perfunctory greeting followed by a rapid conversation. But now he thought that his wife looked beautiful in the sunlight, her hair a cloud of red about her small, rather anxious face. It was sad that their second child had come to nothing, been aborted at that doleful place where he had been terrified as a child. One of his greatest desires now was to impregnate her and let the seed be successfully carried. But there was no sign of the longed-for happening as she escorted Anne on to the royal barge, in fact Rose looked thinner than usual. Whereas the Queen by contrast was blooming, the Prince of Wales well established and grown five months in her belly. Only the flowing swathes of gold hid the fact from the world that the monarch's new consort was going brazenly pregnant to her Coronation.

The Queen's barge was slipping its moorings as the musicians aboard it gave the loyal fanfare and, with this signal, the oarsmen of the whole small fleet stood by to row their occupants in progress to the Tower where Anne would rest for the night and the day to follow.

The players on board the barge of the Knights of the Bath struck up with a lively jig and Francis saw the shores of Greenwich begin to move away as he and his companions headed out for mid-river. Looking over his shoulder and accepting more wine from Lord Monteagle's son William, Francis watched his father and mother – she very unsmiling – complete with their two daughters and sons-in-law, their Fool and their musicians, set out behind him in Sir Richard's private barge, transformed into an arbour of fresh flowers by Walter Dennys. He raised his glass to them and called out a greeting to which they responded with waves and shouted messages. Further behind he saw the crafts of the Duke of Suffolk and Anne Boleyn's father, the Earl of Wiltshire. Everybody fit to bear arms was present except for the Duke of Norfolk who had found it suddenly necessary to be abroad at this important time. But what matter? The Court had set forth and the Coronation had officially begun.

The light was just beginning to dim from the afternoon when they reached the Watergate of the Tower to the sound of booming salutes from its cannon. The Lord Mayor's barge, which had led the floating cavalcade all the way, moored at the steps and he and the scarlet-clad city men alighted and stood at the top waiting to join the King. Here at London's heart the river was packed almost solidly with boats and skiffs while up on the bridge the citizens were crammed together in a gawping, curious, noisome huddle.

The Knights of the Bath, jostled just as tightly in their barge, were rowed to the wharf immediately behind the royal vessel and stood waiting as Anne, with the slower gait of a woman half way through her expected time, went once more onto dry land amidst the shrill trumpet fanfare of the state heralds. Francis was overcome with admiration for her. As ever she dominated the scene; even the King – who had left the fortress and stood in attendance – was diminished to second place.

He watched as the royal procession moved solemnly into the fortress and he and his seventeen companions, followed by a few privileged members of the Court, were free to land and make their way in.

Despite the clarity of the evening and the resplendent capers of a fire-spitting dragon, despite the sweet sound of the players – synchronized now that they had lessened somewhat in number – Francis shivered. He had never before set foot in the Tower and he thought it a wretched place, too full of past anguish to be truly merry. And freshly decorated for the royal occasion though it might be it still had an air of chill that not even the roaring log fires in the banqueting hall could dispel.

And thought he slept well enough that night – in a chamber next to those occupied by the other seventeen – it was on the following evening after a banquet given by Henry and Anne in honour of the eighteen Knights elect that he had a nightmare so vivid and frightening that he woke sweating and shouting, reaching for the candle and panicking like a child when he was unable to find it. And its light when he eventually managed to locate it brought him little comfort. For despite all the luxurious hangings and appointments he saw that he was still in the confines of the fortress that, for no logical reason, disturbed him. He even jumped violently and his hand flew in the direction of his sword as the door opened and John Mordaunt appeared saying, 'What's happening? Francis, are you attacked?'

Francis saw in the dim light that Lord Mordaunt's son stood as naked as at the moment of his birth except for his sword belt which had obviously been buckled on in some haste.

'No, no. I'm sorry, John. A pestilent dream, that's all. Did I cry loudly?'

Mordaunt sat on the end of Francis's bed ignoring his lack of clothes.

'You screamed like a girl. I thought some assassin must be in the place.'

Francis shook his head.

'No, only a nightmare. It's the Tower. I don't like it.'

Mordaunt stared at him blankly. He was a huge young man, as tall as the King but without the excess flesh that Henry was now gaining rapidly.

'Really? I don't agree. I'm enjoying myself – very much. I could do with a woman – I like a woman at night, you know – but other than that I find the whole occasion splendid. Have you any wine?'

Francis motioned to the table and Mordaunt crossed to pour himself a glass.

'Do you want some?'

Francis nodded.

'It might make me sleep.'

'I never thought you would be the type for dreams, Weston. I don't like men who dream. I always think they're he-lovers; mince-walking pretties.'

It suddenly occurred to him that Francis was very fair-haired and long-lashed and he put one hand hastily over his genitals in such a protective manner that Francis grinned and said, 'Don't worry, John. I don't find you appealing. I prefer someone less tall.'

He gave Mordaunt a simpering smile which had the other young man on his feet and hurrying rapidly out leaving Francis laughing alone in the stillness. But despite the drink and the sudden merriment he did not sleep again for an hour, his mind too full of the dream of he and Henry Norris falling down and down into an endless black night, eternally together in a terrifying oblivion.

But in the morning he was fast asleep and had to be shaken awake by his servant. A steaming tub had already been brought to his room and he shaved his face while sitting in the scented water before stepping out and dressing carefully in the violet robes of a Knight of the Bath. From the other chambers he could hear his companions calling out to one another in an atmosphere of excitement which, at last, caught him up. For the first time he was able to shake off the gloom of his surroundings and think of the day ahead with pleasure.

At exactly ten minutes to ten o'clock Francis walked with the other Knights to the banqueting hall which was now filling up fast with members of the Court coming to see the investiture, for over eighty men were to be knighted that day. Looking up to the two high chairs of state Francis saw that Rose stood already in position just behind the Queen's, dressed in satin of a slightly paler colour than his robes. Francis smiled at her but she didn't see him, too preoccupied with Anne's imminent arrival. But as he knelt before Henry and was tapped with the ancient sword so that he might arise Sir Francis Weston, Francis felt her looking and was able to catch her eye.

At midday the great procession which had formed up at the gates of the Tower moved off to journey through the City of London to Westminster Hall. Glancing back over his shoulder Francis could just make out Rose over half a mile behind him, riding with thirteen other Court ladies behind the chariots of the old Duchess of Norfolk and the Marchioness of Dorset. He wondered briefly why Anne's uncle of Norfolk had suddenly found it so vital to be abroad, though everybody knew why his unhappy wife refused adamantly to leave Kenninghall Castle to attend. She had openly declared her allegiance to Katharine of Aragon, regardless of the consequences. So the only senior representative of the Howard clan was the old Dowager, the Duke's stepmother, sitting painted like a strumpet and pouter-puffed with pride.

All along the route were pageants of both adults and children acting out scenes to delight the new Queen but yet, despite the colourful displays and the fact that most of the fountains were running with red and white wine, the crowd was as sullen and as silent as it had been two days before when the Court had come up-river. Any doubt about Anne's lack of popularity in the eyes of the common people could be at an end. The dark, thin Queen would never be forgiven for ousting kind Queen Katharine. Francis could not help but wonder how his friend felt riding in her cloth-of-gold litter, a circlet of glowing rubies about her head. Did the cold reception of London's citizens wound her, did she really want to be a good Queen and popular, or was she so filled with triumph that she cared not a fig for the feelings of the English people who were now her subjects? But another quick glance only showed him her smile and the gleam of the black hair which was flowing down over her shoulders. As he turned back Francis saw John Mordaunt eyeing him suspiciously and could not resist giving the stalwart young man a wink.

It was a relief to leave the silent streets behind and arrive at last at Westminster Hall where the cavalcade dismounted and Anne was carried in on her litter. After being offered wine and refreshment she left for Whitehall Palace to join the King for the night.

Exactly two months to the day after the Coronation the Court was disbanded at speed. An epidemic of that dreaded companion of summer, the Sweating Sickness, had broken out as virulently as it had in 1528, five years before.

The King hurried to Guildford secretly to convene a meeting of his council at Sutton Place, the Duke of Norfolk was sent for from Kenninghall, the Duke of Suffolk was already on his way. And it was not only the Sweat that forced the Councillors to meet so far from

London for the Queen was now installed at Greenwich awaiting the birth of the Prince of Wales and His Grace was going to unprecedented lengths to shelter her from anything that could possibly upset or annoy. Council meetings were discreetly labelled 'hunting trips' and though it was true a certain amount of time was spent in the chase, no measure of sporting activity could take from the minds of those gathering at Sir Richard's mansion the disturbing news that George Boleyn had brought with him from Europe only three days before. The Vatican had declared Henry's marriage to Anne null and void. The Prince of Wales was destined for bastardy.

'A complete break,' said Suffolk hurrying his horse on so that he drew level with Richard Weston's. 'It's the only way. The Pope's a foreigner. He must not be allowed to meddle in English affairs. God's blood, if a man can't be allowed to wive with whom he chooses then we're all prisoners of Rome.'

Weston's face was inplacable as he thought, 'Wretched old hypocrite.' His wife had not been two months in her grave when Suffolk had ordered his son to give up his betrothed so that he – Suffolk – might marry her himself.

And the girl was at Sutton Place – only fourteen years old and obviously still a virgin. A sorry sight indeed walking beside the grey-bearded old man that Suffolk had now become, despite the fact that he was considerably younger than Sir Richard.

'Revolting!' Anne Weston had not minced her words. 'I pity that poor girl in the marriage bed. Such sweet flesh, Richard, to be jointed to that sagging creature.'

Sir Richard had looked at her impassively.

'High influence can purchase almost anything, Anne. Even one's son's bride.'

'Then he has bought resentment along with her.'

'Oh indeed – and perhaps even hatred. But he won't

care. Charles has never let anything stand in his way. Not even His Grace.'

For Suffolk's first wife had been the King's sister, Mary Rose, and there had been royal fury when she – the young widow of the elderly King of France – had virtually eloped with the virile and dashing Duke. It had exercised Charles Brandon's disarming manner to the full to talk his way back into Henry's favour. But he had done it and had been a loyal King's man ever since.

Now he wheeled his horse round so that he could look Weston straight in the face.

'What do you think, Richard, eh? Don't give me that blank stare of yours. Do *you* think we should be Popish puppets?'

Sir Richard looked non-committal.

'We certainly can't allow the legitimacy of the Heir to be questioned.'

'Indeed not! A Prince for England at last. It has been worth all Henry's struggle to marry her to see the Queen great with child. *I* should like more children you know.'

Richard shuddered inwardly. That poor girl – her only hope to be a wealthy young widow. Naturally considerable age gaps were not uncommon in the Tudor marriage game but this particular instance was raising eyebrows everywhere, the innocence of the girl making it all the more sad.

To Suffolk Richard said, 'Well, you've certainly picked a bride young enough.'

The Duke looked at him sharply. He knew full well the whispering that was going on behind his back but Weston wore his usual blank expression. Taken at face value the remark seemed innocent.

'Yes, yes,' he said into his beard. Let them think what they liked. He had wanted her ever since she'd been twelve but had resigned himself to merely eyeing her from afar as a father-in-law.

'A Prince for England,' he repeated.

Just for a second there was a spark of feeling in Sir Richard's eye.

'It seems to have occurred to no one,' he said drily, 'that it could be a girl.'

Suffolk gave him a furious glare.

'By the Mass, it had better not be. Henry has staked everything – everything – for a son.'

His horse moved uneasily beneath him.

'And if it is female, the Queen must resign herself to a child a year until the King is satisfied.'

Sir Richard's eyes were inscrutable once more.

'But His Grace is getting no younger, Charles. It takes youth to sire a stable.'

Brandon received this remark badly thinking of the virgin bride shortly to lie beside him and hopefully to carry his seed.

'By Christ, you speak treason, Sir Richard. Men have gone to the Tower for less. It is as well that we are alone. Guard your tongue!'

Weston remained calm. 'You read too much into my words, Lord Duke. I merely hoped, for the happiness of the realm, that the Lady breeds fast and successfully.'

'That is not how it sounded to me.'

'Then forgive me. I would not offend against His Grace.'

Suffolk laughed shortly.

'No, not you of all men. You tread too warily for that. Well, be careful old man. There will be rocks ahead if the Queen bears a daughter. We will all need our diplomatic skills to weather the aftermath.'

'Yes,' said Sir Richard, 'it will not be easy.'

He turned his horse towards Sutton Place the call of

summer birds filling his ears as he headed home in the sweet pink of the evening. Behind him Brandon said more reasonably, 'I envy you your house, Richard. A magnificent place.'

'It is supposedly accursed.'

Suffolk snorted.

'What patent rubbish! Surely you don't believe that?'

Sir Richard said, 'No, of course not.'

Suffolk was about to answer when he remembered the face of his betrothed as she had spoken to him earlier in the day.

'Lord Duke, I don't like this house. How much longer are we staying?'

'A few days. Why?'

'I heard such a weeping in the Long Gallery last night – but there was no one there. Nothing mortal that is. Yet in the darkness something sobbed alone. It frightened me.'

'Silly girl,' he had said. 'Come here.'

And he had perched her on his knee and given her sweets and patted her head. And she had looked bewildered and wet-eyed, all the while her little pink tongue working a goody round in her cheek and the small hands clutching the fur of his collar. He had felt he would burst with the feelings she aroused in him. So much so that he had hardly heard what she was talking about.

But now he remembered. His sweetheart had been frightened by a ghost – or thought she had – and wanted to leave Sutton Place. The only way to calm her eventually had been to give her a trinket to put around her neck. It was as well for the Duke that he had not seen the look on her face as he had turned away. The babyish expression had become hardened by the pleasure of avarice. Fourteen-year-old Frances was going to make him pay for spoiling her life and the joyful path she had hoped to tread as the wife of his son.

It was quite obvious that the lute player was in love with the Queen. His whole manner with her, the open adoration in his expression, the way he trembled when she laid her hand on his arm or gave him a smile that tilted the corners of her eyes, revealed it for all the world to see. He was very handsome – tall and strong with thick curling brown hair and large dark-blue eyes. He rivalled Francis as the best-looking man at Court but did not quite succeed for his features lacked the fineness of good breeding. His were the physical attributes of the peasant class for his father's hands had striven at saw and lathe, though nobody could have guessed from the delicacy of the young man's touch on the lute. In fact it was considered by Anne's set and by most of the Court that he was the finest lutanist that had ever been born.

He had joined them just after the Coronation found, of course, by the Queen herself with her talent for gathering about her all who were witty and gifted. The rest of her clique – Francis Weston, Wyatt, her brother George, Brereton, Francis Bryan, Henry Norris – thought him an upstart but pardoned him for the sake of his musicianship. Mark Smeaton had gained admittance to the Court's most elite faction and, as a result, worshipped the woman who had rescued him from obscurity.

Now she sat trying to find a comfortable position, her huge belly throwing her slight frame totally off balance. As she fidgeted Mark watched her out of the corner of his eye wishing that she carried his child; wondering if he would ever get an opportunity even to kiss her and then explain it away as a joke, a game. He studied the small curving mouth, wanting so much to feel it beneath his own. His voice in the love song he had written specially

368

for her was bright with the desire he could only just conceal.

Francis thought, 'Smeaton's not concentrating. He's playing well enough but his thoughts are elsewhere. He's in love with her of course.'

But then he thought that the King's gaze had been wandering as well recently. He would not have believed it possible but the fact was now quite clear. The old pattern of flirtatious glances, little squeezes of the hand, over-familiar pats, was starting up again just as it had when Katharine held sway and Anne Boleyn had never been heard of. He presumed that it was the natural reaction of any robust male having a wife great with child and temporarily unavailable but nevertheless it seemed odd. That Anne could lose even a fraction of her power was inconceivable to him.

Mark finished his song and the small group listening applauded enthusiastically. The Court was diminished because of the Sweat and in her present condition the Queen had just a few of her favourites to attend her. So only Francis, Rose and William Brereton were there to help her as she got to her feet. All three of them noticed how strained she looked, how little lines round her eyes that had never been visible before showed quite clearly in the bright summer light.

'Are you well, your Grace?'

'Yes, Rose, yes. But anxious to discharge myself of this burden.'

She put her hand to her stomach.

'Not much longer to wait.'

'About two weeks, I think. Now I must ask you all to leave as Dr Zachary has arrived and I wish to consult him privately.'

They bowed their way out, Mark Smeaton raising her hand to his lips as he did so.

'I hope to God he tells her what she wants to hear,' said Brereton.

'But every astrologer in the land predicts a boy,' Smeaton answered.

'You are new to Court, Mark,' Francis said with just the merest hint of an undertone. 'Dr Zachary is not "every astrologer". He is a very clever young man. And what is more he will tell her what he sees.'

'Why hasn't she consulted him before?' Smeaton asked.

'I believe he has been in Calais and at the French Court. He has a great following in France.'

'I should like to see him.'

'You can pick him out by his hair and his colourful garb.'

But for once Zachary was soberly dressed in black and the expression on his face matched his sombre appearance. As he kissed Anne Boleyn's hand his eyes were unsmiling.

'Why have you been avoiding me?' she said directly.

'I have been with the French King, Majesty. And also in Calais.'

'Where you keep a mistress . . .'

'Your Grace is very well informed.'

'. . . who is with child.'

'Yes.'

'And these were your only reasons for not answering my letters?'

'My mistress is near her time, madam. I should have stayed with her longer.'

Anne moved irritably in her chair.

'It's as well for you that you did not. I wrote three times, Zachary Howard. I am not used to being ignored.'

Zachary raised his shoulders.

'No, you have come a long way, your Grace.'

Anne's fine dark brows creased with annoyance.

'Remember to whom you speak, astrologer. I'm not one of your giggling maids-of-honour. Don't try my patience too far.'

'Forgive me, Majesty, how can I help you?'

'God's blood and body, you know how you can help me! Consult your stars and your glass. Am I to have a son? Does a Prince leap in my belly?'

Zachary hesitated.

'Well?'

'No, your Grace,' his voice was a whisper in the quiet room.

Anne stared at him blankly.

'What are you saying?'

'I am saying, Majesty, that you will bear a girl. A girl so mighty that she will become the greatest Queen this country will ever know.'

But Anne was not listening. Her eyes were dilated in a face drawn and haggard.

'You lie! Every other astrologer says a boy. You have not even looked at a chart, studied your crystal. How can you know?'

'I have always known,' he said humbly. 'Forgive me – I hate to bring such bitter news.'

'God damn you,' she said, 'you cannot understand what this means.'

'I do, your Grace, I do. The King has done the impossible. He is losing interest. You desperately need a son to strengthen your position.'

He had gone too far. The Queen stood trembling from head to foot. She seemed to have shrunk into herself, the only large thing about her belly which she now beat with a clenched fist. Down her contorted face poured tears but no sound came from the mouth which was drawn back from her teeth in a wicked snarl.

'Christ help you, Dr Zachary,' she hissed. 'You know

too much. You are condemned to the Tower pending trial. Let your sorcery save you – for nothing else will.'

He bowed his head. He had realized that morning the outcome of the interview for he had done something he rarely allowed, knowing the ill-fortune it could bring. He had drawn the Tarot on his own account. The answer had been plain enough. There was every possibility that he would meet death at the hands of the Queen.

He could have shirked the issue, told her a lie, not kept the appointment. But some inner pride in his own reputation had compelled him to be honest with her. Even as he had spoken he had known the possible consequences but could not help himself.

Now he said, 'As your Grace commands. But know that once I loved you.'

She gave him a look that froze him to the heart.

'Then you may take your love with you to the hell which conceived you.'

Zachary crossed himself.

'No, madam, do not wish me there. My soul is pure as was my mother's. God grant you mercy for your malediction.'

'God grant me a son – that's all I care about.'

Zachary's last glimpse as he was taken away was of her stricken face as she stood with her arms clutched round herself like an abandoned child.

17

'In the Tower?' said Norfolk. 'But on what charge?'

His daughter-in-law, Jane, looked at him dispassionately.

'High treason.'

She had days ago cried herself out and now existed only from hour to hour. She had no smile, not even for her children, and merely stared blankly at the unfamiliar tears running down the weather-hardened cheeks of Thomas Howard.

'But how?' he said. 'What was his fault?'

'He predicted a girl for Her Grace.'

The Duke brushed his furred sleeve across his eyes.

'And that was all?'

'Yes.'

'Then I must go at once to the King and secure his release. The charge is ridiculous.'

'Do you think you will succeed?'

Suddenly very tired, Thomas sat down. He had been in France since just before Anne's Coronation arguing interminably the cause of Henry's divorce amongst the bishops and princes and now he was exhausted. He felt nothing any more about his tiresome niece and her brat which could be a prince, a girl or a bastard for all he cared.

'Christ knows,' he said. 'Sometimes I wish Her Grace six feet below the earth.'

'As she will be.'

'Aye, Zachary's prophecy, God help us. If that one

were mooted publicly he would be dead a hundred times over.'

'As he may yet be. My Lord, go to the King at once. He has no argument with Zachary. He will lend his ear to you.'

'He must,' said Norfolk darkly. 'I have been his liege man, staunch and true and argued his cause with foreigners till I could scream at the sound of French and retch at over-blown scents. He is in my debt I assure you.'

His grandchild Sapphira who had come noiselessly into the room suddenly spoke behind him, making him jump.

'Let me go with you, Thomas.'

Despite all correction she had always insisted on addressing him by his name. He turned to look at her, bending down so that his eyes were level with hers.

'Nay, little maid. His Grace does not wish to see thee.'

The child's blue eyes stared at him solemnly and he saw nothing but the face of his old love who had haunted the meadows of Norfolk and his dreams these past twenty years.

'Lord Duke, I would do as she says,' said Jane quietly.

Thomas stared at her.

'But she is only three, mistress. I cannot go to His Grace with a babe clinging to my hand.'

His daughter-in-law stood up and crossing over to Sapphira put her hand on the fine blonde hair.

'She is not an ordinary child.'

'What do you mean?'

'She has power.'

'A gift like Zachary's? Clear sight?'

'More than that, sir.'

In his mind the Duke heard the sound of the mob crying out in superstitious fear, heard the voice of the judge saying, 'Death by burning', saw his innocent love turn her head away and felt again the rage of his own impotence, for even the Dukes of Norfolk were powerless to save a condemned witch.

'Do you mean . . .' He could not bring himself to say the word.

Jane nodded.

'Zachary says she is greater even than he.'

Norfolk shuddered.

'Then she will need mighty protection.'

Jane looked at him squarely.

'She is your acknowledged grandchild, sir. Let us pray that that is enough. Now I will get her cloak. See, she has made a poppet.'

From behind her back Sapphira brought a doll crudely fashioned from straw. Yet despite the blobs that served for its nose and eyes and the crazy stitchery that suggested a grinning mouth there could be no mistaking its long cloak nor the mass of wildly cut black wool that crowned its straw head. The Duke's eyes bulged as he saw it and for the first time Jane smiled.

''Tis naught but a child's plaything, father-in-law.'

'No, no – you are right. Dress her quickly then. My barge is at its mooring.'

The oars of his liveried rowers were raised as one and the crest of the Duke of Norfolk tugged at the masthead as he stepped aboard his vessel and heard his servant give a spontaneous cry as the breeze caught Sapphira's hair, sending it flying like a sunflower about her head.

'Why, she walks in beauty already, my Lord. But whom does she resemble? 'Tis not you nor your black-locked boy.'

''Tis someone from the past, Will. Someone from another time altogether.'

* * *

In the still dark waters of the Queen's womb the child that was to be her ultimate death warrant stirred and prepared itself for its journey into life. And Anne Boleyn, sitting in her apartments, passing yet another interminable sun-filled day listening to the pleading of Mark Smeaton's lute, moved uncomfortably as a strange sensation rippled over her. And as if there was a mental communication between them the carpenter's son stopped his playing and stretched out his hand to take hers which lay, just for a second, quite small and still in the midst of his.

'Is all well with you?' he whispered.

Momentarily a frightened girl looked back at him and then she withdrew her fingers and it was the Queen of England who answered, 'Play on, Mark. 'Tis naught for which you should concern yourself.'

'. . . and in short, your Grace, you need not fear that you have lost the French King's affection. As I told you on my return it is merely that King Francis has no wish to appear to be taking sides.'

'Mmm!' said Henry absently.

He was in a state bordering on the ecstatic; wild with joy that Anne had finally taken to the glorious bed that had once been part of the ransom for a French Prince and was now prepared especially for the birth. And his strange soul bounding like a schoolboy's with sentiment because his brother-in-law and friend, the Duke of Suffolk, was to marry a child bride.

'So, your Grace, I most humbly hope that your Grace feels that my mission was a successful one.'

Somewhere within his exhilarated brain it occurred to Henry that Norfolk was being unusually obsequious. He looked up sharply and caught Howard sighing – a habit which the Duke had fallen into more and more of late.

'That remains to be seen, Tom,' he said.

Norfolk looked anxious.

'But, your Grace . . .'

'No buts, no buts. Time will prove all.'

'Yes, your Grace. Of course.'

Henry half rose. He was not yet dressed for the wedding which was to take place within the hour. But to his astonishment Norfolk, who should have known better was continuing to speak.

'So if your Grace considers it fit I would like to present my grandchild to you.'

Henry was so surprised that he said, 'What?'

'My granddaughter, your Grace. Poor, unfortunate Zachary's child.'

'What about her?'

'She is here and wishing to be presented.'

And without further ado and not even waiting for the King's permission Norfolk had hastily bowed his way out only to return a minute or two later with a very small and very beautiful child who clutched the Duke's sleeve in one hand and a ramshackle doll in the other. Henry's annoyance died on his lips. The little maid was advancing on him and handing him a single rose but when he looked down at his hands he saw that it was not a rose at all but the straw dolly.

'Well, well, little girl,' he said jovially, 'is this a present for me? Have you made it for me?'

Instead of the hesitant childish speech he expected from such a mite a well-modulated little voice said, 'No, your Grace. I just wanted you to touch him and then to set him free.'

It was a very odd choice of words. In fact the atmosphere in the room suddenly seemed fraught and Henry found difficulty in breathing. He longed to go but Norfolk was looking at him very directly and saying, 'Your Grace,

I have one further favour to ask you. A favour for which I would gladly give my life.'

'What is it?'

He moved irritably in his chair but the feeling of the child standing so close to him that he could literally sense her breathing made him experience a totally unreasonable clutch of fear.

'Well?'

'My son, your Grace . . . my bastard, Zachary. He is in the Tower. I beg his release. His crime is some prediction to Her Grace. Such foolishness.'

Norfolk sighed again deeply.

'What did he predict?'

The Duke looked vague and slightly reminiscent of an old ruffled eagle. In fact he cocked his head to one side rather like a bird as he pondered his reply to his sovereign.

'He said that the Queen might bear a girl,' said Sapphira, in such an adult way that Henry felt completely unnerved. 'But 'tis well known how much your Grace loves *all* children.'

'I beg you to release him, sire.'

Norfolk was on one knee before him, head bent. So it was full into the eyes of the child that the King's ruthless Tudor gaze found itself drawn. And it was then that he felt himself fall down a million stars and swim the depths of every ocean in the world.

'Who are you?' he heard himself saying.

Without speaking at all she answered, 'I am the eternal secret.'

Henry closed his eyes. He could not bear to look for one second more. But when he opened them again all he could see was Norfolk making obeisance before him and a very pretty, quite normal little girl standing quietly beside her grandfather. Abruptly he rose from his chair and crossing to his desk scratched some words on a paper, gave his great flourishing signature and pressed his seal into the wax.

'Here,' he said thrusting it under Norfolk's nose. 'Here is your son's release. Now go. I am to dance at my brother Suffolk's wedding.'

But the Duke needed no hastening. He was already bowing in the doorway with the child bobbing beside him as ordinary and as every day as you please. Without understanding why Henry VIII gave a violent shudder.

The draperies of the French Prince's bed were drawn against the bright September sun, muffling the far distant sound of the musicians playing for the Duke of Suffolk's wedding. But in the room itself nobody spoke, the atmosphere heavy with the press of humanity as the physicians, midwives and ladies of the Court jostled each other in their frantic sole purpose – to deliver the Prince of Wales alive and safely into the world.

Dwarfed by the mighty hangings and gilt carvings Anne Boleyn lay amidst the splendour, her head lolling back on the pillows, her hair sticking damply to her face, her features strained and drawn. Occasionally she licked her parched lips and then Rose Weston would put a silver goblet to Anne's mouth and let her take a few drops of the spring water that lay within. She was stationed on the left hand side of the Queen, up by her pillows, her task to wipe the sweat from the royal brow.

Despite the rigours of labour – for it seemed possible to no one present that such delicate, thin hips could produce a full term babe – she made no sound. The iron will that had brought her the throne would not allow a whimper and an unearthly silence prevailed, interrupted only by a particularly loud blow on a far away crumhorn or a shout of laughter from the revellers, though even these had grown less in the last hour as word had swept the palace that the Queen was advanced in labour and more and more courtiers had left the wedding feast and gone to wait in the ante-room with the King.

In fact now very few guests remained so that Suffolk found himself virtually alone with his fourteen-year-old bride and his young son Henry, Earl of Lincoln. And despite all the drink he had taken to try and lift himself above the knowledge that his body was old and tired and unable to satisfy, he could not help but notice the way that the two of them looked at each other and then at him. Warm glances turned to winter's chill. Was it his imagination that his half Spanish bride – for her mother was one of Queen Katharine's most loyal attendants – whispered to his son, 'There will be time enough for us'?

The Duke experienced a pang of self-pity. He had stolen his son's betrothed and now, like a judgement, his wedding was over-shadowed by the great events in the Queen's apartments. He felt very old indeed as his shaking hand spilled wine upon the tablecloth.

Anne Boleyn mouthed the word 'Water' and obediently Rose passed the chalice only to have it knocked flying as the Queen seemed to go suddenly into a spasm, letting out a great cry as she did so. The longed-for child was near at last.

And so Rose held Anne Boleyn in her arms as she heaved and sweated in the final moments of labour. Then Anne, eyes closed and body exhausted, gave the ultimate effort and the baby, eased by sturdy hands, lay on the bed before them all.

Margaret Lee and Rose Weston stared at each other in horror as the new born infant girl was cut from its mother's cord and handed in silence to the King's chief physician. And outside the King turned his head away so that his uncontrollable tears should not be seen as the physician gave him the news. Was it for this that he had defied Rome, the Pope and perhaps even God Himself?

'Come, your Grace, come,' muttered Dr Butts in his ear. 'The child is one of the strongest I have ever seen. In three months Her Grace could be pregnant again – and next time a Prince. Take consolation in this.'

With a tremendous effort Henry rallied and called for a great celebration throughout the land. The Queen was safely delivered of a Princess who would be named Elizabeth after the King's own mother. There *would* be rejoicing.

It is a strange day at Moresby. The sun so bright on the white sands that it was impossible to see where the sea and sky joined each other. Lying on his side looking out into the shimmer, Francis felt that he was living in a bubble cut off from the rest of time – a stand-still world only inhabited by he and Rose who was just visible in the distance, riding naked on her horse. It had always been their custom to remove their clothes on this particular part of the beach but he had no recollection of her riding like that before and, despite the fact that they had been married nearly five years, he caught himself watching her through half-closed eyes and thinking that he would give her a tumble in the sand when she drew close enough. He had almost forgotten, in fact, just how desirable she was and wondered if there were truth in the adage about familiarity breeding contempt. Recently, though he would have admitted it to no one, he had considered bedding a maid-of-honour – any maid-of-honour – just to bring a little change and colour into his activities. After all, was he not still called the most handsome man in England and probably, he thought wryly, the most faithful! It would be pleasant indeed to pursue another woman just to prove that he was capable of attracting someone other than his wife.

Nonetheless Rose looked very beautiful as she drew nearer, the warm April sun reflecting on her skin and her hair a mass of flying red.

'Come here,' he called, as soon as she was within earshot.

'Why?' she answered back.

'What? So innocent?'

But ignoring him she slipped out of the saddle and ran into the sea throwing some sand at him as she went. He realized at once the meaning of the game and ran after her, enjoying the feel of the still cold spring ocean on his body. Rose was just in front of him swimming strongly into the tide and laughing with the excitement of the love chase.

'You are like a little girl,' he shouted.

For all the calmness of the day the sea was unusually strong; quite high, with heavy breakers rolling into the shore. Rose leapt over one and then paused, daunted, before the sheet of water that the next presented. But she timed her jump well and the sea lifted her up so that she appeared briefly on the crest, an emerald mermaid shrieking to the sun. Francis was too late. The thunderous wall of foam descended on top of him and he was swept beneath the clamorous tide. He regained the surface gasping for breath and dashing the water from his eyes to find that Rose had been placed at his feet by the gurgling currents.

'I'll have thee,' he said and fell down beside her in the shallows. And it was so harmonious to lift her a little, so that she would not be bothered by the undertow, and make her body one with his and love her so that she could never forget him – all the carnal lust and gentleness that combined to make him for ever irreplaceable.

They lay for a long time afterwards in the warmth of the dunes, sleeping a little and chatting of this and that. But one subject that neither of them would mention was the child they both wanted. Dr Zachary had promised Rose a son within two years but that time was almost up and there was still no sign of him. Yet the astrologer's reputation had become legendary since the prediction of Elizabeth's birth. It was said in Court gossip that even the Queen – who had fallen out with him so badly – was considering consulting him again. For since the birth of her daughter eighteen months ago there had been nothing but two miscarriages.

'Surely he can't be wrong,' was the thought that came to Rose again and again. 'He told me four children.'

Aloud she said, 'Francis, do you think the Queen will bear another living child?'

He was wary at once.

'Yes, I expect so,' he said in an off-hand voice.

'I hope for her sake she does. I believe that His Grace is growing tired of her.'

'Rubbish. He will never tire of her. She has always fascinated him.'

'Yes, but all the signs are there, Francis. He is looking at other women.'

Guiltily Francis said, 'That does not mean that he doesn't still love his wife. A man likes diversion occasionally.'

Rose sat up.

'Do you?'

'No, of course not.'

'Hm,' said Rose.

'Anyway the King will never lose interest in Anne while there is a chance of her giving him a son.'

'If he decides that she can only produce dead children she will be gone, mark my words.'

'I don't think so,' said Francis.

It was typical of him Rose thought. Everyone at Court with half an eye to see had noticed the King's growing irritability with the Queen but Anne's set of friends remained in their rose-coloured world, singing songs and acting masques and generally squandering life on trivialities. It seemed as if they would never learn.

'Think what you will,' she answered rather crossly and standing up began to pull her clothes on. It was then that she noticed the chain bearing the two amulets was missing from Francis's neck.

'The magic stones!' she exclaimed. 'Where are they?'

Francis's hand shot to his throat.

'God's mercy, they must have come off in the sea.'

And he was off running to the shallows and searching among the debris of shells and seaweed. Rose continued to dress and then went to help him but though they wandered up and down for an hour there was no sign of the mysterious eye that had once belonged to Zachary's mother and Giles's carbuncle blessed by the wise woman of Salisbury. Francis shook his head disconsolately.

'I would rather have lost a diamond than those.'

'We must get *new* amulets,' said Rose.

'Bought from a beggar at a street corner? A deal of good they'll do! Mine were powerful – they belonged to Giles and Zachary's mother.'

'We will see him when we return to Court. Perhaps he will help us.'

And with that they had to console themselves. But the shadow of the amulets' loss hung over the rest of their stay and made their journey back to Surrey an unusually quiet one. For though they rode side by side their conversation was sporadic and the usual games of horse racing forgotten. Rose thought that she had never seen Francis so pensive in all the years she had known him.

They arrived at Sutton Place in the midst of an April shower.

'Let's race to see who is first out of the rain,' she shouted, spurring her horse and looking back at her husband, desperate to raise his flagging spirits before they went into the house. She saw him begin to come after her and went at full flight towards the Gate-House arch, shooting straight through it towards the Middle Enter – which was already being opened by the Steward – and jumping off her horse and rushing into the Great Hall where she collapsed, breathless and a little faint. Francis, right behind her, caught her as she doubled up and was relieved to see that she was smiling.

'I am only out of breath,' she said. ''Tis naught but a stitch.'

Nonetheless Lady Weston insisted that she go to bed and that Dr Burton should be sent for.

'I have a feeling that Lady Weston the younger is with child,' she told him.

'And why is that, madam?'

'I have an instinct for these things as I am sure you have. Let us put it down to a mother's eye.'

He laughed knowing exactly what she meant. Diagnosis was probably the most difficult problem facing him and his fellows in an age where one relied upon touching and looking as one's only guide. And if one was blessed, as he was, with a retentive memory that stored up symptoms and could identify them, perhaps many years later, one became known as a good doctor, and could earn a fair living.

Rose was lying fast asleep in the bed in which her marriage had been consummated. Looking down at her Burton thought, 'Her mother-in-law is right. There is a certain bloom about her, a bloom I have seen from great ladies like she to the most wretched hedgerow dwellers.

But this time the child must live. Not for the sake of the infant – for born untimely they are naught but a little heap of carrion flesh – but for her sake. She is a good young woman, loving that silly Francis with her whole heart, and deserves something for her to treasure when he goes a-wandering among the Court trollops.'

He woke her very gently so that she would not be afraid.

'Why, Dr Burton,' she said, 'this is all wrong. I am not ill, only tired. We have ridden from Cumberland in three days.'

'Wouldst let me look at thy belly Lady Weston?'

'My belly!'

'Aye.'

'But there is naught amiss. The moon's cycle was upon me five weeks ago. Five weeks . . .'

Her voice turned into a question and she gave a delighted smile.

'Do you think . . . ?'

'Let me see, madam. You are not afraid?'

'Of course not,' and she had stripped off her nightdress like the unabashed country girl she was.

The doctor rinsed his hands in her washing bowl. Though many of his fellow members of the College of Physicians laughed, he believed that dirt on the fingers could do a patient no good. He bent over her till he found what he was looking for. Pressing and prodding her stomach he had no further doubt – in her womb was a little ball not much bigger than a child's marble.

'Yes?' she said. 'Is it there?'

'Aye, my Lady. And bigger than you think. I think the last flux was one of nature's tricks.'

She sat bolt upright and threw her arms over her head as she cheered.

'I am the happiest woman in the world, Dr Burton.'

'Yes, and so it must continue. Listen to me Lady Weston. You have aborted twice and this third time we must take no risks. I want you to remain in bed from now on.'

'But . . .'

'You want this child, do you not?'

'Yes.'

'Then you must do as I say. You must stay lying still for the full time. I don't want you even in the gardens. In this manner we can hope for the child to be carried the proper term.'

'It is the only way?'

'I am afraid it is.'

'Then of course I will do it. But Francis . . .'

'Sir Francis is quite old enough to look after himself,' said Dr Burton firmly.

It was the change in the balance of sound that struck Francis as soon as he entered the royal apartments in Whitehall. From the Queen's rooms came nothing but the sweet, sad notes of a lute – though whether played by Anne herself or by Mark Smeaton he was unable to tell. The busy hum of voices and the bursts of laughter that had filled the corridors a few months ago were silenced and he was uncomfortably reminded of the time, many years ago, when he had first come to Court as a boy and witnessed the same thing. The ever-growing stillness in the chambers of Queen Katharine; the merriment and activity increasing daily in the humbler rooms of Anne Boleyn.

Just for a moment he was uneasy, remembering Rose's words at Moresby and his own reply that Anne would never lose her popularity with the King. But then he shrugged it off. She was probably just taking her ease – perhaps there might even be another child on the way demanding the uttermost care lest she abort again. And this reminded him of Rose, sitting up in bed in their chamber at Sutton Place, red hair tumbling round her shoulders and pulling a great woeful face that she must remain thus for another seven months.

'And you are not to gamble too greatly or drink yourself into a sot,' she had said as they parted.

'How could you think it? Why, thou art the greatest shrew in the world.'

'Nor go rolling in bed with the maids-of-honour.'

'I?'

He had opened his eyes wide feigning great innocence but the wicked thoughts he had been having recently were still there.

'Aye, you. I've never known you to abstain for a month – let alone seven.'

'I shall devote myself to the reading of learned books.'

Rose had groaned.

'God's holy life but thou has a sickening look when lying. Now begone. I'll torture myself no more with such thoughts.'

But then she had smiled up at him in such a delightful way that he had said, 'Rose, how could I take another into my bed when I love you?' And he had really meant it. So they had left each other with fond kisses and promises of daily letters and constant devotion, and he had set out for Court full of good intent and had only winked at three of the farm girls who had called out 'Hey, pretty fellow' as he had passed – and had most certainly not stopped to dawdle with them.

A sudden roar of amusement brought his mind back to the present and for a moment he wondered if he had been mistaken, if the Queen were visiting her brother. For the sound came from Viscount Rochford's apartment and he could hear several male voices and one female.

But listening more carefully he realized that it was not Anne, for this was not a husky voice full of light and shade but a pertly sulky tone like that of a little girl demanding sweetmeats. Full of curiosity he knocked and was shown into an ante-room and then into George Boleyn's receiving room where he stopped in his tracks, mouth agape at what he saw. Sitting on George's knee in the most familiar manner and surrounded by an admiring circle of men including, of all unlikely people, the staid Sir Henry Norris was an exceptionally pretty girl. Long hair the colour of ash leaves surrounded a small pointed cat-like face complete with large green eyes and a feline's secret smile. Furthermore, the cut of her gown revealed a full round bosom and pleasantly curving hips. It was second nature to Francis to bow and catch her eye as he kissed her hand.

'George, you must present me,' he said.

'Of course.' And Rochford stood up, popping the girl onto her feet. 'Madge, may I present Sir Francis Weston, courtier extraordinary, gambler par excellence but, alas, a married man – not that that should bother you! Francis, this is my first cousin Margaret Shelton, new maid-of-honour to the Queen.'

She dropped a well-rehearsed curtsey giving Francis a good glimpse of her breasts and said, 'Sir Francis, I hope that we shall become friends,' accompanied by a look that left him in no doubt as to her meaning. He raised her hand to his lips again allowing his tongue to stray over her knuckles for a second or two.

'If my lady would but honour me,' he said.

'We shall see,' she replied and turned her attention to Sir Henry Norris who was staring at her like a dog at a beef bone.

'God a'mighty,' said Francis to William Brereton, 'how long has she been about?'

'Since February but you will have to fight for your turn if you wish to dally there.'

'Oh?'

'His Grace heads the list. In fact he serves her daily and Anne but weekly if the rumour is to be believed.'

Francis stared.

'I pity Anne if it's true.'

Brereton gave a short laugh.

'Pity her indeed! It was Anne's own father and brother who brought Madge here. The Boleyns and their friends were so out of favour that they had to reinforce their influence. So they replaced one of their clan in the King's bed with another. Very clever.'

'You are sure of this.'

'Unfortunately, yes. A cynical little plot – but effective.'

'So she's the King's whore?'

'She's everybody's,' said Brereton raising his glass to her, happily aware that she could not hear a word he was saying.

'I believe that George is favoured – Lady Rochford is spitting teeth with fury – and he is not alone.'

'Not Norris?' said Francis, doubling with a laugh.

Brereton grinned.

'I shouldn't think so. He's been a widower so long I believe he has forgotten its usage. But anyone who feels so inclined can spend a pleasant afternoon.'

'You?' Francis asked.

Brereton winked.

'Dear God. I can see that I am hopelessly out of date.'

'I'll wager you put that right in a week.'

'How much?'

'Ten crowns.'

'Make it twenty that I do so by tomorrow night.'

'Agreed,' and they shook hands.

'And the proof?'

'Some lace from her pillow.'

They were sniggering like schoolboys when a shift in the focus of attention told them that Henry had come into the room. His new mistress had obviously pleased him well for there was an air about him that Francis had not seen in a long while. His laughter boomed, he slapped backs, he even executed a nimble dance step or two.

'God be praised,' he said looking genially about him, 'what pleasant company this is.'

'You seem in good spirits, your Grace,' said the impudent Madge. 'May we know the secret?'

'It's the fine new mare I have to ride,' he answered with a definite leer in her direction.

'Aye, I've heard of her,' said Madge. 'Young but spirited they say.'

'Holy Mother,' muttered Francis to Brereton. 'They are not trying to conceal a thing. I think I've lost my twenty crowns.'

'Too late to withdraw, Weston. The wager stands.'

'Indeed it does.'

As fate would have it the King retired early that night so Francis was free to spend the rest of the evening as he pleased. There still being a short amount of daylight left he decided to stroll where the Privy Garden joined the Brake – the open tennis court. As he walked – for once alone and quiet – he found himself thinking not of Margaret Shelton nor even of Rose but of the Queen whom he had visited as soon as he had withdrawn from Lord Rochford's assembly. He recalled vividly that wonderful creature of mystery sitting laughing in the tree, the wind whipping her hair, her thrilling voice raised in song – was it really only eight years ago? And now what had he just seen? A woman thin to the point of ugliness with a pinched mouth and frowning forehead. A snapping-eyed shrew worn out with worry, reduced to conniving in corners with her hated sister-in-law, Lady

Rochford. Francis would almost rather she had died in childbed with Elizabeth than come to this. He had never thought that he could feel pity for the woman who had been the most brilliant creature of her time. But now he did. In place of all that vitality desperation had grown in her like a canker.

He could hear the sound of a late tennis game as he approached the court and was not surprised to see Mistress Shelton firmly ensconced with her admirers, watching Henry Norris play Thomas Wyatt. Norris, only too aware that the eyes of the woman who had finally replaced Anne in his heart were fixed upon him was skipping about like a twenty-year-old, while Wyatt, as lackadaisical as ever, was scarcely bothering to play even adopting the pose of yawning between shots.

'Thomas!' shouted Francis over-loudly and was delighted to see the younger man lose what little concentration he had and drop a point so that Norris won the match.

Everyone turned to see who had arrived and by the gleam in Madge's eye Francis guessed that his stunning appearance all in black and sporting a diamond earring – a fashion he had copied from Sir John Rogers – was having the desired effect.

'Well, you rogue,' the poet shouted back, 'where have you been? I haven't clapped eyes on you these two months past.'

'At my estates in the north,' said Francis grandly, 'Kendal and Moresby.'

All the time he was watching Mistress Shelton to see how she responded but it was obvious that she was not interested in his land ownership but only his appearance.

'Young Weston,' said Sir Henry Norris coming forward a trifle possessively, 'I had no chance to speak to you this afternoon. How are things with you? How is your wife?'

For all his experience and maturity it was obvious that this last question had a slight undertone.

'She is with child,' Francis answered, 'and remaining at Sutton Place from now on. I have seen Her Grace and she has given permission for Rose to retire.'

'Rose – that's a pretty name and unusual too.'

'Her real name is Ann, mistress. She changed it for clarity's sake. There are so many Annes in my family.'

'And in mine,' and Madge laughed obviously referring to the Queen who, as Francis had already heard, detested her pretty cousin.

'May I escort you on a short walk before nightfall, mistress? If you have no objection Sir Henry?'

Norris huffed a little but had no excuse for stopping them so Madge gave her cat-like smile and curtseying said, 'How very kind of you Sir Francis. The evenings can be lonely times when Her Grace retires early.'

'And how about you?' said Francis in an undertone, 'do you ever retire early?'

'As Their Graces command.'

'And do you listen to any other commands?'

'I prefer requests,' she answered, coolly putting him in his place.

They were now out of sight of the Brake behind a thick privet hedge so Francis raised her fingers to his lips saying, 'Then I implore, madam. I desired you the moment I saw you.'

She turned to him with the most extraordinary look in her eyes, her tongue licking at her lips and her cheeks a little flushed.

'Well, you saucy fellow, here's a turnabout. I heard that you were an admirer of Her Grace's beauty.'

'And so I am, mistress. But she is naught but a friend to me. With you I could wish for something – more.'

393

She was pinker than ever as she answered, 'Greater suitors than you Sir Francis have set their caps for me.'

It struck him that she not only lusted for every man she met – something he had heard of but never come across – but desired to hurt and humiliate her cousin. A cat with claws indeed. For a moment he was ridden with guilt that he was betraying both Rose and Anne but what the eye could not see the heart would not grieve over. And if somebody had to satisfy him it might as well be a woman he could never love. In that way his marriage could not be harmed nor his loyalty to the Queen. And so, bolstered up by the easily-found comfort of a natural philanderer, he smiled and said, 'Then if I am too lowly I must take my leave, mistress.'

Rather too quickly she answered, 'No, no. I would discuss it further.'

'Perhaps in your chamber then for it grows mighty cold.'

She pressed against him and said, 'You may follow me at a reasonable distance. Remember that I am mistress to His Grace and dare not have scandal spoke of me.'

Thinking of his earlier conversations with Brereton Francis grinned openly but said, 'Your reputation will be cherished. Remember that I too wish this matter secret. I have a wife with child.'

The cat flashed in her eyes.

'Men who speak of wives and children are dull beyond measure. Do not bother to pursue me, Sir Francis.'

And turning round she was gone in a rustle of skirt. He stood wondering for a moment what he should do and then, pausing absent-mindedly to pick a flower, he followed silently and secretly.

She entered the palace by a small hidden side door and made her way up a stone spiral staircase to a corridor at the end of which lay the royal apartments. Francis, concealing himself behind a tapestry, watched her go through a carved opening and vanish. He hurried forward and found himself at the entrance to an ante-room. A serving woman sleeping on the floor before the fire raised her head as he went in but after looking about her for a second or two was still again. The door to Madge's bedroom lay invitingly ahead of him, open an inch or two. Stealthily walking forward he pushed it and it swung noiselessly giving him just enough room to ease through and close it again behind him.

Madge must have undressed at breakneck speed for she lay naked on her bed apparently fast asleep. Francis was immediately suspicious. How anyone could have lost consciousness quite so quickly was beyond his understanding and looking more carefully he saw her peeping at him through lids that were meant to be closed. So that was what she wanted to play! Hoping he fully understood the rules he threw his clothes off and, still as quiet as a mouse, crept on top of her and put his hand over her mouth.

Her eyes flew open in mock astonishment as he sunk his shaft but struggle and pound him as she might nothing could disguise her outright pleasure. She was the lustiest woman he had ever had and a strange delight filled him. Nothing to compare with his love for Rose but yet a darker side of him was ecstatic.

It was only in the morning with the fire of passion burned to ashes that he felt sick with shame and remorse. He was so consumed with his wife and the babe-to-be that he physically choked. He had betrayed them both; he would never touch Margaret Shelton again. But even as he thought it he knew it was untrue. A part of him that had always been lying dormant had been aroused and he would pursue the King's trollop to the ends of the earth if need be just for the pleasure of one more night with her.

18

In his sloping room beneath the stars Zachary Howard sat staring blindly at the view from his window. The Thames flowing at the end of the meadows was at full ebb, the skiffs and barges bobbing along cheerfully, their owners intent on their business. It was July, 1535, and probably very few realized that this day Sir Thomas More was waiting in the Tower for execution and Anne Boleyn was arranging a great masque, ostensibly not to celebrate but a happy coincidence that it should fall upon the same day.

Very slowly – for nowadays it was an experience that he did not enjoy – Zachary took his crystal glass into his hands. At once the weight as he moved it from palm to palm told him that there was sorrow. He smiled a little wryly. Anyone in the Kingdom with intelligence would have known that without a gift of clear sight. On the surface all might be well but scrape beneath and there was decay.

Anne, of course, had made a great effort, had recovered and rallied from the blows of two miscarriages, had forced her mighty will against the onslaught of Margaret Shelton, had had her hair brushed until it gleamed and put lotions and creams on her face so that once again she outshone every woman at Court. Her laughter had never been gayer, her dancing never more fleet of foot, her brilliant manner never more noticeable. It was spoken of in whispers that when More in the Tower had asked after the Queen and been told that she had never fared better – dancing and sporting her days away – he had answered, 'These dances of hers will prove such dances, that she will spurn our heads off like footballs, but it will not be long ere her head will dance the like dance.'

A sinister prophecy from the man who had refused to swear the Act of Succession – that the future rulers of England should all be issue of Anne's body – and the Act of Supremacy – that Henry Tudor was now the Supreme Head of the Church.

The scrying glass was the black of mourning as Zachary hunched over it. And as he looked the odd thing that sometimes happened to him at such moments took place. It was as if he stood there in the future, observing but unobserved, leaning against the damp miserable walls of Kimbolton Castle and watching the last breath of life eke out of Katharine of Aragon who lay on a small, hard-looking bed, only her lips moving in prayer betraying the fact that she still lived. There were several people in the room, one of them a priest, and round the bed knelt the last of her faithful Spanish ladies. And it was on one of these that Zachary found his eyes fixed. For as Katharine let out her last gasp and her dead eyelids sprung open that all might see the glazed sadness of her look, the little dark woman raised the Queen's hand to her lips. She said not a word but in his trance-like state her thoughts were audible to the astrologer.

He heard her think, 'Let there be revenge. Let the Queen herself smite back at the great whore who sits upon the throne. Let there be divine justice. Let my hatred bring it about.'

And then he saw the black spiral that was force, that was power, come whirling into the death chamber and gather itself round the kneeling figure. And then he was back in his own room and just before the crystal finally misted over he saw his father's face quite distinctly and knew that in some mysterious way it was Norfolk who would not only pronounce sentence of death upon Anne but would be instrumental in her downfall.

The distant sound of a drum roll and the shout of a crowd wafted up the river by a trick of the breeze told him that Sir Thomas More was finished, that the most honest man in the realm had died for his convictions. And Zachary knew that Anne, on hearing the news, would hug herself with relief that an implacable enemy had been removed. Unaware that, like a monster, for every adversary that fell six more would grow in his place.

The merging of the great forest of Windsor with that of Sutton was indefinable except to those who knew almost to the first oak tree where the Manor boundaries lay. Francis, who had ridden this way so often and in so many differing moods, was vaguely aware that he was now on his father's land, the place where the Saxon Kings had once hunted with hawk and hound. But with his eyes he noticed nothing for he had never in his twenty-four years felt such desolation of soul as now swept him.

He had for the last seven months been in the grip of the most feverish love affair of his life. And yet to call it love was in some ways an insult to the word. For Madge Shelton possessed him in a way that was not healthy. He was besotted, enflamed, sick with desire. When he was in her bed, in a secret part of the gardens, in a cornfield – anywhere so long as he could have her – he was exultant. When he was apart from her all he could do was plot and scheme as to how soon he could be with her again, what different ways he could please her. It was like an illness the cure for which was detestable. He felt that if Madge was taken away from him he would rather be dead.

And in this terrible world he had created for himself

there was simply no time to think of anything else but his voracious mistress. Rose, his parents, his sisters, even Sutton Place itself, had ceased to exist other than as grudging thoughts that took him away for a few precious minutes from his feverish contemplation of the ravishment of her wicked embrace. He had not even bothered to replace the amulets that had protected him for so long, afraid to face Zachary lest he should know the overriding desire that was slowly destroying him.

So when he was suddenly given a letter just as he was preparing himself to go to her for a snatched hour he was angry at the interruption. But when he had opened it he had felt fit to vomit with self-disgust. It was from his father and dated the 6th day of December.

'Right trusty and well-beloved son, May it please you to be advertised that on this day at one hour past first light your wife, after labouring mightily, did for your pleasure and comfort deliver and bring forth a son. And that both he and his mother are in good health at this time. Trusting that you will be soon once more at Sutton Place.
Your most loving father,
Richard Weston'

And then after reading such tidings he had – as far as he was concerned – plummeted to the depths of degradation for he had gone to Mistress Shelton just as if nothing had happened and heaved and sweated and shouted with joy as if Rose and the sweet suckling babe did not exist.

When he had returned to his apartments he had been ill, bending over the basin and retching with loathing and despair. Then he had wept and held his head in his hands. He was a betrayer, an offender to God, as low as the beasts in the field. But he was powerless. He coveted Margaret more than life itself. He could see no way to save himself from this nightmare of lust and rapture.

And now he was going home. The Queen on hearing his news had granted him a week's leave from duties. The smile she had given as he had told her that he was at last a father had been radiant for was it not rumoured all round the Court, though Anne herself had said nothing, that she was once again pregnant and restoring herself in Henry's affections? And it was true, Francis thought miserably, that Madge had been more available lately. Dear God, what was he coming to that he waited his turn for favours like a pig at a trough?

Sutton Place was visible in the distance as his horse climbed a hill and he paused for a moment on the summit. He had felt many emotions on first glimpsing the manor house but never before had he experienced dread. What had become of him that the normal pleasures of mankind had gone? That the joy he should be feeling on first seeing his newborn son completely eluded him? Heavy with despair, he walked his horse slowly towards home.

As soon as he entered the bedchamber Rose could see that he had changed. He was as beautiful to look at but there were lines about his eyes that she had not noticed before and in the eyes themselves burned a look that she could only think of as frenzy. Even as he bent over the cradle to gaze at the babe – as yet unnamed – there was a distance about him, an indifference that was hardly credible.

'What ails you Francis?' was the first thing she said.

'Why nothing, nothing.'

And the very way in which he said the words told her that it was everything, everything.

'Are you not pleased with him?'

'Of course.'

'It has taken us long enough to get him.'

And something of the inexplicable depression that she had felt since the birth, but which Dr Burton had told her was a normal part of motherhood and she should ignore as best she could, swept over her and set the tears stinging behind her eyes. Francis seemed to make an attempt at rallying.

'He is beautiful, Rose.'

And he bent over to kiss her but instead of caressing her mouth his lips brushed her forehead. With the certainty of someone who had known him since childhood Rose realized there was another woman. She hesitated for a second as to whether she should play the minx but her old country ways got the better of her and she said directly, 'There's no need for pretension, Francis. Nor am I in the mood for falsehoods. You care as much for the child as you do for your hound's whelp – probably less – and as for me, I am naught but a distraction to your thoughts. Thank God I know not her name for by the Mass I would tear her eyes from her head.'

Just a glimmer of the old Francis showed for he gave a fleeting smile and said, 'Still the wild Rose of Cumberland, I see.'

She sat up in bed pulling the counterpane tightly to her chest with an angry fist, the tears of a few moments ago banished.

'Roses have thorns, Francis – remember that. Tell me her name.'

He hesitated on the lovely cold brink of confession. To cleanse himself. To slide into the waters of say-too-much and reveal the shadowy depths of his benighted spirit. And then he remembered his father – the thick thatch of hair, the widely-spaced eyes, the hard look – as he said, 'Never tell aught, Francis. Admittance is a feather bed for the weak. A man carries his own cross to the grave. Think about it.'

And he had. Foolish, empty plaything he might be but Sir Richard's wisdom, both political and human, he had never doubted. So he looked his wife as evenly in the eye as he could and said, 'There is no one Rose. Your imagination is over full. My mind is packed with Court affairs which swing extremely from one hour to the next.'

Again she hesitated. The lie was patent yet the game was obvious. Her lips played with replies but finally she said, 'Ah well! So what shall we name the child?'

'Henry – for the King?'

'Henry.'

The child destined to fight for Mary Tudor at Calais and entertain her half-sister Elizabeth at Sutton Place slept on in his crib.

'And there shall be entertainments like none His Grace has ever seen,' said Anne.

She stood just a trifle defiantly as was her stance these days. The twelve festivities of Christmas were soon to be upon them and this year above all she must prove her resplendence. From everything she had heard – and there were so many glad to whisper in her miserably willing ear – Margaret Shelton was out of esteem and a certain pale young woman of double receding chin, daughter of the house of Seymour and as sweet as a stinging hive, sat with downcast eyes awaiting His Grace's bluff laugh and alighted blue gaze. So she – dark and glowing and pretending the confidence of long ago – must entertain. But in her belly lay the key to it all. She was pregnant and past the immediate fear of abort. Once again Henry had focused the power of his concentration upon her so the cards stood favourably stacked. With the husky laugh of yesteryear Anne ordered fruits and sweetmeats and tinsels set in gold. All would be in bright array to catch her sovereign lord's notice and set his foot dancing in her direction.

* * *

On the eve before Christmas it was so cold that Norfolk almost decided against the river as a means to journey to Zachary's home in Greenwich. He had already visited Kenninghall Castle some days previously to give a fur mantle to his wife and had seen both Surrey and the Duchess of Richmond – his legitimate son and daughter – at Court. So now it was the turn of his bastard. He looked at the many gifts he had assembled for them; a doublet and hose in a bright but passable shade of red for Zachary – would he ever, he wondered, educate his son in the way of sober dress? – a great muff of ermine for Jane, toys, games and fine stuffs for Sapphira and Jasper, to say nothing of the cured hams, the capons, pies and wildfowl. The mound was more than a horse-load and despite the bitter wind and the lowering sky, heavy with unshed snow, he decided that his barge was the only sensible means of travel. The oarsmen were blowing their fingers, their noses blue with cold, as he went aboard and sat in the cabin wrapping his great fur-lined cloak around him and pulling his hat down to cover his ears.

And it was just as he was about to make mooring at Zachary's wharf that he noticed another barge pulling away and thought far more of it than he would have done normally because of the cruelty of the bitter day. Who else would venture out on the eve of Christmas on a Thames that was beginning to freeze in places? To his great surprise he saw an insignia flying from the masthead and recognized it as that of Sir Richard Weston but the figure huddled in the cabin could have been anyone, swathed as it was in a voluminous wrap, the hood obscuring the face of the wearer. Norfolk peered, rubbing the ice-frosted glass of the cabin window with his sleeve and, as if aware of his scrutiny, the muffled figure huddled into itself even more. And then, just for a second, he saw a glimpse of ember red hair stray out from beneath the head covering. So Rose, Lady Weston had risen from her childbed and made the hazardous journey to London in these bleak conditions.

'And not just for a forecast of events,' thought Norfolk and wondered immediately if that very old but very wise dog Sir Richard was up to some new trick at his advanced time of life.

Zachary stood waiting for him before a fire that roared half way up the chimney, sniffing the herb-sweet cooking smells that came from the kitchens and thrusting a poker into the wine that mulled on the hearth.

'So, Lord Duke my father, the year ends,' he said.

'And will all be as prophesied?'

'Aye. The strands of the web are beginning to tighten.'

'And the house of Seymour?'

'Their star rises – as that of Boleyn descends.'

The Duke sipped from the steaming tankard in his hands.

'I shall not be sorry,' he said. 'If I were never to set eyes on a Boleyn again I would not shed a tear, for a more ruthless mob of self-seekers have never been born.'

'They have – and worse. Watch for the Seymours. They will bear you no love.'

Norfolk shook his head.

'That I expect from no one – except perhaps you.'

'That you have. But remember your words to Thomas More, Lord Duke. It is perilous striving with princes.'

'But I will survive?'

'I have told you – by a cat's whisker only.'

There was silence between them for a few minutes, only the distant sound of the children's voices and the small explosions of the summer-dried logs breaking the quietness.

'Zachary,' said Norfolk eventually, 'I want to ask you about the Queen – Katharine. She was ill two weeks ago.

What ails her? My spies are hot tongued with talk of poison.'

His bastard gazed into the fire, the flames reflecting strangely in his amber eyes and casting the broad Howard nose into shadow.

'Of that I cannot say,' he answered, 'but she will only be on this earth another fifteen days and her heart will be rotted black through when it is cut from her body.'

Howard shuddered.

'Then it will be poison?'

Zachary raised his shoulders, his black hair a nimbus lit by fire glow.

'Yes, I think so. To be honest I have not delved too deep. There are certain things that it is wiser not to know.'

But the Duke was already conjecturing.

'But by whose hand? Yet need I ask! That she-devil will be behind it. If men like Fisher and More can perish then what price the woman who stands between her and her stinking ambition.'

His dislike for his niece was now public after a bitter quarrel between them during the previous Christmas season. He remembered the involuntary raising of his hand to smite that clever dark face and how he recollected just in time who she was and where they were and had lowered it again, striding from the room in the most violent rage of his life.

'By Christ, I hate her,' he said to Zachary. 'I shall never forgive her for what she did to you. Never.'

His son sat silent again, thinking how every piece of the intricate pattern of life fitted in one with the other. How every action, however small, caused another to ensue. How the laws of giving and receiving back – whether it be for good or for ill – were clearly charted in humanity's pre-destined allotment so that the cycle of events must ruthlessly be acted out by all the participants.

Aloud he said, 'Yes, I understand.'

'But you do not detest her?'

'It is not my role to do so.'

Norfolk made a small 'Tut' of irritation.

'Sometimes you are too good by half. I like my love, and my hates and my allegiances clear cut.'

Zachary gave him a grin.

'Perhaps I am getting old. But let me reassure you. Tonight I shall perform a little magic, cast a small spell. Dabble in the arts that are not practised by those who are truly good.'

'A love potion I suppose.'

'Then you suppose wrong. On the contrary. I am getting rid of a mistress on behalf of a wife.'

He winked at the Duke but Norfolk was a leap ahead of him. The curl of red hair which betrayed Rose Weston and the obsessive love affair that Francis was having with Madge Shelton made the connection abundantly clear.

'So Rose resorts to magic to get rid of her rival?'

'Indeed. It is very effective I assure you, Lord Duke. Within a day and a night Sir Francis will be cured for ever. When all else fails a few words to a wax dolly . . .'

He did not finish the sentence but burst into his captivating laugh rather relieving Norfolk who did not care for philosophy and other such cant.

'Well the King's tired of Mistress Shelton anyway. He thinks of naught but Jane Seymour who stands waiting to make her entrance with much high talk of virtue and virginity.'

Zachary rolled his eyes.

'As good a mouth-of-meal as any.'

The Duke guffawed.

'Why thou art a cynic. But what will become of Madge?'

Zachary's face clouded momentarily.

'She will end with none of her present lovers. They will all – go.' Something about his look prevented Norfolk from pursuing the subject.

'And Katharine is doomed for sure?'

'I fear so. But she will be revenged, Lord Duke my father. A power will be summoned up, not by her because she is too pious but by one of her household.'

'What do you mean?'

'I don't know. I was not permitted to see. But you unwittingly will have a hand therein.'

'I? How?'

'Sir, I know not. Question me no more for my wife comes and this must be spoken no further. I have experienced the Tower once in my life – I have no desire for it to happen again. You will keep the secret?'

'Of course.'

But it seemed to Thomas Howard that the night outside had grown even colder and he who feared the dark not at all asked to stay beneath Zachary's roof rather than face alone the freezing river and the thought of Katharine of Aragon's death-blackened heart.

Anne Boleyn could never quite pinpoint the moment when she realized that Henry was no longer in love with her. Was it when Elizabeth had been born? Or was it when he had fixed her with his freezing eye and said, 'Thou art the cause of this man's death' at the news of Thomas More's execution? Or was it earlier? Not that it mattered. She had never loved him so the loss of his affection was immaterial. But what was frightening was to realize that without his protection she tottered on a yawning cliff face. The enemies of the Boleyns stood massed behind her uncle of Norfolk, behind Katharine and the Princess Mary, behind anyone who had the courage to speak out against her. She had risen from the gardens of Kent to royal estate too cleverly for many people's liking. Even her cousin Sir Francis Bryan had deliberately picked a quarrel with her brother Rochford so that he might be allied with the opposing faction. It was disquieting to sit, pregnant and a little unwell, and know that only the possible birth of a Prince could keep a spark of interest burning in the King.

Christmas had not been the success that she had hoped. She had been unable to take much active part in the festivities, terrified lest the slightest thing should jerk the child out of her womb, and had been obliged to remain sitting down, watching her husband cavort with every woman he could lay his hands on.

Last year she had had to suffer the humiliation of her sluttish cousin Shelton hastening from bed to bed and grinning from ear to ear and now, as a final insult, with Twelfth Night only four days gone the sickly Seymour girl had arrived from Wolf Hall in Wiltshire as a lady-in-waiting.

'And she waits,' thought Anne. 'God help me to have a son, for the King wears his falsehood like a new feather in his hat.'

She stood up feeling sick suddenly though whether through pregnancy or general unease she was not sure. Crossing to a basin she lent over it but the malaise wore off and pouring some water in she began to dab at her face. Tears were mixing with perspiration and she was glad that she had wiped them off for her door was being thrust open very impudently and instead of her brother or one of her set of friends Sir Richard Southwell, pompous but mouthing with importance, was coming in. He wore a curious expression – solemnity mixed with a scarcely subdued smile.

'Like a pall bearer telling a joke,' she thought.

He went on one knee and kissed her hand.

'Madam, I come from His Grace. There is news from Kimbolton Castle. The Dowager Princess Katharine died there yesterday afternoon.'

She could think nothing except that those who had steadfastly maintained that Katharine was Queen of England and that Anne was nothing but a whore, a concubine, would not longer be able to do so.

'So I am indeed Queen,' she said rather stupidly.

Southwell stared at her.

'Yes, your Grace,' he answered as if she were a backward child.

But then, oh then, the door was filled with Henry's immense bulk and he was smiling and walking towards her with his arms outstretched and picking her up very gently, just as if Jane Seymour did not exist, and saying, 'She's gone. That weeping sore, that blemish. Sweetheart – she's dead. We shall wear yellow for the mourning.'

It was so comforting to feel safe again, to have the reassurance of his warmth protecting her from ill wishers. But just at the back of her brain a small thought nagged.

'If he can say this – can actually rejoice – over the death of a woman devoted to him for twenty years then what might he say about me?'

Even as he swung her carefully off her feet the chill of fear struck.

Henry was in the lists. In plumed armour he loomed astride his mailed horse, a laughing destroyer, for in truth he hadn't felt so much joy in many a month. The old hag of Kimbolton was dead. Anne was pregnant and Jane offered sweet surrender when he had pandered to her virtue long enough. And he had been feasting and dancing ever since the news of Katharine's death had reached him. The Court had just finished Christmas, had just removed the cold cloths from around their throbbing temples, when he had declared a new bout of celebrations. So they had all picked up their feet and gone on the round of pleasure once more. And none louder – or more tasteless, so many thought – than the King himself.

And now it was time to joust, to show the world that at forty-four he was still the strongest and the toughest – and to give Mistress Seymour food for thought about his capabilities in the bedchamber. His opponent had raised his lance to him, the powerful horses, heavy mailed, stood at the ready and with a kick from his sturdy spurred legs they were crashing towards one another. And then nothing – falling, a huge weight upon his chest and oblivion.

'Dear Christ, he's dead,' said Norfolk starting to run. 'The King is dead.'

Somebody pulled the mighty horse from across Henry's still body and yet another bent over to put his ear to the King's chest. But through that mass of armour there was silence.

'He's finished,' said the Marquess of Exeter, his raven face suddenly pinched and grey.

With a sinister familiarity, as if he was speaking lines from a play, Norfolk said, 'I'll tell the Queen,' and was moving off towards the royal apartments before anyone could advise him otherwise. Again there was that feeling of pre-determination, of something immutable, as he pushed past the gentlemen ushers at her door, strode through the Queen's ladies and arrived before her. He gave the most peremptory of bows, looked into the tilting dark eyes of the woman he disliked most in the world and said shortly, 'Madam, the King is dead – killed by accident in the lists.'

Anne's future passed before her in a flash. Elizabeth

too young to ascend the throne; Mary, smarting and vicious with the many insults heaped upon her and with the great Catholic lords of the land rallying to her side, as the new Queen. And for Anne no mercy at the hands of Katharine of Aragon's daughter. Why should there be? Mary had been shown none.

'Oh Christ help me,' was all she said before she fainted.

'How could you be so brutal, sir?' snapped Lady Lee angrily. 'She is in the fourth month of pregnancy.'

Norfolk gave her a dark look. Nothing ever again would make him feel one whit of sympathy for his niece.

'Facts are facts, madam,' he answered curtly and in silence strode from the room. But when he went back to the tilt yard it was to find that Henry was only unconscious and had been carried to his bed with every physician in scurrying distance sent for. And after two hours of his life seeming to hang in the balance he woke up with nothing more than cuts, bruises and a thundering head.

It was Dr Butts himself who took the news to Anne and, though the look of relief on her face amazed him with its intensity, he nonetheless didn't care for the pinched, white lips that smiled their thanks.

'Stay in your bed, your Grace. Just for a day or two. You have had a severe shock.'

'Yes, yes,' she answered a little weakly. 'It has all been very distressing.'

He wondered what she meant by 'all' and if there was any truth in the rumour that Anne had caught the King with Mistress Seymour perched on his knee and had actually watched him run his great hands over the lady-in-waiting's eager breasts before her shout of rage had warned them of her presence.

'May God grant your Grace good health.'

'Thank you, Dr Butts.'

Another drawn smile made him think that the girl he

411

had once attended at Hever for the Sweat had almost vanished now, all that power and vitality quite subdued. Life was a humourless jest when all was played out and yet there was a certain grim justice to it. The mantle of Katharine had fallen like iron on the shoulders of Anne and silly, plain Jane now trod Mistress Boleyn's path.

'Ah well,' said Dr Butts to himself.

But within six days he who, like all his kind, had made himself hard and uncaring gulped in sickness as he was summoned to the Queen's apartments and saw what lay waiting. On a towel, minute but with formed hands like a delicate star fish, was a dead foetus and he needed no careful examination to see that it was a boy. And as if this wasn't enough the room was filled with the most terrible sound for the Queen was howling. Not crying or sobbing or weeping but baying like an animal. It sent his spine into a tremor and it was as much as he could do to part the heavy curtains of her bed and mutter the familiar phrases of comfort that he used to women in such circumstances. But she did not hear him anyway. She was a knot of grief and pain lying like her dead son, knees drawn up to her chin, eyes staring straight in front of her, mouth open and that unearthly sound coming out.

'Give her this, give her this,' said Butts urgently, searching in his chest for the strongest opiate it was safe to administer. 'She must be composed by the time His Grace comes.'

'Does he know yet?'

'Yes he knows,' and he thought of the cry of fury – not of anguish or concern – that had burst from Henry's lips.

'How dare she, how *dare* she, lose my boy?' he had said. 'The woman must be unable to bear sons. I do believe I am always to be plagued thus.'

And he had stormed round the room muttering and cursing beneath his breath.

Eventually the palace had grown calmer. Anne had fallen into a drugged sleep, the little cadaver that was all that was left of the Prince of Wales had been taken away, Henry had got drunk. And when he had consumed enough and when he had been told that Anne was fit to be seen he had stumped along the corridors still wincing from the bruises of his fall, and flung open the door to her bedchamber, his eyes blazing with hatred.

'So he's dead,' he said. 'You lost my boy.'

She knew then, even with her drug-clouded brain working slowly, that everything – her love for Harry Percy, her revenge on Henry and Wolsey, the capricious teasing that had gained her a throne – had been for nothing. It was over. The trap of her own making had finally snapped shut. It was only a question of time now before he got rid of her in some way or other.

There was nothing to lose, so she said in a voice made flat by the sedative, 'It was not my fault.'

He laughed frighteningly.

'Then whose was it? Mine?'

'Yes!'

He looked as if he would like to choke the life from her but he remained standing where he was.

'Explain that.'

'When you fell in the lists my uncle of Norfolk told me that you were dead. It frightened me into aborting.'

'But that was six days ago.'

'You overlook the fact that I also caught you in the arms of the Seymour woman and that had already put me in a state of shock.'

'You should have been like Katharine and not looked for trouble,' he said shifting his weight from one leg to the other.

'Perhaps Katharine didn't love you,' she answered flatly.

His fury erupted.

'I now see that God does not intend me to have any sons by you and I intend to obey His command. You'll have no more boys from me, madam.'

She just stared at him blankly with those great dark eyes of hers and said nothing. She neither wept nor pleaded which would have been more acceptable than her air of resignation and faint disgust.

'Then so be it,' she said.

It was only as he re-entered his own apartments that the King suddenly realized the significance of the date – January 29, 1536. It was the day of Katharine's funeral! Even as Anne had thrust that pathetic, unformed heap of flesh into the world, the leaden coffin may well have been lowering to its resting place. It would seem that the Princess of Aragon had leaned from her grave and had the last and final revenge after all. It was in a grim mood that Henry Tudor went limping off to console himself with the virtuous primrose Jane Seymour.

And it was with a shiver of amazement that the Duke of Norfolk realized that Zachary had been right. The play was drawing to its close. The Queen had aborted with a fright caused by his own rough words and in so doing had lost her final clutch at supremacy.

19

As if at a touch from Oberon's wand Sutton Place which had been brooding before him, dark and oppressive, was suddenly illuminated by the moon. Francis drew breath. He had never seen da Trevizi's masterpiece more beautiful. The tower of the gateway soared into the night sky, each pane of its many windows sparkling with crystalline iridescence; the triumphant shape of the east and west wings rolled back seemingly for ever; the stained glass of the Great Hall glowed with fire from a thousand rainbows; and each amber brick, each fantastic ornamentation, each moulded pediment glittered like quicksilver. The mansion had never been more graceful yet more exciting – transformed by lunar magicianship into a castle for immortals to dwell in, for fairies to claim.

And this thought put Giles into Francis's mind; that pudding-basin haircut, the split-pumpkin grin that had been so much an everyday part of his childhood; the jumps and somersaults done with such anxiety to please. And now he lay, God alone knew where, his bones long since picked clean, his empty eye sockets gazing for ever up at the sky beneath which he had lived so long. He had believed in the unseen people, in the power of the mystic carbuncle blessed by the woman of Salisbury. But its magic was gone into the sea and Francis was protected no longer.

He looked once more at Sutton Place and saw it fall beneath a shadow as the moon flirted amongst the clouds. And in that extraordinary light he had the illusion that the house was partly ruined – lonely and sad and decaying.

415

And he who had never worried too greatly about what lay ahead felt racked with an unfamiliar concern for his father's mansion and for the people, yet unborn, who were destined to live there. Of course it was just the gloaming that made him think he saw two young girls run through the Gate-House arch and deluded him into hearing them laugh and call to each other.

'Melior Mary, wait for me.'

'Then hurry, Sibella. We must find Brother Hyacinth.'

The voices were echoing, faint. He rubbed his eyes and naturally the girls were not really there but his horse moved restlessly as if he, too, had sensed something. Francis spurred him forward. It was nearly midnight and as it was the whole household would be abed with only the sleepy lads who kept night watch to let him in.

And so it was that he walked through the great slumbering house with no companion except the lighted taper in his hand and, on some strange impulse, crossed the length of the Long Gallery and stood gazing out of the windows at the far end before he turned back towards his bed-chamber. And it was then that he heard the crying and knew that it was Giles. And though he had loved him in life he was afraid of him in death and stood transfixed, every hair on his scalp rising.

'Why do you weep?' he said out loud. 'What is wrong?'

There came a sob so sad in reply that Francis could only feel a frightening sense of impending disaster.

'Dear Christ,' he said, 'I am afraid. Giles go away. In the name of our Holy Mother go.'

The crying ceased so abruptly that Francis was shocked by the stillness and then he felt a presence beside him and knew that the Fool was trying to comfort him. To his shame he ran and did not look back.

And that was how he arrived in the bedroom of the wife he had not seen for four months and to whom he had been wretchedly unfaithful – dripping with the sweat of panic and gasping for breath. And he had wanted to make such a sweet impression, to redeem himself in his own eyes as much as hers.

She woke up very gently and said, 'Who's there?'

Realizing that she was not afraid he said in the darkness, 'It is Francis, sweetheart. I have come straight here from Greenwich. Her Grace gave me leave on the sudden.'

Still not fully awake she answered, 'But that was kind and thoughtful. Is it really you?'

He laughed, the old easy feeling there had always been between them returning with such joyful simplicity.

'Nay, 'tis your lover, Mistress Rose. Now let me in thy bed for I believe Giles is walking tonight and I am cold with fright.'

In the flame of the candle she had lit he saw her eyes regarding him seriously.

'He has been weeping a great deal of late.'

'You have heard him?'

'Aye, in the Long Gallery. For some reason his spirit is not quiet.'

'Enough of it,' he said. 'I have come to see thee and my son and to tell thee of my love and fill your belly with another child. Will you have me?'

She laughed with some secret amusement.

'Art cured of all thy troubles Francis?'

'What troubles?' he said innocently.

She gave him a mocking look and said pointedly, 'I am glad that you have come back to me again.'

Ignoring the underlying meaning Francis got in next to her, his mind going back to a conversation he had had only that morning and the almost identical phrase that the Queen had used to him – 'It is time you went back to Rose again.'

They had been standing in her apartments, neither of them attending the St George's Day investiture at Windsor at which, markedly, her brother Rochford had been passed over as Knight of the Garter and in his place Nicholas Carew – a firm friend of the Seymour faction – was to be elected. The snub to the house of Boleyn had been obvious and Anne had stood moodily with her back turned, gazing out of a window, as Francis had come in. She had glanced over her shoulder to see who had entered but had returned to her listless contemplation of the gardens and the river.

'Well?' was all she had said.

Francis had waited silently for a minute, looking at the droop of her shoulders and remembering that mad March morning so many years ago when she had picked up her skirts and run and run, her hair spinning out like a velvet web, her joyous laugh ringing over the daffodil fields. Now Anne of the million secret smiles had no light-heartedness left for him or anyone else; all merriment spent.

'Your Grace,' he said, 'I came to see how you fare today.'

She had turned to look at him then, her face tight with some barely controlled passion.

'Only as well as any deserted wife,' she said. 'The cuckold's horns are on my brow. Do you see them, Francis? I wonder how they sit on Rose.'

He had stared in astonishment and repeated, 'Rose?'

'Aye. Mince not your words with me, Sir Francis. You sported your lust for the great whore Shelton like a sleeve marker. Thought you then of your wife, cared you a sweat drop from a beggar for her? Mankind is a lowly thing indeed when all its old loyalties go under heel at an aching between the thighs.'

'But I . . .'

'Give me no defences. Everything went for her; your love for your wife, your allegiance to me. Damn you – you are as base as the rest of your sex.'

'But I do love you,' he had answered and down the mill of destiny a pebble had begun its unremitting descent. 'More than anyone in this house.'

Her hand lashed out like a whip and caught him a smarting blow on the cheek.

'What do you mean? More than Rose?'

'No, no.' He was wretched with his sudden lack of words. 'I love Rose – the Shelton affair is over. I meant as my Queen I love you more than anyone else. Oh God help me. I cannot speak today.'

Her glint-eyed stare softened a little but she said nothing.

'Please try to understand,' he went on miserably. 'Madge is no longer my mistress. It ended overnight. I looked at her and suddenly she seemed so revolting that I could hardly force myself to speak. It was as if something that had possessed me was gone.'

Briefly she smiled. 'Perhaps it did,' she said.

'Anyway Sir Henry Norris has her now.'

'Aye, they will be married soon.'

She had turned back to the window again, her anger run out.

'I think he loved me once, you know.'

Francis remembering the strange attacks of weeping and paleness that had at one time beset the King's Principal Gentleman said, 'I think he still does. I don't think he could ever stop. I do believe he still comes to your chamber just to get a glimpse of you.'

Anne laughed though something inside her bruised soul stirred with an old thrill of vanity.

'Well, whether he does or does not he will shortly have a young wife dragging him atween the sheets.'

'Forgive me, your Grace, but I pray that God will grant him strength.'

She pretended not to understand but she laughed once more and just for a moment the old Anne was back, filling the room with her fire and vitality.

'On that note of married harmony I grant you immediate leave, Sir Francis. And it is my wish and command that you return on the instant to your home and your wife. It is time you went back to Rose again.'

He bowed.

'But you must return for the May Day tournament. I wish to see the friends of Boleyn well represented.'

He raised her hand to his lips.

'Be assured of my eternal devotion,' he had said.

And now the sun had run his course and by the light of his sister moon Francis and Rose were making love, enjoying the feel of skin upon skin, hardness and softness, the ever entrancing sensation of shared culmination. All was restored, Madge Shelton banished for ever as had been her waxen likeness.

The days passed contentedly and idly, Sir Richard gazing from his window on the sight of Francis and Rose – heads gleaming like gold and autumn – walking amongst the daffodils, the baby hoisted high on Francis's shoulder staring with ever learning eyes at the shapes and colours about him. There was nothing to mar that week. It stayed like a brilliant in their memories, every facet examined with joy, never dulling or growing tiresome in the continued looking. And when at last the time came for Francis to leave Sutton Place and return to the inevitable conclusion of all that had gone before, the final severance, none of them knew.

The horse pawing at the cobbles of the quadrangle, the turn to wave in the Gate-House arch, the running to the Long Gallery to watch from the windows, the flourish of his hat in the distance and the moving of the baby's arm up and down in silly, sweet imitation of the father's salute – all were done with no more than the usual sadness of departure. And after he had gone from view Rose smiled at her son and said, 'He will be back soon and then he will remark how you have grown,' and the milky mouth smiled back as the eyes closed in unconcerned sleep.

It was the first of May and in every village in England that ancient symbol of fertility – the maypole bedecked with ribbons – had been hoisted at dawn and the festivities and processions were already forming up. It was Beltaine – the first hours of the Celtic summer – one of the most magic days of the year. Maidens were out washing their faces in the dew, the mystic order of Druids were donning their white robes and Zachary had returned to Norfolk to pick the wild flowers and herbs of his childhood wanderings and watch the children of the village which had burned his mother whirl through the intricacies of the ritual dance. There was even a hobby horse catching the young women and dragging them under his skirts in a symbolic gesture as pagan and primitive as any witchery.

At Greenwich the sun gleamed on the armour of the challengers who waited ready to tilt for the King's pleasure picking out the emblazoning of their shields and devices. Sir Henry Norris sitting astride his heavily protected mount, his visor pushed back, watched the stands as Henry and Anne made their entrance amidst a clarion from the royal trumpets and thought that despite the really extraordinary atmosphere at Court during the last week there was no visible sign of bad feeling between them, for they smiled at one another as they took their seats. He was too far away to see that the King's lips curled back from his teeth in something more like a snarl and that Anne's response was the quick, nervous grimace of a child that fears it may have caused offence.

Sir Henry, who had loved Anne for so long and had only now become betrothed to Madge Shelton in the strange hope that it might please the Queen if her amorous cousin was settled as a wife, mentally shook his head. He knew there was something badly wrong but could not put into words, let alone coherent thought, what it might be. First of all there had been the odd conversation that he had shared with Anne a few days before. Laughing and flirtatious, she had asked why he did not marry sooner and when he had told her there was no hurry she had made the tantalizing remark that perhaps he was waiting for her, hoping that the King might meet with an accident. He had stared aghast. His little love of Hever, his *idée fixe*, must have taken leave of her wits for high treason was babbling out of her mouth.

'No, no,' he said wildly. 'I would not dare look so high. Please, your Grace.'

'Francis Weston thinks otherwise,' she said still in the same teasing manner. 'He says you come to my apartments just to get a glimpse of me.'

The fact that it was true had made him gulp with nerves.

'Please don't speak like this. It's dangerous,' he had said.

She had given him a stony stare.

'So you don't love me?'

'I didn't say that. I just implore you to watch your speech. Master Cromwell has his spies abounding. It would not do either of us any good if word of this should be repeated.'

She had seemed to calm down then.

'Yes, you're right. I am being foolish. My tongue runs away with me when I am alone too much. But really I am what is called honourable.' She laughed humourlessly. 'So if you ever hear rumours to the contrary you can deny them with impunity.'

'You know I would,' he had said hotly. 'I would die for you if need be.'

Again that humourless laugh.

'Let us hope that will not be necessary.'

It had all been very disturbing and the King's manner had not helped Harry Norris's growing sense of alarm. He had never known Henry so quiet, so restrained and so consistently preoccupied. Norris, who had been beside his royal master through so many differing situations and had seen the entire range of his moods, had not come across this one before. There was something almost sinister about the King's stillness.

And the third thing – though of no importance at all – was that Mark Smeaton had gone missing the night before and when they had looked for him everything, including his lute, had been found lying casually around as if he were due back at any moment. Norris supposed that the musician had had some secret assignation and would return in the morning but looking up into the stands he could see no sign of him. Young Weston, however, was back from his leave and looking well pleased with life. Seeing Harry gazing over he gave a cheerful wave and grin and Norris smiled back before lowering his visor and walking his horse to where his squire stood ready with his lance. The tournament was about to begin and his opponent, Lord Rochford, was already in his place.

Norris never knew why he should glance up at the Queen as he crossed beneath the stand. Perhaps it was the habit of a lifetime – to steal a look at the object of his love – a habit that his betrothal to Mistress Shelton had changed not at all. But he did so now and through the slit of his visor he saw that she was looking at him and was smiling and was dropping her handkerchief for him to wear as his favour. And then he saw the expression on the King's face – goat-like and leering and sharp with cruelty and looking at him – Norris – with something bordering on hatred. The kerchief was on the point of his lance before he realized that it was this old and traditional gesture which had infuriated Henry Tudor.

The joust went splendidly, Norris unseating Rochford with no ill effects. And after them came other competitors who crashed at each other with sparkling lances and ringing swords. The King seemed quite restored in spirits and laughed and clapped his hands affably enough but at the end he stood up abruptly, simply said one word – 'Farewell' – to Anne and mounted his horse. The Gentlemen of his household also took to the saddle as the cavalcade prepared to move off towards the Palace of Whitehall.

Riding near the back Francis could not help but observe the King draw Henry Norris to one side and the two horses stop beneath a tree. As he passed he gave them a casual glance and saw to his amazement that Norris had gone the white of ash. In fact he looked as if he might vomit. The King leant forward speaking in a low voice, his hand holding Harry's elbow, his eyes like agates. Though unable to hear a word Francis felt his stomach lurch with unease. There was something about the attitude of the two men, the way their heads were held, the rigidity of their backs, that showed that this was no ordinary disagreement between the sovereign and one of his household. At the risk of incurring royal displeasure he craned his neck for another look and to his amazement saw Norris was now surrounded by a group of men – just as if he were being arrested – and Henry was galloping off, spurring his horse with vicious satisfaction as he passed his startled followers bellowing, 'Come gentlemen, let us make haste to London.'

In the woods of Norfolk Zachary picked up the bags of herbs and flowers that he had collected and quite suddenly slung them over his saddle. The glory of the afternoon was just beginning to fade and he knew that at Greenwich the light, too, was starting to dim on the life of Anne Boleyn. If he rode through the night he could reach the palace by morning and play his part in the final savage episode.

Francis stared at William Brereton in horror.

'I can't believe you,' he said.

'Keep your voice down, for the love of Christ. I tell you it's true. Norris was taken to the Tower straight from the tilt and Smeaton is already there.'

They stood in a gallery at Whitehall having both excused themselves briefly from the May Day Banquet to visit the jakes.

'Your informant must be wrong.'

'I think not. He has excellent connections. Anyway if not there where are they? Smeaton's been gone two nights and you must have seen Norris go off under escort.'

'Yes, I did. But what is the charge?'

'Nobody seems sure but that it is something quite gross is the rumour.'

Francis looked at him disbelievingly.

'I can credit that Smeaton might well offend His Grace but Norris – never.'

Brereton pursed his lips.

'Norris has always been a supporter of the Boleyns. And it is the house of Seymour that holds sway now. Think about it.'

'You believe this is some move against the Queen?'

'Anything is possible. But say nothing, Francis. I believe idle chatter could be dangerous to all concerned.'

Francis felt his heart thump in his chest as the full portent of the words became clear.

It was midnight and there was no sound anywhere. Anne, Queen of England, lay fully-clothed on her bed and thought, 'This is what it will be like. This quiet is a foretaste of the death that inevitably waits. God help me the soaring bird of my life has broken its wing at last; all fallen to earth and done for.'

At ten o'clock a messenger had come to her with the news that Mark Smeaton had been taken to the Tower and an hour later the same man, even more grim-faced, informed her that Sir Henry Norris was also under arrest. The charges had not, as yet, been made public. She had known then that the forces were massing against her, that Henry's fury was about to be unleashed. Yet she could not understand the means. The connection between herself and two of her loyal friends was, in this context, difficult to fathom. Perhaps they were all to be accused of a plot to kill the King.

She thought of her conversation with Norris and her coquettish behaviour. If that had been overheard and the wrong construction put on her words . . . Her brain felt as if it would burst with stress. If only her brother or Thomas Wyatt or Francis Weston were there to help her. But they were all at Whitehall with Henry. The single companion she had nearby was a daughter, not yet three, on one of her rare visits from her own household at Hatfield. A wild notion of snatching the child and leaving Greenwich by means of the river went through Anne's mind. But she knew the hopelessness of it even before the idea was cold. Even if she could struggle her way across the Channel nobody would pity her. The monarchs of Europe would send her back to the King with murder in his heart. All she could do was wait to see what charge would be brought and then pray that the inflexible determination and natural brilliance which had given her the crown could combine to save the head that wore it.

In the cold light just before dawn Zachary stood at the Watergate of Greenwich Palace. He had ridden through the darkness, crossing the river by moonlight, and now he huddled in the sharp early breeze, his ears alert to every stirring, awaiting that first distant sound of oars pulling that would tell him the Duke of Norfolk's barge was making its inexorable way from Whitehall, its owner aboard, frozen-faced with the import of judgement.

All the river noises abounded. Somewhere a heron stood, wings flapping over its nest; a cob called a secret dawn message to his pen and stretched his white neck up into the first primitive light; the river gurgled childlike as a fish stirred itself and jumped in driplets of luminescence. And Zachary thought of them all as parts of life, as incomprehensible particles of a galaxy so magnificent in scope that only a God amongst gods would even dare to grasp the key. And then he knew that to try and change the pre-determined course was to blaspheme – and yet he must endeavour. But who was he to interfere with that great march, the great sweep of events that led mankind to the stars?

'Lord Duke my father!'

The hand on his shoulder was utterly familiar even in the gloom. He had heard nothing of the arrival of the ducal barge nor the stamp of landing feet.

'Zachary, why are you here?'

He had never known his father's voice so hard as it was in the streaking morn.

'I have to speak to you, sir. It is imperative.'

427

Norfolk turned to look out over the river, his cloak billowing in the wind, his hand grasping the staff of office that showed him to be the premier peer of the realm.

'My son, has it occurred to you that I am not meant to hear what you have to say?'

'Yes, yes,' said Zachary in torment. 'But I must tell you the truth.'

The Duke turned back to look at him and his eyes were stony with the responsibility that lay before him.

'Zachary, I do not wish to listen. Many years ago you told me that it was my destiny to sentence Anne the Queen to burn or to meet the blade. Then amen. But I must do what is decreed armed by what *I* believe. Do not try to tell me.'

'Then God help me, Lord Duke.'

'My son, it is difficult and sometimes dangerous to know too much. Go home and sleep. You pitted yourself like a child against . . .'

But Zachary had interrupted. 'The universe,' he said.

'Aye. Now farewell.'

And Norfolk had turned and walked, without looking back, into the sleeping palace.

In the silence of Sutton Place Anne Weston dreamed, only this time she was walking away from the mansion in the direction of the old well of St Edward. And walking was not the right description for she glided above the ground, her feet moving but not touching the earth. In this journey of her nocturnal mind it was daylight – bright and jolly – and she could hear the sound of laughter and music. She turned towards it out of a fearful curiosity. She would never, could never – even in sleep – understand who these people were who came to her house and treated it with such fond familiarity.

Rounding a corner she saw them; men and women in

outlandish clothes and – surely not! – the game of tennis being played by both sexes. And a strange box with a horn blaring out the words 'Bye, bye blackbird' lying on the ground beside the court. She stood, mutely aghast, as one of the players looked up and straight into her eye. She recognized him from the dream in the moonlit apple loft. He had been called Alf then by his wife; Lord Northcliffe by a servant. And now it happened again. He went suddenly white and the woman facing him across the net said, 'What is it, Alf? Are you all right?' And a discreet man appeared from nowhere and said, 'Is anything wrong, Lord Northcliffe?'

'No, no,' he said. 'The weather, I expect. It's damned hot today.'

'Damned close,' agreed the female voice which laughed and added, 'God, I could do with a cigarette.'

Something about the way she spoke told Lady Weston she was a woman who strived for attention.

'It *is* warm,' answered Alf's wife. 'Shall we call it a draw and have some tea?'

'Splendid idea,' said the visiting man. 'Come on, Elsie. Give it a rest.'

They all went off and Lord Northcliffe was left alone with his servant.

'M'Lord, I'll ask you again. Is everything all right?'

'It's her, James – that bloody White Lady of my waking hell. She's standing there and she's looking at me.'

The man stared over and straight through her and Anne Weston shook with dread fear of the inexplicable.

'There's nothing there sir, really. I do believe it's this business of not sleeping that's upsetting you. I honestly think you should have it out with your doctors once and for all.'

Lord Northcliffe sat down wearily and the box-like

machine stopped playing its music and began to make a continual scratching sound.

'You're right, of course. It's destroying me. I truly believe I shall go clean off my head if I don't get something organized.'

'We'll see to it tomorrow. Now come indoors, sir, and have some tea.'

They disappeared in the direction of the house but not before Lord Northcliffe had given Anne one last look over his shoulder and that same dark, mutual terror had been struck between them. She hurried on and had only left him a few minutes when she passed the man called Getty. He walked with an instrument attached to his leg which was apparently registering how far he had gone for he was looking at it and saying, 'Two miles already, George. What do you think of that?'

The man with him simply shook his head and said, 'There's no keeping up with you, Dad. You'll outlive us all – you're a health fanatic!'

Getty just gave a lop-sided grin and went lolloping off apparently quite unconscious of the fact that Lady Weston had walked right beside him. And now she had left all sight of the house behind and was in the open parkland.

Coming towards her in a gown of mulberry velvet and a hat that trailed enormous black feathers from its brim was the woman that Anne had thought the most beautiful she had ever set eyes on. And now seeing her in the sunlight she was sure of it. The great nimbus of silver hair gleamed like a moonburst, the eyes were the colour of wild violets, the bones of the face placed there by a master sculptor. Even the movement of her body as she came towards Anne were pleasing to see. Behind her, running to catch up, his arms full of wild flowers, was the man who had shared the beauty's bed in Anne's earlier dream. The same delicate features, the heavily lidded eyes, the discontented mouth, all transformed now by his obvious adoration. He threw the flowers at the woman's feet and then knelt amongst them, raising her skirt's hem to his lips. But she was protesting, 'Highness, it is I who should be kneeling to you. Please rise, sir.'

'No, no – for you are my Princess, my Queen. Don't you understand that I love you Melior Mary?'

Then Anne saw the most curious thing. Surrounded by mist as if they were cut off in some way from the beauty and her lover, a sad-faced young man and woman also observed. And the girl called out, 'Melior Mary, we're here. Why don't you talk to me anymore?' But the boy said nothing, merely shaking his thick red curls in a gesture reminiscent of Dr Zachary. Anne was painfully aware that neither couple could see her nor could Melior Mary see anyone but her lover. It was a frightening feeling, as if time had turned in on itself and had thrown them all together by accident.

With the girl's voice still ringing out and Melior Mary's joyful laughter drowning the plaintive sound, Anne Weston hurried on towards the well. And now she knew that time had truly gone out of step for from the sunshine of a second before she found herself in a damp and miserable downpour. And the sound of the thundering hooves of a hunting party and the sight a minute later of men dressed in the garments of England's past, the hooded falcons clawing at their wrists, showed her something that she could at last recognize.

The clothes of Alf and of Getty and of Melior Mary's lover had all been different one from the other, and none familiar at all, but these men wore garments from an earlier time.

Without seeing her the hunters crashed past and were eventually lost to the eye and ear but she had, at last, come within sight of the well. And there a strange scene awaited her for a young woman lay on the ground, her body jerking in rending spasms. And out of her mouth was coming a terrible voice – hoarse and frightening. Anne could comprehend little of what the girl was saying but she knew that she – Anne – was in the presence of something dark and primitive. That some power from the dawn of time was being called up not only in the name of Odin – a word she did not understand – but in all that malevolently festered in the world that lay just beyond the fingertips of mankind. And that it was Sutton and the future of Sutton Place and all the heirs thereto who were being imperilled at this bleak and awesome moment.

'Christ, protect us,' she called out. 'God the Father, God the Son – stop this malediction.'

But time had played its ultimate trick and nobody heard for as Richard Weston said to her a second or two later, 'It's only a dream, Anne. Why do you weep?'

Francis thought, 'I must write to my father. He will advise me what to do because I can no longer think properly.'

The Palace of Whitehall to which he and his fellow courtiers had returned after the May Day tournament had become crypt-like in its silence. The buzz of everyday life had been reduced to hushed whispers and nobody dared sing or play a lute. Rumour chased rumour and the place seethed with unpleasant gossip.

Francis sat down and took up his pen, dating a piece of paper May 4, 1536.

'Most trusty and well beloved Father,

I do beseech you and earnestly entreat you to reply to this letter forthwith as I am now in great puzzlement as how to best conduct myself. As you may know Mark Smeaton was arrested on April 30 and on May 1, Sir Henry Norris. And the next day the Queen appeared before the Council at Greenwich and her uncle of Norfolk placed her under guard and she was taken to the Tower at two o'clock at high tide. It is reported here that the child Elizabeth was snatched from her arms where Anne the Queen did fondle her and the Queen begged His Grace – who had come secretly to Greenwich – to show her mercy.

At the same time as this Lord Rochford was arrested from this palace (Whitehall) and also taken to the Tower where now languish all four. The charges are that the Queen did commit adultery with Mark Smeaton – who confessed to same under torture – and with Sir Henry Norris, who denies this vigorously. Rochford is accused of having connived with her wickedness.

All who were her friends are now treated most coldly and I am in a torment of . . .'

The knock at his chamber was gentle but persistent and after waiting for a moment to see if the unwanted caller would take his leave Francis reluctantly rose from his chair. The door was starting to open even as he got to it and he saw the face of Sir William Fitzwilliam – a man he had never liked owing to his annoying habit of sliding his pallid eyes off the person to whom he was speaking. He was doing it now, slewing his gaze into the corner and saying, 'Sir Francis Weston.'

He had never noticed before that Sir William's voice was slightly effeminate.

'Yes?'

'I have here a warrant for your arrest. And I would ask you to accompany me now to the Tower.'

The world which had begun to grow grey and cold went black for a second and Francis prayed that he wouldn't lose consciousness in front of the band of men standing before him. He clung to the doorway to steady himself.

'May I see the document?' he said.

'Yes, Sir Francis, you may.'

The eyes went off at a tangent again and a parchment was thrust within a few inches of his nose. The King's signature and the opening words were enough to confirm his fears.

433

'The charge?' he said, in what he hoped was a calm reasonable voice.

'Adultery with the Queen's Grace.'

'I would like you to note, Sir William, that I deny this completely. It is a falsehood. Are you listening?'

'Yes,' said Sir William, staring at the ceiling.

'Then with your leave, I will fetch my things.'

'Very well.'

'And I would like this letter taken to my father.'

Just for a second the watery eyes met his before they went wavering off. 'And that, sir, you cannot have. No prisoner may make communication with his family.'

And he took the paper from Francis's fingers and rolled it into a ball which he threw away.

'Now conduct yourself like a man, Sir Francis. Your every move will be watched. And you will be accompanied by William Brereton who has also been placed under arrest. There is to be no conversation between you incidentally.'

'Brereton!' said Francis. 'Then, God help us, the world has gone mad.'

The skewing eyes went down to the floor.

'I would not worry about the world, Sir Francis. Think more of your neck, sir.'

Into the small silence that followed Francis said, 'There is nothing I can do but pray God that innocence will prevail. And if it does then I have no fear for head nor neck.'

'Take him away,' said Sir William his eyes on the tips of his shoes. 'He always did talk too much. Fools and blabbermouths. Well, they've chattered themselves into a sweet fish kettle now.'

The last Francis saw of him was playing a child's game of football with the letter that had been destined for Sutton Place.

20

Sir Richard was breaking the seal of the letter and, even though he held the paper a fair distance away, was reading the contents without difficulty. He stood like that – reading and re-reading it without saying anything – for quite a long time and then he finally sat down. Or rather he creaked down and the rider from London noticed for the first time that it really was an old man he was dealing with and not someone reputed to be nearly seventy yet whose grasp on life and vigorous manner gave the lie to the passing of time.

'Do you know what is in here?' Weston said eventually.

'Yes, sir.'

'Tell me everything you have heard.'

'Simply that this afternoon Sir Francis and William Brereton were taken to the Tower to join Lord Rochford, Sir Henry Norris, Mark Smeaton – and the Queen.'

'And the charge?'

'It is not made public yet but on challenging the arresting party Sir Francis was told that it was for . . .'

'Adultery with the Queen?'

'Yes – and conspiracy to kill the King.'

An unaskable question hung in the air between them till Sir Richard finally said, 'No, there'll be little truth in it. Francis could not conspire to kill a dog and as for adultery – apart from one little indiscretion his mistress has always been gambling. For the others – Henry Norris has been the King's man all his life, Brereton is a likeable idiot, Rochford is too clever by half to put a foot wrong. Smeaton – perhaps.'

'Sir?'

'A commoner made good, in love with the Queen beyond doubt. She might have used him. Peasants make good breeding stock you know.'

Aware that the old man was speaking high treason but aware also that his paymaster was Sir Richard's agent and therefore he was in a position of trust, the messenger merely stared.

'Those sons of the soil can sire boys, think on it.'

'I am, Sir Richard. I am also thinking that if the King is determined to make such a case as this then there is little hope.'

Sir Richard's shoulders straightened.

'We are running too eager,' he said. 'The indictments have not been drawn yet. And the accused must be tried by jury. I intend to fight for my boy's life. Now get to bed. You have ridden hard and tomorrow you must return with various letters. Be so good as to ask my Steward to send my wife and daughter-in-law to me at once. Do not tell him the reason.'

Anne came into the room first, an unmistakable resemblance to Francis seeming clearer than ever in the candlelight.

'What is it?' she said, sensing bad news by her husband's straight expression.

'Wait,' he answered. 'Please wait until Rose arrives. I have no wish to say it all twice.'

But she persisted with 'What is wrong?' and he was only saved by his daughter-in-law whirling into the room in a flurry of flying curls and rolled-up sleeves gasping, 'I cannot stay for long for Henry is screaming fit to wake the dead and his nurse is already a-weeping.'

Then she grew quiet as she sensed the stillness about her.

'What is it? Has ill befallen Francis?' she whispered.

their separate ways, each one's heart full to a greater or lesser degree with that tragic mixture of hope and despair from which life itself is made up.

On the most significant morning of his life, the day when, as principal royal commissioner he must sit at the trial of four Englishmen accused of adultery with the Queen, Norfolk overslept and was woken shouting 'What? What?' and staring stupidly at his servant. Only on the previous evening had he been informed what he must do the next day and then by his own special request.

'I will not, I cannot act without specific orders from the King,' he had said to William Paulet who had shrugged his shoulders and shaken his head when asked what was afoot. But his worried message had merely brought instructions direct from the arch manipulator Thomas Cromwell. He was to sit in judgement the following morning. Even as he dressed he had caught himself in his habit of sighing. The whole future of the monarchy lay in the balance for, whatever the verdict today, it would willy-nilly reflect that of Anne Boleyn. If the four were found guilty then so must she, and then Henry would be free – a widower – to marry his chinless Jane Seymour and probably beget a new breed of princes to wrest power from the embittered Princess Mary and her half-sister Elizabeth.

'Oh God,' said Norfolk as he mounted his horse and headed it towards Westminster Hall, 'I wish it were a year from now. I wish I lived in lighter times. I wish – I wish I had been born to a lesser degree.'

The building, when he arrived, was already packed with people – the commissioners, the judges, most of the Court and others of rank and influence who had been able to buy their way in. Taking his seat Thomas Howard looked around and was shocked beyond measure to see

Lady Weston and Rose, both dressed in starkest black, sitting amongst those who had come to listen. The presence of the two women was disturbing enough but for them to be the wife and mother of one of the guilty men . . . He paused in his thoughts. Why had he used that word? But then he knew, of course, that the accused must be guilty even before he had heard a word of evidence, even before he had actually listened to the full loathsome detail of the indictments. Nothing so terrible, so monumental could be false. And then he had one frightening, shivering moment of doubt. He stood again on the steps of Greenwich Watergate with Zachary in the rose-bright dawn and remembered the words that had passed between them; remembered how he had walked away to summon his niece to the Tower. All he had believed had been summoned up in that gesture – and he must believe again now. Otherwise he must rise up and leave this Hall in the sight of his fellow peers and – indirectly – his monarch.

Realizing that he was frowning deeply he looked up and caught the eye of Thomas Boleyn, Earl of Wiltshire. Norfolk was sickened. All the Tudor Court ran with the victim and hunted with the pack – it was part of life's survival – but this was beyond the limit of human dignity. That the man could sit there and listen to the filth that must necessarily be spoken of his daughter was bad enough. But to set himself up in judgement of her alleged lovers was too great a blow at paternal feeling. Despite the awesome occasion, despite his position in the hierarchy Norfolk found himself sneering and running his eyes over his upstart brother-in-law in a manner that could have no false interpretation. He mouthed the word 'Hippocrite' and looked away.

The time had come for the swearing in of the jury. King's men; all twelve of them His Grace's Knights brave and true. Norfolk felt another prickle of unease followed by a tension shared by every person present, for the sound of the crowd outside the Hall – part of the background, not consciously listened to – had suddenly stilled. And faint but sure was the noise of marching feet. The accused were being walked through the streets from the Tower to Westminster. Coughing into his hand to mask his feelings Howard heard the end of the oath taking.

The Lord Chancellor Sir Thomas Audley's voice rang out loudly. 'Bring up the prisoners.' And with Sir William Kingston, the Lieutenant of the Tower beside them, there they were. Such silly, human things went through Norfolk's mind; that loyal Henry Norris hadn't shaved well, that Smeaton – always so bright and full of song – had lost a great deal of weight, that Francis Weston had buttoned his doublet on the wrong fastenings, that Brereton was really quite short.

He watched their faces during the reading of the indictments, saw the shared look of disbelief, and wondered how this could equate with guilt? But the answer was quite simply really. She had done it all – sidling and seducing and procuring. He could see her in his mind; those exciting dark eyes promising so much, that sensuous mouth curving into a secret smile. She was the biggest bitch, the biggest whore in the land. That was the *real* truth. She would have sent his son to death and now she had ruined the lives of four honourable men.

Though he was not a juror he found himself in total agreement with the verdict – guilty on all counts. Without wanting to, he glanced across at the two ladies as sentence – hanging by the neck, disembowelling and quartering while still alive – was passed. Anne Weston sat staring in front of her as if she had died where she sat but Rose . . .

441

Rose was looking at Francis and he at her as if that look would never end.

Norfolk would never know, could never know, what passed between them in that final gaze. Everything they had ever shared. Memories – their first childhood meeting in the Great Hall of Sutton Place, their innocent love, the boy and girl decreed for each other but bonded by feelings never dreamed of. Passion – the lust and desire, the virgin and the courtier, the pain and beauty of consummation and the loss of two unborn children. Betrayal – the longing for Margaret Shelton, the flirtatious glances at Henry Knyvett and the absences and inevitable returns. Fidelity – the true love of mind for mind, heart for heart, and the utter totality of pure affection.

All these things and more were exchanged in the last look they ever gave to each other. For they both knew that this was indeed the moment of farewell, that there was no hope, that the way which they had trodden together so joyfully was about to be brutally forced asunder. He shook his head very slightly to show her that he had not been guilty of the terrible things she had just heard, and she gave a tiny nod in return to show that she understood. And then they smiled and continued to smile until he had vanished from her sight and she stood alone, frozen and white, while part of her died with despair.

A touch at her elbow made her look down and she saw that her mother-in-law had turned into an old lady who needed helping up. And even while she struggled with a woman whose legs seemed suddenly useless the Duke of Norfolk – rather strained-looking – was at her side and assisting Lady Weston to her feet saying, 'Come, come. Come, come.'

'Lord Duke,' said Rose.

'Yes, my dear? Yes, yes?'

And he was patting her hand and sighing and shaking his head like a gossip at a fair.

'Will you help me?'

A look of caution entered the heavy-lidded eyes.

'If it is possible to do so, my dear.'

'I want to see His Grace. You must gain me an audience with the King.'

'But it would do no good. You would only distress yourself.'

'Every man has the right of appeal, sir. Is that not so?'

'Certainly.'

'Then let *me* appeal on behalf of my husband. Where's the harm? I can only be shown from the building.'

Norfolk hesitated and then quite distinctly, as close as if he had been standing beside him, Zachary whispered in his ear. 'Do it. Help her.' The illusion was so strong that the Duke glanced round.

'What is it?'

'I thought I heard something. Very well, I'll do what I can. But he's at Hampton Court. 'Tis a fair way.'

'Not by water. May we journey with you?'

The Duke considered. The court had risen for though the hearing of Anne Boleyn and her brother still awaited they must, by the law of the land, be judged by their fellow nobles and there were simply not enough present at this sitting. So the trial of the Queen had been postponed until Monday and Howard was bound, in all truth, to report immediately to the King.

'The postponement – coincidence or tactic?' he thought. 'I cannot summon the peers until tomorrow and then they will have a whole day to think about the findings against her lovers. If it is contrived it is shrewd.'

But Rose Weston was looking at him with a ghastly face, forcing him to concentrate his attention on her and

443

say, 'Yes. We will go now. But be prepared for the worst. His Grace's temper is choleric.'

'There is nothing to lose,' she said.

But despite their apparent calm the silence of the two women unnerved him as his great barge rowed through the beautiful reaches of the Thames past the quiet dreaming villages of Chelsea and Richmond and the grazing land beyond, to where the most magnificent of palaces – once the property of the long dead Cardinal Wolsey – stood in the distance. It was then that Rose finally broke the uneasy stillness.

'God will thank you for this, Lord Duke,' she said. 'Though it may avail us nothing, you will at least have tried.'

But his effort was in vain for though he knew that the interview would be brutal even he was not quite prepared for what actually happened. Anne Weston, who had not spoken at all since leaving Westminster, suddenly cried, 'Let him live,' prostrating herself at the feet of the King who sat lolling in the chair of state eating a sweetmeat.

With a face like a death's head – the bitter black of mourning in cruel contrast to her ashen skin – Rose too knelt before Henry, her hands clasped as supplicant's, whispering in a tone that the Duke found vaguely menacing.

'Sire, I have come to plead for the life of my husband – Sir Francis Weston. He is not guilty as charged because he is incapable of such a monstrous act.'

'That finishes her only hope,' thought Norfolk. 'She should have said anything but that. Henry will have no doubt thrown on his jury.'

'Your Grace, if you will pardon him the Weston family will give up everything of which they stand possessed in the world – one hundred thousand crowns, the manor of Sutton, my manors at Kendal and Moresby, all the houses thereon including Sutton Place, all the lands belonging thereto. We will go penniless if you will sign his reprieve.'

Just for a second the Duke saw Henry was tempted. She was offering him a fortune in return for the stroke of a pen – and it would still leave him three guilty men, with the trial of the Queen's brother yet to come. But then he saw that little mouth – slightly obscene, folded in as it was amongst the fat and the beard fuzz – grow hard. Greedy the King might be but stupid not at all. One dubious verdict could throw the whole of these trials of state into disrepute. A look of irritation, partly because just for a minute he had considered the idea, crossed the once handsome features now lost in a sea of blubber. Then testily Henry dragged himself to his feet staring down at Lady Weston as if she were something from the dung heap.

'Let him hang,' he said. 'Let him hang.'

And stepping over her as if she were a footstool he stalked from the room shouting, 'I'll see you at once, sir,' in the general direction of Norfolk.

'God help us,' said Rose. 'Will he change his mind?'

'No,' said Howard bluntly. 'I'm sorry. There's no hope.'

'The French Ambassador is going to . . .'

'The French Ambassador can try what he likes but nothing short of a miracle will turn events about. You saw the King's face.'

'Then, Lord Duke, I have one final favour to ask.'

Howard shifted from foot to foot. Henry was in a wicked mood and obviously blamed him – Norfolk – for the Westons being at Hampton Court at all. The last thing he should do now was keep his royal master waiting.

'Madam, I must take my leave – His Grace has urgent matters to discuss.'

'I will delay you no more only ask if you will give this to Dr Zachary tonight.'

And she took from a pocket in her cloak a sealed letter.

'But I intend staying here tonight.'

'Then I beg you not to do so. I would go myself but I don't know what to do with my mother-in-law.'

Her face suddenly crumpled like a little girl's and a single tear ran down the side of her nose and hung on the end in a way that, in any other circumstances, would have made him smile.

'Please,' she said.

'Oh, very well. Now be gone. Return to Sutton Place quickly. It will be dark soon.'

'Tell Dr Zachary I shall await him there.'

Norfolk looked at her very straightly.

'I don't think even he can alter what is meant to be.'

She looked at him with eyes like rainbows.

'But he could try,' she said.

Anne Boleyn sat in a high chair in the Great Hall of the Tower and thought about beginnings and endings. And how, in fact, neither existed for all life went in a circle because the point at which this extraordinary adventure had begun – the love of a girl for a clumsy young man and her desire for revenge on those who had parted them – had just clicked neatly into its final place. For opposite her, amongst that sea of faces which represented the peers of the realm come to try her for her life, was Harry Percy.

All the magic, all the dreams and longing, ending here in this terrible place and he so gaunt of eye and slack of skin, his face the colour of decaying parchment, and unable to even so much as look at her. Was he remembering, as she was, the abandoned kisses of youth, the smell of blossom wafting through the night, the feel of his arms about her, the nightingale singing 'Harry loves Anne'?

Was he wishing that the circle had swung off on another course and that she would have been waiting at home for him now, the Countess of Northumberland, surrounded by tall boys with their mother's dark hair and eyes and mild-mannered girls as gentle as their father? Instead of which he – the touchstone of her life – must soon be part of the ritual which would take that life away; the game of love and death which had been pre-determined for them played out to the full – the wheel of fortune come to rest. What had begun with Anne and Harry was ending similarly. Everything was complete.

She stared impassively at the faces of her enemies. Suffolk with his great flowing beard and mean eye, the Marquis of Exeter hunched like a bird of prey, the Earl of Derby and his two fellow plotters Lords Montague and Sandys who had worked tirelessly to bring her down. But her father not there? Probably afraid of what might be said if he showed the last indelicacy of all and sat in judgement on his own son and daughter. Oh, how power corrupted. He had been so gentle once – long, long ago when he had been nothing but funny old Thomas Boleyn, a Kentish knight with a small and beautiful castle, who had actually dived into the moat to fish out Mary and George. And she who had stood on the drawbridge, the sun warming the top of her head, had never felt more secure than then. Her brother swimming like a puppy to the shore and her sister safe in the arms of the father who could be relied on to save and protect them.

That was probaby the cruellest part of all – the joyous childhood romping, the genuine feelings she had for George and he for her, made disgusting. Spoilt by this stinking court's fevered minds. It was hard to bear – that, and the fact that Harry wouldn't look at her.

Her uncle of Norfolk was rising to pronounce sentence and they faced each other eye to eye, like two cats finally come to confrontation. He stood in silence for a moment and she thought how sweetly he must be savouring this morsel of time wasting. And she saw that his eyes were wet, that the great Thomas Howard – standing beneath the cloth of state – was crying. For her! Her lips quivered very slightly as he said in an uneven voice, 'Madam, you are sentenced to be burned – ' he paused momentarily and rustled the papers in his hand, ' – or beheaded at the pleasure of the King's Highness.'

She glanced over at Harry and just for one second he glanced back. She could not tell whether it was sweat or tears or both that ran down his face. A ghost of a smile played round her mouth and something in his stricken soul responded. A fleeting glimpse of the old warmth showed itself before he got to his feet and staggered from the room, too sickened to see or hear any more. And with that, with his leaving, the dream of Anne – his love witch – finally shattered into a million fragments and the song bird was silenced for ever. The game of chance was over.

On the day that the Queen was sentenced to die a summer storm formed over London and stayed brooding for an hour or so before it eventually moved off towards Surrey, seeming to follow the course of the river. To Zachary as he made his way to Sutton Place – first by water and then by horse – it was like an ever-present menace symbolizing something far more sinister then mere thunder and lightning. In fact as he and Sapphira came within sight of St Edward's well it muttered distantly, at odds with the clear blue sky and the May blossom.

The decision to take her with him, to use his daughter in the fearful conflict with evil that must be carried out if the manor of Sutton was to know lasting peace, had been impossibly difficult. On the one hand was Rose Weston's letter:

'Right well beloved Dr Zachary,
I most humbly petition you for the sake of Francis's soul to help me. Of the great malevolence that lies upon this land and upon those – in especial the male heirs – who dwell thereon, you know. But surely by ancient rite and counter evocation of good the spell can be lifted? Is it true of this span of life that all events are heretofore decided or can events be shaped by mankind? I know not but trust that you will act in wisdom. And if not for Francis then for the sake of my babe I do most zealously beseech that you bring about an end to this cruelty by the power given to you at your birth by God Almighty.'

But he had known as he read it that his strength was not great enough; that an accursed place gained force with each victim claimed; that a cry long ago from a wretched woman had now assumed the ferocity of a vortex as it fed over the centuries. And his eyes had turned then to Sapphira and he had remembered the night when he had stood in the pentagram with Anne Boleyn – powerless and frightened – and one command from his child had halted the demonic fury. It was then that he had said to his wife:

'It must be Sapphira who lays the curse of Sutton to rest. I knew it three years ago and I know it today. Only she has been granted the force.'

'And if it kills her?'

'It will not, it cannot. She is more in touch with the source of life than even my mother. She is the master – we the apprentices.'

'But Zachary she is a six-year-old child.'

He had looked away.

'Jane, I cannot let this evil persist.'

'But is it not decreed that Francis Weston will die? Can any power – however great – change that?'

449

'I don't know,' he had said wretchedly. 'I have not solved the riddle.'

'And you would risk our child for a question mark?'

'The risk is negligible. She is mighty.'

Then for the first time ever his wife had taunted him with his bastard.

'I suppose that your daughter in Calais – the babe of your whore Banastre – could take her place? Remember that I do not have another daughter.'

And she had left the room and it was thus that he had taken Sapphira to Sutton Place, with Jane removed to Allington Castle with Jasper, their son, and a black mood stalking. And every part of Zachary torn between the natural love and protection of a father and the wish of a white magician to see wickedness destroyed. And as they had approached the well Sapphira, unprompted by him, had said the ancient words to ward off the evil eye and then snuggled close to him – the two gestures summing up everything that was tearing at his conscience.

A servant from the house had brought down a trestle table as he had requested and it was on this that he now set two white candles and the crucifix that had once adorned the walls of Kenninghall Castle, and then took from his saddle bag the bowls and phials of water and salt that would make his rite close to the elements of the earth.

'Sapphira,' he said, as he placed them on the basic table of God, 'wilt make the water holy?'

It was frightening to see her go forward, so small and so vulnerable, and pour the water and the salt together in purification, dip her thumb in the mix and paint the sign of the cross on his forehead as he knelt before her head bowed. And he knew, even as he bent over and similarly crossed her, that his blessing was not as strong, that the holy water on her brow could not hold such protection as his for in the end the command came from within and he was but a humble servant of nature in comparison with the catalyst that stood before him.

'Come, give me thy hand,' he said, and together they walked to the well lying so calm and so innocuous beneath the dying sun.

'The evil dwells here,' she said.

'Aye, and has for centuries. Canst root it out?'

She turned to look at him for a second and he did not know if it was his mother or his child who said, 'I cannot tell. The Old Serpent is well entrenched.'

He made the sign of the cross.

'Try.'

She raised the bowl of water over her head and poured it headlong into the well, not bothering with sprinkling or delicacy, and then said, 'Father, there is something very ancient here. Something of the old gods that were not tempered by our Lord.'

'But the Beast?'

'He is here too. And yet the woman who did this was pure. It is a strange occurrence.'

In the distance the thunder rumbled again and the sun glowered behind a tree.

'Call him out, Sapphira. Call him out and then let us depart.'

She stopped where she stood and all of time went spinning. 'Zachary, Zachary,' she said, 'should we not play in the meadows?'

He did not know where he was or what he was saying as a joyful madness possessed him.

'Mother – it *is* you! Can we run with the wind?'

'Aye, now and for ever. But there's a danger here. Should we go on?'

He was a boy again and the hand in his was strong and adult.

'If I am with you I am safe.'

He did not hear her say 'Yes, but I am not', because the dream was upon him and it was only as the sun went out of his eyes that he saw he was with his child at the well of St Edward and the last few moments had been a dance of his brain.

'Begin,' he said. 'Call up and dismiss that which haunts.'

She bowed to him like a novice nun and stood before the altar.

In her clear child's voice she called out, 'Depart, thou foul demon to the place appointed for thee. I command the evil to leave this place. Depart the Beast rooting up the vine of the Lord.'

It seemed as if all life had grown still. No bird sang, no leaf moved, all wind dropped – the storm which had followed them throughout was about to break.

Sapphira took up the bowl of salt and crossing to the well, poured it in as it was.

'With this salt I make this water holy. Begone, thou power of long ago, begone the curse as old as time, begone, thou ancient Master of Darkness, begone . . .'

But she stopped speaking. From out of the well was arising what Zachary could only describe as a mist, white and thick and formless. For a second he gazed and then he hurried forward to protect Sapphira in his arms. But it was too late. She had thrown herself on the ground and was rolling about in convulsions, her voice growling in her throat. The caged hare, which he had brought with them to receive the evil as it left the well, sat with whiskers and nose a-twitch – unharmed. The malevolence had entered his child.

'Odin, Odin,' came the terrible gruff voice and as she spoke ectoplasm poured from her lips in a torrent.

'Christ protect us,' called Zachary. *'Salom arepo lemel opera molas. Sator arepo tenet opera rotas.'*

Sapphira writhed in agony.

'Death, madness and despair, for ever,' she shouted in the voice of a man. 'So it is decreed.'

'Depart Old Serpent,' Zachary screamed. 'I command thee to leave this child in peace. Christ, have mercy on her soul. Christ, protect your lamb.'

The ectoplasm was turning to slime and despite himself, despite the fact that this was his beloved child the sight of her brought vomit to Zachary's mouth and forced him to turn away retching and trembling. Behind him he could hear Sapphira snarling frightening obscenities and overhead the skies gave up their burden and with a wild flash of sheet lightning the rain started in full spate.

Suddenly he remembered the crucifix. Picking it up from the altar he wielded it over his head like a broadsword, turning back to where his daughter lay, her face leering and goat-like.

'In the name of Father, Son and Holy Ghost I command the evil to leave this child.'

And then a deep roar of thunder inspired him.

'Thor, god of men, protect my daughter. Rescue her from the violence of Odin. As the runes are consecrated in your name save this maiden that she may dedicate her reading of them to thee.'

He never knew whether paganism or Christianity saved her but to him – the Romany, the seer of hidden mysteries – it was all one anyway. God of gods, one force of infinity – only silly, tiny man to make dogmas and sects.

He saw the ugliness drain from her and then for a second she was transformed. A young woman with hair the colour of wild strawberries lay where his daughter had been and said, 'Oh Edward, if only you had loved me. If only . . .'

Then Sapphira was back again and he bent over her, raising her in his arms.

'Oh, sweetheart,' he said. 'Thou art restored.'

She opened her eyes and looked at him; the saddest, most pitiful glance he had ever seen. Then opening her mouth she tried to say something but no sound at all came out.

'Sapphira,' he shouted, shaking her despite himself.

The tears trickled down her cheeks and she shook her head and he knew at once what terrible vengeance had been wreaked. His daughter would never speak again. Her wonderful gift had been cut off at a stroke for she would never more be able to communicate her clear sight and her mystical knowledge. The child was dumb.

'Oh God, God, God,' he said, cradling her to him and weeping. 'I should not have brought thee. I should have had the courage to come here alone.'

She had lost consciousness again as he swung her over his saddle leaving everything behind but the cross and the trembling hare, which he released unharmed into the forest. And as he mounted, knowing that he would never set foot in this place again, the tempest burst furiously overhead as if all the universe was screaming. The sound of distant hooves amongst the savage thunder made him peer through the rain and coming towards him he saw Rose Weston, her hair streaming out behind her like a burst of flame and her face livid in the storm flashes. Like that, and astride a great white horse she seemed to be one of the Norse maidens herself; a Valkyrie come to take a dead warrior to Valhalla.

'Is it done?' she shouted above the tumult.

'Aye.'

'But is it exorcized? Is it free from the curse?'

Zachary looked back at the well and for once he was powerless. His clairvoyance eluded him. Then he looked down at the child which hung over his saddle like a broken doll, arms and legs trailing down, fair hair almost touching the mud below.

'I hope to God it is,' was all he said as he galloped away.

Rose stayed perfectly still and watched him threading a path amongst the trees until he was lost from view. And as she turned back and came within sight of Sutton Place it seemed to her that the house reached out to her, that its massive structure, its tower, its mouldings and transoms, were trying to tell her something.

She looked up at it knowing that it would stand when she and descendants to whom she would just be a name had long since mouldered into dust. When others had come who would know little and care not at all about the tragedy of Francis Weston. When the King and his Court had turned into names in history books. Would the house reveal its secret to the people destined one day to live there?

'What are you going to do to them?' she shouted into the storm. 'What lies ahead?'

And it seemed to her that the wind, moaning through the quadrangle, answered, 'Wait . . . wait . . .', but that Sutton Place made no reply.

Epilogue

It took him a long time to focus properly after he opened his eyes. At first he couldn't see the room at all and then, very slowly, outline after outline became clear and he realized that he was in his study, softly furnished and warmly lit. And his brown speckled hands feeling about him cautiously told him that he was in his working chair, recognized the wood of the desk before him. So they had put him in his favourite place to die. He supposed that that was what the world would call a fitting end – if it ever knew! The great magnate, the colossus of all tycoons, making his exit from the place where he had spent so many hours, making or losing what other men would term a fortune with a single phone call, a signature on a document.

With difficulty he began what he knew must be his last proper look about him. He had always loved the room, had chosen it at once for his working place. But its history was a bit dull, apparently no more than a kitchen or storeroom. At its best the room where the working lads and the Fool had slept. Nothing really romantic.

But the house, oh the house, that had never let him down. He had bought a bit of English history and it had never disappointed. The cunning old devil who had built it – initials R.W. all over the stonework and some sort of pun on a barrel known as a tun. West-tun. That had style, that had what he would call a bit of cheek, a bit of class. Pity they – the Westons – had all known sadness. But maybe that was the lot of everybody – a few laughs and several tears.

456

Funny thing that, that people generally thought how well the world had used him. They couldn't have bothered to piece together the pattern of his life. So much death, so much sadness. He'd been so low sometimes he'd even thought there was some kind of curse on him. But when he looked in the family archives there was nothing.

But Timmy and Talitha's deaths, Paul the third's ear cut off by kidnappers and shoved, without respect for flesh, into an envelope and posted – and then George. That had been the worst. To love a boy, to trust him with your inheritance, then the son dying before the father – that was cruel. Somebody else had thought that in Sutton Place. Strange he should know!

And thoughts of George set dates going through his mind. May 17 Francis Weston executed – if his memory was right – and June 6 George's sad end. And then his eyes focusing on a desk clock and a rickety calendar that one of his grandchildren had made him for Christmas made it all inevitably clear. It was two minutes to midnight and it was June 5 and he had woken up on purpose, come back from that strange half-world – out of which he could have wandered like a lost child finding its way home – not only to bid farewell to his mansion but to keep his rendezvous with George. All he had to do was stay alive till midnight and then his son would come for him. One needed no particularly strong religious convictions to see that. If it wasn't meant, if it wasn't part of some plan of such infinite proportions that no one dared think about it too much, the cancer would have taken him away long before. That was why he was sitting here now with the Old Reaper grinning in the shadows.

And there *was* something in the shadows, somebody standing there and watching him. His eyes, longing to stare at eternity, tried hard to see but there was so much mist about. Then it became clearer. It was a man with

457

eyes set widely apart and a thick thatch of dark hair and a woman with long eyelashes. He stared speechless, not sure if his voice would come out even if he wanted it to.

And then there were other people. Standing round his chair and smiling at him and being at one with him and coming to escort him. A handsome young man hand-in-hand with a red-headed girl; a woman with hair like a silver cloudburst and with her a man whose face he had seen in history lessons – a famous man. And more people still. Names went through his mind – Richard, Melior Mary, Hyacinth, Francis, Sibella, Rose.

And then, unbelievably, a jester sat at his feet and looked up at him with a great split grin and shook his stick with the belled head on it and he saw that the face on the stick was that of death. The Fool put out his hand but he wouldn't take it because George wasn't there and it was too soon.

'Wait,' he said and his voice was a rasp, like no sound he had ever heard in his life before. It was impossible now to look at the clock because his eyes were growing fixed and he could only sense that they were all still standing round him silently. All he could see was the jester's waiting hand and a bright light in the room – like dawn.

In the Great Hall a clock chimed midnight. And then, oh God, and then the door opened. The final effort, pain upon pain, a million years to turn his head and look and see the outline of a man. George had come and was walking towards him. He opened his mouth and soundlessly said his son's name. And then it wasn't difficult at all. He took the Fool's hand and stood up. Something like a discarded dressing gown was lying on his chair but he ignored it as he stepped out with the others into the morning.

* * *

The doctor saw him die as he walked towards him but couldn't catch the last word he said. But though he had already diagnosed he felt for the pulse. All quiet – like the room. Empty and silent except for the huddled figure in the great chair. He made a note of the time – two minutes past midnight on June 6, 1976 – then looked once more at his patient. Sad little corpse – all his dynamic power made a joke by death's inexorable levelling. Oh well, the reign of the oil king was over. Sutton Place must look for a new master. The richest man in the world was dead.

Bibliography

The Chronicles of Calais (printed by The Camden Society); *Anne Boleyn*, Paul Friedmann; *The Divorce of Catherine of Aragon*, J. A. Froude; *Annals of an Old Manor House*, Frederic Harrison; *1066 – The Year of the Conquest*, David Howarth; *Lives of the Queens of England*, Agnes Strickland; *Henry VIII and His Court*, Neville Williams.